Big
Spankable
Asses

Big Spankable Asses

Angie Daniels
Kimberly Kaye Terry
Lisa G. Riley

A

APHRODISIA

KENSINGTON BOOKS

http://www.kensingtonbooks.com

APHRODISIA BOOKS are published by

Kensington Publishing Corp.
850 Third Avenue
New York, NY 10022

All Kensington Titles, Imprints, and Distributed Lines are available at special quantity discounts for bulk purchases for sales promotions, premiums, fund-raising, and educational or institutional use.

Special book excerpts or customized printings can also be created to fit specific needs. For details, write or phone the office of the Kensington special sales manager: Kensington Publishing Corp., 850 Third Avenue, New York, NY 10022, attn: Special Sales Department, Phone: 1-800-221-2647.

Aphrodisia and the A logo Reg. U.S. Pat. & TM Off.

ISBN-13: 978-0-7582-2181-0
ISBN-10: 0-7582-2181-9

First Kensington Trade Paperback Printing: October 2007

10 9 8 7 6 5 4 3 2 1

Printed in the United States of America

CONTENTS

Just Lay Down

Kimberly Kaye Terry

To my girls, Angie Daniels and Lisa Riley, thanks for joining me to write BSA over late night conversations, apple martinis, and grape Kool-Aid!
Much love, chicas!

And to my cool-ass editor, Hilary Sares: Thank you for diggin' the concept!
—Kimberly Kaye Terry

Prologue

"Just lay down, Lilly, and take this big dick. We both know you want it and nobody else can give it to you the way I can," Marcus said as he sweated and grunted above Lilliana's prostrate body.

With all of that sweating and grunting, she was afraid he'd have a heart attack if he wasn't careful. The thought of him falling out in a state of cardiac arrest did absolutely nothing to evoke sympathy from her. Those days were long past. She refrained from grimacing as his body slammed into hers. Not from his "big dick" did she feel the discomfort, but from his large body slamming into her much smaller one.

Big dick. Yeah. Right. Marcus's dick reminded her of a brown Tic Tac with two juju beans dangling behind it . . . yet he insisted on taunting her on her inability to handle his big cock. Whatever unfortunate rooster he got that thing from, he needed to give it back.

As soon as he'd come home from work, he'd started yelling her name, searching her out, until he cornered her in the kitchen and all but dragged her into the bedroom. He stripped out of his suit and told her to "take that shit off," referring to the long caftan she wore. Without conscious thought she did what he demanded, familiar with the routine. Her mind was already a million miles away.

Within moments of penetration, he was rearing his big body away from hers, sweat pouring down his face like he'd just been in a decathlon and roared, literally roared, his release as he slumped down on top of her.

All that roaring and she hadn't felt a doggone *thing*.

She forced herself not to scream as he lay on top of her, breathing heavily with his nasty sweat transferring to her body. She waited for a full five seconds before she couldn't bear it any longer.

"Marcus, get *off* of me!" She tried to shove his body away from hers, but he was too big. Helpless, she waited until finally he pushed himself away from her and moved off the bed.

He grabbed his shorts dangling from the end of the bed, stepped into them, and turned to face her, an ugly expression of disgust plastered on his handsome face. For someone who always proudly proclaimed to have such a big dick, she noticed that he was quick to pull his shorts on as soon as they'd finished having sex.

"Just who in hell do you think you are, Lilly? You think somebody else would want you?"

"What are you talking about now?" she asked wearily as she pulled her caftan back over her head and sat on the edge of the bed.

He always went on the attack after sex. If she didn't go through the motions and fake it, pretend like it was off the hook and the best she'd ever had, he'd verbally attack her. Lately he'd been doing that a lot more.

"Who else is going to put up with your lazy ass like I do? You don't work, don't go to school, don't do a damn thing but sit your ass around the house, sucking my pockets dry! You're just a damn leech, that's what you are! I work all day long so you can have the finer things in life and all I ask is that you give me some good pussy when I get home. Quit laying down like a damn limp rag! Is that asking too much? Damn, girl . . ."

As the insults rained down on her head like so many blows, Lilliana took them like she usually did, like a prizefighter. Stoically. No grimace, no cringing; nothing. No emotion crossed her face as he got through his familiar rant. She listened but tuned out the exact words, as if they were the lyrics of a familiar song. She'd heard it all before, wasn't nothing new. The words no longer registered on her consciousness as they once did.

She'd put up with Marcus's bullshit for twelve *long* years.

Of course in the beginning, the first year or so, he hadn't been as bad as he was now. He'd wooed her, made her feel special and made a home with her. He'd told her how unique, how beautiful she was. It had been just what she needed to hear. At just the right time.

She'd been working hard at the diner as a waitress, long hard hours avoiding old drunk men and aggressive truck drivers with their groping hands and lustful looks as she worked the late shift. It had been hard work and she'd done it for nearly two years before Marcus stepped into the diner late one evening.

He'd been so smooth with his game. Could lay it out nice and sweet. Damn. The man could sweet talk a woman straight out of her panties without saying a word. He had that dark, naughty, *I need to be tamed* look. The kind of look women were drawn to like stink on shit, as her great-aunt Margaret used to say. Made a woman long to "tame" the beast.

And stupid her, she'd fallen for the look and the man, hook, line and sinker. And then he'd started abusing her. It had been little things at first. He'd cuss at her for not cleaning the house the way he wanted and call her a leech.

Then he started rough-handling her, a light smack here, slap there. Until he'd tied her up and left her for hours once because she didn't fake an orgasm and he wanted to teach her a lesson.

"Are you listening to me? I swear, Lilly, you'd better not be tuning me out again! Don't make me have to hurt you." Marcus snapped her out of her reverie with his low, ugly, threatening words. Words that sent a chill racing down her spine. When he grabbed her by her arm and hauled her up against his thick chest, a determination and resolve filled her spirit, forcing her to shake off the fear and boldly look him in his dark eyes.

This was it.

She knew it was only a matter of time before Marcus decided it was time to take things to the next level and raise his hands to her. A few weeks ago he'd slapped her face so hard she'd sported a large, ugly red bruise on her eye for two weeks before it had finally receded on her chocolate brown skin, leaving a dark purplish mark for days afterward.

Lilliana raised her eyes to meet Marcus's, and calmly, with no inflection in her soft voice, said, "Put your damn paws on me again, Marcus, and I swear to God I will slap your ass back to your mama's womb."

1

"What we *really* need is a man who knows what the hell he's doing! I am so tired of faking it, not getting any, or turning to Big Tom to catch a thrill! And lately Tom has been eating into my budget, for real. I've bought more batteries than you can shake a stick at."

"Simone girl, please! I don't know about *you* two, but I think it's all hype anyway," Melinda said in disgust as she sipped her drink.

"What's all hype? Orgasms?" Simone frowned and asked as she paused to take a sip of her drink.

"Orgasms, multiple orgasms, G-spot, whatever . . . all of it!"

"So says the woman who has never had one," Lilliana piped up and laughed.

"Oh, and you're an expert?" Melinda raised an eyebrow.

"No, but I've had a couple here and there," Lilliana said, sipping her margarita as she sat with her two best friends, Melinda Carlisle and Simone Thomas, in their favorite booth at Hooters, drinking, gossiping and winding down with the rest of the early evening crowd.

"Well, I don't know about you two but I'm no stranger to the ultimate thrill, it's just . . . been a while, that's all. And for a chick like me? A toy can only provide so much relief. I need a man. A real man. One that doesn't require batteries," Simone said on a sigh as she sat back in the booth, her eyes restless as she surveyed the crowd.

"Ummm. Yeah, I know what you mean, girl. Since I've returned home, well, actually since I left Marcus two years ago—"

"Thank God you saw the light and finally left that loser."

"Simone!" Melinda cautioned.

"What? We all know that jackass was a sorry excuse for a man. No man puts his hands on a woman. Period. End of subject. He was lucky all our girl did was give him a black eye with that vase she bashed over his head when he tried to hit her again. He should be thanking God that when she knocked him out, she didn't lay his ass out to rest! I would have," Simone said grimly. The women were silent for a minute.

"You're back home and we're thankful for that. I missed you, girl. Long distance calls and occasional visits are nothing like having you here at home." Melinda reached over and enveloped Lilliana in a hug.

"Thanks, Mel. It feels good to be home," she said, returning the hug and giving a small half-smile.

"I missed you too, Lil. It's kind of like old times, the three of us together again. Remember how you'd sneak out of the house, when your brothers and your mom were asleep?" Simone asked and all three women laughed in memory.

"That was the only time I ever had any fun! If it hadn't been for you two, I don't know what I would have done."

"I tell you what you would have done. Watched your brothers twenty-four-seven. That's what would have happened," Melinda finished and shook her head. "Girl, I still don't understand why your mother did that to you. You and Glenn are only a year or so apart, aren't you? And the twins weren't that much younger than Glenn."

"She worked late nights sometimes and she was beat. She said she didn't have energy to deal with us, especially the younger ones, after working twelve-hour shifts at the factory," Lilliana answered with a shrug.

"Why do you always do that?" Simone asked after a slight pause.

"Do what?"

"Excuse your mom."

"I don't excuse her. It happened and I don't want to dwell on it. It was in the past, it has nothing to do with the present, so can we just not go there tonight? I thought we were talking about men, anyway, not my mama." Lilliana barely refrained from rolling her eyes. She glanced down at her drink and caught the subtle elbow nudge that Melinda gave Simone, and Simone's answering grimace.

"Like I was saying. I am in total agreement with you on the whole *it's been a while* syndrome!"

Melinda laughed. "I had no idea that lack of sex was a syndrome."

"It is when it's been a while since you had any."

"Hmmm. Especially when it's been a while since you had it put on you right! And the official name for it is PID," Simone returned drolly.

"Pelvic Inflammatory Disease?" Melinda was a nurse and naturally applied a medical term to the acronym.

"Hell no! Pussy In Distress Syndrome," Simone said.

"Okay? Girl!" Lilliana agreed and all three women laughed.

"So what do we do about it?" Melinda asked after they'd stopped.

"Do? What do you mean?"

"Hold on . . . let me get the waitress over here." Simone raised her arm to capture the woman's attention.

"Do you think Hooters would hire me?" Lilliana asked out of the blue.

"What in the world? Why do you want to work at Hooters? Don't you like the temp job I set up for you?" Melinda asked Lilliana before she turned to Simone. "I don't think I need another drink, Simone! My head is reeling from the two I've already had!"

"Girl, please. It's Friday night . . . what else you got planned?" Simone turned her head. Her long, honey-blond, relaxed hair whipped around as she snapped her fingers to try and get the waitress's attention.

"Yes, I do like the job. It's going really well . . . I'll have another one, Simone," Lilliana laughed, easily moving back and forth with the conversation. She turned to Melinda. "I was just wondering if they'd hire me. I mean look at these chicks."

They all glanced around at the midriff-baring, T-shirt wearing waitresses bustling around the bar and grill, big boobs bouncing as they served drinks and food.

"What about them? What are you complaining about? You've got more than enough going on up top. Both of you heffas do. It's my behind they wouldn't hire. All ass and no tits!" Melinda humphed.

"Yeah, I got the boobs, but it's the rest of me they wouldn't dig, girl. Not only do I have the tits, I got the ass, thighs *and* hips to go along with it," Lilliana argued.

"Well, at least you're evened out. Got a nice small waist. I'd love to have more on top to go along with this butt of mine," Melinda insisted.

"Girl, whatever! I don't know what kind of man you're used to . . . oh, wait. That's right!" Simone snapped two fingers together. "You were married to that bougie fool, Edmund. His wannabe ass wouldn't know a real woman if she came up behind him and pimp-slapped him! That's why he didn't know what to do with you, Mel. You're a real woman, and once you stopped living in his image he didn't know *what* to do!"

Lilliana couldn't help smiling at her friends. It felt good to be home with friends who knew and loved her. She'd been back in Chicago for less than a month, yet it already felt *right*. She'd felt nervous returning home after being away so long, but her girls had made her feel comfortable in no time.

All three women had known each other since they were teens, attending the same private school. Melinda and Simone had been friends before Lilliana came along in the tenth grade. She'd received a scholarship to attend St. Mary's Catholic School. Well, that's what they'd called it, a scholarship. It was a more polite way of phrasing what it really was: a handout. The only qualification for the "scholarship" had been based on financial hardship.

In other words, for broke folks.

But she'd been glad to get away from the public school she'd attended in her own neighborhood. St. Mary's was a far cry from West Central, where she'd attended her freshman year of high school. At Saint Mary's all-girls academy, she didn't have to worry about being harassed by the older boys, teased because of the size of her breasts and told what they'd like to do with them and her.

Lilliana had always been slightly uncomfortable with her large breasts and tended to slump forward to hide them. Her own mother had teased her relentlessly about them, saying that was all a man would want from her. It had taken until recently before she'd finally kicked the ugly habit of hiding her body. But even now, she'd catch herself slumping and Simone would bust her out every time.

Her gaze traveled over her friends as they discussed the pros and cons of tits versus ass.

Simone was beautiful, vivacious and didn't give a damn what anyone thought of her. She spoke her mind without being mean, although sometimes Lilliana wondered how much was bravado and how much was real. No matter what, the woman had it going on. She loved her girl and although she didn't feel jealous of her, Lilliana wished she had a tenth of Simone's sheer nerve.

Simone wore her hair long, relaxed and blond. Bold. Just like she was. The color complemented her caramel skin and chestnut-colored eyes. It worked for her. Like Lilliana, she was short. Actually, Simone was petite, with nice firm breasts and butt, but she was thin. She often tried to hide her actual height, Lilliana rarely saw her wear shoes with a heel less than three inches.

On the other hand, Lilliana didn't consider herself petite, although she was short, and she had never been thin at only five feet three inches tall. The difference between her and Simone was that she was curvy *all over*. Her waist was small, but that was it. Thighs, hips, behind and tits ... nothing but curves.

Where she and Simone were shorter in stature, Melinda was tall and thin. But no matter how thin she was, sista girl still had an ass. Not as much as Simone, and nothing compared to hers, but she wasn't flat by any stretch of the imagination.

Before Melinda divorced Edmond, she too wore her hair long and relaxed as did Simone ... and fake. But unlike Simone, Melinda wore her additions to please her husband.

Although Lilliana lived her life by the motto "to each his own" she liked that her friend now wore her own hair short and twisted. In Lilliana's opinion it suited Melinda much better than all that fake stuff she used to sport.

Lilliana had worn her hair natural most of her life and had no desire to relax it. She'd used a relaxer once as a teenager and when all her hair fell out, that ended her desire to straighten her nappy kinks. If she didn't have it braided she usually wore it as she had it now, big and nappy all over her head, she thought with a laugh.

"Are you listening, Lilly? What do you think?"

"I think that's cool," she said, although she didn't know what in the world they were talking about.

Lilliana turned her attention back to her friends and hid her embarrassment. She'd developed the habit of going into her own world and thoughts as a teenager when her mother went on one of her rants, cussing her out for some perceived slight or other. The habit had been strengthened during her twelve years with Marcus, when he'd done the same thing to her.

"Are you serious? You want to do it? Okay, Melinda, that means you're going to be left out, girl! Come on, it'll be funny as hell if nothing else. Just think if someone actually answers the ad! Damn!"

"What ad?" Lilliana asked.

"*What ad*? You just said you thought it was cool! I knew you weren't paying attention. The ad we're going to take out to find a man who knows how to handle a big spankable ass! While you were spacing out, we were talking about taking out an ad . . ."

"*You* were talking about taking out an ad," Melinda quickly interjected.

"Fine, *I* was talking about taking out an ad in the *Reader* to try and find a man who knows how to, uh . . ." Simone hesitated.

"Don't act shy now, " Melinda laughed.

"I'm not shy about it! To try and find a man who knows what he's doing in bed. One who knows exactly how to please a woman," Simone said and paused to take a sip of her drink.

"Wait a minute. First off, are you serious? An ad in the *Reader* looking for a man? And how many of those have you had?" Lilliana asked, referring to the oversized margarita in Simone's hand.

"This is my third . . . I think," Simone disregarded the question with a wave of her French manicured hand and continued. "And not just any man. We want one who knows how to—"

"Yeah, I *got* that! One who knows how to handle a big spankable ass! Girl, what?" Lilliana started chuckling and before they knew it all three women were cracking up with laughter.

"Hold up, hold up! I'm serious!"

"Okay, so explain this to me. Ooh, Lord. Simone, you are nuts!" Lilliana gasped trying to get her laughter in check.

"Welll . . ." Simone started and dragged the word out. "We've all been complaining lately about not getting any good loving. I, for one, am tired as hell of relying on my vibrator for relief. I'm also tired of being alone and my love life sucks serious monkey balls. The brothas I've been dealing with lately are working my last nerve! The latest one lost his job *and* his erection! I can deal with one, but I damn sure am *not* dealing with both! I tried my damnedest to be sympathetic but when he started taking it out on me, that's where I draw the line! I want a living, breathing, man. *A real man.* I want to try things I've never tried before. I want adventure. I want a man to *lay it on me.* I want him to spank my fat ass . . . and *make* me like it," Simone paused and looked directly at Lilliana.

Lilliana felt like a deer caught in the headlights.

"How about you, Lil? Aren't you tired of the game? Are you with me? What better way to find exactly what we're looking for than to advertise? Are you both with me?"

Simone sat back in the booth. With one eyebrow raised and a half-smile on her face, she slowly raised her margarita high in the air and waited.

"Here's the rules," she continued when her friends didn't answer. "First date in public. During the day. No exchanging personal info until we check the man out. No hopping into a stranger's car. Keep it safe—and then go crazy."

Lilliana felt a curious excitement settle in her lower belly. The kind of tingle that meant she was going to do something bold, crazy, and unlike anything she probably would have thought of on her own. She laughed out loud.

"Hell yes, girl . . . count me in!" She raised her glass and they both turned to Melinda.

Melinda had a small smile on her face and she raised her glass as well. "What the hell, what can go wrong? It's not like anyone is going to actually answer the ad correctly," She laughed and with a clink all around the ladies toasted in agreement and ordered another round of margaritas.

That night as Lilliana lay in bed she thought back over what she and her friends had discussed and wondered what it would feel like to have a man really know what the hell he was doing in bed. To know what it would feel like to have a man do her real slow, take his time and work her until she cried out in mercy, pleading for him to take it *easy* on her. Make her call his name and like it. No faking, no pretense. A real man would know what she wanted. He'd know just how to handle her.

As her mind brought up images of an unknown stranger's large hand caressing her, she opened her legs and withdrew the vibrator from her side table drawer and soon a low hum filled the air. She leaned back against the pillows, licked her lips, closed her eyes and allowed her imagination to take over.

Slowly, he'd climb up her body, his dick thick and strong as it slid along the inside of her thigh. As it rubbed against the outer lips of her pussy, the head would be damp with pre-cum before it would thump a happy welcome against the curvature of her belly.

He'd lean down and kiss her. Slowly, skillfully, and completely . . . kiss her. He'd make love to her mouth like a porn star, sucking and nibbling until the kisses were no longer enough.

She brushed the vinyl-skinned vibrator against her aching, wet pussy, imaging it to be her dream lover's stiff dick. He'd play with her at first. Tease her wet lips, rubbing and torturing the hidden nub of her clit with the round knob of his penis until she was breathless in anticipation, waiting to see when he'd stop toying and give her what she needed.

Lilliana reached up and lightly cupped a breast in her hand and massaged the large globe and imagined how good it would feel to have a man's big hand in the place of hers. Lilliana pinched and pulled her nipples until they stood out in stiff peaks while she feathered the rubbery end of the vibrator against her clit. Slowly she eased the broad head of the apparatus into her vagina and groaned out loud as the smooth hardness of being filled to the rim with ten inches of vibrating sensation filled her.

She spread her legs far apart and allowed her knees to fall to the bed as she moved the plastic apparatus, bucking her hips and allowing her mind to imagine a man was riding her . . . to imagine it was the perfect man, making perfect love to her.

As she ground against the vibrator, she placed the palm of her hand above her pelvic bone and applied slight pressure and soon felt the heady sensation of an orgasm just out of reach. She quickened her pace and roughly massaged her breast and within minutes she cried out long and high as she came.

Once her heartbeat returned to normal and her breathing was once more under control she curled on her side and hugged her body pillow tight.

Lilliana wished with all her might that the sex she'd just had hadn't been a solo experience and the pillow she was hugging was a real man who'd just made love to her, instead of the fantasy man in her imagination.

A man who knew what to do with a big spankable ass, she thought with a humorless laugh.

2

"Oh, *please* hold that elevator!" a low, feminine voice cried. Josh reached out just in time to prevent the doors from closing shut.

"Thanks!" The woman rushed inside the jam-packed elevator, the occupants inside pressed shoulder to shoulder, all trying to make it in to their respective offices before eight A.M.

Josh was normally in the office himself much earlier, but he'd had a late start to his day trying to get off the phone with his mother, listening to her badger him about when she could expect a grandchild or two from him.

At twenty-eight years old, marriage and children were nowhere on his to-do list for the near future. No matter what lectures his mother gave about sperm count and his ability to father children decreasing with every year, he didn't produce a grandchild for her.

As the woman moved inside, Josh's gaze absentmindedly raked over her small body and an appreciative, purely male smile spread across his face. The elevator was so packed that she'd somehow gotten squashed between a very large guy and the wall, and from his vantage point, he didn't bother to pretend *not* to check out her breasts, full and flowing over in the peasant-style blouse she wore.

The blouse pushed them together and the soft-looking, large brown globes were high and firm-looking, her nipples straining against the bra she wore. Josh loved it when a woman's nipples poked her bra, unable to be contained . . . the sight was hot as hell. And this woman had his mouth watering when he saw the way her nipples were almost revealed through her gauzy blouse.

She kept her head down and her gaze averted and Josh looked down at the soft curls covering her head. He stopped himself from reaching out to see if her hair was as soft as it looked.

He inhaled, deeply, her fragrance reaching his nostrils. She smelled like a mixture of cinnamon and nutmeg. Either he was hungry from missing breakfast, or she smelled good enough to eat. Either way, she'd caught his attention. The thought of eating her appealed a lot more to him than his healthy rice bran cereal did. He subtly adjusted his pants.

The elevator jostled when the door opened up and as passengers left, more entered the overcrowded space. The woman stumbled when the large guy she was pressed against all but shoved her aside as he tried to get out of the elevator door before it closed.

Josh reached out to help steady her. Her skin felt smooth as butter when his fingers sank into the soft brown skin of her upper arm.

When she mumbled a thank you and glanced up at him, he felt sucker-punched.

It was her.

He'd seen her off and on for the last two weeks and this was the closest he'd ever come to seeing her up close. The first time had been in line in the large cafeteria the firm provided, during a late lunch.

She'd worn a badge clipped to her blouse, so he knew she worked for Longmire, Lieberman and Strauss, the same financial investment firm that he worked for. But unlike the sexy, curvy woman, he didn't have to wear a nametag identifying who he was. That was something he'd not had to wear since he'd been promoted to upper management.

He'd been two people behind her in line and had done his best to get closer, to get a better look at her. But his uncle had chosen that moment to find him and pulled him away to discuss a new client's portfolio.

Josh rarely ate at the cafeteria, but after seeing her there the first time, his interest had been piqued. He'd gone in every day over the last two weeks to try and corner the elusive woman who'd captured his attention, and find out her name.

Josh had an appreciation for all women, no matter their race, color or hue . . . fine was fine. And this woman was fine as *hell*. Her skin was the color of rich milk chocolate and her large, light brown eyes—almost too big for her face—were framed with thick, dark eyelashes. His gaze quickly slid down to her lips and he restrained a groan.

Her lips weren't exactly large, but they were lush enough to send his libido into hyper-drive, imagining what inventive things she could do with them . . . what he could do *to* them.

Especially when she pulled the lower, lush one into her mouth with her top teeth and slowly allowed it to pop back out as they stared at one another.

Although they could have only been looking at each other for a moment, Josh felt as though he'd lost track of time, not sure, really, how long he had been staring at her, gazing at that luscious mouth of hers. Imagining how good it'd feel wrapped around him.

He saw the way her eyes widened, as though she were startled. She was staring at him as though he was the big bad hunter and she was prey. He smiled, exposing all his canines, feeling like a hunter indeed. He didn't miss the way her breath hitched, her large breasts heaved, and her chest filled with fortifying air.

The intense, brief moment ended when she motioned to move away from him. Josh reluctantly released his steadying hands on her shoulders and with a nervous smile, she stumbled away.

Shit. What the hell had just happened? The acute disappointment he felt when she made a move to get off on the next floor didn't make any sense either, but damn if he didn't feel it.

She left the elevator, but before she did, Josh noticed that she paused and cast him a look on the sly, from the corner of her eye, before she rushed off the elevator. He canted his head to the side and admired the way her full hips swayed back and forth beneath the long green skirt, before the elevator doors shut, taking her away from his view.

Joshua glanced down and his eyes caught the flash of a silver clip with a name badge attached to it. He quickly bent to retrieve it. It must have come off when she'd been jostled to the side.

Hmm. He knew just who to talk to . . . to find out more.

Lilliana rushed away from the elevator as fast as her legs could take her, feeling flustered and ridiculous. Here she was, a grown woman of thirty-two . . . almost thirty-three years and she'd allowed herself to get all hot and bothered just by looking at a man. Okay, so he wasn't just *any man*. He was a big, blond, *ooh-baby-do-me*, fine as *hell* man. And she really, really wanted to be done. It had been way too long since she'd felt the caress of a man.

She'd noticed the way he'd been checking her out in the elevator although she'd done her best to pretend as though she hadn't. The way he'd been staring at her tits, her lips . . . Lilliana shivered.

She'd taken side peeks at him a few times, but she'd had to look away for fear he'd catch her eyeballing him. She noticed right off the bat how tall he was. He had to be at least six two or three and had a body like a linebacker. His dress shirt had been tucked neatly into the tailor-made slacks, showing off a trim waist, no doubt courtesy of the gym.

His hand had been the one to stall the elevator as she'd made the mad dash to get inside, trying to avoid being late for the second time.

She'd noted how nice the man's hands had been, with the neatly trimmed fingernails and a barely discernible dusting of hair over the backs. Not too much hair, like a Neanderthal, just enough to be sexy.

When he'd helped steady her and she'd looked up to say thank you, she'd felt like someone had kicked her straight in the gut. He'd smiled down at her and two dimples flashed in his lean, lightly tanned cheeks and she'd offered up a weak smile and hopefully mumbled *something* back. But in all honesty she hadn't a clue what she'd said, if anything, as she'd looked into his eyes, feeling like a women in one of the erotic romance books that she secretly read.

Lord have mercy, if he wasn't fine, though.

He was white, but although it was early in the summer, his skin was a nice golden tan as though he'd spent time in the sun.

His dark blue eyes were deep set and the look in them when he'd held her gaze made her think, for one moment, that she was the only woman in the world. The way he'd given her an almost quizzical half-smile, the flash of dimple and way he'd stared at her mouth, had her imagining what she'd like to do to him with her mouth.

No two ways about it, the man was fine.

"Okay, so you said that part already. He's fine. Now move on," she said to herself.

"Hi Lilly! Ooh, girl, thanks! You like my new blouse? I bought it yesterday at Macy's one-day clearance sale! But don't tell anyone that. Gotta protect the diva image," her co-worker said as she passed his desk.

"Lee, you nut, I wasn't talking to you. I was just talking out loud," Lilliana laughingly answered.

"Oh poo! I thought you were talking to me!" The Hispanic man made a small moue with his lips and Lilliana reached over and patted him on the back.

"I'm sorry, sweetie! Yes, I like your blouse ... although, Lee—women wear blouses, men wear shirts."

"Um well, not this man. Don't I look *fabulous* in it?" he said and promptly jumped up from his chair and did a small pirouette for Lilly and curtsied.

"Of course you do! Now sit down, before Ms. Hillman sees you out of your chair! If you want to get hired on as a full-time administrative assistant, you need to fly a little further under the radar!"

"As if! Girlfriend, all this fineness *can not* be contained." He laughed and leaned against her partition, examining the nearly clear coat of polish on his manicured hands.

"Lee," she began.

"Please call me by my diva name. That's Ms. Leesia to you, ma'am." He tooted his lips out and gave her an air kiss.

"Do you *have* to be the stereotype?" She tucked her large hobo bag underneath her desk and started pulling out documents in her inbox to prepare for the day.

"It's what I do best, sweet thing! Why be a drear queer?"

"I guess," Lilliana said as she readied her desk and situated herself.

"Life is too short to try and live up to someone else's expectations of who you should be. Been there, done that, got the friggin' badge, *mami*," he laughed. Lilliana heard something more than humor behind the laugh. Lee noted the look and answered her unasked question.

"Long story short, I grew up with a father who didn't exactly take well to his ten-year-old son telling him he preferred Ken over Barbie, and ballet to football. Added to that, there's the bizarreness of my mother who continually caught me dressing up in her stilettos, makeup, *and panties*. Her only response was 'It's just a phase. He'll grow out of it!' " The happy, carefree veneer dropped from Lee's handsome face, leaving a disgusted sad look in its place.

"I'm sorry, Lee."

"No biggie. I'm happy now and my parents are slowly coming around. Eventually maybe they'll accept who I am. And if they don't . . . oh well! I'm not missing Macy's one day sale for anyone! I'd sell *mi abuela* to get that new Versace blouse I've had my eyes on for the last month. It's going on sale twenty percent off for one . . . day . . . only," he dramatically stretched out the last three words.

"You are so stupid!" Lilliana said with affection.

She and Lee had taken to one another quickly during the last two weeks of her employment with the firm. Lee too was a temporary hire, and like her, he wanted to be hired on full time. When Lilliana had been assigned the cubicle next to his, he'd taken the sole responsibility of hipping her up to what went on at Longmire, Lieberman and Strauss, and the beginning of their friendship.

"But you love me anyway. So what did you and those heffas you hang out with decide to do?"

"About what?" She didn't bother to check him on calling her girls heffas. He'd ignore her anyway if she did.

"Honey, don't play with me! You know what I'm talking about! Big, spankable . . ."

"Sshh, Lee! Someone might hear you!" Lilliana said and stood up at her cubicle and glanced around. She caught the supervisor's eyes, and quickly sat down. "You'd better sit down, Lee. Ms. Hillman is eyeballing you all the way from her office. And this time, I don't think she's got her eyes on your new bag." Lee swore up and down that the woman was jealous of his collection of Louis Vuitton bags.

"Whatever, chica. I'm not afraid of that overgrown rat." He talked a good game, but Lilliana noticed he sat down anyway.

"That's not nice, Lee. She can't help her overbite," Lilliana said automatically.

"Braces. How about a nice set of braces? Hmmm? And you know she's making mucho dinero! The heffa's been working for Longmire since the Stone Age. Not married, no kids . . . uh huh, she got money, *mami*, trust me. She needs to use a few of those greenbacks and get her damn mustache waxed . . . with her ole evil self." He quickly turned to his work when the woman turned her eyes on him, a deep frown settling across her mustachioed face.

"Lee," Lilly hissed, trying to make him be quiet. If he kept on, she knew she'd end up laughing out loud and drawing more attention to herself and give Ms. Hillman a reason to come over to their cubicle.

"We'll talk about this later!" Lee promised in a low voice.

She turned her headset on and listened to Kem croon low in her ears. Music always helped her work go by faster and she was surprised when they were allowed to listen to headsets in the office.

Lilliana happily began on the mountain of statements she had in her inbox that needed to be processed into the computer and bounced a bit in her chair as she worked.

"So . . . did you?"

"Boy, you almost gave me a damn heart attack! Did I what?" She'd been concentrating for several minutes when Lee plucked one of the earphones away from her ear and asked the question.

He frowned at her and poked out his lips and she sighed. "You are not going to let it go, are you?"

"No, I'm not! I just don't think you have the balls to actually go through with it, that's all."

"Don't have the what? Pulleeze! I not only have the balls to contemplate it . . . I did it! I took out the ad!" Lilliana stated proudly. She lowered her voice when a few co-workers turned their heads in her direction at her confession. "And not only that . . . it comes out in today's issue of the *Reader*!" She smirked when Lee's mouth literally dropped.

"Close your mouth, you'll catch flies!" she laughed.

"I don't believe it! Prove it!" he hissed back over the partition and promptly sat back down when Ms. Hillman came out of her office.

Lilliana dug out her bag from underneath her desk in the cubicle and plopped it into her lap. "I have the proof right here," she said and rummaged around inside until she came out with a folded piece of paper. She wheeled herself away from her desk and toward Lee's cubicle and shoved the cut-out to him. "Check it out!" she giggled.

Lee quickly scanned the contents of the ad and raised approving eyes at her. "Oh, snap! You did do it! Girl, I can't believe it! Oh, how funny, Big Spankable Asses!" he chortled at the words she'd handwritten across the top of the paper. "Did your girlfriends do it as well? I want all the details and don't leave anything out!" He settled back in his chair with an excited look crossing his handsome face.

"I'll give you the scoop at lunchtime—right now, give it

back! Ms. Hillman is headed this way." She grabbed the paper and stuffed it into the top drawer of her desk and got busy before their supervisor busted them.

"Fine, but I want all the details!" He went back to work as well, before the woman reached them.

3

"Josh, I want you to take the Bradley case over from Ben," Allen Longmire told his nephew as they left the top floor suite of offices and entered the elevator.

"No problem, Allen. Is Ben okay with that?" Josh asked and punched the elevator button for the third floor.

"He's *going* to be okay with it." The way Allen said it left no doubt in Josh's mind that it wasn't Ben's idea to be replaced. "You've got a proven track history with these particular investments. Ben's been fucking up lately and we don't want to alienate the Bradleys. They bring big money to the firm. We need to keep them happy, and money keeps them happy. Making money keeps everyone involved happy, particularly this firm. You'll do a great job with it, I have confidence in you, boy." Allen patted his back as they left the elevator. Josh managed not to grimace at the hearty pat and the way his uncle called him "boy." At twenty-eight, he'd left boyhood behind a long damn time ago. Actually, since his father left his mother when he was six years old, he hadn't felt like a boy for what felt like eons.

"That's fine with me, as long as you let him know it was your idea and not something I approached you with."

"Of course I will, just leave Ben to me! I'll take care of it." His uncle patted him on the back again. "Look, it's lunchtime, do you want to head down to grab a bite to eat in the cafeteria? I don't have the time to go anywhere else today."

"I was thinking the same thing. Let me go back upstairs, I need to grab my wallet."

"I think I can afford to buy my own nephew a five dollar sandwich," Allen laughed.

"Yeah, well, I have enough shit to deal with as it is, with some thinking I don't really belong here. I can buy my own lunch, but thanks, Uncle Allen. Besides, I have an errand to run after lunch and I need my wallet," Josh hedged.

"Hey, you deserve to be here just like anyone else. Nothing was handed to you. You work damn hard, make more money for this firm than any other senior exec, and to hell with what they think. Your father helped me build this firm and you have the same skill and knack for making money that he did . . . does."

"I appreciate the words, but it won't take long for me to grab my wallet from my office. I'll meet you down there," Josh said, avoiding his uncle's eyes.

"Sure. I'll meet you down there," he agreed. Josh caught the flash of *something* in his eyes before he exited the elevator.

Wallet retrieved, Josh waited before he pressed the down button. When the second elevator slid open, he stepped inside and withdrew the badge from the pocket in his jacket.

"I wouldn't have believed it had I not read it with my own two eyes," Lee said around a mouthful of tunafish salad he was trying to swallow.

"Well . . . I'm not all that sure I believe it myself and I took the ad out!"

"But you're going through with it, *si*?"

"You mean if someone actually guesses the right answer? Yeah, I think so," Lilliana said and laughed. "But what's the likelihood of that?"

"You mean of someone coming up with the right reply?"

Lilliana paused to take a sip her of green tea and answered after she swallowed. "I mean . . . who would guess?"

"Girl, you been away from Chi-town *way* too long! We got some serious freaks here too, just like Cali!"

"What? What do you mean, freaks here like in Cali?" she spit his words back to him.

"I don't know—I guess I would say don't be surprised if *somebody* guesses what B.S.A. stands for . . . or comes damn close. We've got some folks into the whole spanking thing, on the down low for real, chica," he laughed.

"What do you mean? And why are they on the down low?"

Lee looked over the top of his slushy at her like she was crazy, and suddenly Lilliana felt just as crazy as she must look. "Lee! I'm serious! What is it?"

"Girl, I thought you were into the whole *tie me up, spank my ass and slap a collar on me while you're at it* scene!" he said in a low voice.

"What?" she said and nearly choked on her tea.

Lee looked around as though he were making sure that no one was listening to them and leaned across the small table. "I just assumed from the ad that you were into spankings . . . maybe a little S&M too."

"No, I'm not! Why would you think that?" Lilliana knew her voice was way too high and squeaky when several pairs of eyes turned in her direction in curiosity, but she ignored their looks and allowed her gaze to stay trained on Lee.

"Okay, for one, I thought you were into it because you took a frickin' ad out asking for a man who knew how to spank your ass! And another . . . well who the hell takes an ad out asking a man to tap that ass if she didn't want her ass tapped?"

"Tapped and hit are two different things! I don't want some man hitting me! I just left one who did that to me! Why in hell would I willingly ask someone to hit me?"

"Hitting and spanking are two different things, chica! Don't knock it till you've tried it."

"What? You've done it? Let a man hit you?" Although the idea of allowing a man to willingly put his hands on her was abhorrent to Lilly, she found herself curious as to what Lee would say.

"Not *hit* me, Lilly . . . *spank* me. Two totally different things," he told her with a smile. "Girl, no one's ever introduced you to the sweetness of submission?" Lee laughed coyly and when she shook her head he looked around again, as though someone was trying to listen to their conversation. "Well, let me be the first to tell you. With the right person, it's a feeling like no other."

"Really?" Lilly asked in a hushed tone, completely forgetting to eat the spaghetti smothered in marinara sauce that she loved as Lee filled her in, with graphic details, on what he called the sweet side of submission.

"Honey, yes. A nice firm but soft hand, applying just the right amount of sting . . . chica, ummm . . . it's off the chain." He smiled what she thought was a very happy, reminiscing grin.

"It has to be with the right man. You've got to trust him, trust that he won't hurt you," he told her thoughtfully as he continued to eat. "Have some candles burning, some Hennessy, maybe a little Luther or Usher playing in the background, and a big beautiful naked man, hard and ready to lay it on you!" he laughed.

The handsome blond guy she'd seen on the elevator instantly sprang to Lilliana's mind. She had no problem imagining how good he'd look, butt naked and standing tall, hard, and ready to give her what she needed.

"Tell me more and don't leave out a thing," she demanded, fascinated, wondering how it could possibly feel good to be totally at the mercy of a man's hands during lovemaking, and enjoy it.

"Anything I can do for you, Mr. Longmire?" Josh nearly jumped out of his skin when the supervisor tapped him on the shoulder and asked the question.

He turned and barely kept the smile on his face when his eyes came into direct contact with Ms. Hillman. He struggled to keep a straight face as he stared at the floor supervisor's obvious mustache.

"No ma'am, I was, um, just looking for someone." Josh had no idea why he stammered, but there was something about the older woman that made him feel all of twelve years old with his hand caught in the proverbial cookie jar.

"Tell me who it is. I'm sure I can help you. Everyone has gone to lunch but I can show you to the cubicle of the person you're searching for. Is there something I can help you out with?" She smiled, showing all twenty-eight of her slightly protruding teeth.

"Thanks, Ms. Hillman. It's really not a problem—well, if you could show me where Lilliana Michaels's cubicle is, I can take it from there."

"Is there a problem? Did she do something?" There was a look of anticipatory glee on the woman's face that Josh didn't find particularly attractive.

"No, actually she dropped something and I simply want to return it to her."

"Oh, well she's out to lunch with that *friend* of hers, Lee Gutierrez. Her cubicle is down that aisle, second to last one on the right," she said, pointing. "But I can return it, sir. No problem."

"Thanks, but I'll do it." Josh was relieved when her phone rang and the woman left to answer. He quickly walked down the aisle as she went inside her office and closed the door to answer the call.

When he located Lilliana's desk he smiled, noting the scattering of framed self-affirmations on her desk. She was obviously into the positive-thinking craze. He placed her name tag on her desk and was turning to leave when he noticed a crumpled piece of paper lying on the floor, slightly underneath the corner of her desk. As he bent down to retrieve the paper, it occurred to him that the woman sure had a habit of dropping things.

When he was about to place the paper on her desk, he glimpsed three words on it that got his attention, big-time. Damn. What in the world? Feeling like a snoop, he opened the crumpled-up paper and quickly scanned the contents.

BF in search of a real man, one who knows just what to do with a B.S.A! In order to prove you're up for the challenge, be the first man to respond to this ad with the right answer and tell me what B.S.A. stands for and we can go from there. Respond at this e-mail address bsa1972@ . . . Hurry up, the clock is ticking.

She'd written in a flowing script at the bottom of the page the words *Big Spankable Ass*, and Josh almost choked. Oh my God. This was way too good. Damn.

She'd written the answer at the bottom of the slip of paper, but the ad itself didn't have the answer. The ad had been placed in the *Reader*, Chicago's free popular weekly periodical. He looked at the date and realized that either she'd just put it in today, or it had appeared in a previous week, as the *Reader* only came out on Thursday and today was Thursday. He took note of the e-mail address, folded the ad, and placed it on her desk.

He looked around to see if anyone saw him and left the office. If the administrative assistant wanted her pretty brown tush spanked, well, Josh was just the man to do it. He laughed outright in a purely male chuckle as he made haste back to his office and his computer.

4

The walk home after she'd exited the bus was only two blocks and Lilly felt safe in the upper-end neighborhood walking in the light dusk of early evening. She counted herself blessed that she'd secured the cottage that she lived in and knew that she owed Melinda a serious debt of gratitude for finding the affordable little house for her.

As Lilliana walked the small distance she had time to think back on her very . . . enlightening . . . conversation with Lee and laughed.

When Lilliana had placed the ad, she hadn't given it as much thought as she obviously should have. What in the world had Simone been thinking when she told them all to ask a man to figure out the acronym for Big Spankable Ass in an ad? Hmmm. Maybe Simone was doing some freaky shit herself on the down low, Lilliana thought.

She reached her small home, opened the door and walked inside. Once in, Lilliana let out a deep breath, kicked off her shoes, and tossed her bag on the chintz-covered sofa that she'd carefully reupholstered and glanced around.

The cottage wasn't large, but it was perfect for her. The living area was large and airy and opened up into a sizable bedroom. She'd separated the two rooms with large bamboo screens that she'd found at a flea market, and set side by side. She loved the ambiance she'd created throughout with her other unique finds.

She and her girls, Simone and Melinda, had spent a weekend sanding and refinishing her tables and whatnot stands, despite the occasional good-natured grumbles, usually from Simone, about messing up manicures and causing calluses. They'd helped her to make the cottage feel like home. The only things not donated or bought used were her mattress and her laptop.

With a happy sigh, she padded barefoot to the kitchen to search for something to eat. She opened the refrigerator and took out the pan of enchiladas she'd made two nights ago and popped them into the microwave and set the timer.

As she waited for them to heat, she checked her voicemail and laughed as Simone's voice came on, complaining about one of her employees, whose behind she was about to kick to the curb if she came in *one* more time smelling like weed and fried chicken.

The microwave dinged and she took out her dinner and blew on it as she walked though to her bedroom, where she had her laptop connected to the Internet sitting on the small desk in the corner of the room.

She sat down, placed the plate of food near the keyboard and logged on, then reached out to pick up the remote control to her small stereo system and hit the play button. The crooning, NuSoul sound of India.Aire came wafting out of the speakers.

Lilliana bounced her butt in her seat and sang off-key along with the singer as she listened to the music and waited. She wished she could afford to get the high speed connection the cable company offered, but she'd have to wait until her money wasn't so funny before she could afford to do that.

"Let's see what's going on in the world," she mumbled out loud as her home page filled the screen.

She read the headlines until she noticed the small envelope icon in the corner that notified her that she had e-mail. She clicked on it and saw a handful of e-mails that had come in response to the ad and felt nervous excitement pool in her gut. She'd created a second e-mail name, solely for the ad, that would redirect to her main e-mail address.

She clicked on the first e-mail from mrbiggs@biggiesworld. com. What the . . . ?

Lilliana was almost scared to see what Mr. Biggs' answer would be. Any man that had to *tell* you he was Mr. Biggs, she'd lay odds he wasn't all that big in the places he wanted you to think he was.

Hey girl, I like what I read and I think I got just the answer for YOU! First let me tell you a little about myself. My name is Tyrese Bigelow, but they call me Mr. Biggs for short, and I bet you can guess why! But don't let the name fool you. Just because I'm big don't mean I don't know how to be gentle. I'll treat you right, baby girl! So let's just cut to the chase. You say you're a BF (black female) in the ad, so I'm guessing that B.S.A stands for Black Smelly Ass! But girl, if I'm wrong I won't tell nobody if you don't. **Wink!** *Hit me up at 555-1920 and we can discuss what you want me to do with that Black Sexy Smelly Ass of yours! I can smell it from here . . . girl, you're ripe for me, you're ripe!*

By the time Lilliana read the last line she was laughing so hard she almost fell out of her chair. "Oh no, the hell he didn't! Oh my God. Black *Smelly* Ass and I'm ripe for him?" But hell, it wasn't any worse than what she, Melinda and Simone had come up with! Lord have mercy.

Okay, one down, two more to go. She opened the next e-mail. This one sounded halfway normal. At least he had a nice screen name, she thought—until she opened up the e-mail and got seriously confused reading the message.

Hello, Ma'am. My name is Clarence John, but my friends call me C.J. I'm hoping that you and I can become friends!

"Ooh, isn't that nice?" Lilliana carefully bit into her enchilada and continued to read.

The minute I read your ad in the personal, I knew I had to answer! I, too, am a Boy Scout of America and was thrilled when I saw this ad!

What the . . .

Now, I'm not sure what you want me to do, but ma'am, I'm up for the challenge. The Scout's motto is to be prepared at all times for all things! I've been a member of the Scouts for over thirty years and I've lived this motto for just as long!

"Okaaay . . ."

I've got some nice new rope and know just how to use it! My last one got really frayed with my ex-girlfriend. If only she'd just sat still! Anyway, recently, as a senior scout leader, I've learned a variety of new knots that I'd love to try on you guaranteed that you wouldn't be able to escape from! I also have some really good, secure hand and mouth restraints, ball gag, the works, that I'd love to put on you!

"Oh no the hell you won't, you damn freak." Lilliana deleted the message so fast she almost hurt herself. "I don't know if I should laugh or call the damn cops on his strange behind!" When she saw that there was one more message she almost deleted it without looking at it. "Oh, well, it'll be good for a laugh anyway . . . or a good long cry."

This one had a normal e-mail address so that was one point in his favor. She reluctantly opened the e-mail, almost afraid to read what this one had to say.

Hello, Miss. I'm not quite sure how to start this. In fact I have to admit that I feel a little silly.

Lilliana chewed her food thoughtfully, swallowed and continued reading.

To be honest, I wouldn't have ever come across this ad had it not been by pure chance. But since I'm a man who believes in chance and destiny and star-crossed lovers . . .

Lilliana laughed out loud at that part.

That was the part that you were supposed to laugh at, ha ha.

She laughed again.

I knew I had to answer the ad. I'm a normal guy. At least my mother says I am. I'm six foot, two and a half inches. (I claim the half inch because I have three older brothers who beat the crap out of me growing up and the half inch gave me the edge a few times.) I have a pretty good job doing what I like to do, make money.

Hmmm, nothing wrong with that!

I like to read, like to collect miniatures . . . oh hell. I probably shouldn't have written that. Now you probably think I'm gay, huh? Strike that. I collect fifties sitcom memorabilia . . . Damn! That was the wrong answer too, I can feel you laughing!

Lilliana was laughing so hard, her side hurt.

I work out and go to all sporting events, particularly world wrestling matches, like to go boating and fishing, among other manly pursuits—how about that? Is that better?

"Loads!" Lilliana said out loud and laughed when she read the next line.

Yeah, I thought so too! As I was saying . . . I found your ad purely by accident and was intrigued. I would love to meet you. But according to your ad, I have to figure out what BSA stands for, right?

Heck, even if he guessed wrong, at this point Lilliana was willing to overlook that part, this one sounded like a winner.

She was left with her mouth wide open as she finished reading the e-mail.

At first I thought . . . hmmm? What could it be? Bright Shiny Apples? Then I thought that didn't make any sense! Okay how about Big Sweet Apples? No? What about Bodacious Succulent Apples? Oh hell. Why did I try and figure this out on an empty stomach? Well, let me go out on a limb here . . . Big Spankable Ass? If any of the answers are correct call me. My phone number is 555-0860. But even if I'm wrong, call me. Please :)
~Josh

Oh my. He'd answered right. Lilliana had been so busy cracking up at his apple answers that she was totally left speechless when she read the right answer. How in the world did he guess? Her lunchtime conversation with Lee surfaced in her mind and she remembered him saying how many folks were into spankings in Chicago! Was this Josh one of them? How else would he have come up with big spankable ass?

She logged off the 'net but not before she'd jotted down his phone number. She quickly went to her side table, picked up the cordless phone, and punched in his phone number, not wanting to give herself time to think and chicken out. Yes, he'd find out her number if he had caller ID, but nothing else, no address or anything like that. She couldn't be found in the reverse directory. As the phone rang, the nervous feeling in the pit of her stomach increased to the point that she felt physically sick and was tempted to hang the phone up and forget the whole thing until she heard a deep voice answer.

"Hello, this is Josh. I'm not in at the moment. Leave a message. Thanks!"

She almost laughed out loud in relief. Okay, so it wasn't meant to be. No way was she going to leave a message. She hung up the phone. The sick feeling in her stomach receded as she lay back against the pillows on her bed.

She turned and curled around the soft body pillow and looked out the large window in her bedroom. What in the world had convinced her to take out that ad in the first place? Loneliness and stupidity were an ugly combination.

She stared out the window, at the pretty lit-up garden in the backyard of the mansion that the cottage belonged to. A lone tear escaped and fell down her cheek. Lilliana smiled a small half-smile and closed her eyes and eventually fell asleep.

5

Josh was too impatient to wait for the elevator and instead took the stairs two at a time until he got to the sectioned-off area that led to his large, open bay loft. He wanted to know if Lilliana had responded to his e-mail, but after work his mother had decided she needed him to drive out to her home, way out in Winnetka, to help her move her sofa.

Josh had reluctantly driven out and, with more speed than he'd thought humanly possible, had helped her rearrange two rooms of furniture, listened to her lament about how his oldest brother Landon rarely came to visit anymore, among a host of other complaints such as the recently released scientific data stating that as a man entered his thirties, his sperm count was greatly reduced.

He'd moved the furniture, commiserated with her about Landon, and reassured her that his sperm count wasn't in jeopardy, before he'd finally left and raced home, making it by ten o'clock.

After he'd let himself into his loft, he headed toward the kitchen and the cold beer in the fridge. He tossed his keys on the center butcher block table and grabbed a beer before going to his computer in his den.

The loft was split-level and over 3,000 square feet, smack in the middle of the Gold Coast near the lake. He'd paid the hefty, half mil fee for the loft with the money from one of his more lucrative commissions, with no help from his uncle.

Joshua was grateful for all that Allen had done for him, but at times he felt uneasy about accepting the handouts, as his brother Landon liked to call them. Although he disagreed with Landon and didn't see them as handouts, he knew his brother said it to screw with him.

He worked hard and was good at what he did, and in his time with the firm, he'd added to their reputation as aggressive brokers who knew how to generate profit.

Besides that, their father had helped make the firm what it was today, as their uncle was always quick to acknowledge, and if he were still around things would be . . . different.

Shit. No use thinking about what could be and why the hell it wasn't. His father wasn't around. End of subject. Hadn't been since he was a kid and there was no use rolling down that particular memory lane. Right now he was curious about whether or not the sexy admin assistant had answered his e-mail, and done with thinking about painful memories best left in the past.

Once inside his den he flicked on the overhead track lights, picked up the small remote on the edge of the desk and pressed a button. Music filled the entire loft from hidden speakers in each room. With the heart-pounding lyrics and bass of Lenny Kravitz to pump him up, he sat down at his desk and touched one of the keys on his wireless keyboard. His large screen filled with his home page on the Internet within seconds.

He saw the envelope icon telling him he had mail and clicked on it, searching for one from Lilliana Michaels. Within minutes of reading junk mail, and stupid forwards he'd patiently asked his mother to stop sending him that demanded he forward the stupid forward to ten people in the next ten minutes . . . he stifled the feelings of acute disappointment when he didn't see an e-mail from *her*.

Maybe someone else had already answered the ad and he'd been too late. Or maybe she'd actually called him. His glance fell to his cordless phone that set on his desk. He picked it up and pressed the dial tone, but when he didn't hear the static tone that indicated he had a voice mail, he pressed the end button. Then he noted that he had several new caller ID notifications and out of curiosity he scrolled down and stopped and smiled.

L. Michaels. 555-1914.

Hot damn. She'd called.

Josh sat back in his desk chair and swiveled around with his fingers steepled together. Should he wait to see if she'd call him back? He looked over at the grandfather clock in the corner. It was already 10:15. Maybe she'd think it was too late to call. Or maybe she'd chickened out and decided not to go through with it.

He doubted that. No way could someone come up with an ad asking a man if he knew what to do with a big spankable ass and be afraid to leave a message. Or would she? Maybe someone put her up to it, or it was all a joke.

Best way to find out was to call her and see if she was all bluff or if she was serious. He quickly pressed the button for last call return and ignored the unsettled feeling in his stomach as he waited for her to answer the phone.

The jarring of the phone woke Lilliana out of a light doze and after she wiped her mouth with the back of her hand, she answered with a croaky, " 'ello."

"Hello, is this L. Michaels?" a man asked in a voice so deep and sexy, Lilliana woke up completely and bumped her head against her wrought iron headboard in her haste to sit up.

"Ouch!" she said and rubbed her head.

"Are you okay?" deep and sexy asked.

"Uh, yes. I'm fine. Thanks. This is Lilliana Michaels . . . may I help you?" She squinted her eyes in the dark of the room to search out the time on her alarm clock, afraid she'd somehow overslept and was late getting up for work. When she saw the time she breathed a sigh of relief. She must have fallen asleep after she'd spoken to Melinda.

"Hi, Lilliana. My name is Joshua. Josh Ellis."

It took a minute for the name to register and when it did Lilliana gasped. "The guy who answered my ad, right?"

"What ad? Oh! The big spankable . . ." He left the last word off and Lilly felt her cheeks heat with embarrassment. "You're the woman who placed the ad in the *Reader*—I was wondering who you were. You called but didn't leave a message. I've been getting a lot of that lately and just decided to call back. Why didn't you leave a message? Did I answer the ad correctly?" He asked the questions back to back.

Lilliana had to clear her head. He had caller ID—well, who didn't? But he didn't have her address and she wasn't going to give it to him.

"Yes, yes you did. I called but . . ."

"Chickened out and decided not to leave a message?"

"No-o," she dragged the word out. "I wouldn't say that."

"No?" He laughed and his laugh was as deep and sexy as his voice. Either it had been way too long since she'd gotten any, or she was one nasty heffa, as she felt moist between her legs from the way he teased her.

She laughed with him, reluctantly. "Okay, maybe I did." She suddenly felt a bit more at ease with the conversation. "And yes, you did answer the ad right," she finished.

"So what's my prize? I believe the ad mentioned the game beginning? I can't tell you what type of images that brought to mind," he said.

"Oh really? Well, I hadn't gone that far in my thinking. I didn't expect anyone to guess it! And after all of your apple answers . . ."

"Yeah, sorry about that. Like I said in the e-mail, I was hungry when I read it."

"Sure you were!" she laughed and continued, "I was surprised when you guessed right. How did you come up with the right answer?"

"I'm kinky. It comes naturally for my mind to think along those lines," he said. She could have sworn he was laughing although his voice was perfectly normal-sounding.

"Kinky? Just how kinky are we talking? Whips, chains—what?" She held her breath waiting to see if he'd confirm her worst fears and say he was some kind of freaky-ass dominant, like the ones Lee had enlightened her about over lunchtime. After he'd told her about spankings he'd gone on a long diatribe about the whole BDSM lifestyle that had scared the mess out of her. Although . . .

The idea of this sexy-voiced man tying her up and doing some of the things Lee told her about filled her with a strange expectation that made no sense at all.

"No, none of that. I'm more into the sweeter side of submission." He laughed again. Lilliana couldn't tell from his voice if he were joking with her or serious. "What about you? I gather from your ad that you've been . . . spanked before?"

Josh waited to hear what she'd say. He was hoping the luscious beauty was into spankings, because she'd captured his attention from the minute he'd set eyes on her. He conjured up the image of her sweet, round ass swaying in the full peasant skirt, which in turn had his imagination running wild with how he'd like to slap that ass and then kiss it till it wasn't sore anymore.

He wasn't into the BDSM scene, by any stretch of the imagination, he just enjoyed a bit of light bondage and spanking and he hoped that she did also. With that nice, full round ass of hers . . . he longed to feel how soft and smooth it was as he smacked her ass and plunged his dick deep inside her warm pussy.

After a significant pause she answered in her soft voice, "No. I've never been spanked. I've been . . . hit, but I didn't like it." Her laugh was in no way humorous.

Her words made him pause as well. That didn't sound good. He wasn't sure if she was playing a game or not, but it sounded as though she'd been hurt. "It can be good with the right person, Lilliana. In the right situation. And a light spanking is a hell of a lot different than someone hitting you. But you have to feel comfortable with it. It definitely can't be forced on you. I would never do something to a woman that she didn't want done."

"That's good to know," was all that she said.

"Can I ask you a question?" As they'd been speaking, Josh had carried the phone into his bedroom and had removed his clothes as they spoke and was now lying down, naked, on top of the light quilt.

"Sure."

"Why did you take out an ad with that acronym if you're not into spankings?"

She paused before answering. "As a lark, I guess. Partially. I don't know." Could he hear the nervousness in her voice? "Like I said, I didn't think anyone would answer."

"Well, I did. So where do we go from here?" As he spoke to her, he cradled the phone between his shoulder and ear, and lay propped against a few pillows.

"Where do you want to go?"

"I don't think you're ready to hear that yet." He laughed at her and laughed even harder when she answered, "nasty ass," and then giggled. Damn, she had a cute giggle. She sounded all of fifteen years old, but he knew for certain she was over the age of consent.

"You'd be surprised," she said and his interest was piqued even more. During their twenty-minute conversation she had already presented an intriguing mixture of innocence and naughtiness that had him ready to explore which side of her would show up in bed. He could only imagine what a combination of the two would be.

"Would you go out on a date with me, Lilliana?"

"A date?" she asked. He refrained from commenting on her clear surprise. From the words and the way she said it, she obviously thought he just wanted to fuck her. Spank her and fuck her, to be precise. Not that he didn't want to do both, but he found himself wanting to do more than that with her.

"Yes, Lilliana, a date."

"Like where?"

"How about the Navy Pier Friday?" As soon as he said it, he remembered the new client that his uncle had assigned to him. He was supposed to meet with the man after work on Friday. No way in hell could he get out of it this soon, although for once the thought of making money didn't hold as much appeal as the desire to get to know a woman.

"That sounds like fun. I haven't been to the Pier in ages." She sounded so excited that he wanted to groan.

"I'm sorry, Lilliana, I have a commitment Friday that it's too late to get out of. I completely forgot. How about something later? Saturday or Sunday?"

"That's fine. Saturday will work for me. During the day. At the Pier?"

"That works for me. What time is best? How about noon? We can get something to eat there." They agreed on the time and meeting point. They also described what they would be wearing and Josh gave her his cell phone number just in case. When she described herself, he almost laughed out loud.

"I'm short, about five feet three inches, African American, dark brown skin. My eyes are my best feature, I think. They're light brown but they're kind of big. I wear my hair natural and it's kind of curly. Nappy curly, I guess," she coughed and continued. "Ummm. I think that's it. Sorry, I must sound pretty average to you."

"You sound beautiful to me," he said sincerely. He already knew what she looked like. He figured that either she was being modest or she really didn't know how beautiful she was.

"I'm tall, and since you say that you're five feet three inches, I'm almost a foot taller than you, and dorky," he said. She cracked up laughing. "What? I'm serious. I'm six feet, two inches tall, my hair is dark blond, my eyes are dark blue, and I wear a size twelve shoe . . . which I've been told makes up for all dorkiness." He waited. After a short pause, it dawned on her what he was implying.

"Oh my God, you are nasty!" she said and laughed so hard she made him laugh along with her. "Dark blond hair and dark blue eyes, huh?" He heard the question in her voice.

"I'm white. Does that make a difference?" He held his breath waiting to see if it mattered to her.

"Nooo, not really." She dragged out the word and he thought he'd lost her. He knew that she was black and it didn't make a bit of difference to him, sexy was sexy. In fact, the image of how their flesh would look naked, white skin against chocolate-brown, was as enticing as hell, but he didn't know how she felt about the racial difference and waited to hear what she'd say.

"The whole size twelve shoe thing would make me not care one way or another, even if color were a consideration," she said and he laughed along with her, relieved.

They spoke a few minutes longer before she yawned and apologized. Josh glanced over at the time on his alarm clock and saw that it was almost eleven o'clock.

"Oh man, I didn't know it was so late. I'm sorry. I'd better let you go," he said, strangely reluctant to get off the phone with her, but it was late and he didn't want to keep her up longer. "Lilliana, I'm looking forward to seeing you on Saturday."

"I am too, Josh." He loved how soft her voice was and how shy she sounded one minute and the next would say something hilarious and off the wall, like calling him a nasty ass, he thought and laughed. He didn't think he'd ever heard someone say that before.

"What's so funny?"

"Nothing. I'm just looking forward to meeting you . . ."

"Me too. I'm looking forward to meeting you as well," she said.

It sounded to him as though she were surprised at how she felt. "And seeing for myself just how spankable that ass really is. See you on Saturday, Lilliana."

He heard her light gasp as he hung the phone up and he smiled in anticipation. He sank down lower in the bed and allowed his mind to bring up images of her.

He could recall how good she'd smelled, how smooth her skin felt when she'd bumped up against him in the crowded elevator, how lush her breasts had looked as he sneaked a peek down her ample cleavage.

As he thought of her breasts, how big and firm-looking they were, he allowed one of his hands to lay on the bed near the outside of his thigh, while the other went to his crotch and smoothed a hand over the hardening length of his dick.

He wrapped his long fingers around the length, and began to work the engorged shaft in short, smooth movements, his thoughts centered on Lilliana Michaels. With his eyes closed, he imagined how good it would feel if her small hands were stroking him.

His balls felt tight, filled with cum as he thought of what he would like to do with her, *to* her, if she'd allow him to. How he'd like to feel the tight walls of her channel clamp down on his dick as he ground into her from the back, holding on to her soft curves the whole time.

He'd do her really slow . . . doggie style, in order to get a good look at her from the rear, fully enjoy the way her ass would jiggle with each thrust of his dick, each slap of his balls . . . each stinging slap of his open palm against her lushness.

She'd be surprised at first, but she'd like it. He'd make sure of it. With each stroke and retreat of his cock, with each stinging slap to her ass, he'd make *sure* she liked it. He'd play with her clit, rub her feminine juices up and over her nub while he stroked into her tight, hot snatch.

Damn.

Just thinking of how good it would feel, how snug she'd feel wrapped around him, sent blood rushing to his head. He could feel the orgasm bubbling up with each stroke of his hand up and over the hard length of his erection, the pre-cum on the bulbous tip moistening his palm.

He groaned out loud as his body took over, his mind no longer able to handle the mental stimuli of imagining what it would be like to make love to the woman he was quickly becoming obsessed with.

His body demanded release, until finally, with one final stroke, he let out a long, harsh groan. "Lilliana!" he yelled.

With his heart pounding, eyes closed, palm cupping his semi-erect penis, Josh knew he wouldn't be able to wait long to make her his own.

No way in hell.

6

Lilliana had awakened the next day with her hands buried in her crotch and realized she needed to go back on the Pill.

That was her waking thought as soon as she'd opened her eyes. After speaking to Josh on the phone Thursday night, coupled with the hot-as-hell dream she'd had where an unknown man had rocked her all night long and she'd woken up playing with herself, she *knew* she'd better get on the Pill. If Josh looked half as good as he sounded on the phone and as long as it had been since she'd gotten some . . . she *just* might be tempted to let him do what he insinuated he wanted to do to her.

Now, approaching their designated meeting spot outside of the Children's Museum—it didn't get more public than that— she allowed the nerves she'd been feeling since their phone call to take over. The day after their communication, she'd debated telling Lee about it, but had decided to wait. She was nervous enough as it was. She didn't need him teasing her, adding fuel to the flames of her nervousness.

They'd agreed to arrive at the Pier at lunchtime, but she had to rely on public transportation to get her there. Lilliana didn't want to take any chances and miss her connection so she'd arrived an hour before their designated time. She'd used the time to walk around.

Couples strolled around the large, popular attraction walking hand in hand, families, teenagers . . . it was an eclectic blend of Chicago natives as well as tourists.

She sat down at the bench and instantly started scanning the crowd after she glanced at her watch. Her eyes came in contact with a man as he sat with a small package in his hand and she glanced away after a heartbeat.

He looked familiar, she thought, and her gaze went back over him, from top to bottom. When he turned around and looked at her directly with his dark blue eyes, she knew it was him. He hadn't even begun to do himself justice when he'd told her what he looked like.

He was tall, she could tell, even though he was sitting down. His face was carefully formed as though he were crafted from an artist's rendition of a perfect man, with deep-set, navy eyes that were surrounded by dark, thick eyelashes that no man had a right to have. He had lean cheeks and an aquiline nose that was saved from perfection by a slight bump in the center. Nicely shaped lips, not too thin, and the bottom lip was a bit fuller than the top, and a shade lighter than his tanned face. Lord have mercy! She felt like a cat in heat just looking at him.

This had to be Josh. And boy, was he fine. And familiar looking. When he smiled and stood, and she caught a flash of a deep dimple, she knew it was him and obviously he'd figured out that it was her. He picked up his package and walked toward her. When he reached her he held out his hand.

"Hello, Lilliana?" He asked the question in his unmistakable, deep, *do me* voice.

She smiled and stood, allowing him to help her to her feet. "Yes, I'm Lilliana. You must be Josh." Lilliana went to shake his hand, but he pulled her to his tall frame and gave her a light hug instead. He smelled like a combination of outdoors and the sea. Did he have to look good and smell so good, too? she thought. Come to think of it, he looked . . . familiar, but she was too nervous to figure out why. She stepped back quickly once he released her.

He allowed her to and asked, "Have you been waiting long?"

"No, not really," she said. "Actually, I got here early on purpose so I wouldn't be late. I took the bus and it's been a while since I've been out this way. I didn't want to chance being late." She felt like a teenager, nervous and jittery.

"I wish I'd known that." He smiled down at her and a deep dimple flashed in his cheek again.

Lilliana forced herself to calm down, and not act like a schoolgirl on her first date. He grasped her arm and guided her through the throng of people, toward the entrance to the Children's Museum.

"Why's that?" She cleared her throat when her voice came out high and squeaky.

"I arrived early too. Didn't want to chance missing you, either," he laughed and put her at ease.

They walked inside and Lilliana felt like a child again as they walked around, examining the statues and the variety of exhibits in the museum. "Wow, this is amazing! I've never been to a children's museum this large before."

"You've been to a lot of them, have you?" he asked.

"I've been to a few. I kind of like them." Actually she'd been to more than a few. She loved museums, particularly children's museums. The few times that she and Marcus had traveled outside of Southern California, she'd always go hunt out the local museum. When she'd look for a children's museum, Marcus would either make fun of her or harass her and tell her she'd "better not be getting any bright ideas about having kids."

As if.

So she hid her embarrassment that she secretly loved museums, particularly children's museums, from him.

"If you tell either one of my older brothers I'll flatly deny it . . . but I love them as well," he told her and she laughed with him.

"Your secret is safe with me," she promised, and her ridiculous embarrassment was eased with his light statement.

"When was the last time you were out to the Pier?" he asked her as they milled around the special exhibits.

"Oh, it's been a while. Not since I left Chicago," she replied softly, caught up in checking out the dinosaur expedition exhibit.

"You've been away from Chicago? Where did you go?"

"Actually, I've only recently returned. Chicago is home. But, I've been away since I was a teenager," she said.

"Oh really? So you've been away for a few years."

"It's been more than a few," she said. "It's been over fifteen years!"

"What do you mean, over fifteen years?" He looked so puzzled that Lilliana felt like laughing.

"I left when I was seventeen. I'll be thirty-three in November." The look on his face was so comic that she felt like either hitting him or kissing him for the obvious surprise.

"You don't look a day over twenty-five!"

"Well, thank you. But I definitely feel almost thirty-three. How old are you?" She suddenly knew she wasn't going to like the answer, from the look on his face.

He didn't answer right away.

Josh was thinking that she was even prettier up close where he could get a good visual of her. Her creamy, cocoa-brown skin looked so smooth he had to stop himself from reaching out to caress her cheek to see if it was as soft as it looked.

Josh had arrived at the Pier an hour earlier than usual, so that he wouldn't miss seeing her when she arrived. He didn't want to take any chances on missing her. When he'd spotted her, that curious clenching he'd felt in his gut came back again, this time stronger than before.

Each time he'd caught a glimpse of her at work, she'd been dressed in a long skirt or flowing dress of some kind. Now she was wearing capri jeans, a striped halter, and tall wedge heel sandals and because he didn't want her to think he was a pervert, he'd tried his hardest not to stare *too* hard at her body.

But damn.

There was only so much a man could take.

Her jeans were soft and molded her round ass and thighs and showed off the perfection of her figure. Although she had a nice sized butt, her waist was small, and he already knew she had great breasts, as the blouses he'd seen her in at Longmire showcased them to perfection. However, in the halter she was now wearing, they jiggled just enough to make him salivate.

She was hot as hell and he didn't think he'd be able to be noble and allow her out of her deal.

He'd known she was nervous about the date and had decided not to press the whole "big spankable ass" thing, but that was before she showed up looking so gorgeous and lush in those tight-fitting jeans, *showing off* her big spankable ass. Now, things had changed.

He smiled and finally answered her question. "I'm twenty-eight," he said. He noticed the disappointed look cross her face, stopped walking and lifted her chin lightly with his forefinger. "And age has nothing to do with what I have planned for us. For today," he amended.

He knew the smile he gave her wasn't exactly . . . sweet as he took her arm. The quick, nervous-looking glance she threw his way as she accepted his arm confirmed that.

"Did you have a good time?" Josh smiled and asked, coming to a smooth halt outside Lilliana's small cottage. He cut the engine on his low-slung Jaguar and turned to face her.

"Oh my God, I had a wonderful time, Josh," she said sincerely and enthusiastically.

Lilliana didn't know the last time she'd had so much fun. After they'd started walking and talking—and figured out that they worked at the same place—she'd become more and more comfortable in his presence.

They'd gone through the Children's Museum before heading off to the Make a Bear store, where they'd both created bears. Lilliana made hers totally retro, complete with seventies leisure suit and pink fedora hat. When Josh looked the bear over, he'd laughed and said he looked like Huggy Bear from *Starsky and Hutch*. Lilliana laughingly agreed although she simply *had* to tease him about not being out of diapers when the show came along. He'd given her a slight smack on the butt in retaliation that had surprised them both and Lilliana had felt a crazy thrill with the tap.

After the whole *smack my butt and I might like it* incident, as Lilliana thought of the occurrence, the rest of the day had been carefree, with him amusing her with his observations of the visitors at the park and the occasional time he'd slip in something serious, like when he mentioned seeing her at Longmire, Lieberman and Strauss.

"Don't you work at Longmire?" he'd asked casually as they waited in line for the carousel at the Pier.

"Yes, I do. I thought you looked familiar. But I didn't know how to ask." Lilliana turned to him and carefully scrutinized his face, not quite sure what she was looking to find in his eyes.

"I think I've seen you in the elevator a time or two, as well as the cafeteria," he said and casually wiped the corner of her mouth, where she had a remnant of caramel sauce from the caramel apple he'd bought for her earlier. Lilliana almost wet herself when he had the nerve to casually place his thumb in his mouth and lick the sauce away, as though it were no big deal. And *then* winked at her. Once again, like all of this was normal.

"I think that's where I've seen you as well," she stuttered and felt crazy. Here she was, a grown woman, totally thrown off because he licked his thumb after wiping her mouth and winked at her. So what if it was the sexiest thing any man had done to her in a month of Sundays?

"Which department do you work in?"

"I'm in the admin area . . . what about you?"

"Management," was all that he'd said. The subject of the job hadn't come up again, until later when he'd asked her if she'd allow him to take her home. It was dark and he didn't want her to take public transportation.

She'd agreed, knowing she was setting aside one of Simone's rules. But her every instinct told her she was safe with Josh. When he'd guided her toward the valet section of the parking garage and led her to the late model Jaguar sedan, she knew that he'd left out how far up in management he had to be to drive a car like the one he was driving.

The drive home, much like the day, was enjoyable and Lilliana was reluctant to see it end, something she hadn't been expecting.

He'd casually flirted with her, often touching her lightly on the arm, the small of her back, grabbing her hand and running with her toward the Ferris wheel like a kid. Throughout the day he was so casually affectionate towards her that she didn't even *try* to tell herself she didn't like his touch. She loved it, along with the attention he showed when she shared information about herself with him, smiling and carefully listening to her as though she was the only woman in the world.

Not once had she caught him eyeballing some hot young thing at the Pier. Not once did his eyes wander from her to some other woman while they were walking hand in hand toward the next exhibit. The man was smooth. And not superficially smooth like Marcus had been.

She'd known him for less than six hours, but she knew he wasn't the slick type. At twenty, she'd been too young to recognize the fake slickness in Marcus's game.

At the age of thirty-four she would run ten thousand miles away barefoot in the snow if she saw it coming her way in any other man. She and Josh had established a connection from the first time they'd really looked at one another, in the elevator ride at the firm.

She hoped he was feeling the same way. He *had* to have felt the connection as well. She pleaded to the powers that be in heaven that this wasn't all one-sided.

"I'm glad, Lilliana. I don't know the last time I had such a good time," he answered her question and began to lower his head toward hers. She knew what was coming and felt the tingle in her belly as she waited impatiently for his mouth to connect with hers.

Joshua saw the way she waited for his kiss and pulled her unresisting head gently toward his, both palms on either side of her face. He covered her pretty, plush lips with his and groaned.

He knew her lips would feel like this, soft and edible. He placed nibbling kisses over her mouth before he pulled away and licked the seam of her lips, forcing her to open her mouth. When she willingly did, he inserted his tongue inside and licked the inside, searching for her warm, willing tongue.

"Ummm, oh god," she mumbled around his lips.

He pulled away from her and smiled before he took her bottom lip in between his and gently tugged on the fullness. He loved how soft they were, how good it felt to caress them.

"You taste so good, Lilliana," he said after several more minutes of licking her lips. "We'd better stop now," he said because kissing her had his dick totally hard. He knew if he didn't stop soon he wouldn't be able to and he didn't want to blow it with her. There was something about her that drew him unlike any other woman.

She was shy at times, bold at others and sexy all the time. He wanted to get to know her better and he didn't want to scare her off by asking her if he could spend the night with her, although he wanted to so badly he felt like howling at the moon. He wanted to take that beautiful, curvy body of hers and do wonderful things to it.

But there was no way in hell she'd be willing to ask him in. No way. If he thought for one minute that she would . . .

"Josh, would you like to come inside?"

7

"Your home is beautiful, Lilliana." Josh looked around her small house and Lilliana was proud of how she'd pulled together her secondhand furniture and accessories and made them their own.

"Thank you, Josh. Can I get you anything to eat or drink?" she asked. The look in his eyes sent those chills racing down her spine again. She motioned for him to sit down and sat down next to him, after she'd turned on the small CD player and the low sounds of a sexy, bluesy sax filled the air as she sat near the arm of the sofa.

"No. But you can come closer. I won't bite, not unless you want me to," he laughed. She smiled and scooted her body closer to his along the sofa, and nervously placed her hands in her lap.

"So why did you leave Chicago when you were younger? Didn't you say that you left as a teenager? You've only recently returned, right?" He casually placed his arm around her shoulder, turned his body and pulled her even closer so that she faced outward and was nestled in front of him. Lilliana allowed the intimacy, kicked off her sandals and curled her feet underneath her bottom before she answered.

"To be honest, I didn't think much about it. I told you I was the oldest of four kids, right?" she asked. He nodded his head and feathered caresses over her exposed shoulder in the halter that she wore, raising goosebumps down her arm.

During their date she'd found it easy to tell him about her family. "Yes, you did," he said and continued to caress her arm.

"I was tired of taking care of my brothers, cleaning the house, making beds, combing hair . . . there was no other alternative for me, I don't think. It was leave or go insane. I mean, I felt guilty about it for a long time," she said and paused.

"Why?"

"Why, what?"

"Why did you feel guilty? You had nothing to feel guilty for. If anything, it sounds as though your mother should feel guilty," he murmured.

"I don't know. Our father wasn't around. My mother needed me, depended on me. I should have stayed and helped her."

"Lilliana, that wasn't fair of your mother to expect you to take on the parent role for your brothers. From what you told me, it didn't seem as though you ever had a childhood of your own. Please don't get mad at me, but I think it was unfair—and that's putting it mildly—for your mother to expect you to care for your brothers like they were your own children. To the point that you never went on a date, never participated in school events, never did anything that normal adolescents get to do. No, I'm sorry, I don't think you have a damn thing to feel guilty for. Now your mother? That's another matter," he said grimly.

This man didn't know her, didn't know anything about her but the injustice of her childhood affected him. He nestled her closer to his body and she felt the unmistakable feeling of his mouth lightly kissing the top of her head, and the small gesture touched her deeply.

"She was a whole hell of a lot better than Marcus," Lilliana sighed.

"The man you lived with before you returned to Chicago?"

The amber glow of the lamp, the low music, and the nearness of Joshua made it easier for her to open up about her time with Marcus and the way he constantly berated her, until eventually his verbal abuse escalated to physical abuse.

"So you ran away . . . to something worse," he said grimly and Lilliana sighed.

"I guess so. I knew it was time for me to go. I may be stupid when it comes to people using me, but I'm nobody's punching bag."

Joshua didn't like to imagine a sad Lilliana growing up with so much heavy responsibility on her small shoulders. He'd grown up relatively free from anything like that. Although he'd had the burden of knowing his father had left his family when he was barely five years old, he had no real memories of his dad. His uncle had stepped in and filled the shoes his father left vacant. Any bitterness he felt at his father's desertion, he'd gotten over a long time ago.

And if he ever had any thoughts about his dad, he quickly shoved them to the back of his mind.

But thoughts of Lilliana taking care of her brothers all day every day, missing out on life, being used as a servant by her mother, was unbearable.

And as he listened to her low words, the way she described the things her ex had done to her to humiliate her turned his stomach.

He felt his hands clenching in tight fists and forcibly relaxed them so he didn't scare her. But the thought of a man hurting this small woman fucked with his mind so badly he wanted to jump up from the sofa and run to California and find his ass and beat the shit out of him.

How anyone could lay a hand on her in anger was beyond

him. Her spirit, her quiet sense of humor, her laugh . . . everything about her was beautiful. He had no idea how or why, but in the short time he'd been with her, their one conversation over the phone, he was falling for her.

He also knew, from the way she looked at him and the way she opened up to him as though they'd known each other forever, that she felt it as well.

Josh turned her around and tilted her face toward his. "Lilliana, you never have to worry about me raising my voice to you, much less lift a hand to hurt you. I swear to you, I would rather cut my hand off than ever hurt you. You can trust me." He lowered his head and kissed her softly on the lips.

He released her when she gently pressed her hands against his shoulders to end the kiss. The look in her eyes was scared, excited, and questioning, and he waited to see what she would say to his declaration.

Lilliana felt restless and on edge as she sat up and away from him. If she didn't get away from his intoxicating nearness soon, she'd do something crazy.

"Would you like something to drink?" she asked again. She didn't wait to hear his answer. Instead she leaped up from the sofa and quickly walked the expanse of the room toward the kitchen. She was two seconds away from asking him to make love to her, what with his nearness, the low lights, sexy music and the way he was looking at her . . .

She knew he didn't want anything to drink, and neither did she. But it was easier than trying to figure out how to ask him if he'd make love to her. How in the world did you ask that? She put to the side thoughts of what she might feel like in the morning if she were to make love to a virtual stranger tonight.

She wanted to make love with this man and she wanted to do it now. She didn't want to think too deeply about it, didn't want to weigh the pros and cons, she just wanted him to sex her up. Like his life depended on it. She wanted him to lay it on her. Just like Simone said . . . spank her fat ass, and *make* her like it, she thought with a heady rush.

She hoped he knew what he was doing, as she wasn't all that experienced. Outside of Marcus, she'd only made love with two other men. One before Marcus when she'd first moved to California, and the other after their breakup.

Both experiences had been less than desirable and had confirmed her belief that maybe Melinda was right and it was all hype. Chill, she told herself. Make some iced tea.

Lost in her thoughts, she missed that Josh had walked up to her in the small kitchen and now stood less than a foot away from her.

When he took the pitcher of tea out of her hand and placed it on the small countertop away from her suddenly nerveless fingers, she stifled a moan. Even that brief contact of their fingers brushing excited her.

She was a hot mess.

"Come here, Lilliana . . . let me touch you," he said in a low voice, in the semidarkness of the room. She had turned on the standing Tiffany lamp in the living room and the only light in the kitchen came from the small bulb in the open refrigerator.

Lilliana released her hold on the fridge and walked the few paces to where Josh leaned against her small counter and allowed him to take her in his arms. He tilted her head to the side and surprised her by kissing her on the side of her neck.

Oh, God. How in the world had he gone to her *spot*? He slowly licked the side of her neck, just underneath her earlobe and . . . Lord, was he going to . . . she groaned.

"Ummm," was all she could say when he lightly took the end of her earlobe into his mouth and sucked it gently, into his mouth. He licked and laved her earlobe and Lilliana felt the wetness pool between her thighs from the simple caress.

He released her earlobe and his mouth traveled along her

lower jaw, delivering warm, wet kisses along the way until he reached her mouth and delivered soft, nibbling kisses that left her weak and wanting. When he took her lips between his, Lilliana felt the wetness increase between her thighs and clenched them tightly together in response. He grabbed her ass, pulling her closer to his body, and she shamelessly pressed against the thick bulge inside his jeans.

He worked her lips, kissing and licking her mindless. The way he kissed her, coupled with the way she was grinding against his dick—Lilliana felt the unmistakable sensation of an orgasm, hovering, just out of reach.

"Oh God, no way. I can't believe this, I can't believe I'm going to come this way," she mumbled, embarrassed, and pulled away from him.

"Baby, it's okay, just go with it." Josh refused to allow her to break away from him—instead he pulled her closer. He lifted her onto the counter, spread her thighs and stepped in to the vee of her legs. He continued to kiss and stroke her, keeping his hand on her ass and pulling her to the very edge of the counter while he wrapped her legs around his waist.

He moved her body up and down along his, working her, helping her to grind herself against him until, helpless, she felt the orgasm as it ripped through her body.

"Ooooooooh, I'm coming! I'm coming . . . I'm comiiiing," she groaned and cried. Josh continued to move her lower body against his erection until the orgasm claimed her completely, leaving her body weak when it was over. Replete, she slumped and he caught her slight body against his chest. He kissed and calmed her before he leaned down and whispered into her ear, "Where's your bedroom, baby?"

Lilliana was still seeing stars and she weakly lifted her head from his chest and pointed. "Right there, through that small hallway." Unresisting, she lay back against his hard chest when he effortlessly lifted her and strode in the direction she pointed.

The light in the room came from the streetlights outside and streamed inside the open, curtained window as he walked to the bed. He laid her gently on the bed and immediately went down on his knees to massage her feet before he walked his hands up her legs to the waistband of her jeans and unbuttoned them, never taking his eyes away from her.

"Do you mind if I undress you?" he asked.

"No, not at all," Lilliana whispered and leaned back against the pillows, allowing him to undress her. It was something no one had ever done for her, undressed her with such exquisite care, removing her clothes slowly, with such anticipation, as though she were a birthday package he was excited to unwrap.

Although she knew she should feel nervous, perhaps scared, she didn't. Surprising.

She had just met Josh, and although she'd been in a relationship for over ten years, she knew she was sadly lacking in the knowledge of how to please a man. Lord only knew how many times Marcus had told her that.

But that didn't matter to her. Not here, and not now. All thoughts of Marcus and his abuse flew out the window as Josh said in his sexy deep voice, "Lift your bottom, sweetheart . . . I need to get these jeans off."

Lilliana laughed, feeling free and happier than she had in a long time. She lifted her butt and allowed him to peel the jeans away from her body, leaving her wearing nothing more than a pair of thong panties. The thong she wore had been a gift from Simone and had a caricature of a sista wearing her hair big and nappy, with the words *"if it ain't rough, it ain't right"* blazoned right across the center of her coochie.

She loved the double entendre. She saw that Josh had been able to read the words in the dim light of the room when he smiled and said, "Do you like it rough, Lilly?"

Lilliana licked suddenly dry lips and stalled. What did he want her to say? She felt an uneasy sensation in the pit of her gut. She hoped he wasn't like Marcus. She silently prayed to God that he wouldn't be really rough with her. That he wouldn't hurt her. Her instincts were telling her no, she'd felt a connection with him like no other, but . . .

"No, I don't. I don't like to be hurt," she whispered.

Josh had sat on the edge of the bed and lightly, with what felt like reverent fingers, brushed his hands back and forth over the front of her panties, before he slipped a finger beneath the edge and started rubbing her clit softly.

She moaned when he kept playing with her clit, before he removed his fingers and allowed her panties to cover her. He continued to play with her through the silk.

"I would never hurt you like that, Lilliana. I told you that, and I meant it. But when done right, rough can be so damn good, baby. It's got to be done right, though," he said.

She moaned when he removed his fingers from her panties and she almost fainted dead away when he took the finger he had been fingering her clit with into his mouth and sucked.

"Sit up, please," he asked gruffly. She leaned away from the pillows and watched with half-closed eyes as he crouched closer to her and deftly untied the strings of her halter, letting the top fall down to her waist. Her large breasts were bare and Lilliana automatically crossed her arms over them.

"No, don't hide them from me, let me see them, Lilliana." He removed her arms from her breasts and stared down at her. The look in his deep blue eyes was intense, hot, and nearly unbearable.

"What? What is it? What's wrong?" she asked when he didn't say anything, and instead continued to stare at her breasts.

"What's wrong?" He laughed huskily as he mimicked her question. "Nothing's wrong, baby. You have beautiful tits, so creamy and brown . . . so perfect," he finished.

His words were stark and blunt. Lilliana felt the intensity of his stare along with the stickiness of her own cream against the inside of her thigh as his words and looks washed over her like warm rain.

"And there is no way on God's earth I would ever be rough with you. Not in a way you wouldn't enjoy," he amended the statement.

"How can rough be . . . enjoyable?" she asked and arched her body in sharp response when he took one of her nipples between his thumb and forefinger and pulled on it lightly.

"Pain and pleasure, when administered in the right way, can be the ultimate in satisfaction, Lilliana." He lowered his head and took her distended nipple in his mouth and delivered a slow, heated lick.

Lilliana cried out from the hot sensation of his tongue on her nipple, the incredible feel of her nipple scraping against the roof of his mouth.

"Do you like that, baby? Do you like to have those long nipples of yours sucked?" Josh opened his mouth wider and gathered as much of the large tit into his mouth as he could and suckled her, before he pushed her back down gently on the bed and, fully clothed, stretched out alongside her.

He promptly took his big hand and cupped both of the large globes and pushed them together.

"I love the color of your skin, so brown and smooth. I like the way your pretty breasts overflow in my hands. I wonder what it would feel like to have my cock sandwiched between them, Lilliana. Would you let me do that to you? Damn, you're sexy."

Lilliana hadn't given much thought to the color contrast of their skin before, but as she looked at his big hands cupping and molding her breasts, the contrast of their colors excited her as well. The thought of seeing his penis nestled between her breasts sent her traitorous pussy into overdrive.

He leaned across the small space that separated them and

with one hand on the back of her head, the other resting at the curve of her hip, pulled her closer to his body and kissed her again.

Josh didn't just kiss her. It was more than that, he *devoured* her. He licked and tugged on her lush bottom lip as though it was some sort of delicacy and Lilliana was a willing participant in the feast.

Damn if his kisses weren't addictive. The way he feasted on her, the way he sucked her lips, made her feel as though she was the only woman he'd ever kissed, the only woman he'd ever want to kiss. She felt special from a kiss alone and she wanted more.

If he could make her feel like this from a kiss, she could only imagine how he'd make her feel if they had sex. If he fucked her like he wanted to. The way his eyes were promising he would. She was beyond ready to find out.

She broke the kiss and looked at him. "Can you take these off?" she asked and although she should probably feel shy about it, she didn't. She felt bold and ready.

"Are you sure you want that? I can stop now, Lilliana, it'll be hard as hell, pun intended, but if we take this any further I can't. And what I want to do to you, I want to make sure you want done. You have to trust me. If we make love, you have to trust that I won't hurt you and that I only want to make you feel good. Want us both to feel good. Can you do that? Do you trust me enough to believe that?" Joshua asked and looked into her eyes, searchingly.

She was tired of being afraid. She wanted this man, and it was obvious from his larger than life hard-on that he wanted her as well. She'd worry about doubts and recriminations in the morning. She knew what he was talking about. She knew from his conversation that Joshua was into . . . spanking, and maybe some more kinky shit. As eager as she was and as tantalizing as the thought was, Lilliana wasn't sure that she was ready for something like that, especially with someone she didn't know very well.

He must have seen the hesitation in her eyes. "We'll take it slowly. If I do anything you don't like . . . just tell me, okay?"

Lilliana took a deep breath and released the pent-up fear and answered, "Okay, I'm ready."

That was all he needed to hear and within moments he'd sat up on the edge of the bed and removed his jeans and shirt. Before he placed his jeans on the floor, he removed a small foil package from his wallet and turned back to her. She hadn't watched him as he'd undressed and when he turned back to face her she tried her best not to stare at his cock.

But damn if it wasn't . . . beautiful.

She knew it had been a while since she'd made love, much less seen a penis up close and personal, but this man had one beautiful dick. It was almost the same light tanned color as the rest of his body and lay long, thick and curved against the muscular plane of stomach. The bulbous tip glistened with pre-cum as it rested on his belly and Lilliana wanted to reach out and lick it like a lollipop.

She must have stared too long, because he coughed and she turned her face away, embarrassed as hell. She felt her cheeks heat with his knowing laugh.

Josh lay down next to her and took her into his arms. "Don't look away, I'm sorry. I wasn't laughing at you. Hell, you can look at it all you want. You can even touch it if you want to." He pulled her on top of his chest.

When he pulled her down, she kissed him willingly. Soon the kisses weren't enough and he pulled away from her, his breathing heavy as he picked up the condom package and carefully ripped the foil package and removed the wrapper.

"Would you like to do the honors, Lilliana?" He handed her the condom with a daring look in his eyes. As though she'd be afraid to take it.

Not likely.

She pushed her body up and straddled him. With both of her legs riding alongside his, she took the condom from his hand. Slowly, she worked it down the long, steely length of his erection and smiled wickedly when he groaned. She'd purposely allowed her fingertips to feather his dick, playing with him, as she sheathed it with the condom.

"You like to play games, little girl?"

"*Little girl*? Boy, I'm your elder . . . you'll do well to remember that!" she laughed.

"Oh yeah? And what are you going to do if I don't? Punish me?" he asked. Her laugh was cut off with a long hiss of pleasure when his large hands wrapped around her waist, lifted her high and eased her back down on the long length of his hard dick.

He reached up and leisurely kissed and licked her breasts, until her nipples stood out stiffly from his ministrations. "Does that feel good, Lilliana? Do you like having those big, pretty tits licked, baby?" He gently bit down on her nipple, and when she whimpered in sensual agony, he suckled the small hurt with his tongue, swirling the tight nubbin in his mouth and then blew on it.

"God, yes!" She cried sharply from the effect of the stinging caress and his hot breath.

Lilliana leaned back on her hands and he placed his hands beneath her ass and helped her raise and lower herself on his penis.

"Ooh, that feels good," she moaned and pressed her clit tightly against his length, sliding herself up and down his dick while his hands rested lightly on her waist, steadying her as she rode.

"Yeah, baby . . . Just like that, fuck me just like that," he whispered.

She reared back and the adjustment catapulted her to a new level, the angle of his dick hitting her spot with unnerving accuracy. Lilliana felt a second orgasm hover as he rocked into her, back and forth, in and out, the pressure building until she gladly reached for it. Suddenly, he lifted her body up and off of his and slid completely out of her.

"Nooo!" she cried, her breathing harsh. "What are you doing?"

Without answering, he wrapped one arm around her waist, flipped her onto her knees and positioned himself behind her. He nudged the broad head of his penis inside her pussy and stroked back into her . . . all in one smooth move.

This time her cry was sharp and high as she felt every long, hard, thick inch of his dick embedded deep inside of her streaming entry.

He covered her back with his chest and started pumping into her as he gripped her hips. In short, tight thrusts he fucked her, moving her body in ways that suited him, in ways designed to make them both feel good.

Ways she never even knew her body could *move*.

As he manipulated her body, he reached between them and carefully separated her vaginal lips with one hand and gently pressed down, applying light pressure with his palm right above her pelvic bone. With his other hand he toyed with her clit, spreading her own cream over and around the small hidden nub, working it until Lilliana screamed from the pleasure.

"Oh, lord—what are you—what are you doing?" she panted.

"You like that, Lilly? Good, baby . . . that's good," he whispered hotly into her ear. After that the only sound in the room was their harsh breathing as he slipped in and out of her wet, slippery folds, relentlessly pumping into her, until startled, she felt the stinging sensation of a hand slap her ass and cried out.

Shocked, she tried to look over her shoulder at him, and he leaned down and delivered a hot lick with his tongue to the side of her neck that made her shiver. "Sshh," he whispered. "It's okay baby, it's okay . . . just enjoy it." After that whispered command, he continued playing with her clit as he flexed into her.

Lilliana was so hot from the way he was fucking her, moving her body and playing with her clit, that the sting on her ass from his hand, felt . . . good. Her heart raced in anticipation.

The second time she felt the stinging slap, she wasn't surprised by the slight pain as Josh popped her on the opposite ass cheek, but this time she stifled her cry, although the tap was much stronger than the first had been.

One of his hands left her pussy and moved to her breasts. He gave a quick massage to the large globes before he pinched one of her erect nipples, twirling and tugging while he continued to thrust into her wet heat.

He didn't move his other hand away from her ass, allowing it to remain resting where it was.

Her heart raced in anticipation waiting to feel another stinging slap.

The wait wasn't long. Joshua popped her on the ass again and continued to stroke into her, the sensual moves between his thick cock and strong hand orchestrated and smooth.

Pop . . . slide. Pop . . . thrust. Pop . . . glide. Pop . . . thrust.

Lilliana no longer felt the harsh sting, instead, the steady feel of his rod inside her soaking wet channel felt so incredible she was about to lose her mind.

"Ooooh," she groaned harshly. "That . . . that feels . . . so . . . good," Lilliana's breath was coming out in harsh gasps as she could barely get the words out.

On and on it went until the feelings of pain and pleasure were so intertwined Lilliana didn't know where one left off and the other began, and neither did she care. The feeling was indescribable and unlike anything she'd ever felt before.

She allowed her head to hang low, completely strung out as she accepted his wild and yet controlled thrusts and the steady whack of his hand on her butt.

Every plunge and retreat, every stinging slap of his hand and balls against her ass, pushed her closer and closer toward orgasm, until finally she felt it. That undeniable feeling came up from her toes and washed over her until it completely engulfed her . . . and she released.

As the orgasm completely overtook her, Lilliana was so weak she could barely keep her body upright.

But he wasn't done.

As soon as she'd achieved her release, he gripped her hips and surged quickly into her, over and over, so many times she lost count until she felt the impossible, another orgasm starting up. This time when she came, crying out until she was hoarse, he joined her with a deep, guttural cry echoing hers.

With his release, Josh held her tightly against his body as their heartbeats raced out of control, together. They stayed in that position for long moments, as the sweat from their bodies cooled on their skin in the chilly air of the room.

"That was incredible. Thank you," Josh said in a low voice as he gently laid her down on the bed, covered her body with the light sheet, and spooned behind her.

"I should be thanking you." Her voice was slightly hoarse and she cleared it before speaking again. "Incredible doesn't even describe how that felt."

There was a heartbeat of silence before he asked, "Are you okay?"

Josh had no idea how she felt. His mind was in a state of mush. He'd just had the best sex of his life, and he only hoped she felt the same way.

He didn't know what thoughts were racing through her mind about the way he'd handled her. He'd had no intention of spanking her, at least not consciously, but feeling that big pretty ass of hers grinding on his dick the way she'd been doing, there had been no way in *hell* he could pass that up. No damn way.

And her response . . . hell, her response had fired him up to the max.

Just the memory of how good her pussy felt, so tight and warm, kept him in a state of semi-arousal. And her smell, that strong heady scent of cinnamon and nutmeg that clung to her, had intensified as they made love, wrapping him in a cocoon of sensuality he never wanted to leave.

And it wasn't only that the sex had been mind-blowing; he'd also made a connection with her. Before the sex, he'd been willing to walk away and leave her alone. Get to know her before they took it to the next level and went to bed together. But then she'd kissed him, and there was no way he was going to stop.

Now as he lay behind her, he hoped to God he hadn't fucked up royally by introducing her to his brand of lovemaking before it was too soon. Before she was ready to handle something like that. She seemed to enjoy it, but . . .

"Lilliana, are you okay with what I did?" He held his breath, waiting for her answer.

"I'm fine. It was ecstasy . . . what you did to me. I never knew it could be like that, a man spanking me."

Her words caused the knot of unease to ache to loosen and he gathered her closer to his body.

"Josh, it felt incredible. And unlike what I imagined it could be. I thought it would be the way it was with Marcus," she admitted in a low voice.

"What do you mean, like Marcus?" he asked. Her breasts heaved. His hands had been resting underneath the heavy globes, and when she blew out a long, shaky breath, he gently massaged her breasts and bent closer to her neck to give her a kiss in the hollow of her shoulder. "Tell me," he demanded quietly.

"I told you that Marcus was abusive," she started.

"Yes. He was verbally abusive before he started to hit you."

"Well, that's not all," she admitted.

When she moved slightly and made a distressful sound he realized that his hands on the underside of her breasts had tightened in his anger. He instantly loosened his hold and murmured an apology.

"When we made love, he was . . . too rough. I told you that. Toward the end, right before I left him, he started restraining me when we made love."

"Had sex. When you had sex," he interrupted. The thought of her making love with that asshole was unbearable to him.

"Sex—yeah, you're right. It was just sex," she said with a humorless laugh.

"What did he do, Lilly?"

"He was a very big man. He tied me to the bed and after he forced himself on me, if I complained too much he'd leave me like that. Sometimes for hours."

"I'm sorry. God, I am so sorry."

"It's okay. It happened a couple of times, and I left soon after that. I can only imagine what would have happened had I stayed."

"You don't ever have to worry about that again, Lilliana," he promised her, as her story came to an end.

Josh gathered her close and held her tight until they both fell asleep.

"Wow, that was delicious, Lilliana," Josh complimented her.

He walked over to where she stood at her kitchen sink, washing the afternoon dishes. He'd made her breakfast earlier and after that, they'd decided to take a nice stroll around Hyde Park and had just returned after a few enjoyable hours.

When Lilliana had woken up that morning, she'd been stiff, knowing she'd used muscles she didn't even know she had as Josh made love to her, long into the early hours of the morning.

At first she'd been awkward with the whole morning-after thing, but he'd put her at ease when he'd kissed her good morning, asked her how she'd slept before, and proceeded to walk bare-assed to her bathroom asking if she liked blueberry pancakes.

How lucky could a woman get, to have a man fine as Josh, give her a night of off-the-chain sex *and* make a mean stack of blueberry pancakes? Yeah, life could be good sometimes, she thought with a giggle.

During their time at the park, she'd shared things about herself with him, such as why she left Chicago and how she felt coming back home. She admitted it wasn't easy, but she'd been taking it one day at a time.

"I met Marcus soon after I left home, I was only eighteen when we hooked up," she told him as they strolled and he captured her small hand within his much larger one.

"That was pretty young. How old were you when you left home?" he asked.

Lilliana normally didn't like to revisit that time in her life, but it felt right to share it with Josh, so she opened up.

"I was seventeen. I'd just graduated from high school and decided to move to sunny California," she laughed.

"Why did you pick California?"

"It was warm there. In my high school geography class, I would always fantasize about what it would be like to live somewhere warm. Nothing like the cold winters here in Chicago, when half the time my family didn't know if we'd have electricity, and there were days here and there when there'd be no heat in the house."

"Damn. That must have been rough," he murmured as they continued to walk.

"It was, at times. I think I needed to get away from all the craziness of growing up in my household, get as far away as I could from my mother and the responsibilities I'd shouldered for as long as I could remember. I helped raise my brothers, I cooked, cleaned, patched up scraped knees, walked them to school, made dinner, tucked them into bed...I felt like *I* was their mother, and I hated it," she admitted. Although she had nothing to be ashamed of, she'd always felt as though she had abandoned her mother when she'd left.

"That would be hard for anyone that age to have to deal with," he said, as though sensing the direction of her thoughts.

"I guess. It sure made me not want children. That was one thing Marcus and I had in common," she told him and allowed him to steer them toward one of the benches that lined the walkway in the park.

"Marcus didn't want kids? Somehow, from what you've told me about him, that doesn't surprise me."

"No, he definitely didn't want kids with me! In fact, he once told me if I 'fucked up and got pregnant,' I'd have to take care of *it*." Although Lilliana hadn't wanted children either, when Marcus had spit the ugly words at her, she remembered how badly it had hurt to hear him put it the way that he had.

"What a jackass . . . to say something like that is really fucked up—excuse my language, Lilly. That had to hurt."

Lilliana looked into his eyes to try and discern any double meaning, but found them open and honest. "It did," she admitted. "For one, as though I would try and trap him into a legal commitment. And secondly, that he would want to end the potential life of his own flesh and blood, out of convenience."

"That says a lot about his character. I could never imagine saying that to you, much less feeling that way about a life we'd created together," Josh said. The shield around Lilliana's heart opened up even more with his heartfelt words.

"Come on, let's walk." He smiled gently at her and tugged her to her feet. They continued their stroll and some of the burden of her past seemed to lift then and there.

During the remainder of the walk, Lilliana also found out that Josh was the youngest of three boys and that he hadn't seen his father since he was small. She'd learned that he wasn't just in management at Longmire, Lieberman and Strauss. He *was* management. His uncle was the CEO as well as one of the partners.

"Your uncle is Allen Longmire?" she repeated, halting their stroll to stare at him.

"Yes," he said, and took her hand back after she'd dropped his, and made her keep on walking.

"Is he your mom's brother? I mean, your last name is Ellis . . . right?" the sudden doubt in her voice made him pause.

"Actually, he is—was—my father's twin brother. My last name is hyphenated. It's Ellis-Longmire. I use Ellis at the job, to avoid certain problems," he said. Lilliana caught the way he hesitated over explaining the connection with his father.

"Is your father still alive?"

He sighed and didn't answer for long moments. Finally he spoke. "I haven't seen my father since I was a kid. He left us when I was around six years old, and none of us have seen him since." This time, Lilliana heard the sadness in his voice, a sadness he tried to cover up.

"I'm so sorry to hear that."

"Sometimes it's tough. My brothers all remember him a lot better than I do. The twins, Hank and Rowan, were twelve when he left, and my older brother Landon was in high school. He was the closest to dad. He never has gotten over it."

"And you have?" she asked.

"Yes. No . . . hell, to be honest I don't know. Like I said I was so young when he left, I don't remember much about him. My uncle has always been a father figure for me."

"It's good that you and your brothers have *him*, at least."

"Yeah, that's true. Although my brother Landon . . ."

"What?" she glanced up and caught the frown on his handsome face. Her first reaction was to smooth the frown away with her fingers and she knew she had it bad for this guy. She brushed the thought away, not wanting to examine the effect he had on her after such a short time.

"Landon never has trusted Uncle Allen."

"Why not? How do you know?"

"It's not anything he's actually said, rather what he doesn't say. He's in the military and the few times he comes home, he always seems to avoid actually being in Uncle Allen's presence. And when he is, he finds some excuse to leave. Or maybe it just seems that way to me." Josh shook his head. "Anyway, I've worked with the company since I graduated from college. I love doing what I do, and I'm good at it. Making money can be better than sex," he laughed.

"Oh really?" Lilliana placed her hand on her hip and gave him a *look*. The universal look women gave men that screamed *oh no the hell you didn't just say that!*

"Baby, that was before I made love to you. Now, I'd rather make love to you than roll around buck naked in a bed full of Imhan shares. That was, before my experience with you, the closest I ever came to heaven in my imagination."

"Rolling around butt naked on a bed of Imhan shares?" she laughed. With the sudden explosion of trading for this up-and-coming new software company, shares were skyrocketing. "Oooh, baby you sure do know how to make a brown chick blush," she laughed. "It doesn't get much better than that!"

The remainder of their walk had been filled with them sharing memories, laughing and walking in the park, as though they'd been lovers for years.

"I'd better head home. I have a ton of work to do, and if I stay much longer, I won't leave."

As she stood at the kitchen sink, finishing up cleaning, Lilliana felt a moment of hesitation. What should she do now? After the weekend she'd spent with him, she was honest enough to admit she didn't want it to end. But did he feel the same way?

Some of her doubts eased when she felt him wrap his arms around her waist, and give her a warm kiss on the neck. She glanced down at his forearms and loved the way his tanned, muscular arms looked wrapped around her body. She wiped the back of her hands on her shirt and turned to face him.

"I wouldn't kick you out." She smiled and stood on tiptoe to kiss him. He grabbed her and held her tight as he returned her kiss, kicking it up a notch. When he released her and took her face between his hands she saw the honest regret reflected in his eyes and was relieved.

"I'd better go. I was just assigned a new client and I have to go over his portfolio before I meet with him tomorrow, or you wouldn't be able to get rid of me. Walk me to the door?" he asked.

She allowed him to take her by the hand and lead her through her small cottage. When they reached the door he kissed her again. "I don't want this to end. I'm assuming you feel the same way," he said. When he kissed the palm of her hand, his tongue giving it a sensual lick, she clenched her legs together when she felt the instant wetness between her thighs that his caress invoked. Her treacherous kitty cat was acting a *fool*. Give her a sample of dick and she didn't know how to act! Although it hadn't been an ordinary sample, Lilliana thought with a silent laugh.

"Yes, you assume right. I don't want this to end," she admitted.

"Would you like to go out to dinner this week? How does Tuesday sound?" he asked and she agreed. After they secured the time and date, Josh kissed her, lingeringly, and left.

After the door closed behind him, Lilliana leaned against the heavy oak, a deep, satisfied smile of contentment crossing her face before she let out a laugh. Wait till she told her girls.

8

"Ooh, mami! Somebody is *way* too happy for a Monday morning!" Lee grumbled as he plopped down in his cubicle, next to Lilliana.

"What are you talking about?" She accepted the coffee he held out for her.

"Please lower your voice! Do you have to yell like that, chica?"

"Okay, first off, I'm not yelling. Secondly, it's Wednesday and not Monday. You've lost a few days, I think . . . still sick?" she asked and turned back toward her work when she saw the way Ms. Hillman was eyeballing her as she stood at the front of their section, speaking to one of the other assistants.

"Something like that. Who in the hell gets the flu in the middle of a heat wave?" Lee blew out a frustrated breath when he couldn't open the bottle of pills in his hand.

Lilliana took pity on him and removed the bottle from his struggling fingers, shook out two of the tablets and handed them to him. With a thankful murmur he swallowed the pills and took a careful drink of his coffee. "Oh, God. The next time

I decide to hook up with a blind date, who I was *warned* was sick . . . shoot me, okay? Just shoot me. The things we do for love, or the potential for love," he groaned.

"That bad?" Lilliana laughed.

"That bad." He focused his scrutinizing dark gaze on her. "Now you, on the other hand . . . you're positively glowing. Care to share why? Spill. Wait a minute . . . ooooh. You got some! That's what's going on with you! I knew it. When you came sashaying in here late last Monday I *knew* something was going on!"

"Just now noticing that? Had you decided to come into work last week, you probably would have noticed the glow then," she told him and rolled her eyes.

"I already told you that wasn't my fault!"

"As far as that goes, had you shown up for work yesterday or stayed the entire time Monday, you'd know the scoop," she continued as though he hadn't spoken. "Now you have to wait 'til lunch. That is, if you decide to stay that long. Get back to work, we'll talk later." She laughed at the moue he made but turned away anyway to start working.

Lee had been ill all of last week and the beginning of this one, and Lilliana found that she really wanted to talk to someone about her burgeoning relationship with Joshua. She'd found herself avoiding Simone and Melinda's phone calls for almost a week, until she'd finally decided to check her answering machine and wasn't surprised that they'd both left several messages.

Actually, between the two of them, they'd left over a dozen. Lilliana had listened but had not called her friends back until her lunch break. Melinda begged for details, but Lilliana hadn't been ready to disclose what happened between she and Josh until just yesterday when they'd met up at Simone's club, and she'd finally told them about her developing relationship.

* * *

"The club is hopping for a Wednesday night! What's going on tonight?" Lilliana asked as she and Melinda threaded their way through the early evening crowd toward the reserved table that Simone had set aside for them.

"This is the second week of speed dating. Remember Simone started it last week? She told us about it last weekend. You should have come, it was fun!" Melinda spoke loudly above the music, loud hum of conversation, and ringing bells notifying the couples when it was time to move on to the next table and the next date.

"Did you go? I didn't know that! Did you actually participate?" Lilliana asked as they finally made it to their booth and she scooted toward the middle of the leather booth and made room for Melinda to sit.

"Yes, I did. It was fun . . . wasn't like I was doing anything else," she muttered with a disgusted look plastered on her face.

Lilliana didn't have time to ask further in-depth questions as Simone came up to their booth, looking flushed and excited.

"Wow, Simone! This is awesome. Was it busy like this last week, too?" Lilliana asked after they'd exchanged hugs and Simone sat on the edge of the booth seat.

"Girl, yes! I think it is the best promotional idea yet! Business on Wednesday night has picked up significantly in just the two weeks we've been doing date night," she said with satisfaction, as she waved her hand to get the waiter's attention, and ordered drinks for them.

"Well, it's hopping, that's for sure," Lilliana agreed and the women caught up with the gossip of what had been happening in their lives.

After they finished playing catch-up, Lilliana was sipping her virgin daiquiri when she felt the burning gaze of her friends. "What?" she asked, suddenly self-conscious.

You know why we're looking at you . . . give up the goodies," Simone spoke around her straw. "We want all the details about this hot young thing you've been hanging around, and you'd better not leave out any details. We want to know the *who, what, when,* and *how. When* you let him rock you, *what* it was like . . . and girl . . . just *how* good was it, and from that grin on your face, my guess is that it was, is, *damn* good!"

With that pronouncement, Simone sat back in the booth, crossed her arms over her chest, eyebrows raised, waiting to hear the juicy details of her friend's newfound love interest.

"Not only was it *damn* good," Lilliana said and paused for effect, "ladies, I had no idea *how* good it could be when the right man spanks that ass . . . just right." She didn't try and stop the blissful smile from crossing her face before she happily gave up the goodies on her relationship with Josh.

9

"Dang it. I need blueberries and all he has is raspberries . . . Simone, have you ever made raspberry pancakes?" Lilliana muttered, looking into the back of Joshua's fruit bin in the refrigerator as she spoke on the phone to her friend early Saturday morning. She'd spent the night with Josh and had gotten up early in order to make him breakfast.

"No, you're not making him blueberry pancakes!"

"Yep, sure am . . . and homemade at that!"

"It's like that, huh? He put it on you so hard you're making homemade pancakes . . . oooh, go girl!"

"Sim! You've *no* idea . . . yum! We already, um, used the strawberries and whipped topping last night so I have to improvise for my pancakes!" Lilliana laughed happily, feeling no shame in her game.

"Ooooh . . . you so nasty!" Simone chortled. "I can see your fast behind now, running around the kitchen in flip-flops, wearing his shirt and no damn panties on . . . damn hussy!"

"Not flip-flops, got on socks instead."

Lilliana looked down at her garb and refrained from laughing out loud. Besides the flip-flops, Simone had nailed it. She'd gotten up less than an hour ago and after she'd kissed a groggy Josh good morning she'd grabbed the nearest thing, which happened to be his T-shirt, and pulled it over her head. She'd pulled on a pair of his socks and scrunched them down. Sans panties, she'd left the bedroom and made her way down to the kitchen to prepare breakfast.

"Well, I'm no culinary expert, you know how I avoid the whole domesticated thing."

Lilliana could picture the look of disgust on her friend's face as she said the word "domesticated" and refrained from laughing. Simone was as far from domesticated as any woman could possibly be and took pleasure in reminding a man of that, if one ever mistakenly thought she wanted more than fun and good times from him.

"Yeah, I know. I could be experiencing PMS—I feel kind of irrational. So . . . speaking of domesticated and all of that, when are you going to place the ad for someone to . . ." Lilliana allowed the sentence to trail off and waited.

"Spank my ass?" The laugh Simone gave was short and to Lilliana's ears sounded forced. "Ummm. Who knows? Soon, I guess. Anyway, tell me what you and the young wonder stud have planned this weekend," she asked lightly.

Lilliana was tempted to call her out but refrained. They'd made the agreement that when they'd placed their ads they would decide when and if they wanted to share the details with each other. So for now, she let it go.

"Ummm. Well, let's see. After I make breakfast I'll go serve it in bed to him. After that, I figure it should be around lunch time . . ."

"Nasty heffa. Go on, I'm listening," she giggled and they both laughed.

* * *

"Uncle Allen isn't as bad as you make him out to be, Lan. I think you need to either come to terms with the fact that dad alone made the decision to leave, or let the shit go. Either way, it's time to move on," Josh said to his brother. He held the phone away from his jaw as he stared at his face in the bathroom mirror and rolled the electric razor over his morning stubble.

Usually when his brother talked about their uncle or their father, a hard knot of stress would ball up in the pit of his gut. He didn't like to think too much about the hows and whys of his father leaving. He'd been so young at the time, and besides, his father had been busy with the business when he was there. The truth was Josh hadn't ever been particularly close with him.

When his father had disappeared, leaving only a note saying he no longer wanted to be a part of the family or the business, Josh had felt the sting of his betrayal like the rest of the family. But for his older brothers, particularly Landon, it had been worse.

"Does this mean you're not coming home this year for the holidays?" he asked, moving his jaw side to side and examining his shave.

"I don't know yet. Depends on this mission. If it's over by then . . . I may," Landon hedged.

In addition to his distrust of their uncle, Landon was in Special Forces. Athough Josh could never tell the exact nature of what he did or where he went, Landon was able to tell the family enough to let them know when he was okay and in the country, which was rare. 24/7, Lan lived and breathed Black Ops, which made his next statement even more surprising.

"Maybe I'll take leave. Come home and check out what's going on."

"You? Take a vacation? What brought this on?"

"We don't call it 'vacation,' you damn pussy," Landon guffawed, "It's called leave. We take *leave* from duties. And I want to check out this woman who's got my baby brother's shorts in a knot," he finished.

"She's got more than my shorts in a knot, man. She's got my heart. And I know you don't like Uncle Allen, but he helped me out and made sure Lilly got hired on full time at the firm," Josh said as he sat down on the end of the bed.

"What did he do that was so great?"

"All I had to do was ask and he made sure it happened. It was pitiful, man. She was working as a temp, no medical or dental, making God-knows-what an hour. Hell, she couldn't even go to a doctor's office to get her birth control pills, she said she went to the damn free clinic to get them! I told Uncle Allen I needed him to get her on full time . . ."

"It's the least he could do. Hell, you own stock in the damn company, it's as much yours as his," his brother interrupted.

"That may be true, but he still helped me out of a jam. I didn't know what I was going to do about Lilliana, but Uncle Allen got me out of that. I knew she wouldn't accept anything from me directly, but she needed medical. She needed a stable job and Allen helped me take care of it. He's not as bad as you think." Josh's voice trailed off when he heard a gasp and looked up to see Lilliana standing in the doorway with a tray, wearing his T-shirt and a murderous expression on her face.

He mumbled a goodbye to his brother and quickly got off the phone and stood to walk over to her. He could tell by her expression she was pissed off. Her next words confirmed it.

"You manipulative son-of-a-bitch!" She threw the tray down, food splattering everywhere, and spun around to leave the room

Damn. She'd overheard his conversation.

Lilliana had never been so hurt in her life. He sounded way too much like Marcus. Just another full-of-himself asshole who hid it better, that was all. She didn't need another man taking care of her. She didn't need another man thinking she was useless. She didn't need another man who would tell her she was a leech and a waste of space. She didn't need another man . . . tears were running down her face when Josh grabbed her by the shoulders and spun her around to face him, his breathing harsh.

"What the hell is wrong? What did I do that was so bad?" he asked, confusion etched harshly on his face.

"I don't need you, or any other man to take care of me! I've been doing that since I was a child! I am more than capable of taking care of myself. So thank you and your rich Uncle Allen," she said, her breathing just as harsh as his, "but no fuckin' thanks! You're no better than that jackass I was with for twelve years! Well, I learned my lesson. It may have taken my dumb behind twelve years, but I finally learned! Nobody has to take care of me! You're just a silly boy trying to be a man . . . no damn thanks!" She tried to jerk her arm away from his, but he held on. His grip didn't hurt her, but she sure as hell couldn't get out of it.

"Oh, okay. You think I'm no better than Marcus? You think I'd hurt you? Make fun of you and hit you? Treat you like shit and demand you fuck me? Is that what you think, Lilliana?" The look on his face was fierce and set. Lilliana panicked and tried to strike him as she increased her struggle to escape his hold. He simply allowed his hands to slip down her arms and held her above the wrist, effectively preventing her from hitting him or getting away.

"Get your damn hands off me, Josh! I mean it, let me go!" She struggled and yelled out in surprise when he suddenly lifted her into his arms and angrily strode back into the bedroom and slammed the door closed.

"Just in case you get too loud, I wouldn't want the neighbors to know what I'm doing to you," he muttered grimly and tossed her on the bed.

Before she could do more than bounce a few times on the firm mattress, he'd reached into a side drawer and withdrew several long strips of black leather. With obvious expertise, he had her bound and trussed, her hands behind her back and her ankles securely fastened, so fast she didn't know what hit her.

"You can't trust me, Lilly? Think I'd hurt you, baby?" he whispered hotly in her ear, just before he ripped the T-shirt she was wearing completely off her body and flipped her onto her belly.

"What—what are you going to do?" she asked, apprehension, fear, and . . . excitement all pooling together in her belly as she waited to see what he'd say, what he would do to her.

He didn't say a word, and in the position she was in, she couldn't see him. All she heard was the hiss of his zipper and the rustle of jeans that he was no doubt removing from his body.

From her side vision, she saw him remove a condom from a wrapper and smooth it over his rock hard erection. The dip in the bed told her he'd joined her and seconds later, he'd taken a pillow and, lifting her by the waist, he'd placed it underneath her belly.

"Are you okay? Are the restraints too tight?" he asked against her ear. Lilliana refused to speak to his crazy ass, and only gave him a short nod telling him she was fine.

"Are you saying 'yes, I'm okay, sweetheart?' Or 'the restraints are too tight, you asshole?' Hmm, Lilly? Which one is it?" he asked and bit down lightly on her earlobe. When she yelped he suckled the small sting.

"I'm fine . . . you asshole," she said, refusing to allow him to pull her in.

He laughed and she caught her breath when he lifted her ass high in the air and bit down on one of her cheeks.

"You really have an ass fetish, don't you?" she taunted him, and hoped he didn't see the cream she felt easing down her thighs when he bit the other cheek.

"No. Not just any ass will do. I need a big spankable ass to set it off for me," he told her as he spread her cheeks apart and lightly massaged each round, firm globe.

She felt self-conscious as hell with her hands tied behind her back, feet trussed up like a Thanksgiving Day bird and her fat behind raised high in the air while he stared and played with her.

Lilliana thought she'd die if he didn't do something soon. Either let her go or stop playing with her—the anticipation was killing her.

Within moments, she felt the long hot glide of his tongue against her anus and she stifled the moan of delight, and instead cussed at him. "Damn it . . . let me go! I don't want this, *or you,* now let me up!" she yelled.

He laughed and ignored her as he continued to lap at her and when his fingers worked around the front of her and started to play with her clitoris, Lilliana gave up the fight and gloried in the feel of him playing both ends of her.

"You like that, sweetheart? Do you like the way I make you feel?" he asked, and when Lilliana felt the tip of his dick against her opening she automatically bucked against the restraints, no longer comfortable with his form of play.

"Yes . . ." she murmured and waited to see what he'd do next.

"Do you trust me, Lilliana? Do you trust that I would never hurt you or do anything to you that you wouldn't want done?" he asked and continued playing with her clitoris as his cock touched the opening of her anus.

Although the feelings he was arousing in her made logical thinking fly out the window, Lilliana thought about what he was asking. Did she trust him?

She'd only known him for a few short weeks. She'd known Marcus for over ten years. How could she trust someone she'd only known for such a short time not to hurt her? How could she believe that he wouldn't take her for granted or manipulate her? She didn't have the answers to those questions.

"I don't know. I . . ." She stopped speaking when she felt the broad head of his penis enter her vagina and she let out a long groan of pleasure. If she felt disappointment that he didn't finish what he'd started, she shoved that thought to the back of her mind as he plunged and stroked her, giving her mind-blowing pleasure.

"Umm," she moaned. "That feels good." Lilliana glanced down to see Josh give her a toothy grin. Seconds later, he'd lifted her foot from where it lay against his chest and take her big toe into his mouth. He swirled his tongue around it before he allowed it to pop back out. Lilliana nearly came from the caress.

After their explosive lovemaking he'd untied her and they'd lain together, silent, for long, contented moments, allowing the sweat to cool on their bodies before he'd lifted her and brought her into his bathroom, sinking down with her in the oversize Jacuzzi-style bathtub. After a leisurely scrub, rosy and content from the bath, he had put her down on the bed and stretched out beside her.

"You like that, Lilly?"

"God, yes," she moaned and slumped further down in the bed, against the overlarge pillows lining the headboard. He chuckled and took each of her toes into his mouth, licking and lapping them, gobbling them up like they were candy.

She cried out when he reached her pinky toe. With a final

swirl of his tongue he allowed her foot to slide out of his mouth and land on his lightly furred, muscled chest. He then began to crawl up her body, on all fours, eyes hot, his erect penis brushing against her inner thigh on the way up.

"You know, no one should have toes that taste that good. If your toes taste like that, I wonder what the rest of you tastes like. Hmmm. How about I find out?" he all but purred.

In that moment, Josh looked to her like an oversized hungry cat and she was the big old bowl of cream he wanted to lick.

He kept his gaze trained on her and the look he gave her was scorching hot. It was mingled with lust and some other emotion she didn't want to examine too closely. The intense stare, the way he felt rubbing against her overheated body, the feel of his dick rubbing along her skin, forced Lilliana to tightly close her eyes, unable to contain the anticipation.

"Uh-uh, Lilly . . . you don't get to look away. I want you to see what I'm about to do to you," he chastened and she forced her heavy lids to open.

When his big body came to rest lightly against hers, she moved her neck to the side, her nostrils flaring as he sensually rubbed his nose, his face, up and down her neck and inhaled.

"I love your smell. Have I told you that before?" he asked and numbly she nodded her head. He leaned away from her, spread her legs gently apart and placed them over his forearms.

"Ummm, yeah. I think so," Lilliana answered although she didn't think he wanted an answer. Good thing he wasn't requiring intelligent conversation. The way he was staring at her mound filled her with such anticipation she could barely get the words out of her mouth.

She *had* to close her eyes when he raised her lower body to his face and stroked her aching pussy with a slow, heated lap of his tongue.

Lilliana arched her back in sharp response, fisted his crisp linen bed sheets, and held on for dear life as he separated her folds with his tongue and began to suckle and grazed his teeth on her clit.

He gently held on to her hood, ferreting out her nub, and carefully worked it with his tongue, lips and teeth. Lilliana lost it completely.

"Oooh, Lord! Boy, you're going to have me speaking in tongues if you keep that up!" Sharp little flickers of delight electrified her entire body as she accepted his oral loving. Long, delicious glides of his tongue over her clit forced moans and whimpers from her throat, with her head tossing back and forth against the soft pillow in sweet agony.

When he placed two fingers alongside the inside lips of her vagina, spreading her wide and completely covered her *entire* pussy with his lips and sucked . . . this time she did lose her mind. Utterly, completely, lost it.

"Stop—please, Josh. This is too much." She barely choked out the words.

"Sshh. It's okay, Lilliana. I'm not done with you yet," he promised and lowered his head back between the juncture of her thighs.

As he laved her with his tongue, he eased two of his big fingers into her wet entry, and pumped them in and out, fingering the swollen folds of her pussy lips so slowly she ached.

He continued to suckle her clit, while he eased his fingers out of her streaming pussy, and one by one, inched them into the tight opening of her anus, carefully working them in, not wanting to hurt the tender tissue inside.

When she moaned in distress, he stilled his fingers.

"It's okay, baby. Trust me, it'll feel good." He lifted away from the nectar between her thighs to croon. He waited until she nodded her head before he continued his journey, until his fingers were embedded second-knuckle-deep inside her ass.

She screamed from the exquisite pleasure/pain.

He played both ends of her, clit and ass, working her, pumping his fingers in and out in smooth rhythm with his tongue, suckling her turgid clit until she broke.

She came long and hard, screaming his name until her throat ached, and he had pulled every last bit of energy she had from her body. Her orgasm was so prolonged she had absolutely no strength left in her body. She had to force her lids to stay open or she would have slid right into unconsciousness without a care in the world.

She lay quiet and content in the candlelit bedroom until Josh finally withdrew his dark blond head from between her thighs.

When he kissed her lightly on her lips she smiled, tasting her own essence on his lips. She watched in languid satisfaction as he rose from his position between her legs and lay down behind her. He cuddled her close. She was near sleeping and almost missed his whispered words. "Lilliana . . . I think I love you."

She felt her heart leap at his words. Silly words. There was no way on God's green earth that he could mean them.

"Lilly, baby . . . did you hear me?" he asked in his sexy, *do me* voice.

"Yes," she finally answered.

"That's all you're going to say. 'Yes?' Damn, Lilliana . . ."

"What? What do you want me to say, Josh?" She turned around to face him fully when she felt him try and move his body away from hers.

"An 'I love you too, Josh' would work," he laughed without his usual humor. "Forget it, I was being stupid. Just a silly boy. Isn't that what you think?"

"When I said that, I didn't mean it, Josh. I was pissed off. I thought you were manipulating me, just like—"

"Don't say it, Lilly. I'm serious. Don't say his goddamn

name." The fire in his eyes was intense, reminding her of how he'd looked when he was angry with her. But Lilliana had no fear of him. He'd proven that she could trust him. Although . . .

"In the future, I don't want you taking care of me, Josh. I don't want or need that in a relationship."

"I'm sorry, Lilliana. I just wanted to help. But I should have told you. I'm sorry. I wasn't trying to manipulate you, I promise."

"I don't think that now, Josh. I never really did. But can I ask you a question?" she asked.

"Yes, of course."

"What is it you love about me?" she asked quietly.

"Why? Don't you think you're lovable?" He gave her a small kiss in the hollow of her shoulder.

When she didn't answer, she heard him take a deep breath.

"Why wouldn't I love you, Lilliana? There's nothing about you I don't admire, don't crave. I love the way you smell, like cinnamon and nutmeg," he said. She shivered when he leaned impossibly closer to her and inhaled long and deep.

"I love how your hair feels against my skin, between my fingers when you let me play with your hair," he went on. She groaned out loud when he placed his hand into her "kitchen," as her grandmother called the back of the hairline, and massaged her scalp.

"I love your body, your pretty breasts, your plump ass, your sexy smile, your intelligence, your loyalty, your shyness, your boldness . . . your everything. I love *you*," he finished simply.

"God, you make it so easy to love you, when you say things like that," she laughed shakily.

"It's the truth. So what is it, then? Do you think you'll ever develop those type of feelings for me?" he asked. Josh sat up and moved to the edge of the bed. He ran a hand through his dark blond hair in frustration.

Lilliana smiled at the way he looked. He was all man, he'd proven that to her several times over the last few weeks, but she couldn't help but smile at the way he sulked right then, thinking she didn't care about him. She crawled toward the edge of the bed and when she reached him, she lightly rested her head on his back and wrapped her arms around him.

"I've never told a man that I love him," she admitted in a low voice.

"No? Not even—"

"Nope. Not even . . ." She allowed her sentence to dangle and smiled against his back.

"Did he say it to you?" He grasped her hands as they lay lightly on his chest.

"He did. I don't think he meant it. It was just another way for him to try and manipulate me. It was one of the things that made him so angry. The fact that he couldn't force me to say those words to him; that I loved him. No matter how pissed off he'd get, no matter how he threatened me, I never gave that to him," she said.

They sat that way for long moments, neither saying anything, until Josh pulled her around and sat her in his lap. He took her face between his hands and stared at her so long she grew nervous and licked her lips, waiting for him to say something. He caressed the undersides of her full bottom lip with the rough pads of his thumbs before he leaned down to capture the lush flesh and draw it into his mouth.

"Where do we go from here, Lilliana?" he asked after he'd reluctantly released her lip.

She settled into his lap and rested her head on his chest. "I don't know, Josh." She felt the way he took a deep breath and laughed shakily. "I have to be honest with you. I won't lie. This is all new for me."

"It is for me, too. I've never fallen for anyone this soon," he interrupted.

"Josh, there are so many things we don't really know about each other. Not to mention the differences." She sighed and suddenly felt all thirty-two of her almost thirty-three years.

"Yeah, we have differences. So what? What's that got to do with it? Race, age difference . . . what the hell does that have to do with us? With how we feel about each other? And no matter what you say, I know that you care about me as well. Nobody could fake that kind of passion you show. No damn way," he said grimly.

"Baby, I'm not saying I don't care about you. I've never felt like this before. I just need some time to think about all of this. I don't want to make another hasty decision."

"Don't compare me—us—with anyone else, Lilly. It's not fair. You already know I wouldn't treat you like he did. I know it's only been a few short weeks, but you *know* I would never hurt you, don't you? Don't you, baby?" With desperate attention he latched on to her lips and kissed her with more feeling than he'd ever given her before.

She felt it. It was all in his kiss.

When he withdrew from her, he rested his forehead against hers. "What are you so afraid of? Won't you at least give us a chance? A chance that you could come to care about me as well, Lilliana? Don't you think you could love me? That you'd trust me with your love, with your body, and know that I would never hurt either?" A small muscle ticked in his lower jaw. He clenched his teeth, his fingers tightened fractionally on her as he held her face inches away from his.

Lilliana completely came undone when she saw the threat of tears in his eyes. To see this strong, vibrant man so strongly affected crashed down even more of the walls she had erected in her heart. The remaining barriers crumbled like the useless waste they were and Lilliana realized this man was for real.

They'd known each other for a few short weeks. Her girls would probably laugh at her, maybe even think she was foolish.

Hell, maybe she was a bit foolish. But damn it if she wasn't going to believe.

Damn it if she wasn't tired, beyond tired of wishing, hoping, dreaming, that she'd find someone just like the man in front of her. She had no idea where this journey with Josh would take her, but suddenly her heart felt lighter than it had in years. She grinned at him, barely able to still her excitement at what she was about to say, and mean every word of, for the first time.

She covered his large hands with her much smaller ones and smiled. "It's already too late for that, Josh."

"What . . . what is it too late for? You don't think you can ever love me?"

She turned her body fully to his and and smiled into his handsome face. The look in his eyes was real, and honest. Lilliana knew she was about to make the best decision of her life. She reached up and kissed him with all the leftover fear, excitement and love she felt for him.

"It's too late to go back," she said and cleared her throat around the sudden restriction before she could continue, "because I love you, too." As soon as the words tripped from her mouth, Josh grabbed her and crushed her body against his naked chest and hugged her hard.

Lilliana wasn't ashamed of the tears she felt easing down her face. Her tears weren't due to sadness, not due to someone hurting or mistreating her. These were plain old-fashioned tears of *joy*. Josh was special and she knew it deep down in that place that defied common sense or description. The same place that insisted that she give this man . . . this relationship a chance. And Lilliana intended on doing exactly that.

She was done running, hiding and crying. That was over. Been there, done that, time to move on.

She intended to enjoy the journey and give them the chance to explore, love and learn . . . together.

Caught

Lisa G. Riley

Acknowledgments

Thank you to all of my family and friends who supported me through this process. I love you and your support was more appreciated (and needed) than you realize.

To my agent Cori Deyoe and my editor Hilary Sares. Thank you guys for being so thorough.

LGR

1

Melinda closed her locker with a soft click, trying to save her pounding head from more pain. "Okay, God, I'll make a deal with you," she whispered from a dry throat. "If you'll just let me get through the next ten hours without falling on my face, I promise that I'll never again let myself be convinced that mixing margaritas and white wine has never hurt anyone." She turned to the mirror to check herself one last time, wondering just when all the water with lemon she'd drank was going to kick in. She needed to drink to replenish what the alcohol had depleted.

"Eesh," she said, looking at her face. She just looked so . . . well, *hungover*. She took another huge swig from her water bottle. She couldn't believe she'd drunk so much—she generally didn't drink at all, really. She didn't like the false sense of reality people got from alcohol and the loss of control it could cause.

Trying to act normal, she made her way from the nurses' locker room to the small kitchen located in the back of the Living Well Health Clinic where she worked as a nurse and nursing supervisor. Dr. Nicholas Pantino stood at the sink with his back to her. Oh, *come on*, not him. Not now, she thought with an inward sigh, and slumped against the doorjamb. Not now when I'm feeling like I've just gone a round with The Rock and lost. She studied him from her position in the doorway. He was just too sexy for her own damned good.

He was the first man she'd been even remotely attracted to since before she'd gotten married, and she'd been divorced for three years. Almost from the moment he'd started working at the clinic four months before, she'd known that things were going to change at Living Well and for her. For one thing, all the nurses and practically all the female patients between the ages of nineteen and ninety drooled over him like he was a giant ice cream cone in the middle of the desert. She was convinced that she was the only woman within ten miles who didn't lust after the man.

Okay, so maybe she did, she forced herself to admit with another inward sigh, but at least he didn't know it. And she didn't plan that he ever would. Okay, so maybe he *suspected* it—again she forced herself to be honest—but she'd be damned if she'd ever confirm it for him. He had enough women swooning over him; she wasn't about to be added to the greedy, ferocious pack.

Dr. Pantino—everyone except Mel called him Dr. Nick—was, to put it simply, one of the finest men she'd ever laid eyes on. He was at least six feet tall, had gorgeous olive skin, thick, luscious black hair, and eyes that were just as dark. His body, *geez*, his body was just a work of art. Looking at it made her go hot and achy almost every time. And then there was the hair on his face. She itched to bury her fingers in that thick, rich, neatly trimmed beard, and she imagined his mustache would be all soft and tickly against her lips.

"Good morning, Melinda."

Mel came out of her daydream at the sound of his voice. She

prayed he hadn't caught her staring. She straightened from against the doorjamb and walked into the kitchen. "Hi, Dr. Pantino," she said, and went to the refrigerator for a bottle of Gatorade. Maybe the electrolytes would help send the bitch of a headache on its way. She carefully closed the refrigerator and walked over to a small table to sit down. Feeling his eyes follow her every move, she tried to act like she wasn't hungover. She was a spectacular failure.

"Hung over, huh?" Nicholas asked her, his voice tinged with amusement. He chuckled when she sent him a dirty look without answering his question. He deliberately sat right next to her at the table. "Well, I hope you feel better soon. The water should knock it out of you. Has the lemon helped to settle your stomach at all yet?"

Mel tried to ignore his nearness. It was like heat radiated off his body, and *her* body was acting like it was a freaking heat-seeking missile. "A little bit," she said, deciding to stop trying to deny the hangover. She opened the Gatorade and took a long swallow, the cold, tangy liquid tasting like manna from heaven as it slid down her parched throat.

Nicholas watched her drink the beverage. It was an unintentionally sexy move and he fully enjoyed the show. Her head was thrown back and her light brown twisted hair brushed her shoulders. Her eyes were closed. The look on her face could only be described as one of pure pleasure. He watched the muscles underneath the skin of her neck contract with each swallow of the drink and felt his heart rate speed up right before his stomach muscles tightened and his penis lengthened to push against the zipper of his pants. Christ, she could make him hard without even trying.

He resisted leaning in to take a bite from the sleek skin of her neck. Instead, he took hold of her arm and waited for her to stop drinking and look at him. "After that enticing little performance, you know I just have to ask you, don't you? For the love of God, Lindy, when the hell are you going to put both of us out of our misery and go out with me?" He used his own personal nickname for her.

She frowned at him. "Okay, stop right there, Dr. Pantino. I can't play with you today. And like I told you before, we are not going to go out. It wouldn't be a good idea, so just stop asking me."

He studied her quietly while he let his thumb caress the soft skin of her arm. "I'll stop asking when I'm convinced that you really don't want to go out with me." He enjoyed working with her, and he wanted to be with her outside of work. It was as simple as that. She was making things difficult and, liking the challenge, he went along with it, but pretty soon he'd rein in all the game-playing. She was a sexy, caring, witty, intelligent woman, and besides wanting to make love to her until she couldn't walk, he also wanted to get to know her better. Seeing her for a few hours a week just wasn't cutting it.

Mel sighed and closed her eyes to avoid his stare. The determination in that stare was a threat to her sense of balance. She sensed, *knew*, that what she was willing to give of herself would never be enough for him. He'd be one of those men who demanded that a woman hold nothing back. She kept her eyes closed, praying for strength as she tried not to let the soft sweep of his thumb across her skin distract her. He *would* have to pick today to mess with her—today when she was just too darned tired and sick to really play with him. He asked her at least once every other week to go out with him. Her answer was no every single time, but that didn't stop him.

It had become a verbal game with them, one she fully admitted to herself that she enjoyed. But she couldn't do it today. Today, she was almost weak enough to give in to his gentle persuasion. "Well, I don't know what to tell you, then," she said in answer to what had almost seemed like an accusation. She winced at the pathetic line. How sorry could she be? As comebacks went, that one fell flat on its face. She gave a mental shrug. Whatever. It was the best she could do.

Nicholas hid his satisfaction. She hadn't denied wanting to go out with him. That was a first and would have to do for now. "Aw, poor baby. You really are hungover. Can I get you anything?" It was obvious that she wasn't up to their little game, and he decided to forgo his usual pleasure of teasing her. She was usually more creative and gave him a verbal comeuppance every time.

He wanted her and had wanted her since he'd seen her all those months ago when he'd first caught a glimpse of her. She was sexy as hell with those long legs; high, firm ass; and smooth, brown skin. Yes, he wanted her, but she was more than a little skittish. He'd heard enough of the clinic gossip to know she hadn't had a happy marriage and hadn't dated anyone since the divorce. He wanted to know what kind of marriage she'd had, and he'd wait for her to tell him, but he wasn't going to let that be an obstacle. She was going to belong to him. "Would you like something to eat?" he asked her.

Mel sighed in relief—relief that he was going to give her a reprieve. She didn't care that he heard it. "I'm fine, thanks."

"So what did you do last night anyway?"

"I went out with Lilly and Simone," she said cautiously. There was no way in hell she'd tell him about the BSA ad. She'd just be asking for trouble. He'd take it and run with it.

"It appears you had a good time," he said.

She winced as she thought about all the alcohol she'd consumed the night before. "Let's just say it was a memorable one."

"Well, you just keep drinking the water, and you should feel better. I've got some paperwork to go over," he said as he stood. "Our first scheduled appointment is in twenty minutes. It just sounds like a bad cold, so I may not need you. You can rest that sensitive head of yours, all right?"

"Yes, thanks, but I'm fine. I just need to sit for a few more minutes. There were no walk-ins when I came in, but Jacinta is on the desk. She'll call back if she needs help." As nursing supervisor, Mel set the schedules for the other three full-time nurses and herself. They took turns working with the three doctors who each worked at the clinic two days a week. This week she was on the schedule to work with Nicholas.

"All right, then. I'll see you later in exam room one."

He stood to leave and she allowed herself to begin to relax. When he stopped behind her chair and she felt the heat of his body against her back she realized she'd relaxed too soon. *Well, damn.* "Do you know how much I want to taste you?" she heard him whisper in her ear and shivered in sudden desire.

"Pretty soon I'm going to stop asking and waiting," Nicholas continued after he'd felt the shiver. He softly scraped his nail across the back of her neck.

Mel caught her breath and did her best not to shiver again as the muscles in her stomach tightened. She swallowed hard before saying, "How do I know you've been waiting?" She felt the vibration from his chuckle flow against her skin.

"Oh, baby, you can be sure that that's all I've been doing since I met you. But that's okay, because when you finally let me catch you, you won't want me to let you go." He straightened and left.

Mel let her body slump in the chair and rested her hot forehead on the coolness of the table. Aw, hell. Good Lord, she was in trouble. A kind of trouble she'd never experienced before. Ever. Until she'd met Nicholas, she hadn't really known what it felt like to be so hot and bothered, regardless of the fact that she'd been married for two years. Sexually, her marriage had been a joke. For the most part, sex between her and her ex-husband had involved her lying on the bed with her nightgown rudely shoved up around her waist while he pushed his dick into her over and over again.

She'd just lie there not making a sound except for the automatic groans that came in response to her body being invaded. She hadn't felt anything either. She'd keep her body as still as she could and her mind as blank as possible while he'd root around inside of her like he was digging for gold. When Edmund was finished, he'd get up, adjust his dick and leave— probably on his way to another woman's bed.

Which was why until recently, she hadn't understood what the appeal of sex was, at least not for women. Sure, she'd heard all the stories about multiple orgasms and the mythical G-spot, but they had never really resonated. She'd even felt some lust when reading romance novels, but it had never gone any further than that. Reading about the positions some of the more risqué novels described had made her hot, but it still wasn't enough to make her a true believer.

She sighed. She'd always believed that either Edmund hadn't been doing his job or she was as frigid as a Popsicle. She hadn't enjoyed sex with her boyfriend in college and she hadn't enjoyed it with Edmund, who'd cheated on her almost from the first day of their marriage. She'd actually believed that she just wasn't meant to have sex. Until Nicholas. After meeting Nicholas, who could make her shiver and moan with just the right look, she could say with dead certainty that she wasn't a Popsicle. And, hell, now sex was higher on her agenda than it had ever been.

"Hey, Mel!"

The voice was way too perky for Melinda and she looked up with a scowl. "Not so loud. Can't you see some of us are trying to die in peace?" she said to friend and clinic psychologist, Dr. Cally Winston, and put her head back down on the table.

"Uh-oh. Are you really ill, or did you enjoy yourself a little too much last night with your friends?" Cally asked as she went to the counter for coffee. She was a small, shapely woman with dark, intelligent eyes that shone out of a pretty, honeybrown face. Despite the fact that she'd lived in Chicago for most of her life, her Southern accent was sometimes still very evident.

Sure now that she wasn't going to get any peace and quiet, Melinda sat up again. "The last one."

"Well, I don't feel sorry for you, then," Cally said as she sat down across from her. "I just saw Nick, and he looked pretty happy. Did you agree to go out with him?"

Melinda had shared her feelings about Nicholas with Cally a couple of weeks before. The two had become fast friends when the psychologist had started working at the clinic a year earlier. Like Nicholas, she offered her services twice a week, while keeping her own practice on the other side of the city. "No, I didn't, but I tell you, I was really close to doing so. Thank God he didn't push it."

"Well, you already know what I think. You should go for it. I know you don't trust gorgeous men like Nick who seem to have harems all their own, but he isn't asking you for marriage. He's just asking for a date, and besides, I know Nick. He's not the type to date more than one woman at a time."

"That is a part of it, yes, but he also scares me," Melinda admitted candidly. "I told you that for the longest time, I thought I was frigid, right? Well, Nicholas has totally disproved that theory, and, well, it feels like my body is waking up from a long, deep sleep. The feelings are so unfamiliar to me that I'm not entirely comfortable with them. I always feel like I'm about to lose control around him, and I don't like it." She'd already told the other woman that her ex-husband had not only cheated on her, but had also been demanding, arrogant, and controlling and had not taken the time for foreplay.

"I get it," Cally said with a nod and an understanding smile. "You've felt safe, so to speak, all these years thinking that you couldn't be sexually excited."

"Well, I didn't necessarily like it, but I got used to it—"

"And then Nick came along and blew that theory all to hell

and back and you're left with all these pent-up, hot, sexy feelings that need alleviating, but you're too much of a lily-livered coward to let that happen. That about cover it?"

"Well, I wouldn't have put it exactly in those terms," Melinda said sarcastically, "but if you, as a highly qualified, board-certified psychologist feel that *you* have to, then who am I to argue?"

Cally just laughed at her. "I'm not speaking as a psychologist. I'm speaking as your friend, and you know I'm right."

"Yes, yes, I know you're right, but that still doesn't make it any easier."

"I'm sure it doesn't, but look at it this way—if you and Nick ever do hit the sheets, you definitely won't be faking orgasms anymore."

Mel looked around to make sure they were still alone. She leaned in, "Be quiet, Cally! I don't want everyone within the sound of your voice to know my business. Don't make me regret telling you my secrets," she warned in a whisper.

"I'm sorry, but it just amazes me how you were able to fake orgasms all those times during a two-year marriage, while your husband thought he was screwing your brains out. One, I don't know how you did it and stayed sane. And two, I don't know how your husband didn't catch on to it. You must be some actress."

Melinda frowned. "I don't know how I did it either, but I did. It's not really something I'm proud of, but it's over now. I didn't fake it the whole two years. We'd stopped having sex by the time the second year rolled around. I realize now that faking it during the marriage was my way of getting back at him for being so damned arrogant and controlling. And as for Edmund not catching on to what I was doing, I think a part of him knew. At one point, when I wasn't responding the way he figured I should be, he got insulted and said that if I thought there were other more interesting things I could be doing, then he'd like to know what the hell they were. I could have given him a full list—reading a book, grocery shopping, watching television, hell, watching paint dry! Anything but having sex. But of course I didn't. When I took too long to answer him, though, he actually bragged that from there on out, he wouldn't finish with me until his 'male prowess' had made me scream and had made my eyes roll to the back of my head."

"No, he didn't!"

"Yes, he did. And that's when I knew that it had become some kind of competition for him or something. And not because he wanted me to have pleasure either, but because he wanted to prove that he could make the ice queen come. Well, what I wanted was *him* off *me,* so I started faking it. I could fake the screams all right, but I never could manage to fake that eyes-rolling-to-the-back-of-my-head thing, so I just closed them so he couldn't see what they were doing."

Cally just looked at her. "The woman that I am wants to crack up laughing that you tricked him, but the therapist in me wants to analyze both of you."

"Okay, well, listen to this and see which one of you wins out. Once, when Edmund was sweating and grunting all over me like an animal, in my head I figured out this really difficult equation that had been bugging me since college. It was the first time during sex that I had ever said anything besides my usual 'yes . . . yes . . . yes, you're the man,'" she said in a bored voice.

Cally loudly guffawed. "I know you didn't sound like that when you were in the midst of it."

"I don't know, but I doubt it. I didn't want him to know that what the words really meant was, 'finish what you're doing, pull the hell out, and get to steppin', you knock-kneed, slick son of a bitch!'"

Full-blown laughter escaped Cally's throat again.

"Anyway, after I'd figured out the equation, I made the mistake of excitedly yelling out, 'Oh, my God, that's it! Yes, that's it!'"

"Oh, Lord. What did your ex do?"

"What do you think? He went ape-shit crazy! He started pumping his hips faster and faster like it was his last chance to fuck before he died. Then he gave me his usual arrogant smirk and said between these hard, panting breaths, 'Uh-huh, that's right. I know that's it. You don't have to tell me. Shit, I'm the man. You hear me, girl? I am *the* man! I know what I'm doing!' Little did he know that it had been numbers that had gotten me excited, while his so-called male prowess had left me all but bone dry."

"Good Lord," Cally repeated with a shake of her head. "What did you do?"

"I said, 'You certainly are,' and just waited for him to finish. When he left, I wrote the equation down."

"Just like that, huh?"

Melinda nodded. "Just like that. Well, actually, after that one time, I tried not to think about numbers anymore because it gave Edmund a false sense of accomplishment. He suddenly thought he had some kind of magic between his legs and he expected me to sound just as excited as I had when I'd figured out the problem. I just couldn't do it and after a few more times of him giving it the old college try and attempting like mad to get that gold star, I just couldn't take it anymore."

Cally studied her for a moment before saying, "Have you ever thought that maybe you value control so much that you don't have orgasms because they would be the ultimate in *losing* control?"

"Yep," Melinda said.

"And?" Cally encouraged.

"And you and I have talked about it before. You said that control is a valuable commodity to me. Okay, I'll buy that. I'm the first to admit that I like having control. But I also know that I didn't love Edmund. I thought I did at first, but I really didn't. And after we were married, I didn't even like him, so any intimacy with him was a struggle for me. I didn't trust him enough. And before you ask why I stayed with him, I'll tell you—because I'd made a commitment and because I thought I could change things. When I realized I couldn't and was just making myself miserable by staying, I left."

"Sugar, please. I'm a psychologist; I already know why you stayed. What I was going to say was, when somebody finally does sex you up the right way, you are going to be so caught up that you're not going to know what the hell to do with yourself."

"Maybe," Mel said with a skeptical shrug as she stood. "All I know is that it's not about to happen right now. I've got to get to work."

"Mel, the right man can have you fienin' for it so badly, you won't be able to think about work or anything else!"

2

"*Umm-umm*! That's the finest lookin' white man I've ever seen in my life!"

Nicholas heard the whisper and shook his head, stifling a chuckle as he stood at the receptionist's desk filling out charts. The woman speaking was a pillar of the community and a volunteer at the clinic who constantly flirted with him. She obviously had a healthy sexual appetite. She was also seventy years old.

"I know that's right," he heard her friend whisper loudly. The two did everything together, including volunteer their time at the clinic twice a week. "If I didn't already have a husband, damn his sorry eyes, and I liked white meat, I sure would get myself some of that!" She was sixty-eight.

"*Oh-kay!*" Wholesale agreement was more than clear in the first speaker's voice. "Dr. Nick is a straight-no-chaser type of hottie. That's the best kind!"

Nicholas finally turned toward the perpetrators, who were sitting in the otherwise empty waiting area waiting for children to arrive. They kept the children occupied while the clinic's staff saw to their parents' needs. "Now, girls," he chastised the two, and smiled when they giggled at the term. "Behave your-selves. What would your husbands think?"

"I don't know, Dr. Fine-as-Wine," Mrs. Johnson said, her brown eyes twinkling and her brown, leathery skin stretching in a mischievous grin. She was the older of the two; no more than five feet tall, and she might have weighed one hundred pounds. She had curly gray hair, looked innocent, and was as cute as a button. "I'm not trying to be bad, but I just can't help myself. Every time I see you, I want to take you home with me and have my way with you. *All* of you," she finished with a grunt.

"Stop that, Mary," Ada Thomas chided, and nudged her friend with her elbow. She was a couple of inches taller than her friend but was just as thin and looked just as innocent. "Can't you see you're embarrassing the boy? You're too old for him anyhow. Dr. Nick needs some young and fresh thing. Some-body like our Melinda," she said innocently. But Nicholas saw the sly look in her eyes when she looked directly at him. "She'd be perfect for him."

"Mmm-hmm. I agree," said Mrs. Johnson. "She's a bit skinny, but I think they would be good together. Even though she's black and he's white, but he's Italian, so that's close enough."

Mrs. Thomas rolled her eyes and sucked her teeth. "Cut out your foolishness, old woman. It doesn't matter what color peo-ple are anymore. This isn't the 1920s, thirties, forties, fifties or sixties. Nothing matters but how two people feel about each other. And Dr. Nick here has got feelings for Nurse Mel. Don't you, Doc?"

Any conversation between the two ladies and him almost al-ways managed to wind its way to Mel. He never discussed her with them, and he didn't now. Saying nothing, he turned back to his charts. The two elderly women were funny and enter-taining, but they could also be trying, especially on a day like today when he'd seen almost double his usual number of patients.

He thought about his office, all nice and empty, and wanted to be there so badly, he actually started walking towards the door. He needed a break before patients started coming in again. In their line of work, they had to take their breaks when they could. People walked in looking for help all the time, and any one of them could be an emergency. They had to contend with them and with the ones who actually had appointments. Whenever there was a lull in the busy schedule, he took advantage of it.

"Ooh, Dr. Nick! I can't believe you're just going to walk away from me like that!"

Nicholas heard the surprised insult in Mrs. Thomas's voice and winced. He'd completely forgotten about the two volunteers. He turned back around. "I'm so sorry, ladies. It's been a busy day. Now, what were you saying?" he prompted Mrs. Thomas, feeling that he had to listen to her talk about Melinda to make up for the earlier insult.

"I was saying that I know you've got the hots for Mel," she said, and made a skeptical sound when he only looked at her. "Now, don't try to fool me. I might have glaucoma, but I'm not blind, man. I've watched you watch her for the past couple of months now. I've just been wondering when you were going to make your move."

Nicholas just looked at her, letting his silence speak for him.

Mrs. Thomas smiled. "Boy, you are so stubborn! I hope you don't think that I'm going to let that stop me. Now, back to our girl. She might be tall and thin but she's proportioned, and the perfect height for a man of your size. That skin of hers is nothing to sneeze at either, what with it being so smooth and clear. And what about her hair? Those little twisty things she wears now are so much better than when she wore it straight. You can see that pretty face of hers even more, don't you think? And they just look so soft. Now let's talk about her eyes and her mouth, why—"

"I get the picture, Mrs. Thomas," Nicholas finally interrupted and stopped just short of rolling his eyes. They acted so much like his mother and grandmother when it came to his love life that he could laugh. "Yes, Melinda is a beautiful woman, gorgeous, in fact. Is that what you want to hear from me? For the love of God, you're not even trying to be subtle about it."

"Well, if you get the picture, just when do you plan on asking her out?" This came impatiently from Mrs. Johnson.

"That, my little busybody, is between the lady in question and me. Now, I'm going back to my office." He looked at his watch and then back up at the two women. "Are you ladies having something brought in for lunch? It's twelve-thirty, you know."

"We know," said Mrs. Thomas. "We brought a little something."

"Okay, then. I'll see you later," he said, and turned to the receptionist, who was trying really hard to act like she was minding her own business. "Will you buzz me in, please, Allison?" he asked her, referring to the security door. He waited for the loud buzz and then pulled the door open. He walked down the long hall, past the exam rooms and bathrooms until he reached the back of the building, where he shared an office with two other doctors; like him, they also worked at the clinic twice a week. They alternated days.

He made his way through the large space, to the corner where his desk was. It was the farthest away from the windows, the door, and the bathroom because he'd been the last doctor to come on board. The others didn't know it, but he preferred to be in the corner—it was quieter and there was at least an *impression* of privacy there.

He sat in his chair and closed his eyes. He'd gotten to the clinic at eight that morning, and he was absolutely exhausted.

So far, he'd seen almost fifteen patients. He only hoped that the calm they were currently experiencing would last for at least a little while longer. A general practitioner, he'd been approached to join Living Well after another doctor had retired and moved to Florida. He enjoyed the work, and he loved being able to help the underserved.

At Living Well, all kinds of patients came in, from the poor to the middle class. Some people had insurance, others Medicaid, and some nothing at all. Living Well had been started several years before for the express purpose of helping those who couldn't afford a doctor's care. A board of directors made up of professionals and activists from the neighborhood oversaw the running of Living Well. Nicholas was taking a significant cut in pay but didn't mind. He was a partner in a successful practice and also did occasional rotations at a local hospital.

He knew that Melinda had been at Living Well for almost ten years. She was full-time and served on the board. When members of the board had approached him to join the staff, she'd been with them. All she'd had to do was smile and he'd been hooked. The deep dimples in her cheeks alone would have been enough, but she also had plump, full lips with a pretty little freckle right near the top left lip. Most people would have called it a mole, but because it was flat, it was a freckle. It didn't matter, though, because being a mouth man, he wanted to feel both the freckle and the lip against his tongue.

Working at the clinic and seeing her at least twice a week, sometimes three times if he could fit in an extra day, he'd started to fall for her. She had the most beautiful doe-like brown eyes, was funny, a little quirky, and sweet—he wanted her. He loved her, wanted to *make love* to her, but he also wanted to fuck her. He wanted to get her alone in a locked room—it didn't matter where—and make love to her until she couldn't walk, talk or think a coherent thought. If she ever found out, she'd probably run like the wind.

Nicholas closed his eyes, leaned back in his chair and let his mind wander into fantasy. He sat in his office chair and in walked Melinda. She closed and locked the door behind her, closing out the noise of the busy clinic. She wore nothing but a shy, anticipatory smile as she walked toward him with long, languid strides, her small, high breasts jiggling a bit with each step. He could smell her arousal, and as she came closer, he saw it begin to drip from the short hair covering the pretty pussy that protected what he was sure was a throbbing, swollen clit.

Arriving around his desk, she peeked at him through her lashes and quickly looked away before climbing onto his thighs to sit astride his lap, her feet flat on the chair and her knees raised up and spread wide on either side of him. Her musky scent made him breathe in deeply. He felt the heat of her through his jeans and looked down. The view was spectacular. Her clit peeked through her slick, wet lips, just begging for his touch. As he stared, her opening contracted with a hungry, grasping sound . . . once . . . twice . . . three times, like it was crying out for his dick to fill it. Juice began to leak out from her opening and slowly trailed onto his thigh.

"Mmm," she moaned, making him raise his eyes. She slowly licked her lips before taking a shuddering breath.

Nicholas made a low, greedy sound in the back of his throat as one of her hardened nipples brushed teasingly against his lips with the releasing of her breath.

"Hi, Dr. Nick," she purred as she began to loosen his tie. "Touch me," she whispered, and leaned in to bite his chin. She then trailed brief, open-mouthed, wet kisses along his jawline until she reached his ear. "Will you—"she paused to lick the inside of his ear and then puffed a soft breath into it before she continued, "—*touch me*, Dr. Nick?" she sighed with urgent need into his ear.

Pressing a tender kiss to her shoulder, Nicholas reached behind her for the large, thick medical books he kept on his desk. "Raise up, sweet—"

His phone rang, rudely jerking him from his fantasy. He picked it up. "Nick Pantino."

"Hello, Nick! How's my favorite son today?"

He closed his eyes in horror and felt his dick quickly slink back to its normal size at the sound of his mother's voice. He cleared his throat and tried not to sound like he'd been up to something. "Hi, Mom. Your *only* son is fine, thank you very much." He was the oldest and his mother and grandmother had raised him and his sisters when their father had died. Nick had become the man of the house at the very tender age of eleven. "What's up? You and Nana okay? Does one of the girls need something?"

"No, darling, everyone is fine. I'm just calling to remind you about your grandmother's party. You have only a few days to let us know who you're going to bring—*if* you're going to bring anyone?"

Nicholas smiled. His mother had been trying to butt into his love life ever since his divorce. "You need to know who I'm bringing? I thought this was just an informal gathering of friends and family—mostly family," he reminded her. "Why would you need to know who I'm bringing? Will there be name placards at this backyard barbeque?"

"Well, no," Sophia Pantino hedged. Nicholas heard her sigh impatiently. "I just need to know, okay?"

"Mom," Nicholas began.

"Don't you 'mom' me in that tone of voice, Nicholas Anthony Pantino. I just want to know. And besides, if I had had any part in picking out your first wife, then you wouldn't be divorced today."

His mother was a dyed-in-the-wool Catholic, and to her, divorce was a sin. Interfering in his love life was her way of trying to save his immortal soul. "Well, I was a grown man when I decided to get married, Mom. Grown men are supposed to pick their own wives."

"Don't you get smart with me, Nicky. I'm simply saying that I could have helped you make a better choice and next time, I will. So I ask you again—who are you bringing to the party?"

Nicholas thought of Melinda. He knew his mother would like her, but a huge family gathering was not the place for a first meeting. He didn't want to scare her away, and if Melinda had to meet his huge family all at once, she'd be running for the hills. He said, "I'm not bringing anyone, Mom. I'll be flying solo."

Melinda made her way to the kitchen for the second time that day. Her stomach had finally stopped its vague rumblings of a threatened revolt, and she was eager to placate it with a mild lunch. Chicken noodle soup and French bread were on the menu. Seeing Cally at the table again, she smiled and walked in. "Geez, didn't I leave you in that exact same spot this morning?" she teased. "Just when do you work?"

"Oh, whatever. How's your head?"

"Better, thanks," Melinda answered as she poured her soup from its restaurant container into a bowl that she'd taken from the cabinet. "I'm hoping this soup will get rid of the last little bit of the hangover and I'm sure you'll be glad to know that I no longer feel like death warmed over."

"Whoo-hoo," Cally said drily, and forked up some of her salad.

Melinda smiled and brought her soup over to the table. "God, it feels so good to get off my feet again."

"Well, now that you are, tell me what else you and your girls got up to last night—that is, besides getting so wasted you could barely walk or see straight this morning."

Melinda laughed. "You don't want to know, trust me," she

said with a shake of her head before spooning up some soup. "I'm trying like crazy to forget it myself."

"Now, I know you don't think I'm going to let you leave me hanging like that? Give," Cally demanded mildly. "Tell Dr. Cally all the sordid details."

Melinda debated about it, feeling kind of stupid and embarrassed about the whole thing. She couldn't believe she'd actually agreed to the scheme in the first place. "Well, one of those crazy loons I call friends—I can't even remember which one—came up with this scheme for all of us, since none of us are getting any, to put ourselves out there, find a real man and get some action."

"Right. Tell me, does this scheme involve you approaching Nick at all? Say, to jump his bones or anything like that?"

"Nope," Melinda said, unconcerned. "Not at all."

"Even though you can't get the man off your mind?"

"Even though," Melinda said in mild agreement, and took a sip of her soup. "It would be easier for me to go out with a stranger than it would for me to go out with Dr. Pantino. Does that make sense?"

"Not to me," Cally said crisply with a shrug. "But I'm sure it does in that twisted mind of yours."

Melinda gave her a stern look. "Do you want to hear about the plan or not?"

"Okay, sorry. I'm ready when you are."

Melinda began her story. "So the idea is a crazy one, and I agreed to it because I'm crazy, too. The gist of it is, we each place an ad entitled 'BSA,' which stands for Big Spankable Asses. In our ads, we'll each say that if a man can guess what BSA stands for, then he can have a date with the woman who placed the ad . . ."

Nicholas rose from his desk, deciding that he wanted a cup of coffee. He left the doctors' office and walked down the hall to the kitchen. Inches away from the entryway, he heard Melinda say "big spankable ass" and stopped in his tracks. What the hell? He turned to leave, thinking that the way she said it—all conspiratorial-like—probably meant that this was something she would prefer no one else hear. Then he heard her say something about placing an ad and decided to stay. He leaned against the wall with his arms crossed, and with no shame at all, listened to the conversation.

3

Cally wiped tears of hilarity from her eyes. "Wait, wait," she said between wheezing breaths. "BSA? Big Spankable Asses? I love it! That's hysterical and just the thing you need. You're not going to back out, are you?"

"No, of course not. I would never do that, no matter how much 'sane Melinda' is telling me that I need to run like I just stole something." She stopped to look at Cally, who was laughing so hard that she looked in danger of falling out of her chair.

Wiping more tears of laughter from her eyes, Cally said, "You're that desperate, huh?"

"No, not really desperate, just sort of weirded out about it. I've never placed an ad to find a date before, and of course, you know that I haven't been on the actual dating scene in years. The last time I dated was before I married Edmund and that was six years ago. The landscape has changed a hell of a lot since then and I'm just nervous about it, to be honest."

"Well, it's only normal that you would be," Cally said. "But just go ahead and do it. You might surprise yourself and actually find someone."

"Right. A lot of freaks, nasties and strange folks. How could I not with an ad titled 'BSA'?"

"Probably, but you could also find someone to have a little fun with."

"I know, and at least there's a safeguard. I'm pretty sure there aren't going to be many people who'll be able to figure out what the phrase means."

"Exactly," Cally agreed. "And besides, you don't have to do anything you don't want to. Things can only go as far as you let them. Have you decided where you're going to place the ad?"

Mel shook her head. "No, not yet, but Simone called me on my cell this morning to tell me about a local online dating site. I'm going to check it out when I get home."

"Did she mean the site was locally owned or that it's for Chicago locals?"

"It's for people who live in the Chicago area, I believe. It would certainly narrow things down for me, if it is. Anyway, the site is called ChicagoLuhvin.com. Ever heard of it?"

"It doesn't sound familiar, no."

"Well, according to Simone, it's supposed to be a lot easier to register with than other sites, and you don't have to commit to any long subscriptions."

"Cool. That should make things simple for you," Cally said. "Are you considering posting on the site?"

"Yeah. I'll either put the ad there or in one of the newspapers, probably the *Reader*. I haven't decided yet. I need to check out the site first."

Cally pushed her chair back and stood to dump her empty container in the trash. "Will you at least consider asking Nick out, Mel? I mean, the whole BSA thing may not even be necessary."

"No, I don't want to ask Dr. Pantino out." She pushed her own chair back and stood to rinse her bowl in the sink. "Like I said, it would be easier for me to go out with a perfect stranger than it would to go out with him. I just don't think I'm ready to take him on."

Nicholas took the sound of the second chair scraping back as a sign that it was time for him to leave. Scowling, he walked unhurriedly back to his office. He couldn't believe she was actually going to place an ad about getting spanked. His frown turned angry at the thought of other men putting their hands on her. "The only man who's going to touch that ass of hers is me," he said in a low voice.

He had to admit that it surprised him that she might want to be spanked. He'd have no problem doing it if that was what she really wanted, but proper Melinda getting spanked? It just didn't compute for him. He supposed, though, that many people would be surprised at some of the things he'd done in the privacy of the bedroom.

"All right, sweetheart, if that's what you want, then that's what you'll get." Oh, he'd spank it, lick it, bite it—whatever she wanted. He had to laugh. She had a nice-sized butt, and he'd always wanted to get his hands on it. It had always surprised him that someone of her small stature would have a behind that size. It boggled the mind.

He had a feeling that it would fill his hands nicely, and he couldn't wait to put his theory to the test. He sat down in his chair. He was finally going to get that date. It was about damned time, too. All he had to do now was figure out which ad was hers and they could stop all the playing around.

Nicholas sat at the computer in his home study. He frowned in concentration as he brought up the ChicagoLuhvin site. "Let's see if she's finally placed that ad," he muttered in frustration. He'd been checking every day since he'd eavesdropped, and there had been nothing yet. He'd missed checking yesterday because he'd been on call at the hospital. But he knew she also hadn't placed anything in the *Reader* newspaper, as he'd yet to find her ad. He'd seen one BSA ad there, but he'd known it wasn't Melinda's and had just assumed it was one of her friends. It just hadn't sounded like anything she'd write.

"You certainly are putting me through my paces, sweetheart," he said as he logged onto the site. First, he'd had a devil of a time finding the damned site because he'd been spelling it incorrectly—l-o-v-i-n'—the normal way, instead of phonetically. Then he'd had to actually open an account, feeling foolish as he'd done so, but glad that the site gave him the option of registering for as little as two weeks, or as long as an entire year. He'd chosen a monthlong subscription and had actually gotten a couple of responses, even without posting his picture. Of course, he didn't expect Melinda to post hers, either. That would just be too easy.

He was lucky that the site was extremely searchable; otherwise he'd be going through thousands of postings by the day. Subscribers could search by gender, sexual orientation (including transgender and bisexual), and sexual proclivities (bondage, dominant/submissive, et cetera). Breaking it down even further, one could search by race and ethnicity and then date of registration onto the site. He always went straight for African American women who'd registered in the past two days—two days was the closest he could get in terms of time. He didn't think he needed to go any further than that. The number of women who were looking for love absolutely astounded him.

"Come on, baby," he mumbled as he typed in his search parameters. "Be here, today, just *be* here." Melinda had been driving him crazy at work. More and more lately, just looking at her made him want to do things to her. Shocking things—the kinds of things that could easily get him arrested in several states. Just the other day, she'd been leaning over an opened drawer of a waist-high filing cabinet and the way the material of the white nurse's uniform had stretched over and cupped her behind had made him have to turn around and go back to his office to hide a sudden hard-on.

He'd actually seen himself walking up behind her. She'd looked over her shoulder at him in surprise, but when it dawned on her what he was thinking about, she'd smiled in anticipation. He'd bent his head and kissed her, pressing his dick into her ass as he slowly bent her over the filing cabinet. She'd dropped the files and held on to the cabinet. He'd lifted up her skirt and pulled down her nylons and panties all in one swoop, palming that perfect butt of hers as he did so. His hand had worked its way to her cleft and she'd moaned, pressing her clit into his hand. She'd been so drenched with need that he'd pulled his pants down and slid his dick into her to the hilt on the first try. She'd pushed back against him in a frenzy of need while he'd pushed forward, and all too soon, he'd exploded into her at the same time that she'd come in a gush of cream. He'd even heard their moans and the banging of her body against the metal cabinet as he'd rammed into her.

In his head, the whole scenario had taken less than a minute. Nicholas frowned. His imagination had gone crazy since he'd met her, and he was becoming a desperate man. Unable to think of anyone but her, he hadn't even had a date in three months and he hadn't masturbated so much since he was twelve. Something had to give. Soon.

As it was, he always seemed to be two seconds away from palming her butt in both his hands, worshipping it with desperate squeezes and then giving it a stinging smack. Ever since he'd learned about the possibility of her allowing herself to be spanked, his mind had been filled with images of it.

The computer finally revealed the results of his search, and he quickly sat up in his chair. He skimmed over the results, reading some of them out loud. "Black beauty looking for stud to tame her." Nope. "Tall and beautiful looking for short and princely." Ahhh . . . no. "I'm hot and sexy. Are you?" He had to stop for a minute because he was laughing so hard.

"Well, at least she has confidence," he said with a disbelieving shake of his head, and went back to scrolling through his results. "There's our girl," he said triumphantly a little later when he saw a title that sounded like something she'd write. He clicked on it.

Her title was "Brand New to the Dating Scene" and her ad read . . .

BSA. Can you tell me what these letters stand for? If you know the answer, I'd like to meet you. Before you start racking your brain in futility, however, I'll give you a small hint. Okay. I'm going to tell you: the letters BSA . . . Oh, wait. First, come closer to the screen; you'll see better that way. There. Ready? Okay, here it goes: the letters BSA don't stand for anything you would proudly write home to your mama about. Unless you and your mama have a super-close relationship—one where you tell her everything, including about BSA. And if you have that kind of relationship with your own mama, then you should forget you ever read this, because . . . uh . . . well, I don't think I want to meet you.

So how about it? Has the hint helped you figure it out yet, smart guy? If you think you've got the answer, e-mail me.

"Yeah, that's definitely Melinda—quirky sense of humor, sassy attitude, and all," Nicholas said with satisfaction when he was finished reading. His glance fell on the counter next to the post's title. It gave the number of people who had responded to the ad. She'd already had twelve responses and as far as he knew, she'd just posted the ad the day before. She hadn't posted a photo, nor had she given any pertinent details about herself. Hell, she hadn't even listed her name. But Nicholas knew why the responses had come so fast.

"Damned freaks," he said lightly. Mildly annoyed that so many thought they were going to get in her pants, he clicked on her e-mail address, which the site had helpfully made into a convenient link. He wasn't worried that he actually had competition. They didn't know her like he did. He began to type his response and finished just as his doorbell rang. Reading it over quickly one last time, he sent it off and rose. He looked at his watch. His cousin was early.

He left his office, which he'd located on the third floor of his restored brownstone. He liked to be able to look out onto the tree-lined street as he was working. He stopped in his bedroom on the second floor to put on his White Sox baseball cap. He and his cousin Griffith were going to catch the team in a game against the Detroit Tigers. Since Nick's house was located in the Bronzeville neighborhood and about fifteen minutes from the ballpark, it was easiest for Griffith to stop by for dinner before they headed to the game.

Making his way down the hardwood stairs, he opened the door to the vestibule and then opened the outer door to let his cousin in.

"Hi, Nick," Griffith Cantori said as he grabbed his hand and pulled him in for a quick hug. "How are you?"

Nick returned his cousin's hug with a smile. He and Griffith were more like brothers than first cousins. Their mothers were sisters and they'd grown up right across the street from each other. Griffith was an only child whose father had been a traveling salesman who'd been on the road all the time. Nick, whose entire family had moved in with his grandmother when his father had died, was the oldest of four children and the only boy.

The two boys had bonded out of sheer necessity, just to keep from being overtaken by what at times seemed to be an entire sea of females. Now, at thirty-eight, they were even closer than they'd been as boys and had often been mistaken for brothers, though they really looked nothing alike. They were both tall and dark, but Griffith was big with it. And while Nick was handsome with his dark eyes and olive skin, Griffith was simply gorgeous and had light green eyes.

"I'm good, Griff. What's new with you?" Nick asked as they walked into the house.

"Nothing much. Work is crazy, and my personal life is even crazier, but other than that, I'm just peachy keen." The sarcasm was evident as Griffith followed Nick deeper into the house, through the living and dining rooms and back to the kitchen.

Nick looked at Griffith as the other man sat on a stool across the counter from him. "Is everything all right?" His cousin was what was known in the business world as a corporate raider. He bought and sold companies that were in financial trouble, turning them over at blink-and-you-missed-it speed for each acquisition. It was a stressful job that sometimes included threats of bodily harm to Griffith, but Nick's quietly intense cousin seemed to thrive on it all.

Griffith loosened his tie. "Yeah," he said with a tired sigh. "The situation is a pain in the ass, but it's nothing I can't handle." He had never been married and liked to trade women almost as often as he liked to raid companies. He was so handsome that he was almost beautiful and had been that way even as a child. He'd started breaking hearts at the age of fourteen, when he'd realized that having a gorgeous face didn't necessarily make him a sissy and could actually work to his benefit.

"Okay," Nick said as he removed a dish of his grandmother's chicken cacciatore from the refrigerator. "Which did you raid? Another company or another man's bed? Is it an ex-employee who's gunning for you or an irate husband?" he asked with a straight face. He was not surprised when Griffith took him seriously.

"I don't sleep with married women anymore, so that should give you your answer," Griffith said quietly.

"Oh, okay. Wanna talk about it?" Nick put the dish in the microwave.

Griffith looked up impatiently, making Nick laugh. "What are we, married?"

"Well, honey," Nick said as he flicked the dishtowel at his cousin, "you just look like you've had such a rough day." He batted his eyelashes.

Griffith's chuckle was reluctant. "All right, all right. I get it; I've been acting like an ass. I'll stop."

"Good," Nick said cheerily, and turned as the microwave beeped. "Now get your surly ass up and fix your plate. We've got to leave soon because I need to stop by the clinic and pick up a file before the game starts."

Griffith rose and walked into the kitchen, his brow rising suspiciously when Nick started whistling. "What the hell are you so happy about? You get laid this afternoon? Is she still upstairs?"

Nick continued to whistle. He shook his head at his cousin's question.

"You win the lottery?"

"Nope."

"Your sisters promise to stay the hell out of your business?"

"Nope."

"Then what the fuck is it?"

Nick finally gave his cousin his full attention. "Let's just say that I'm about to get what I've been wanting for months."

"Just as I thought," Griffith said. "What's her name?"

4

"Okay, so I've gotten some responses to my ad," Melinda said into her cell phone to Lilly. She'd stayed to finish some paperwork after the clinic had closed for the day and she now sat at the receptionist's desk.

"You have?" Lilly asked. "That's cool. How many have you gotten?"

"At least a dozen so far. I set up an e-mail account through Yahoo! like you suggested, instead of using my real e-mail address, and they've been coming in pretty steadily."

"Good," Lilly said. "Wow, twelve responses; that's pretty good. Have any of them even been close to guessing what BSA stands for?"

"Nope." Mel laughed into the phone. "The only reason I've gotten so many responses in so little time is because there are some freak-a-deaks out there who are just excited that they may have found the one person who might share their interests."

"Exactly. That's the purpose of signing up on those sites. I forget, did you post a picture?"

"No, no pictures. I didn't want to, and I just figured the ad itself would be enough."

"And it turns out you were right. So tell me about some of the responses you got at ChicagoLuhvin. Just how far off base were they?"

"Oh, you're gonna love this. One guy actually wrote and asked me if BSA stood for 'Big Stankin' Asses'! I couldn't believe it! He said if it did, then he was the right man, because although it wasn't something he ever talked about in polite circles, he'd always loved big, stinky behinds. He actually wrote that he loved the smell of unwashed flesh and that it was a huge turn-on for him." She grinned when Lilly burst into laughter.

"Okay, that's just nasty," Lilly said when she finally stopped laughing. "What the hell kind of pervert is he?"

"Oh, I'm not done yet. It gets better. He went on to say that he thinks it goes back to his childhood when his mother used to give his sister and him baths. She would concentrate on their butts first, telling them that she just couldn't abide the smell of a rank and dirty behind."

"Oh, shit, Mel, that's just plain old disgusting! I can't talk to you, 'cause I know you're just making stuff up now!"

"No," Melinda said definitively with a firm shake of her head. "I'm not. I won't even tell you what he went on to say about the size of his sister's behind. It's just too perverted. One thing I'm learning through this whole process is that people will tell you anything online. Absolutely anything."

"Yes, more than you could possibly want to know. Have you checked the site today yet?"

"No, it's late. I'm still at work and can't check from here. I had some paperwork to finish up. I'll be leaving in a bit, but I thought I'd take a minute and call you. Anyway, I'll check my e-mail when I get home."

"Well, I wish you luck with it. Maybe if nobody answers it

right, you should just try to make it with that fine doctor you work with. And before you ask which one, you know which one I'm talking about. That fine Italian one—Dr. Do Me Hard, please."

"He is fine, isn't he?" Mel asked contemplatively as she thought about Nicholas. "You know how much I love his beard, right?"

"You only talk about it every time you mention his name. How could I not know how much?"

"Okay, so anyway, the other day he was absent-mindedly pulling at it with his long fingers like he always does when he's trying to figure something out," Mel said as excitedly as a schoolgirl talking about her first crush. Leaning forward in her chair, she pressed her thighs tightly together. "It was incredibly sexy and I felt this heavy, dragging heat in my stomach. You know what I mean, don't you? It's the way we used to feel in high school when we'd sneak and watch sexy movies at Simone's house, except this was more intense for me. Way more intense."

"Yeah, I know what you mean," Lilly answered. "It's called lust, you big goof!" she said teasingly. "So what are you going to do about the good doctor?"

"Nothing for now. I'm not ready to do anything about him yet."

"Well, you should probably make up your mind soon. I mean, for God's sake, Mel, he's fine as all get out *and* he's a doctor. Do you know how many women would trip over themselves trying to get their claws into him?"

"Five thousand, nine hundred, and sixty-nine," Mel said, jealousy swirling through her system as she thought about all the women at the clinic who came on to Nick. Her eyes narrowed, and the jealousy became more intense as she wondered just how many he'd actually gone out with.

"Uh . . . okay," Lilly said through her startled laughter.

"Just kidding. No, of course I don't know how many, but I know they would probably number in the hundreds. Anyway, if I ever considered letting anyone spank me, it would be Dr. Pantino."

There was complete silence coming from the other end for a few seconds, and then in a scandalized whisper, Lilly said, "For real?"

"Well, maybe," Mel hedged. "I did a little research on the Internet and read that just the right intensity of pain can help increase the pleasure, but I don't know if I believe it. It seems too contradictory." An image of Nicholas bending her naked body over his knees while he prepared to spank her with the flat of his hand suddenly filled her head, making her so hot, her breath caught in her throat. She gripped the phone tighter to her ear to keep it from slipping from her suddenly slick hand. More than a little surprised, she shook her head to dispel the image and cleared her throat. "Uh, I'm sorry, Lilly, I've been talking so much about myself that I haven't asked how things are going for you."

"I kind of don't have time to talk to you about it now. We'll talk later, okay?"

"Okay. I need to get out of here anyway. Talk to you later." Melinda clicked off the phone and stared into space for a minute. The image was back. This time, his hand actually made contact with her behind, and she flinched as if she actually felt it. "Whew! Is it hot in here, or is it just me?" she muttered as she began to fan herself with her hand.

Feeling like he was caught in a snare, Nicholas stopped his forward progress into the room and watched Melinda. She obviously wasn't aware he was there. He was completely arrested by the sight of her arm lifting gracefully to gather up the hair that rested on the nape of her slender neck. His eyes narrowed. *Mine*, he thought fiercely, *all mine*. The material of her blouse stretched to emphasize the contour of her breasts, and he felt his stomach muscles clench in tension and anticipation.

He watched some more as she grimaced. That gorgeous little freckle beckoned to his mouth. She began to fan herself and he frowned, wondering why she was so hot. The air was on. Now she was unbuttoning her blouse. One button slid through its buttonhole, exposing smooth, silky, brown skin. The second one slid through and he caught a glimpse of pink satin and lace. He held his breath, wanting to see more and at the same time knowing he was playing a dangerous game. He'd have to jump over that desk and grab her if he caught even a glimpse of the swell of her breast.

Her long, tapered fingers hovered indecisively over the third button. Saliva abruptly filled his mouth. The fingers landed, gripped the button and were still. Sweat broke out in beads on his forehead. One last caress and the fingers were gone, fluttering away to fan at her throat, taking his fantasy with them. His body slumped in a curious mix of disappointment and relief.

He began to feel lightheaded and realized he was still holding his breath. Damn, she'd literally taken his breath away. He cleared his throat and watched as her head swung quickly in his direction. She blushed and dropped her hands.

"Oh! Hi, Dr. Pantino," Mel heard herself say in a barely audible voice. She knew she was blushing.

Nicholas stopped in front of the desk. "None of that 'Dr. Pantino' crap, Mel," he said harshly. Suddenly he was sick of her holding him at arm's length. "I've asked you time and time again to call me 'Nick' or 'Nicholas.'" He watched her rear back in her chair and give him a look that was designed to make him feel less than dirt and show that she was insulted at the same time. He frowned back at her. "Now, don't get your back up about it. I've asked you repeatedly to call me by my first name, but in order to keep distance between us, you refuse to, don't you?" He deliberately leaned in closer and lowered his voice to a more intimate level.

Okay, I'm a goner, Melinda thought. He'd knocked her completely off balance. That, coupled with the knowledge of what she'd been thinking about before he walked in, made her lower her eyes in curiosity and embarrassment.

"It's all right, Melinda," Nicholas said softly to her bent head. "Soon, none of it will matter. None of it."

Curious now, Mel quickly looked back up at him. The way he was looking at her, like he had a huge appetite that could only be satisfied by him taking a bite out of her, sent a message straight to her core, which in turn sent it to her pussy, which promptly began to gush its greedy appreciation into her panties. Mel sat up straighter in her chair in somewhat delighted surprise. What the hell? That had *never* happened before—at least not so much at one time. *Good Lord.*

"Are you all right, sweetheart?"

Flustered by the tenderness in his voice and the endearment, she squirmed in her chair but suddenly stopped when she squished a bit. Okay, this had to stop. She took a deep breath and looked him dead in the eye. "Just what are you doing, Dr. Pantino?" she asked him suspiciously.

Nick leaned in even closer. "It's Nicholas. Just say it," he commanded.

His breath whispered across her lips, sending tingles down her spine, and Melinda closed her eyes for a moment. When she opened them again, they were direct and just as intense as his. "Nicholas," she whispered obediently.

A hairbreadth away from her mouth, Nicholas closed the space between them and nibbled at her lips. He felt her catch her breath in surprise and felt her stiffen, but she didn't pull away. "Say it again, Melinda."

"Nicholas." Her heart racing with confused longing, Mel was barely able to remember her own name, let alone say his.

His mustache felt so soft and good against her lips and skin that she found herself rising out of her chair to get closer to him.

"That's it, baby," Nicholas encouraged as he cupped her face with both hands. He let his tongue laser in on her beauty mark and he licked and sucked at it until he was pulling it and the corner of her lip into his mouth.

Melinda marveled at the kiss, his sucking causing a corresponding pulling low in her belly. She quivered in delight. She'd never experienced anything like it before, and she loved it, but she wanted more. There just had to be more. Going by instinct, she brushed the top of her tongue along the underside of his. Loving the slick, silky texture of it, she did it several times more, until she was moaning into his mouth. "Oh, God, Dr. Pantino," she mumbled between kisses.

Nicholas broke away from the kiss. Still cupping her face, he looked down at her. "Nicholas, Melinda. From here on out, it's just plain Nicholas, especially for you. All right?"

Mel could only nod once in agreement.

"Good," he whispered, right before he enveloped her lips with his.

The voracious kiss made Melinda weak in the knees and she swayed toward him, gripping his shoulders in her hands.

Nick ate at her lips, his teeth clicking against hers while his tongue snaked a path through her mouth. She was delicious, tasting just like he thought she would. He slowly broke away, pressing kisses to the corners of her mouth and on her chin. He couldn't get his mind off that small swath of skin he'd seen earlier, and he released her face to let his hands wander to her blouse. Bending his head, he pressed his lips to her neck as he undid the third button on her blouse.

Mel threw her head back, the sensations sweeping through her body almost too much for her to handle. Her hands went from his shoulders to grip his wrists; unsure if she wanted him to stop or not, she held them in her hands.

Nick looked up and met the hesitant curiosity in her eyes. "Can I have a taste?"

Shocked by the idea of it, Mel's eyes nearly went opaque with need as she thought about what it would feel like to have him suck her nipple into his mouth. She felt the heat twist and tighten in her stomach and let out a shuddering breath. Looking into his hungry eyes, she gave a jerky nod.

Nick wasted no time and released two more buttons right before bending his head. "Perfect," he murmured when he saw that beneath the pink silk and lace, her small nipples were already hard and poking against the material. He transferred his hands from the blouse to her rib cage and gently pulled her forward. He kissed the nipple and heard her catch her breath just before he felt the nipple strain some more against the material.

Mel let out a squeak of delight when she felt his mouth and pressed her hands to the back of his head, hoping he would suck the nipple inside. She felt him blow on the wet spot he'd made and desperately tried to hold back a cry of need, but couldn't.

Teasing the nipple some more, Nick licked it repeatedly through the silk and tightened his hands when she flinched in response. Unable to stand the tension any longer himself, he pushed the material aside with his tongue and pulled the tight little bud into his mouth where he sucked it hard against the roof of his mouth.

Melinda went wild, soft cries escaping her mouth as she alternately pulled at his hair and pushed his head against her flesh. The pleasure was too intense, and she didn't think she could stand much more of it. More liquid gushed into her panties and she pressed her legs together in an attempt to stem the flow. "Oh, Nicholas, don't stop. Please don't stop," she begged.

Feeling greedy and hungry for more, Nick held her in an almost bruising grip as he tried to bring her closer to his mouth. He lifted her onto her toes and bit down on the nipple, causing her to jerk in his hands and cry out in surprise at the sting.

Melinda thought she was going to die from the pleasure and, in an effort to get a grip on her waning sanity, began to push his head away from her body. The desire coiling and tightening low in her belly was so powerful that it was almost completely unfamiliar and it scared her. She sensed a total loss of control coming and didn't think she could handle it. "Stop, Nicholas. Please, stop." She pushed away some more until he released her. She looked down to button up her blouse.

She grabbed her things and hurried around the desk and through the security door, avoiding Nick's eyes and his touch the entire time.

"Talk to me, Melinda."

She heard the quiet words, but she did her level best to ignore them. Of course, that didn't sit well with him, and he grabbed her arm as she tried to rush past him.

"Are you going to explain?"

Still refusing to look at him, Mel felt his frustration and heard his confusion. She finally looked up and winced at the look in his eyes. There *was* frustration and confusion, but there was also concern. "I'm sorry, Nicholas," she said, and tried to explain something she barely understood herself. In the end, she mumbled, "I felt . . . you made me . . . that is . . . I've never . . ." The frustration on top of the embarrassment was too much and she said, "Oh, *come on*, Nicholas. You have to know what I'm trying to say."

After a moment of simply staring at her in silence, Nick suddenly looked like he was having what Oprah called an Aha! moment. But instead of the moment being something as socially important as "Aha! I think I've found another solution to global poverty!" she was sure his was, "Well, I'll be damned. This woman has never had an orgasm!"

Leaving him to digest his sudden revelation, she slipped out of his loosened grip and escaped through the front door. He didn't follow her outside, and she gratefully slid into her car to scurry home in embarrassment.

5

Melinda lay in bed staring at the ceiling. Conveniently, she had the next two days off after her episode with Nicholas, and now, on the morning after it had happened, she was still kind of reeling from the experience. She'd guessed correctly that what she'd been on the verge of experiencing had been an orgasm, and from the way it had felt, it would have been an explosive one. But how was she to know when she'd never in her life experienced one before?

"Damn it," she said, and rolled over to her side. She couldn't believe she'd reacted that way. She moaned in embarrassment when she thought about what Nicholas must have thought of her. "He probably thinks you're a sexually repressed lunatic, Mel. What the hell else can he think when you freaked out like a virgin who'd been drop-kicked into a prison yard full of hard-up convicts?"

Sighing dejectedly, she sat up in bed. "Yeah, you have your precious control, you idiot, but can it bring you to the brink of orgasm like Nick's tongue? I think not." She went into the bathroom to perform her morning hygiene. In the middle of brushing her teeth, she decided that she'd worried over the situation long enough. She tried to push it out of her mind. It was hard because she couldn't help but feel that she'd messed up something with Nick that had the potential to be spectacular, something that went beyond sex. She left the bathroom for her home office. It was time to check the responses to her ad.

She logged on to her computer and tried to get comfortable in her desk chair. She really needed a new one. She'd gotten the current one at a discount furniture store and realized now why it had been so cheap. The seat was made of a rough, knobby material that scraped against the skin. When she was logged onto the Internet, she went straight to the ChicagoLuhvin site. "Eight new messages! Good Lord, these people are desperate for some companionship!"

On the fifth e-mail, her face formed a thoughtful frown as she read what the author thought BSA stood for. He'd written that he thought it stood for: "Bring your Silly Ass on, bitch." And then he'd written "LOL."

"All I can say is whatever floats your boat," Mel murmured, and continued to read the rest of his message. The writer went on to say that he liked to dominate his women at all times—before, during and after sex—and if he was correct in his assumption of what BSA meant to her, then she obviously liked to be dominated. He left his phone number for her to call him.

Mel's response was a simple "No, thank you," before she closed out of and then deleted the e-mail.

The next two were also incorrect and Mel sighed, resigned to the fact that no one would probably answer it correctly. The subject line of the last one said "From Smart Guy."

"Let's just see how smart you are." She clicked to open it. Her mouth dropped wide open before she'd even finished reading the first sentence. "Oh. My. God," she whispered in shock.

Smart Guy had written:

*Do you really want it **Spanked**, or are you just teasing me? And just how **Big** do you think your **Ass** is? Okay, Brand New, I'm not going to lie and say that the size of it doesn't matter to me, because I like a nice-sized booty just as much as the next man. But, as long as it's got even a little bit of heft to it, I can spank it good. Real good. And as the song goes, I can even slap it, flip it, rub it down . . . Whatever you want me to do to it, I can.*

Amazingly, Melinda found herself giggling at this last part. She used to love that old song from the 1990s. "Slap it, flip it, rub it down, ohhhh noooo!" she sang happily with a big grin on her face.

She continued to read:

*Let's get serious, Brand New. I'd love to get together with you. You've got a crazy sense of humor, but it's just the kind I like. Your wit and intellect draw me in, too. The fact that you have a sense of the daring is obvious because of your post. So, how about it? Want to meet me? E-mail me back, I'll give you more details about myself and we'll set things up. Before I go, I should mention that you don't even have to let me spank your **Big Spankable Ass** if you don't want to.*

He'd also signed off with "Smart Guy." Melinda had to squint her eyes and get closer to the screen to read what he'd typed under his signature.

Fine Print: The last sentence of the last paragraph applies to the first date only. And failure to read the fine print does not, I repeat, DOES NOT, excuse you from future spankings.

She couldn't help it: she burst out laughing. "Oh, more than just a smart guy, he's a very clever boy," she said with a smile before she hit reply and started typing her message to him.

Hi, Smart Guy, or should I call you "Clever Boy?" I really enjoyed your message and you were correct: BSA does stand for Big Spankable Ass. And so far, you're the only person to actually figure it out. How did you do it?

At this point, her fingers hesitated over the keys as she thought about Nicholas. She realized now that she'd been hoping she hadn't scared him away and that maybe they could start again. After all, he'd been after her for months for a date. She sighed again. "At any rate, whatever he wants, I have to at least see the game through," she murmured, and finished typing her reply.

Actually, I didn't think that anyone would ever figure it out, but now that you have, let's do meet.

Now she figured she'd just plunge right in. If she didn't, she knew herself well enough to know that she wouldn't do it at all. "In for a penny, in for a pound."

Shall we meet for coffee or something? Tell me your name and describe what you look like—maybe you could send a photo—so I'll know who I'm meeting. Does that work for you? Let me know when you're available.

P.S. Thank you for your compliments. I like your sense of humor as well. But know this, Smart Guy: I read your fine print. Twice. I'm on to you big time. Don't be so sure that there will even be anything more than a first date.

"Take that, Smart Guy," she muttered, and pressed send. She tried once again to get comfortable in the chair, and deciding she didn't have anything better to do for a little while but wait for a response, she began reading the news headlines on the Web site.

Nick laughed out loud as he finished reading her e-mail. He, too, was at home for the day. It had taken all of his willpower not to call her after what had happened in the clinic. But he kept recalling the panic he'd heard in her voice and that had been enough to keep him from calling. She needed some space, and he didn't want to scare her any more than he already had, the poor baby. He'd been somewhat surprised to learn that a sexy, vibrant woman like her had never had an orgasm, but when he'd thought about it, he realized that it wasn't all that surprising, given how much she liked to be in control. He'd let her go because she'd looked so devastated, but he'd planned to call her and then had decided not to, sure that she wouldn't talk to him. He decided to wait and see if she answered his e-mail.

He began furiously typing his reply, hoping she'd get it before she logged off the computer. He wanted to get things rolling as soon as possible.

Hello, Melinda. Yes, I do know your name, and before you panic and write me off as a stalker, just finish reading the e-mail and you'll know exactly how I know it. I'm going to answer your e-mail from the bottom and work my way up.

Of course there's going to be more than a first date, dear heart. Make no mistake about it. I'm happy you read the fine print twice. I'd expect nothing less from you. I'm even happier that you're on to me; that way there can be no confusion later on.

As for meeting for "coffee or something" I'd prefer the "or something." But I won't tell you what that is right now.

In your e-mail, you ask for my name. It's Nicholas. Yes, it's me, the Nicholas you work with at Living Well. As for what happened yesterday, I don't want you to worry about it; I'm not. We'll fix it, and if you're agreeable, before our first date is over, I'll show you that orgasms can be your friends.

Now, back to the "or something" I referred to earlier. I want to cook dinner for you. If you'll trust me enough, I'd like for you to come to my house for dinner—tonight, if you're available. Nothing sexual has to happen if you don't want it to. Or a whole lot can happen if you want it to. It's completely up to you. I'm sure you already know just how much I want you, Lindy. I've made no secret of it. But you have control, and I'll follow your lead. If you'll let me, I'll teach you how to enjoy your sexuality and your body. I can pick you up for dinner at seven.

I think you've probably already figured out just how I knew what BSA stands for, but just in case you haven't, I'll tell you. I eavesdropped on your conversation with Cally. I want you, Melinda. I took my time over the past couple of months, playing our little sexy word games, letting you lead the chase while I tried to catch you. Quite frankly, I was already tired of waiting by the time I overheard your conversation. I had planned to make my move anyway, so when I heard you talking about BSA, I took my opportunity where I found it.

Let's go back to the confusion that I mentioned earlier. To further eliminate even the possibility of there being any, I'm going to make my intentions very clear right now. I want to do more than spank that firm ass of yours. I want to taste it and your clit. I want to watch you while you touch yourself and me. I want to lick your pussy, suck your nipples, and feel your opening squeezing my dick until it's squeezed it of every drop it has. And after that, I want to start again. I want to do it all, Melinda. Will you let me?

May I have your address?

Mouth wide open, Mel read Nick's e-mail again; just to be sure she'd read it correctly the first time—and the second. She ignored the little voice that said she was only reading it again because it turned her on. Her breathing was fast, choppy and loud in the quiet room as she finished reading the last paragraph for the third time. She felt hot, even though the air conditioning was on. The sleeveless short nightgown she wore was too much and its satiny material seemed to chafe against her suddenly too-sensitive skin. She felt an urgent need to peel it off her body, and before she realized it, her fingers were at the bottom of the gown, preparing to lift it over her head. At the last minute, she stopped herself.

She sat in the chair, a confused mass of longing. Her breasts bobbed in time with her breathing, her nipples beading and turning hard as she read the last paragraph again. And again. *I want to taste your clit. I want to lick your pussy.* She imagined Nicholas saying those words to her in his rumbling, sexy baritone and she cried out as the heat twisted and grew in her stomach. She smelled her own arousal in the air and moaned. The intense ache she felt was spreading and demanding to be appeased.

Her thighs fell open of their own accord, as if telling her that she knew what she needed to do.

Eyes wide and nervous now, Mel squeezed her legs back together, trying to concentrate on what she should do about Nicholas. Her hand wanted to wander down between her legs, but she restrained herself. *I can't*, she told herself. She closed her eyes, counting and picturing equations in her head until the urgent need to touch herself had passed. A few minutes later, she opened her eyes and sighed, realizing what she'd done.

"You always were a chicken, Mel," she murmured. "This can't be a healthy attitude."

Nicholas had tricked her. She couldn't believe it. She had to admit, though, that she was glad he was the one who'd answered the ad correctly. Especially after what had happened at the clinic the night before. He'd known all along about the ad but hadn't said anything. She didn't know if she should feel embarrassed or pleased. He certainly deserved some sort of comeuppance for being so damned sneaky. She sighed. He was solely responsible for all these new feelings she was having—for her newly awakened body.

She clicked on reply, briefly typed her answer to his e-mail, and quickly sent it off into cyberspace before she could change her mind. "Persistence pays off," she murmured. She was more nervous than she'd ever been. In fact, it was bordering on fear. But she knew that this step was long overdue for her. She *needed* to take it. She wanted Nicholas.

Nick heard the ding from the computer that signified he had new mail and impatiently clicked out of the Microsoft Excel document he was working in and back to his e-mail account.

"It certainly took her long enough," he said as he opened Mel's response. Reading it quickly, he chuckled to himself.

She'd typed three lines:

I now think I prefer the term "sneaky bastard" to "clever boy." I'd rather drive my own car to your house. Send me your address and I'll see you at seven.

He typed his own answer. After giving her his address, he typed:

This sneaky bastard will see you promptly at seven, sweetheart.

6

Melinda sat across the dinner table from Nicholas in his gorgeous dining room. The entire house was beautiful. He'd given her a tour of the restored brownstone when she'd arrived, and she'd been thoroughly impressed, especially since he'd decorated the place himself. The house was located in Bronzeville, a neighborhood given its name because of the many blacks who'd lived there in the 1920s through the 1950s. The area had been a self-sufficient city within a city, because black people had been denied services in other parts of the city in the first half of the last century.

The area had fallen on hard times in the sixties and seventies when new housing laws had forbidden discrimination in housing and the wealthier residents had left for the suburbs and other neighborhoods. Many of the beautiful old brownstones and historical buildings had fallen into disrepair. Nicholas had told her that he'd bought his brownstone years before when he realized the value of the real estate. He hadn't been the only one. Bronzeville had seen a resurgence of business and residential interest, and now the area was fast becoming one of the most expensive in the city. The only color that mattered now was green.

She fixed the skirt of her little black dress around her knees and thought about how nervous she'd been on the drive over. She'd even felt a little shy, wondering what exactly was going to happen that night. Going back and forth in her head about whether or not she'd have sex with him, she'd decided that she was sick of being in her own special kind of limbo and that she would take that final leap and stop being so worried about being in control. She wanted to experience what other women experienced and what she'd read about time and time again in romance novels. Why shouldn't she? If she changed her mind, at least she could drive herself home.

When she'd arrived on his doorstep, he hadn't given her much time to focus on being nervous or shy, because she'd barely said hello before he pulled her into his arms and kissed her mouth as if it contained some type of life sustenance. She couldn't put it all off on him, though, because she'd been a willing participant.

"So, Melinda," Nicholas said as he forked up some cake from his plate. "Are you enjoying the meal?"

Mel looked over at him with a lift of her brow. The linguini and shrimp had been delicious, as had the Caesar salad before it. Now they were enjoying a chocolate torte with espresso. "No, I hate it. I only suctioned it up like a Hoover because I couldn't think of anything else better to do," she teased, and picked up her coffee. "Who taught you how to cook like that?"

Nicholas smiled. "My grandmother. She would always have me in the kitchen while she was cooking, telling me to lift this or get that ingredient and before I knew it, I was a good cook," he said with a shrug. "Anyway, we've talked about work and your friends; will you tell me about yourself now?"

"What do you want to know?"

"Anything you want to tell me. I'm all ears, and I want to know everything there is to know about you."

"Everything?"

"Absolutely."

"All right, then. I was born at Osteopathic Hospital on the South Side. I weighed six pounds, five ounces. My mother was in labor with me for twenty-two hours. I'm told that she almost reached down and pulled me out herself; that's just how desperate the pain was making her—" Mel stopped and laughed at the expression of chagrin on his face.

Nicholas shook his head at her in exasperation. "All right, so that wasn't quite what I meant and you know it."

"Well, you did say *everything*," she said when she finished laughing. "So, I thought I'd start at the beginning."

"Okay, so I deserved that. And as curious as I am about your auspicious beginnings, I don't think there's enough time tonight to hear about all of that, so let's start someplace sensible. Do you have any brothers or sisters?"

"No, I'm an only child. What about you?"

"I'm the oldest of four."

"All boys?"

"No, I'm the only boy. I have three younger sisters."

"King of the castle, huh?" she asked.

"Hardly. Those girls ran me ragged with demands. You try being the only guy in a houseful of females. My father died when I was eleven, and my mother, sisters, and I moved in with my grandmother. She babysat while my mom worked."

"You were close to your dad, huh?" Mel asked. She'd seen the wistful look on his face when he'd mentioned him.

"Yeah, it was the two Pantino men against the world. We were protectors of the Pantino women. Anyone who dared to upset them or make them cry had to deal with us." He smiled fondly as he reminisced.

"Bet that didn't stop for you when your father died, did it?"

"No, not really," Nick said, and took a sip of his coffee. "All games aside, it was my duty to take care of them, so I did."

Mel cocked her head as she studied him. "I bet you were such a serious kid. How old were you when you got your first job?"

"Twelve. It was in the summertime. I did stock at Santori's Grocery. I made a whopping two bucks an hour!"

"That's a lot of money to a twelve-year-old."

"Yeah, it was, but I contributed to the household finances, as much as my mother would let me. She worked as a secretary downtown, and I knew she needed the help with us."

"Did your mom ever remarry?"

"No. She always said that no other man could take the place of Pop."

"Wow. What a lovely sentiment."

"Yeah, it was," Nick said. "But tell me more about you."

Mel wiped her fingers on a napkin. "Well, I had a pretty good childhood. My parents kind of spoiled me. I didn't have everything I wanted, just what they thought I deserved. I had my two best friends instead of sisters. They're like my sisters, though."

"What did your parents do?"

"My mother was a teacher, and my father was a taxi driver. They're both retired now."

"Do they still live in Chicago?"

"Yeah. They always talk about moving to Florida, but I'm sure they never will. They'd be too worried that I'd be here alone without any family. Moving to Florida would make it very difficult for them to check in on me. They'd have to worry from a distance," she said wryly.

"Are they overprotective?"

"A little, but they're much better now. When I was a kid, they were really bad."

"Would they be concerned that you're dating me?"

"Maybe, but only because you're divorced. Marriage is a huge deal to them, which is why they took it hard when I announced that I was getting divorced. Well, my mother did anyway."

"Your dad didn't?"

"No. He'd never liked Edmund. He thought he was too arrogant and a know-it-all."

"And was he?"

"Yeah," Mel said with a nod. "Pretty much. What about your ex-wife? Why'd the two of you divorce?"

"Maria and I had known each other since the fifth grade. She was my first kiss. She was also the first girl I'd ever slept with. We dated off and on throughout high school, and then I went away to college; when I came back, she was still there. We thought we were in love, but we really were just comfortable with each other. We never should have gotten married. We were meant to be only friends."

"Where is she now?"

"She's in Italy. She married some minor count there, and they have five children."

"How sweet. I love children."

"So I take it you want some of your own."

"Yeah." Mel's eyes went wistful. "I always have."

"So why don't you have any?"

"Because it wouldn't have been a good idea to bring children into the kind of marriage I had. I wanted to, but I just couldn't bring myself to be that selfish."

Nicholas looked at her empty plate. "Would you like another slice?"

Mel placed her hand on her stomach. "Good Lord, no. I

don't think my stomach could take another thing. But thank you, it was delicious. All of it."

"You're welcome, and thank you for the compliment." He rose and walked around the table to stand behind her chair. "Let's finish this conversation in the living room. We'll be more comfortable there."

Mel stood after he pulled back her chair. "Thank you."

"Should I bring the wine?" Nicholas asked.

"Sure, why not?"

They walked through the dining room and into the living room where they sat on the long sofa. Nicholas poured them each another glass of wine, placing the bottle on the table in front of them. He turned to face her and handed her a glass. "So, finish telling me about your marriage."

Mel frowned into her glass as she thought about it. "There's not a whole lot to tell, except we were miserable together."

"Why?"

"To put it simply, he was a control freak, and I didn't like to be controlled."

"Then why did you marry him?"

Mel raised her eyes to look at him. She shrugged. "I really thought I loved him and when we were dating, he wasn't so bad. But looking back on it now, I can see that there were signs. There always are."

"Is that why at thirty-four and after having been married for two years that you've never had an orgasm—because your husband was controlling?"

Startled, Mel almost choked on the sip of wine she'd just swallowed. "Boy, you don't pull any punches, do you?"

Nicholas studied her. She'd worn a silky-looking dress that had no straps and barely reached her knees. She'd put on black high-heeled sandals to match. Her fingernails and toenails were both polished a hot red. She looked good enough to eat and he was still hungry. He answered her question. "I assumed you were ready to talk and get things out in the open. Am I wrong?"

"No, not really." She took a deep breath and said, "Yes, my husband was controlling, but I'd dated before him. I had a steady boyfriend in college, and I'd never been able to have an orgasm with him either." She shrugged. "I'd just assumed that I was one of those women who can't feel . . . well, I thought I was frigid."

Nicholas set his wine down, then took hers and set it down, too. Moving closer, he took her hands in his. "You're joking, right? A woman like you? Frigid? That's impossible."

"I know that *now*, but before I met you, I just thought there was something wrong with me."

"Well, I'm glad I could be of help." Nicholas bent his head to place a kiss on her shoulder. "What do you think," he asked between the kisses he was tracing on the skin leading to her neck, "of my being even more helpful and showing you just how much pleasure this beautiful body of yours can give you?"

Mel shivered from the feel of his beard and mustache brushing against her skin. Her eyes fell shut, and she unconsciously let her head fall back when his lips reached her neck, granting him better access. She licked her lips, and her hands clenched when he took a nip of her ear. "I think . . . mmm . . . I think that I would like that."

Nicholas allowed the relief to surge through his body before he said anything. Pushing her gently away from him, he looked into her eyes. "Are you sure, Melinda?"

Mel nodded. She realized that she'd come tonight for just that. She wanted him to be the one to give her an orgasm, which is why she hadn't done it herself earlier that day. "I want you to make me come, Nicholas."

Nicholas smiled. Somehow, that just didn't sound right

coming from proper Melinda. "Talk about not mincing words. All right, sweetheart. Your wish is not only my command, but it's my pleasure. First things first," he said as he twirled some of her hair around his finger. "I want you to strip for me."

7

Mel looked at him. "Excuse me?"

Nicholas smiled again. He rubbed her arms soothingly. "I said that I need you to strip for me. If this is going to work, you have to give up some control. And if you're going to give up control, you have to trust me first. Melinda, do you trust me?"

Her eyes flashed a combination of fear and indignation before she swallowed and looked away. "I guess I wouldn't be here if I didn't," she mumbled. "But I don't see how taking off my clothes will help the situation." He chuckled and she realized what she'd said. She sighed and rolled her eyes. "Oh, you know what I mean, Nicholas. Of course I would *need* to take off my clothes—"

"Good," Nicholas said, and pressed a kiss to her forehead. "Now, take off your clothes, sweetheart."

Knowing how difficult that would be, Mel scooted away from him on the sofa, frowning when he simply followed her. "I don't think I can do that."

"Will you at least try? If it's something you just can't do, I promise I'll leave you alone about it."

She studied his face, trying to gauge his sincerity.

He leaned in and pressed a kiss to her mouth. "You can do it, Lindy." He knew he was pushing her, but he also knew that stripping was one of the ultimate ways to give up control. Without her clothing, she'd feel completely exposed.

Taking a deep breath, Melinda frowned as she had a conversation in her head between who she'd come to think of as sane Mel and horny Mel, who talked in italics.

Giving a striptease would take a lot of courage.

But I want Nicholas, more than anything I've ever wanted before.

You'd be naked and it doesn't look like he's gonna take his clothes off any time soon.

But I want Nicholas.

You'd be naked.

But I want Nicholas.

You'd be *naked*.

He can give me an orgasm. That'll do it, she thought and stood. "Where do you want me?" she asked resolutely after taking a deep breath.

"Hold on." Nicholas quickly stood. "Don't move, I'll be right back," he threw over his shoulder as he hurried from the room.

A little angry now, Melinda scowled. "Well, I like that. He'd better hurry up before I change my damned mind." Sorely tempted to sneak out the door to her car and safety, she subconsciously let her eyes search the room for her purse.

"Okay, I'm back," Nicholas said as he entered the room again.

Both of Melinda's brows arched at the sight of what was in his hands. He carried a wall mirror. It was about four feet tall. "Uh, just what do you think you're going to do with that?"

"You'll see." He leaned the mirror against the couch and turned to the table. Lifting one end of the heavy piece of furniture, he pushed it back a few inches and then walked a couple of feet to his left so that the table was at an angle to the sofa. Picking up the mirror, he leaned it against the table and sat back down. "Perfect," he mumbled as he checked his reflection. "Okay, now, Melinda, please take off your clothes."

Her eyes still stuck on the mirror, Mel threw a startled look his way. "Just what kind of freak do you think I am—"

"You promised to trust me," he interrupted her softly.

"Yes, but—"

"No buts. Either you trust me or you don't. I promise, I won't hurt you."

Nervous, Mel licked her lips. She looked at him again. His eyes seemed to promise her the world if she'd just let go. She reached over her shoulder again for the zipper to her dress. She'd better get a damned orgasm out of this!

Nicholas watched as she licked her lips, her tongue briefly touching on her freckle. He narrowed his eyes against the heat that was invading his body. She pulled the zipper down as far as she could reach and then turned the dress around so she could have better access to the zipper. He saw a brown nipple peek out through the opening and stifled a groan, glad he hadn't known earlier that she wasn't wearing a bra. He'd have tortured himself just thinking about it during dinner.

She slid the zipper all the way down, her hands holding the sides together over her breasts for a moment. His eyes went to her face again. He was surprised to find her eyes on his. He smiled reassuringly. *Come on, Lindy, you can do it*, he thought. She went back to concentrating on what she was doing. He watched as she pushed the dress down her body, first exposing both breasts, then her flat belly, slim hips covered in a brief bit of black silk, and finally her feet. She bent both knees and stepped out of the dress, straightening again to lay it over the arm of the sofa.

Mel felt thoroughly self-conscious and wanted nothing

more than to put her clothes back on and go home. Her hands went to her panties, and, realizing they were the final barriers protecting her, she paused and couldn't move them. She looked over at Nicholas, who didn't say anything as he looked into her eyes. His eyes didn't urge her to do it, nor did they show disapproval or disappointment. They were just accepting. Quickly, because she needed to do it before she changed her mind, she pushed the panties down her legs and stepped out of them. She kicked off the sandals.

With nothing on but earrings now, she stood with her arms hanging tensely at her sides. Nicholas could do nothing but stare. His breathing labored and sweat breaking out on his brow, he let his eyes travel the length of her body several times.

Feeling so vulnerable and exposed that she wanted to hide, Mel did her best to resist covering her body with her hands. *Besides*, she thought irrationally, fighting the urge to giggle, *which parts would you choose? You've only got two hands.* She swallowed, wishing he would say something. *Anything.* She knew she was on the skinny side, and her breasts were kind of small, but things weren't that bad, were they? She wished she knew what he was thinking, but she couldn't tell because his lids were at half mast as he stared at her body.

This trust thing is for the birds and Nicholas can kiss my ass, she thought. Scowling now, she was on the verge of reaching for her dress when he finally spoke. The words vibrated through her and she looked at him again. His eyes were full of what she could only describe as greedy lust and she felt her knees go weak.

"Christ Jesus, you're beautiful," he finally growled after staring at her for long moments. He'd planned to take things slowly so that he could ease her into the pleasure. Now he wondered how in the hell he was going to do that. He was ready to plunge deep.

"Come here, Lindy," he said and held out his hand.

Blindly, Mel took it and climbed into his lap when he tugged on her hand. Feeling a little awkward, especially because she was nude and he was still fully clothed, she turned sideways— away from the mirror—raised her knees to her chest, and buried her face in them. "What are we doing, Nicholas?" she asked in a stifled voice, strangely feeling even more vulnerable now that she was in his lap.

Nick rubbed her thigh from knee to butt and back again, smiling when he felt her tremble slightly before she leaned into the caress. "You, my sweet, are about to be pleasured beyond your wildest dreams. Now, bend down here and give me your mouth."

Mel blinked once before comprehension dawned. She leaned down and softly laid her lips on his, sudden hunger for him making her open them. She let herself be free to explore, even going so far as to rub her lips over his mustache before sucking his top lip into her mouth like he'd done hers the day before. Moaning, she moved closer and wrapped her arms around his neck and felt her hardened nipples push into his chest and rub against the material of his shirt.

Her nipples puckered some more from the movement, and liking the sensation, she deliberately made sure they rubbed across the material again . . . and again. At the same time, she was sucking his tongue into her mouth and biting at his lips, unable to get enough of him. Excitement thrummed through her body, and the feather-light touches of his fingers on her thigh were only making it worse.

"You like to have your breasts touched, don't you?" he asked.

Mel nodded, too breathless to speak.

"Tell me how." He pinched one lightly between his fingers. "Like that?"

Mel's mouth fell open on a small gasp before she was able to speak. "A little harder," she whispered.

Nicholas pinched the nipple harder, giving it a little twist. "How about like this?"

Mel couldn't speak. Her eyes fell shut as he gave the other nipple the same treatment, and her head fell back on a long, drawn-out groan. She purred her agreement instead.

She heard him groan as he leaned forward and kissed the exposed skin under her jaw, nipping and sucking it as he trailed his lips down her throat until he reached the hollow of her neck, laving it repeatedly with his tongue. He followed the natural line of her body to the swell of her breasts, making her arch her back and push her flesh against his mouth.

A short shriek escaped her throat when he sucked her nipple deep into the caverns of his mouth and plied it with his tongue. The bite he gave her nipple was just enough to make her feel some pain.

Mel was beside herself with pleasure and could only think to lift her other breast and brush that nipple back and forth around his mouth until he released the first one and sucked the second one in. Oh, God! She needed so much more, she thought as she slid her ass on his thigh and felt how wet she'd already made his pants. She lifted her other breast and rubbed it against his beard, moaning at the dual sensations she was receiving. "Nicholas, please," she begged him.

"It's okay, baby. I'm going to take care of you," he assured her, and slipped his hand between her thighs.

She squirmed in his lap, feeling his rock-hard penis through his jeans. His fingers traced a path down her inner thighs and she let them fall open. One finger slowly circled her clit, teasing her, and she fell forward to rest her forehead against him. "Please, Nicholas," she said again, unable to stand the waiting.

He snagged her lips in a kiss. "What do you want me to do, Melinda?" he asked against her wet lips.

She closed her eyes, breathing harshly against his mouth. "I want you to touch...to touch me. Will you touch me, Nicholas? Please."

Unaware that her husky words were reminding him of his fantasy of her in his office chair, she moaned when greedily, he let his finger zero in on her clit and gently slid it against the smooth, throbbing little nubbin. Her fingers clenched on his shoulders when he took another finger and dipped it along her slick folds before bringing it to join the other. His fingers dripping with her essence now, he took her clit between the two and pinched and rubbed.

She let her head fall to his shoulder and pushed against his hand frantically, loving the feel of the rough material of his jeans against her naked skin. She was quickly working her way to an orgasm, the rough material exciting her more and helping her along. When he pressed the pad of his thumb on her clit, she screeched and came halfway out of his lap.

"You like that, baby?" he growled, and pressed the little button again.

She couldn't answer; the pleasure was too exquisite. She bit his shoulder and opened her thighs wider, feeling like she was coming out of her skin when he pinched her clit between his fingers again. Now he was back to rubbing it, and she strained to keep up with his rhythm, her hips pushing and jerking spasmodically. The emotions rioted inside her, bringing with them such a forceful heat that for a moment she was afraid that the inferno would burn her alive. The feeling that she was going to break apart and lose herself was imminent, and while she strained to beat it back, she was also a little scared.

Subconsciously, she squeezed her thighs together, trapping his hand and the feelings.

Using his other hand, Nicholas gently pushed her knees apart, forcing her thighs open again. "It's all right, baby, just roll with the feelings. Let them take you over," he crooned.

She heard his voice as if from a distance and lifted her head to look at him. Her eyes were drawn to his mouth; unable to stop herself, she bent to kiss him, rubbing her lips across his mustache and her breasts against his chest again. His fingers were still driving her mad, and she stopped fighting the heat and the swirling emotions, sliding her ass back and forth and pushing her flesh against his fingers. Suddenly all the heat and the emotions gathered to thump heavily in one spot and then broke apart to explode and travel to other parts of her body. She stiffened from the force of the impact, throwing her head back and letting out a series of screams that carried one distinct word. *Nicholas.*

8

Nicholas rubbed his hand soothingly down Mel's back, wondering just how long she planned to keep her face hidden in his neck. It had already been at least two minutes. He knew the orgasm had shaken her and that she was probably also embarrassed, but it had been beautiful to watch and had made him even harder and hornier. And he wasn't finished with her yet.

Mel knew she couldn't stay like that forever, but she honestly couldn't move. She felt lethargic, her limbs and neck too heavy to lift. She sighed, actually feeling like she could take a brief nap. She resisted snuggling, but only because she wanted more of what he had just given her. Tiredly she lifted her head to look at him.

"Ah, Sleeping Beauty stirs," Nicholas teased her and laughed when she blushed. He rubbed her back some more. "Are you all right, Lindy?"

Mel arched a brow. "What do you think? Aren't you the one who told me that orgasms are our friends?" She smiled when he chuckled. "I didn't know it could be like that," she said, her voice a little awed.

"It can be even better," he assured her.

Her look said *stop playing*. She pressed her lips to his with a murmured "thank you."

Nicholas bit her lip, taking the kiss from chaste to amorous in a matter of seconds. He slid his hand under her ass and fingered the small swath of skin that separated her vagina from her anus, holding her tightly when she jerked against him and moaned into his mouth.

Mel lifted her head and looked at him in surprise. Her eyes were drenched with renewed need, and she tried not to squirm as he continued to finger that incredibly sensitive skin. "Again, Nicholas?" she barely gasped out before closing her eyes and concentrating on the pleasure. She wiggled against him and scooted back so that her butt rested between his thighs, and his fingers could move with more freedom.

He gently swiped the pad of his fingers across her perineum one last time before sliding his hand a little farther up to slip his finger inside her opening; her eyes popped open in surprise. They were soon closing again in pure delight as he slid the finger in and out.

Mel hummed low in her throat, her heart beating in time to the slow movement of his finger. In and out. She planted her feet more firmly on the couch, her toes digging into the leather as she began to move her hips in rhythm with the sliding of his finger. In and out. She concentrated fiercely on this and began to feel the heat rising in her stomach again. She looked at Nicholas through her lashes, unable to even lift her lids. He looked to be enjoying it as much as she. In and out . . . in and out . . . in and out.

She actually felt her clit begin to strain upward, getting harder and harder with each stroke of his finger. Begging for his touch now, it pulsed with need. Mel swallowed with difficulty. "Hmm . . . Ni-Ni-Nicholas." She stopped because the last stroke felt too good for her to do anything else. She tried again. "Nicholas . . . ahhh . . . ohhhh . . . will you . . . um, touch it?"

He hugged her around the waist with his free arm and turned her in his lap. Her breath quickened in surprise and need as her eyes popped open again. They widened when she saw why he'd turned her. She'd forgotten all about the mirror. She saw herself in his lap, her legs hanging on either side of his while she ground her mound on his finger, which he was still working inside of her. Stunned, she found his eyes in the mirror.

He put his chin on her shoulder. "Open your legs," he commanded.

Mel closed her eyes and turned her face into his shoulder, too embarrassed to look anymore.

Nicholas pulled his finger out and tried to ignore her cry of protest. She still didn't look at him. Softly, he ordered her again, "Open your legs." He growled in satisfaction when she slowly opened her thighs, and he saw her labia, her clit, her opening— the heaven between her legs. "That's a good girl," he said, and fed his finger into her pussy again. He opened his legs so that hers opened even wider, exposing her even more to his gaze. "Perfect. Now, lift your arms over your head and wrap them around my neck."

Still refusing to look but almost desperate for an orgasm, Mel did everything he wanted. She tried to ignore the mirror, but her curiosity finally won out over her embarrassment, and she opened her eyes. He had her stretched out and wide open so that she couldn't help but see everything. Her eyes traveled from the top to the bottom and she saw how lust-filled her eyes were, how she had whisker burns around her mouth and chin. Farther down she saw the hickey in the hollow of her neck and more whisker burns on her breasts and puckered nipples.

Lower still, she saw her stomach quivering in time to her

breathing and as wide open as he had her, she saw her hair-covered pinkish-brown lips, and the tip of her clit peeking through those lips, and she moaned. What caught her attention, however was the sight of his finger pushing in and pulling out of her entrance and the way she contracted around his finger and greedily milked it, her hips rising and lowering to bear down on that one finger.

All of this took less than a minute and she continued to stare at her cleft and his finger as it disappeared and reappeared again and again. She wanted to look away but couldn't. Even as she watched, he pushed another thick finger inside. The stretch was almost unbearable and she felt her internal muscles resisting, yet she loved the tight fit.

"That's right, sweetheart. Look and see how beautiful and responsive your body is," she heard him say and her eyes flew to his face.

"Oh, God, Nicholas," she told him as she picked up speed with her hips, working her opening furiously on his fingers. "It feels so good!"

"I know it does, baby, and you look beautiful. Keep concentrating on the pleasure," he said, just before moving both fingers in a circular motion inside her. He felt her arms tighten some more around his neck and noticed that her nipples hardened even more.

She screamed and moved faster. The heat was spreading and threatening to consume her. She actually heard the wet sounds her pussy made as it accepted his fingers and it made her feel even hornier. The sense that something larger than anything she could ever imagine was building inside of her increased her urgency. She wanted to feel it, wanted to be consumed, and it wasn't happening soon enough. "Nicholas, please!" she begged, her behind slapping up and down on his thighs. Even the sound of that turned her on. "Help me!"

Nicholas's response was to squeeze another finger in on her next downward thrust.

"Oh my God!" she screamed, her arms unwrapping themselves from around his neck so that her hands could find a better anchor on his thighs at this new mind-blowing sensation. She hooked each of her feet around each of his legs so that her position would be even more secure. With her hands clenching and pushing against his thighs, she rode his fingers like her very life depended on the ride. When that little nubbin of flesh at the apex of her thighs briefly scraped against the back of his hand, she was brutally reminded that there could be more. Much more. "Nicholas," she said between panting breaths. "I need more."

Nicholas knew what she wanted and he wanted her to ask for it. "What do you need, sweetheart?" he asked and made sure with a flick of his wrist that her clit brushed his hand again on her next time downward.

Mel found that she couldn't say it. She released his thigh long enough to find his free hand and place it on that bundle of nerves that so needed his attention. She looked at him in the mirror, her eyes begging him to just do it.

Nicholas watched the pleading turn to demand when his eyes told her he wouldn't do it. "Say it, Melinda. Tell me what you need."

Mel closed her eyes when a particularly effective thrust made her toes curl. "Nicholas," she breathed. "I want you to touch it. Just touch it, please."

"Touch what?" He asked.

Frustrated beyond belief, Mel opened her eyes to look at him. "My clit," she forced out between licking her lips. "Please, touch my clit, Nicholas." It was ridiculous that she found it difficult to say the word, especially since she was letting him finger-fuck her in front of a mirror and thoroughly enjoying it.

She thought this even as she emitted a soft, glad cry when he curled his middle finger so that it lightly scraped her inner wall.

The words were barely out of her mouth before he was stretching his thumb upward to sweep across her needy flesh. Frantic cries escaped her throat, the sight of herself in the mirror only making the pleasure streaking through her body more intense; but she wanted more and was ready to tell him so when she heard his zipper and a barely audible, "Lift yourself up, baby," from behind her.

Bracing herself on his thighs, she lifted her body. Her eyes went back to the mirror and she watched as the swollen head of his dick pushed into her entrance as she slowly lowered herself onto it. He was so long and thick and she bit her lip at the size and feel of him. The double sensations of watching and *feeling* him stretch her were too much and she closed her eyes. Panting now, she lowered herself more, thrilling at the feel of another centimeter entering her.

"Ah . . . ah, Nicholas. Ooh, it feels so tight and so good!"

She moved some more, taking in a little more of him, realizing that nothing had ever felt so good before. She moaned and let her head fall back for a moment as she savored the fullness. She felt Nicholas's arm wrap around her waist and seconds later an impatient upward thrust sent half his dick tunneling through her and sent her spinning out of control. She reveled in the loss, sliding herself up and down on those few inches as her fingers clawed at his thighs and her internal muscles clutched desperately at his length. God, she burned and the scorching heat of the orgasm raged through her, making her scream his name over and over again until she felt that there was nothing left and she fell back against him.

Nicholas felt her slump against him and used both hands to lift her by the waist. He lowered her until her body automatically adjusted to take him—all of him. She looked back at him, her eyes dazed with pleasure as he easily slid into her drenched opening again and again. "My turn," he growled right before catching her mouth in a ravenous kiss. He hadn't planned on taking her this soon, but his need rode him too hard. He worked her furiously up and down on his dick, plunging deeply like he'd been wanting to since he'd met her. Soon, she was panting into his mouth. "That's it, Lindy," he said when she began to gyrate her hips and grind her pussy against him.

He could feel the pressure from an orgasm building and he took the tip of his finger and scraped it once . . . twice . . . against her clit, making her come again, just when his own orgasm ripped straight through him.

Mel lay in his lap with her arms wrapped around his neck. Sighing in pure bliss, she curled her body deeper into in his lap. Damn, life was good! Nicholas was wonderful. She had actually had three orgasms. It was perfect, and she couldn't ask for anything more, she thought just before tears pricked her eyes and she began to cry.

She tightened her arms around his neck. She felt his surprise and then felt his hand soothingly rub her back. She cried harder. She knew he probably was wondering what the heck was going on, but she couldn't stop the tears. A thought occurred to her as he continued to rub and she chuckled. The hand stopped moving. She lifted her head to look at him. "You weren't rubbing my back with the hand that just got to know me so thoroughly, were you?" she asked wryly and wiped the tears from her face with her fingers.

Nicholas grinned. "Trust me, if I had, you'd have known. That hand is still wet."

She gasped and leaned farther in because said hand was currently resting on her behind. "No, it isn't," she whispered and looked over her shoulder to be sure.

Nicholas laughed and turned her back around to face him. "Why were you crying, Lindy?" The tears he'd felt on his neck had surprised him at first, but not for long. Having grown up in a houseful of females, he'd learned never to question tears, even when they made absolutely no sense to him. He'd also learned that there was usually an explanation.

"Because I've never experienced anything like that before in my life," she answered without hesitation. "It was exhilarating. I never knew it could feel so good."

"And you were so happy that you cried?" Nicholas tried to clarify. This was not a first for him. One of his sisters cried from happiness all the time, and this he understood.

"Exactly. Well, almost exactly. I was happy, but I was also sad because I've let so many years go by without experiencing that. I was so worried about protecting myself that I couldn't experience it."

"And what's different now?"

Mel snuggled back down in his lap and rested her head on his shoulder. "You are, of course. I trust you. Before, I never could trust anyone else enough to let go."

"Why do you trust me?"

She fiddled with one of the buttons on his shirt and stifled a yawn. "At first I didn't because I thought you were too handsome for your own good, and all those women at the clinic are always chasing you. Then I realized that I'd never actually noticed you giving chase, and a part of me had known it all along. This is going to sound odd, but you almost seemed too interested in me, and you were so sincere. Also, I'd learned to trust you just from working beside you all the time."

"Those are a lot of reasons, Melinda."

She shrugged. "You asked."

"Why didn't you trust other men?"

She chuckled. "It wasn't like there was a whole truckload of them. There were only two—a college boyfriend and Edmund, my ex-husband. With Edmund, I didn't trust him because he started cheating on me almost as soon as we were married."

Nicholas stiffened. "And you knew?"

"Yeah, I did. I think most people know almost immediately if their spouses are cheating. I confronted him and he denied it at first, but then he admitted it and promised to stop, which he did for a while. But he was cheating again within a few months, and I couldn't trust him. I stopped having sex with him after that."

"But weren't you married to him for two years?"

"Yes, I was, but I couldn't make myself have sex with him again. So, I moved my stuff out of the bedroom, and we lived as strangers in the same house for the next year. I woke up one day and asked myself why I was waiting to divorce him. I mean, it wasn't like I could ever trust him again. So, I filed the papers that very day."

"And he didn't fight you over it?"

"Oh, no," she said sleepily. "He didn't want to be with me any more than I wanted to be with him, so it was easy. Hell, it was all over but the shouting by then."

Nicholas said nothing as she made herself even more comfortable. She shifted again, and he caught a glimpse of the curve of her hip in the mirror. He narrowed his eyes and leaned toward the mirror. "Is that a tattoo?" he asked in surprise and bent over her body to get a closer look.

Half-asleep now, Mel mumbled, "It's a phoenix . . . symbolizes my freedom . . . got it to celebrate divorce."

Nicholas rubbed the small tattoo a couple of times. She was just full of surprises. He felt her slump against him and knew she was asleep. *She won't be for long*, he thought, and lifted himself to pull his pants up. He rose with her in his arms to carry her to bed. He scooped up the dress from the arm of the couch, and unwilling to bend so low to reach her panties, he left them on the floor.

9

Melinda woke up to find herself being lowered onto the bed. She grabbed on to Nicholas to bring him down to lie beside her. She turned to face him. "I'm sorry I fell asleep," she whispered as she traced his mustache with her finger.

He kissed her finger. "It's all right. You were probably asleep for five minutes at the most."

"Oh. What time is it, then?"

"About ten."

"No wonder I fell asleep so easily. I'm usually in bed by now. Well, that and the fact that thanks to you, I've had more excitement in one night than I've had in years," she teased with a smile as she tangled her bare legs with his jean-covered ones. She'd expected to feel embarrassed by her nakedness, but felt only contentment.

"Years, huh?" he asked as he captured her lips in a slow, thorough kiss.

"Mmm-hmm. Years," she managed to whisper when he released her mouth. She arched closer to him as his hand massaged her back, tracing her spine until he reached her behind, which he caressed until she felt the heat that never seemed to quite disappear when she was near him slowly building again in her belly. She stretched into the caress and moved even closer to him, her body automatically seeking the fulfillment that the caress promised. "Why are you still dressed, Nicholas?"

Nicholas arched a brow at the question and sat up. "Because I've got a greedy wench in my bed who until now hasn't given me enough time to really do much of anything but quench her insatiable lust." He unbuttoned his shirt and slipped it off.

Mel grinned unashamedly as her hands went to the front on his jeans. "Is that so?" she asked.

"Exactly so," he said, and completed the job himself, pulling his boxers off with the jeans and tossing them both to the floor.

"Why, that selfish bitch," she teased as he pulled her into his arms. "Did you at least enjoy it?"

"Mmm-hmm." His response was muffled against the sensitive skin at the back of her ear. He rubbed his mustache and beard against it and did it again when she shivered with need. "I enjoyed it, and I'm going to enjoy her some more." His voice was gruff with the strain of holding himself back. Her smell, the little sounds she was making, her fingernails biting into his skin, the picture of intense pleasure on her face when she came earlier were all getting to him, and he eased his hand between her legs to see if she was ready for him. She was drenched. Automatically, he dipped a finger inside, working her clit until her hips were bucking up against his hand. Quickly, he gave her another orgasm.

Mel could not believe how skilled he was at working her into a fever pitch. The emotions rollicking through her body were so intense that she could do nothing but close her eyes and ride them out. She felt his hands on her knees, and eager to feel him stretching and filling her again, she opened her legs for him. *Good Lord, yes*, she thought when she felt his hands at her hips and the thick head of his cock at her entrance. She lifted her hips and felt herself close around that first inch like a fist. She bit her lip to keep a scream of unadulterated joy locked behind her teeth.

Eyes still closed, she accepted his tongue into her mouth when he licked her lips for entrance. She loved the feel of him inside of her, she thought, just before she winced as he pushed another inch inside. She felt him shift so that he leaned over her more. Abruptly, she was reminded of old times and was back to being the old Mel.

Her body suddenly went dry. Her fingers lost their tight grip, and suddenly, instead of Nicholas leaning over her, it felt more like he was looming and she wanted him off of her. Old habits died hard, and without conscious thought, she stopped participating and lay there. "Yes . . . yes . . . yes," she mumbled.

Even in his frenzied state, Nicholas felt the change in her immediately. He studied her. Her face had lost all excitement and lacked expression completely as she just lay beneath him. She mumbled a monotone series of yeses again, and he frowned when the reality of what she was doing hit him. Angry and insulted, he pulled out with a slick sound and moved off her and to her side. "What the fuck are you doing, Melinda?"

He didn't yell the question at her, but there was no doubt he was furious and wanted answers.

Still caught in the grip of her past, Mel opened her eyes to find Nicholas staring down at her with a scowl on his face. He was livid. She realized what she'd been doing and flinched. "Oh, my God," she said in horror, and scrambled into a sitting position. She averted her gaze.

"I want an explanation, Melinda. In the past hour, I've given you at least three orgasms. Did you really think I wouldn't recognize the difference between a real one and a fake one?'

"It was four," she mumbled without thinking, still not looking at him. She risked a peek at him and flinched again when she saw the disgust on his face. Suddenly, she didn't feel comfortable in her nakedness anymore and looked around for something to cover herself up with. Her voice was stifled when she asked, "May I have something to put on?"

"No." Nicholas was implacable. "The next thing you're going to do is explain what the fuck just happened. There will be nothing else until you do."

Mel looked at him like he'd lost his mind. Defiantly, she pulled at the light spread that covered the bed, prepared to pull it up and wrap her body in it.

"Don't even think about it," Nicholas said as he grabbed her hand. "I'm not finished with you yet."

She tried to snatch her hand away and couldn't. "What is this? Some kind of perverted payback?" she asked angrily.

"If you like," he conceded with a nod. The truth was, he knew that her response to him a few minutes before was all about her needing to keep control. The response had probably been automatic, which was all the more reason, as far as he was concerned, to keep her vulnerable now. If this was going to work between them—and he was determined that it was—she needed to learn to give up control during intimacy. She needed to know that she could trust him even when she was at her most vulnerable. "Start talking, Melinda."

Mel scowled at him. "You can kiss my ass," she said.

"I will. Later," he promised. "Now, talk."

Melinda's eyes went to the door, and she wondered if she could make it down the stairs to her clothes before he caught her. She felt bad for what she had done and knew she owed him an explanation, but now she was angry with him for treating her like this and just wanted to leave for home and safety. Who the hell did he think he was? She looked at the door again, trying to gauge the distance.

"I'd catch you, so don't even think about it," Nicholas said, and trapped her gaze with his when she whipped her head around to look at him. "You're not going anywhere."

Seeing that he wasn't going to give in and feeling completely powerless and exposed, she looked away as tears filled her eyes. She moved away from him until her back hit the headboard, where she raised her knees to her chest and buried her face in them. She wrapped her arms around her legs, wishing she were anywhere but there with him.

Nicholas couldn't stay angry. She just looked so miserable and alone. He moved closer to her and brushed his hand over her hair several times, letting his fingers massage her scalp. She didn't respond. He continued to stroke her for several more minutes. "I thought you said you were going to trust me," he reminded her softly.

She sighed but still didn't lift her head. "You don't understand," she said plaintively.

"You're right. I don't understand," he agreed before sliding his hand between her knees to grab her chin and lift her face. "Make me," he said softly as he looked into her eyes. He saw that although her lashes were wet, her face was still dry, and used his thumbs to brush the tears away.

"I don't know if I can."

"Try. Let's start with what happened a few minutes ago. What the hell, Melinda? You laid there like a corpse."

She saw the hurt and the confusion and grimaced. "I'm sorry about that, Nicholas, I really am. It was just habit."

"Habit?"

She nodded. "Edmund and I didn't have sex until we were married. I'd wanted it that way because of past experience. As you already know, I've never had an orgasm until tonight. I figured that it hadn't happened with my college boyfriend because I didn't love him. With Edmund, I did love him, or at least I'd convinced myself that I did, and at least I felt those first feelings of heat in my belly with him. It just never got beyond that. Anyway, I thought waiting until after we were married would make the act even sweeter."

"And he went along with this?" Nicholas asked in disbelief.

"Yes. He didn't want to, but he did. Besides, we'd only known each other for six months before we got married, so he didn't have long to wait."

"Sweetheart, when sex is done right, six months can feel like a lifetime."

She smirked but continued. "Anyway, the first time we had sex, I didn't . . . couldn't feel anything, and I just laid there until he finished. He didn't touch me like you did tonight, he just pulled my clothes off and had at it and I hate to say this, but it felt more like an invasion than anything else."

"The stupid fuck didn't prepare you?"

She shook her head. "No, but I didn't demand it, either. I just assumed that he would. I thought it would be like they described it in romance novels and movies; when it wasn't, I became disillusioned and thought that there was something wrong with me, so I just laid there. He became angry, of course, and told me that . . ." She stopped there, feeling ridiculous at the thought of telling him exactly what Edmund had said. "Well, uh . . . let's just say he said he would keep at it until he made me come. He couldn't do it, and I got tired of him trying so hard, so I started faking it, which is what you saw tonight."

"Unbelievable," Nicholas said.

"I guess," she said with a shrug.

"But I still don't understand how that happened tonight. I need you to give me details."

"I really don't know how it did. I was really enjoying feeling you inside of me. There were all these sensations that I'd never felt before with anyone else. You were so big, and it felt so tight; then it felt more like you were looming over me and taking over, and I just went on automatic Melinda pilot. I felt like I had lost control, and I wanted it back, so I took it the only way I knew how."

"Looming over you? That's when you felt like you were losing control?"

"Yes, and I'm sure I was just going back to old habits. I'd never liked to feel Edmund's—"

"Don't even think like that," he interrupted her. "When I get my dick inside of you again, which will be very soon, it's going to feel so good, you won't want me to pull out," he said as he nibbled at her mouth.

"Really?" she asked between nibbles.

"Really," he confirmed, and unbent her knees, stretching her legs out. Taking her by the waist, he scooted her down on the bed until she cleared the headboard, then he laid her back against the pillows. "You see, what that idiot Edmund failed to understand is that a woman's body is like a delicate instrument." He kissed her forehead and then her eyelids, followed by her nose, her cheekbones, and finally her lips, where he sipped gently at them until she was trying to kiss him back.

He ignored her efforts and continued to move his lips over her, tasting and savoring as he went along. Her chin received stinging little nips, and her neck was treated to a thorough licking and sucking until her legs were moving restlessly against the bedspread. "It's a delicate instrument that needs to be wooed and worshipped until it willingly, happily, gives up its beautiful music," he finished, right before he bit down briefly on a turgid nipple, causing Melinda to let out a keening wail and arch her back clear off the bed.

"Like I said," he stated between the kisses he was trailing across her chest to her other breast, "music." As he gave her second breast the same treatment as the first, his fingers found their way between her opened thighs. "And if a man is skillful and . . ." he began as he took his mouth down her torso and back up again.

Melinda didn't think she could take much more of his torture. His hands and mouth were everywhere, leaving burning heat in their wake. She moaned when he let his finger just barely trace her opening. She wanted to beg when he scraped his nail on her clit and then teasingly took it away. "If a man is skillful *and*," she reminded him desperately as she pushed her pussy toward his hand. She knew he wouldn't let her come until he finished his explanation.

He tongued her navel several times, further stirring the heat that was just below the surface. "If a man is skillful and very, very lucky," he said as if she hadn't said anything at all, "he'll get—" he pushed a finger inside her opening and pressed his thumb hard against her clit, "several encores before the night is over." He finished just when she started to scream his name over and over again as she began to shatter inside.

Moving quickly, Nicholas removed his finger from her vagina, kneed her legs even farther apart, and slid his dick into her until he filled her to the hilt, taking her legs and wrapping them high around his waist. He watched as her eyes popped open in surprise and felt her begin to stiffen. Eyes narrowed, he took the flat of his hand and gave her a slap to one raised buttock.

Melinda let out a sharp little cry and her eyes, widened by shock and pain, looked into his. She didn't acknowledge the little shot of pleasure she felt and she slapped at his shoulder. "Stop it!"

"Don't you dare stop, Lindy."

When she tried to push away from him, he smacked her ass two more times, right on the exact spot of the first slap. Each smack brought a rush of white-hot pleasure to the forefront and made her squeeze his dick a little more.

Melinda tried to ignore the frisson of pain-induced pleasure the stinging smacks sent through her system. *She* tried, but her body didn't, and it was bucking wildly beneath him, leaking out its joy and appreciation all over his plunging dick. *Traitor,* she thought even as a long moan of yearning escaped her throat. She closed her eyes to enjoy the dual shots of pleasure and pain.

Nicholas could tell that the light spanks had added an element she hadn't expected and that she liked it. He leaned down to whisper against her lips, "You like that, don't you, sweetheart? Want me to do it again?" She opened her eyes, and he saw the lust that filled them at the thought. He knew she wanted him to, but he wanted her to tell him that.

Melinda licked her lips in indecision. The slight pain really had felt good, but that she could find pleasure in the pain scared her a little bit. She licked her lips again.

Completely turned on by the sight, Nicholas bent down and kissed her, biting that tongue gently between his teeth. "It's okay, sweetheart. I won't do it again."

For once grateful to have a decision taken out of her hands, Mel kissed him, her nails digging into his back as he continued to thrust forcefully into her.

She was so tight, Nicholas thought, as she squeezed around him like a hot, sweaty fist. This alone more than made up for all the months he'd waited for her, and it was much better than any fantasy he could have dreamed up. He felt his orgasm begin to build at the base of his spine, the force of it so explosive he knew instinctively that he'd have to rest for quite a while when they were finished. He looked down at Melinda. She seemed close, but he couldn't wait much longer and decided to speed things along for her.

He reared back, simultaneously lifting her torso so that her nipples were level with his mouth. Sucking one nipple into his mouth, he bit down on it just as she bore down on his penis, unknowingly manipulating it into contact with her G-spot.

The resultant full-body pleasure stunned her into a speechless void and she couldn't move for a moment. But as the storm raged through her, instinct took over, and she blindly followed it, riding him hard and hungrily until she thought the absolute bliss would make her lose her mind. As it pounded through her body and left her weak and gasping, the only thing she could do was sob out his name.

Nicholas wrapped his hands around her waist and forced her down on his cock as he lifted his hips to thrust into her one last time. His orgasm crashed through him, taking him cleanly and completely over the edge.

10

Melinda awoke to feathery caresses trailing down her spine. She turned her head to look at Nicholas and smiled when she was greeted by a wicked grin. "Hey," she whispered.

"Hey, yourself," he said, dipping his head for a morning kiss.

She turned her head at the last minute so his lips landed on her cheek. "I haven't brushed my teeth yet," she reminded him softly.

Nicholas chuckled and leaned back into his pillows. "Okay, stinky," he teased.

Smiling, Mel rolled over into his arms and rested her head on his chest. She let her toes tangle with his under the covers. "You're on the schedule today, aren't you?"

"Yep," Nicholas said, and pressed a kiss in her hair, which now smelled like his shampoo. They'd showered together the night before, and he'd had her a third time against the tiled walls as steamy water flowed around them.

"How much time do we have?" She didn't see a clock anywhere.

"Just enough time to talk about you. Are you all right this morning?"

"I'm fine," she assured him. "Just a little sore." Her voice softened and trailed off as she remembered him taking her against the wall on their way to the bathroom for a shower. He'd been carrying her with her legs wrapped around his waist, she'd rubbed herself against his swollen dick, and he'd backed her against the wall and had been balls deep in her within seconds. The memory of it made a tremor pass through her body. Sighing, she rubbed her breasts against his chest.

"Uh-uh, none of that now," Nicholas chastised her. "As much as I'd love to accommodate you, you're much too tender for what you have in mind."

Mel thought about it. She only felt a little sore. "Maybe you could just use the tip of it," she whispered, suddenly feeling horny.

Nicholas looked down at her with a teasing smile, thinking that she was joking, but the lust that shone clearly in her eyes told him otherwise. Quickly, he let his finger find her clit, and when she winced, he said, "Just as I thought. Lindy, you're too tender for me to do anything down there—even touch you."

She pouted for a moment, knowing he was right. Saying nothing, she put her head back down on his chest. "Okay, Doctor, I'll accept that," she grumbled. "For now."

Nicholas laughed and got out of bed. "You stay there. I'll be right back."

He was naked and Mel thoroughly appreciated the glorious view from the back—and the one from the front when he returned from the connecting bath.

"Lay back." He threw the covers off her body. "Now open your legs," he commanded. "Oh, baby, you're so red." He pressed a cold compress against her flesh.

Mel sighed in relief when it made contact, closing her legs around it. "Thank you," she said when he got back into bed.

"Now," Nicholas said as he settled in next to her, "Tell me why you have such a strong need to be in control."

"I've been talking to Cally about it, and she thinks it could have something to do with the way I was raised. And thinking about it, I can see her point."

"I thought you said you had a good childhood," Nicholas reminded her.

"I did. My parents were and still are wonderful. It's just that they didn't have me until they were forty. They had been trying for years, and when I finally came along, they felt so happy and lucky that they were overprotective. They felt like I was the only one they'd ever have, and they needed to be extra careful with me, which they were. At the same time, they were really involved in my life, almost too much so. I was never allowed to go outside alone until I was twelve, not even to just go next door to my best friend's house. Let's see, what else? They put me in Catholic schools because they knew that I'd be watched over carefully and that the nuns would not let me leave the building unless my mother or father was there to pick me up.

"There was just a lot of stuff they did that made me feel powerless, so as a consequence, Cally said, I became a control freak. She says that control became a valuable commodity to me the way that money and power are to other people." She shrugged. "Like I said, I can see her point. I remember that during the college application process, I only picked the ones that were out of state so I could get away from everything. I loved my parents but they drove me crazy. I was pampered and spoiled and quite possibly could have been a useless adult if it hadn't been for Lilly and Simone. They, especially Simone, kept me grounded. They let me know in little ways that the way my parents treated me wasn't normal."

"That's interesting," Nicholas said. "So Cally thinks that you just transferred your need to control to the bedroom?"

"Yes, the most intimate of places, when you're at your most vulnerable."

"Well, I'll say one thing for Cally, she's still as smart as she was when she was a kid."

"You guys knew each other when you were kids?" Surprised, Melinda lifted her head to look at him.

"Yeah. She didn't tell you?"

"No. I mean, she said that you guys had known each other before Living Well and she's the one who recommended you, but I just assumed that it had been from working at the same hospital."

"Oh, no, I've known Cally since she was a little bitty ten-year-old Southern belle, when her family moved to our block from Atlanta. She was so funny, and my sisters loved her. She was at our house all the time. I even thought that there might have been something going on between her and my cousin Griff when they were teenagers, but then when she was seventeen, she just disappeared."

"Disappeared? Her family moved?"

"No, her family didn't move, but one day she just wasn't there anymore. Her family wouldn't talk about it. I always suspected that Griff knew something, but he would just clam up when I asked him about her, so I stopped asking. It became the big mystery of Taylor Street."

"Interesting. And you never asked her as an adult?"

"Nope. When I ran into her at the hospital about five years ago, I was so pleased to see her that I didn't think to ask her. I told Griff about her return later that day, and he asked me to promise not to ask her anything about her sudden disappearance. I could see it was important to him, so I promised."

"Whatever it is, it must be pretty painful or bad, because she never told me she knew you from when you were kids, and she knew that I assumed otherwise." She shrugged. "I guess if she had wanted me to know, she would have told me, so I won't ask either."

"Good."

They lay like that for a while, and Mel was falling asleep again when he said, "Well, it's time for me to get up and start the grind. Feel free to spend your day off here, sweetheart. I'll take you out to dinner when I get home tonight."

Mel looked up at him with a smile. "Oh, good, I'd like that—oh, but I can't. I don't have any clothes here, and I don't want to even consider wearing the dress I had on last night. It's clearly for after five P.M."

"And?"

"*And* if I put it on now, anyone who saw me would know that I'd had it on last night and had spent the night having sex."

"What does it matter?"

"It just matters, okay? I guess I'll have to sneak out to my car," she said, and moved to get out of bed. Pain from another area made her wince. "Ow."

"What's the matter?" Nicholas asked. "Is the compress not working anymore?"

Mel's frown showed her embarrassment. "Oh, it's working fine. It's not that, it's my—" She cut herself off and turned over on her stomach, deciding it was best just to show him. She waited for his laughter.

And was not disappointed. Nicholas laughed so hard, tears rolled down his face. She frowned up at him. "It's not funny, Nicholas! Just tell me how red it is!"

Nicholas stopped laughing long enough to say, "Yes, it is funny. I told you to take it easy last night, but you just kept begging for more." He made his voice a falsetto. "Harder, Nicky, please. Just a little harder," he mimicked her before he started laughing again.

Mel grimaced. During the last time they'd made love, she'd thought about the light slaps he'd given her earlier in the night and wanting to experience the sensations again, she'd asked him to spank her. He'd agreed and had put her across his knee like she'd asked, but he'd refused to hit her any harder than the light stings she'd already experienced. When he wouldn't make the slight slaps any harder, she'd begged him to keep spanking her instead. He'd cautioned her that it was too much, but she'd obviously gotten carried away, as had he.

She blushed.

"Oh, look, now your face is the same color as your ass," he teased, and started laughing again.

Mel's lips twitched, but she clamped them together so she wouldn't laugh. "Nicholas!" she said sulkily. "Stop laughing at me. How red is it?"

Nicholas stopped laughing and sat next to her hip. "I'm sorry, babe." He pressed a kiss in the dip of her back. "I shouldn't have laughed so hard, but you've got to admit, it is funny. Now, let's see what we've got here." He pressed a finger gently against her skin, watching for her reaction as he did so. She didn't move. "Does that hurt?" he asked.

"No, I just felt a little pressure."

"Okay, it's just a little pink, so you'll be fine. It will be uncomfortable to sit on for long periods of time, though. Stay here today. Unless you think you can take the pain, you shouldn't drive home just yet."

"Yeah, I was thinking that too. If I gave you the extra set of keys to my house, would you go over and grab me some clothes for dinner after you leave the clinic? I know it would be out of your way, but—"

"Don't worry about it, Lindy. I'd be happy to. I'm happy to do anything that will keep you trapped in my bed for hours at a time, which reminds me—" he rose and walked over to his closet "—I bought you some presents."

Mel perked up, resting her head on her hand so she could see better. "You bought me presents?" Her eyes widened when she saw how large the bag was that he was carrying. "What on earth is it? And when did you buy them?"

"Well, *they* are some things that I thought might be fun to try while you learned about the pleasure different parts of your body can bring you." He sat on the edge of the bed, then reached into the bag and brought out some striped material. "I got them after what happened the day before yesterday. I was determined to get you in my bed and show you just what we could do with that body of yours."

Mel scooted over to get a closer look. "A thong? You bought me a thong?"

"It's not just any thong," Nicholas said and pulled out a remote control. "It's a remote-controlled vibrating thong."

Mel laughed. "Get out!" she said, and snatched the thong from his hand. It started pulsing against her palm and she looked to see Nicholas working the remote. "So I would wear it while you had the remote?"

"Yep, or you could use it by yourself."

"Ooh," she moaned. "That would be really kinky, wouldn't it? I never knew they even made stuff like this!"

Nicholas reached into the bag and next pulled out what looked like a plastic butterfly. It was purple and had black straps on either side.

"What is that?"

"Another vibrator."

"But it's a butterfly," she protested, and reached out to touch the antennae.

"A *vibrating* butterfly."

"Yes, but it's still a *butterfly*, plus it's purple. I'd feel like a pervert using that one. It looks like a toy for kids. What else you got?" she asked eagerly.

Nicholas laughed in sheer delight. He'd had no idea that the toys would go over so well. He'd only thought to get them to help ease her into the world of sex in a playful way, but clearly she didn't need any easing. He reached down again. "Pull the bag off when I lift this last one," he told her. "It's a big one."

Eagerly, Mel reached over to grab the bottom of the bag, pulling it off of what looked to be an oddly shaped cushion. Shaped like a bowl, but long, the piece was royal blue in color. She poked it with a finger. "What is it?"

"It's called the Liberator, and this particular piece is what's known as the scoop," he told her. He set it on the floor and pushing it down at one end, set it to rocking. "Imagine all the fun we could have on that."

Mel watched it rock and suddenly blushed. "Oh, wow," she said as various positions flashed through her mind. She looked at the Scoop, then at Nicholas and back at the Scoop again. She blushed some more.

Nicholas laughed at the speculative, lusty look in her eyes. "I think I've taught you too well."

Still looking at the rocking piece of furniture, Mel mumbled, "When do you think we can use it?"

"Oh, God. I've created a sex fiend!" Nicholas snatched her up by her waist and planted a hard kiss on her mouth. "I've got to start getting ready. Find a comfortable position on the bed, and when I come out from the shower, I'll rub some salve on your butt. But first, I'll need you to get me those extra keys to your house, and you'll need to use the bathroom if you have to, because I don't want you to move much until the salve dries."

11

Mel spooned the last of her breakfast yogurt out of its container and halfheartedly put it in her mouth. It was nourishment and she had to eat. Sighing, she took a sip of water, picked up the novel she was reading, and tried to concentrate on what was on the page. The book was written by one of her favorite authors, and she'd been trying to start it for days, but she couldn't concentrate on it long enough to follow what was happening in the story.

She thought about Nicholas. Now, she had no problem concentrating on him. She'd been avoiding him for days, even switching shifts so she wouldn't have to work with him. She was running scared, and she knew it but couldn't help herself. When she was around Nicholas, she lost all sense of propriety and some of herself. She was in love with him and in lust. He inspired her to do all kinds of things she didn't think she'd ever do with someone else, and that scared her.

"Hey, it's today's resident sourpuss!"

Melinda looked up at Cally as she entered the clinic's kitchen. "Hey, Cally," she said without much inflection.

"Um-um-um," Cally said with pity as she sat down across from her and looked at her miserable face. "Girl, you are just a sorry sight to behold. What in the hell is going on, and what are you doing here on your day off?"

"I switched shifts with Tory this week."

"Well, judging by the other sourpuss's disposition this week, I guess I don't have to ask why. Okay, two questions. When did the two of you break up, and whose idea was it?"

"We didn't exactly break up, and I'm the one who's been avoiding him."

"Why? You told me that you guys were going like gangbusters. That you had fun together and you loved being with him."

"We were, we did and I do."

"Okay," Cally said slowly, not quite comprehending. "So, my original question stands. What in the hell is going on?"

"I just couldn't take being with him. It scared me, so I decided that I needed some space, that's all."

"What scared you?"

"Do you remember when you told me that the right man could have me fienin' for sex so badly that I basically wouldn't be in my right mind?"

"I don't remember using those exact words, no, but I do remember the conversation," Cally said in confusion and then the light dawned. "Girl, has Nicholas Pantino turned you out?"

"Out, in, sideways, upside down," Mel confirmed mournfully. "I don't think there's a way he hasn't turned me."

"Well, good for Dr. Nick! And for you, of course!" Cally said excitedly; then another light dawned when she realized that that was why Mel was miserable. "Wait. It's not good?"

"Not for me, it isn't. Cally, it scares me—the things I'm willing to do with him."

Cally's eyes widened and she leaned in closer. "Do you want to give me an example?" she whispered.

Mel looked at her and burst out laughing. Even through her misery, she could see the avid curiosity on Cally's face. "You're so nosy!"

Cally didn't even try to deny it. "Hey. I am what I am."

"Well, the details are none of your business, Popeye, but let's just say that Nicholas inspires me to forget every bit of decency that my mama, my daddy, and two different Catholic schools spent a lifetime trying to teach me."

"Damn," Cally drew the word out for several seconds.

"Exactly," Melinda concurred with a nod.

"Well, just answer these questions. Is what y'all have been doing illegal?"

"Maybe in some states," Melinda said with a secret smile, "but not this one."

Cally grinned before she continued. "Is what you're doing hurting anyone?"

Melinda thought about the couple of times he'd spanked her and almost answered with an "only me and only for a minute," but stopped herself "No," she said, and blushed.

"Is he *making* you do things that you don't want to do?"

"Oh, no," Melinda said in surprise and frowned. "Nicholas would never do that."

The insult she heard in the other woman's voice made Cally smile. "Then what exactly is it, girl? I'm not getting it."

Melinda sighed and leaned in to whisper, "It's just that I want to do it *all the time* with him. And when he's not around, I'm *thinking* about doing it with him. Once I was thinking about him and *it* so much that I couldn't wait for him to get home and I masturbated."

"Oh, girl, that's normal," Cally dismissed her worry with a wave of her hand.

"Twice in twenty minutes, Cally?"

Cally paused but recovered quickly. "Yes, it's still normal."

"He came home and caught me just as I was finishing up," Melinda said, "and he took me on the floor and against the wall before we even made it to the bedroom."

Cally's mouth hung open in shock for a moment. "Well, damn! You guys are just a couple of freaks! And I don't know what to tell you."

"Cally!" Melinda said in shock before she tried not to laugh.

"What? Don't look at me. You need help that only a sex therapist can give you."

Melinda really looked worried then. "Really?" she asked despairingly.

"No, Melinda," Cally said. "I'm just messing with you. What you and Nicholas have is a healthy sex life. It might be more active than others, but it's still healthy."

"Well, that's a relief, I guess."

"What is it?"

"I've just never felt this way before, and it scares me. All of it."

"Ah, so we're back to your control issues," Cally said with a nod.

"I don't know. Maybe."

"My advice is for you to just let go. You can't get any more miserable than you are now." When Mel didn't answer, Cally stood. "My first patient will be here in ten minutes, and I've got to prepare. Are you going to be okay?"

"Yes, I'll be fine, thanks."

"All right, then. I'll see you later."

"Thanks for listening, Cally."

"Just think about what I said before you panic and sabotage a good thing, Mel."

Mel thought about how much that sounded like the advice Simone had given her, except Simone had been her usual blunt self on the phone the night before. "Don't fuck it up, Mel," she'd said before hanging up.

Mel sighed and thought about the last time she'd seen Nicholas. Every summer, the city sponsored an outdoor movie festival in a downtown park. The movies played every Tuesday starting at dusk, and she and Nicholas had attended the showing of *Rebel without a Cause*. Her face hot with embarrassment, Mel remembered the things she'd done on that last date that had scared her enough to send her scurrying into hiding.

She'd sat next to Nicholas as he'd lounged back on the blanket he'd brought. He'd also brought a picnic dinner, pillows, and a second blanket in case the night turned cool. Butler Field in Grant Park was crowded with hundreds of people, and they'd set their things up as far away from the crowd as possible.

Nicholas had already eaten most of the cold chicken, cheese, and fruit they'd brought and was licking a vanilla ice cream cone that he'd bought from a nearby stand.

"Want some?"

She shook her head no as she swallowed the grape she'd just chewed. She heard a noise and looked towards the huge screen just as the movie was starting.

"Hey, Lindy. What does this remind you of?"

When she'd turned to look at him, he'd stuck his tongue out, which was covered in heavy clumps of dripping white. Since she'd just watched him eat her out in the mirror the night before, she'd had no problem guessing what he was imitating. Heat had exploded in her stomach before traveling downward to tease her clit. She'd been horribly turned on. "Stop it, Nicholas. Not here."

He'd swallowed the ice cream and laughed wickedly. "Why not?"

She'd scooted away from him and leaned back on a stack of pillows. "Because, super freak, it's not appropriate."

Laughing some more, he'd moved closer to her and slipped his hand under the skirt of her halter dress to squeeze her knee. He'd looked up at her and lasciviously wriggled his eyebrows.

She'd giggled. "You're incorrigible."

"I'm also eager to see what you're wearing under this little yellow dress."

"Seeing as how you asked me to wear it, you should already know what I'm wearing," she'd reminded him.

"Ah, yes, the vibrating thong," he'd teased, and she'd watched as he'd slipped his hand in his pocket.

Suddenly she felt a vibrating buzz against her clit and stiffened. "Nicholas, don't you dare," she begged him.

"Why'd you wear it if you don't want me to?"

"I thought that maybe you'd do it in the car on the way home. Not here, you idiot!" Another buzz, this one much stronger. She fell back against the pillows with a soft moan.

He leaned over her and bent his head to kiss her, just as he hit the switch on the remote control. The vibration this time lasted much longer, and she'd helplessly groaned into his mouth, her hips beginning to jerk as she tried to get closer to the vibration.

He'd raised his head and she'd grabbed his hand that held the remote. "Don't do it again, Nicky, please. People will see."

"The movie's just started. No one is paying attention to us. Besides, I can use the other blanket to cover you," he'd said, already reaching for it. "No one can see."

"It's eighty degrees out here! We don't need a blanket." But he was spreading the summerweight blanket over her body and she was letting him, because the risky nature of what he was proposing turned her on.

When he'd untied the halter of her dress so that it fell open to expose her nipples to his fingers, she'd let him do that, too. And right there, under the night sky in Grant Park and amidst hundreds of people, she'd come violently, screaming into his opened mouth and scratching at his shoulders as he'd pinched her breasts with one hand and remotely stimulated her clit with the other.

They'd also made love in the front seat of the car on the way home because neither one of them had been able to wait to feel him moving inside of her. He'd pulled over into a deserted parking lot, and she'd straddled his lap. Later, he'd dropped her off at home because she'd had to work the next day and that was the last time she'd seen him.

Melinda brought herself back to the present with a shake of her head and a deep breath. She rose, dumped her empty container in the garbage and prepared for another long day without Nicholas.

Nicholas let himself into the dark clinic with his extra set of keys. Cally had called him earlier and told him that he should get his ass over there pronto if he wanted to save his relationship. She'd told him that Mel had planned to stay late. He looked toward the receptionist's desk, expecting to see her there working and frowned when he didn't.

"Damn it," he muttered. "Where the hell is she?" He opened the security door and began walking down the hall, checking the nurses' locker room first. He'd been trying to reach her for days. She wasn't answering her cell or house phone, and the couple of times he'd gone to her house, she hadn't been home. It was almost like she'd disappeared.

Almost. He'd figured out what the problem was soon after she'd made herself unavailable. He'd remembered what they'd done, remembered how she'd been before they'd started seeing each other, and he'd put two and two together. "And I came up with five," he muttered with a shake of his head as he looked into the empty kitchen. "Just like she, in all her crazy logic, did. A saner person would have come up with four and at least talked to me about the problem." He left the kitchen and made his way toward the only place left to check. The doctors' office.

Melinda finished working out the nurses' budget and leaned back in Nicholas's chair with a tired sigh. His scent surrounded her, and she breathed it in. She'd decided to work at his desk because she missed him so much and thought that sitting in his chair would help her feel better. "Of course it didn't," she said aloud as she rubbed her neck.

"Of course what didn't?" Nicholas asked her as he walked into the room.

Startled by his voice, Melinda jumped. "Nicholas! What are you doing here?" Her heart raced. He'd asked an innocent question, but the look on his face belied any sense of calmness she might have fooled herself into thinking he felt. She could only describe the look as furious.

"What do you think I'm doing here, Melinda?" He asked this question just as calmly as he continued to walk in unhurried strides toward her.

She stood as he came closer, feeling like she had to in case she suddenly needed to flee. "Um, I don't know. Did you have to pick up a file or something?"

"Nope," he said as he continued to stalk her. "Guess again."

Melinda watched him carefully, feeling more and more like prey to his predator the closer he got. "I don't know," she tried to say calmly; then she blew it by saying shrilly, "Stop doing that!"

Nicholas stopped in his tracks and placed his hands on the desk. "Stop doing what, Melinda? I don't know what you mean."

All the guilt she felt for being such a coward and the lonely achiness she felt from missing him so much combined to make her nervous and irritated. "Yes, you do! So stop it!"

"I see. I'm supposed to stop doing what I'm doing because it upsets you," he said sarcastically. "Yet, you didn't *stop* to call me when you decided that you didn't want to continue our relationship. You didn't *stop* to tell me what was wrong. You didn't even *stop* long enough to try and work out the problem, whatever it is. All those things bothered me, Melinda. In fact, they almost killed me. But I'm supposed to stop what I'm doing because it upsets you. Is that right?"

Melinda's eyes nervously darted to the door. *With a full-out sprint and surprise on my side, I could probably make it,* she thought.

"You wouldn't get very far," Nicholas promised her in a low voice as he walked slowly around the desk.

She held a hand out to ward him off. "Now, Nicholas," she began, but stopped when he grabbed her hand and pulled her to him.

"Just tell me why you left, Lindy," he said softly. "Whatever it is, we could have worked it out. All you had to do was talk to me about it."

Melinda sighed and gave up the fight. "I was scared," she mumbled.

Nicholas sat in his chair and pulled her into his lap so that she faced him. "Scared of what?"

"The way you make me feel and the things I do when I'm with you. I have no control when I'm with you," she confessed.

Nicholas sighed. "So we're even. I don't have any control when it comes to you, either."

"It's not the same," she insisted.

"Yes, it is. Try being in the middle of a consult with a patient and have your dick strain to say hello, just because a certain nurse walked past the room and you caught a glimpse of the freckle near her lip."

"Stop it," she protested as she looked at him through her lashes. "That didn't happen."

"Yes, it did. Worse, try having your dick pick the time to say hello just when you're in the reception area standing in front of the all-seeing, lusty Mrs. Johnson."

"I don't have a dick," she said through her chuckles. "And I know that didn't happen."

Nicholas was nodding his head. "Yes, it did. It was that day a couple of weeks ago when you came in wearing that little blue miniskirt. Remember? I saw the shape of your ass through that skirt and it was 'Hello, Mrs. Johnson. Have you met my dick?'"

Her laughter pealed out again, and when it subsided, she couldn't meet his eyes. "Is it really that way for you? Do you ever feel so uninhibited that you lose yourself and feel you could do absolutely anything? And at the same time you're terrified because you don't feel you're thinking with your right mind?"

"All the time," Nicholas assured her quietly.

Melinda looked at him, and when she saw that he was sincere, she hugged him around his waist and laid her head on his chest. "God, Nicholas, I'm so sorry." She blinked back tears that sprang to her eyes from a rush of relief. "I was just so scared, and I thought I was the only one who feels this way."

Nicholas hugged her back. "All you had to do was talk to me, Lindy. The next time you feel scared, just talk to me and I'll do what I can to make it better. Understand?"

Melinda nodded and pressed a kiss to his chin.

12

"Now," Nicholas began as his hands slipped under the short, floaty skirt she wore to pull at her panties, "did I ever tell you about this fantasy I used to have about you, me, and this chair?"

"Ah, no," Mel said as she felt him tear the panties from her body.

Nicholas rolled the chair closer to the desk. He grabbed the first of three thick medical books that sat on his desk. "Raise up, sweetheart." When she did, he placed all three of the books on his lap. "Okay, now sit back down." One by one, he took her feet and placed them on the arm of the chairs. "Beautiful," he growled when he was finished.

Mel sobbed in pure need when she saw what he'd done. Her vagina was right on level with his mouth, and she was wide open for access. She closed her eyes and waited for that first sweep of his tongue. When it didn't come, she opened them to look questioningly at him.

"Tell me you love me," he said.

"I love you," she said without hesitation, and was rewarded

with one greedy lick. She grabbed hold of the desk behind her and pushed toward his face. She looked at him again when she felt nothing but cool air.

"I love you, too," he said, and slurped at her. His tongue and lips made suctioning, wet sounds against her flesh for a few moments before he stopped, making Mel sob again, but this time in pure frustration.

"Oh, God, Nicholas!"

"Tell me what you want me to do," he demanded.

Mel looked at him. "Please, Nicky."

"Please, Nicky what?" he asked and blew softly on her clit, making her jerk in response.

Stunned, Mel really looked at him. *Not again*, she thought. *Bastard*. She tried to bring her legs down, but his hands were pressing into her feet so that she couldn't move. "Come on, Nicholas. Please," she begged.

"Tell me what you want."

Mel could tell that she wouldn't get satisfaction until *he* was satisfied with her surrender. Closing her eyes, she said, "I want you to lick—"

Then she was screaming as he swept his tongue from bottom to top several times. And then he started nibbling, his teeth gently biting and scraping at her clit and his beard and mustache brushing against her every nerve ending. She felt him hungrily lapping up every drop of cream that flowed out of her and she fed herself to him, pushing and grinding into his face.

Nicholas lifted his head to look at her again. His lips were shiny with her essence. Mel looked back at him, barely restraining herself from grabbing his head and closing her legs around it so he could finish what he'd started. She waited.

He pinched her clit lightly between his fingers and released it just as quickly. "Look at me and tell me," he said softly when she rolled her eyes in frustration.

She kept them on him as she said, "I want you to lick my clit and then I want you to take it between your teeth and suck it into your mouth until I'm losing every bit of reserve and control I've ever had."

Nicholas went back to feeding and Mel went back to screaming, and as her eyes began to roll to the back of her head, she thought, *oh, my gosh, it actually can happen!*

Nicholas held Melinda's hand as they walked out the back door of the clinic. He turned to lock the door.

"Wait! I know you've set the alarm, but we have to go back in," Melinda suddenly said as he inserted the key.

His mind on other things, Nicholas looked at her. "What? Why?"

"I left my panties in your office."

He smiled and turned the key. "You did, but I didn't. They're in my pocket," he assured her and started to walk through the well-lit parking lot to her car. The plan was for him to follow her to his place.

"Oh, okay," she said. "I'm glad one of us was thinking. In fact, my brain still isn't operating at full capacity," she teased. When he didn't respond, she looked at him. He was frowning. "What's wrong, Nicky?"

Distracted, he said, "Hmm? Oh, nothing." They were at her car and he took her keys to unlock the door. He hesitated and turned to look at her. "You are going to marry me, aren't you, Lindy?"

Stunned, Melinda could only stare at him. Unable to take it in, she stumbled back until her butt hit the front of the car.

"I know we've only been going out a short time, but we know and love each other." He placed an arm on either side of her. "Are you going to marry me? Tell me you're going to marry me, Lindy."

Melinda cupped his face in her hands to stare into his eyes.

What she saw there made tears fill her eyes and slowly flow down her cheeks. "I'm going to marry you," she choked out.

"That's wonderful," he said as he kissed her. "You've just made me the happiest man in the world." He laughed when, still crying, she brought his head down for another, more thorough kiss. "Now, tell me you're going to have my babies," he said softly when he came up for air.

She felt the heat that had started to flame inside of her make way for a bunch of mush. "I'm going to have your babies."

Nicholas took a deep, shuddering breath as the idea that he was going to have everything he wanted took root and began to grow. Hardly able to believe it, he put his hands on her waist, closed his eyes and rested his forehead on hers. "Oh, baby," he whispered reverently.

Melinda closed her eyes as well, silently grateful that she had been well and truly caught.

Fienin'

Angie Daniels

*This story is dedicated to my freaky-deaky partner in crime,
Kimberly Kaye Terry. Thanks for asking me to be a part of
this anthology*
—Angie Daniels

1

_____

"Oooh-weee! Damn, baby, you feel good!" Bernard howled between broken breaths.

I wish I could return the compliment.

Simone Thomas rolled her eyes while she rocked her hips back and forth. She was beginning to think there was something wrong with Chicago's drinking water because good dick had suddenly become hard to find. But she wasn't ready to give up hope just yet. Somewhere out there had to be a man that could satisfy her mind and body.

"That's it, baby. Ride this dick."

What dick? she thought as she squeezed her muscles tightly around an erection that didn't go deeper than a Vienna sausage. *I can't believe this!* she screamed inwardly. Bernard had promised her a Ball Park frank. Weren't they supposed to plump when you cook them? *Humph!* His dick had been basting in her wet, hot pussy for over twenty minutes and, damn, it was still the same size.

A headache was inevitable. She had wasted an entire

evening of flirting, touching, and teasing with the retired basketball player only to discover Bernard didn't have anywhere near enough to scratch her itch. What a waste, she thought as she gazed through lowered lids at the two-hundred-and-fifteen-pound, rock-hard body lying beneath her. He couldn't even reach her G-spot. *Whatever.* As soon as she got home, she was pulling out her vibrator and finishing what he'd started.

Simone tilted her face toward the ceiling, causing her hair to tickle her shoulder blades. While she rode what little he had to offer, her heavy breasts jiggled. Bernard rubbed at her nipples, then lifted his head and captured one in his mouth. His touch did nothing for her. In fact, Simone hadn't met a man in years capable of making her feel anything but disgust and regret. She didn't know why she even bothered anymore, especially since she no longer found any satisfaction in one-night stands.

Bernard held onto Simone's hips and urged her to ride harder. She tried, but damn, he kept slipping out, and after a couple more awkward strokes, she gave up and ground her hips instead. Closing her eyes tightly, Simone forced the tears back. What happened to her? She was no longer that sassy outspoken girl with the love-'em-and-leave-'em attitude. She had changed, and not necessarily for the better. For the last two years men had been in and out of her life. If she needed sex, she never had a problem getting it. Yet none of the men she encountered did anything to fill the emptiness in her heart. Clamping her lips tightly together, she fought off a surge of frustration. *This was not the way it was supposed to be.*

No, her life didn't have to be this way, but it was because she couldn't risk falling in love again. It hurt too much. And as a result, she was in for a life of flings and meaningless sex when all she wanted was to find one man with a dick her pussy fit like a glove; a simple sexual connection that didn't involve the heart.

Last night she had taken the time to think back over her numerous sexual encounters and a crush of realization hit her square in the face. After two years of riding dicks of different shapes and sizes, as much as she hated to admit it, sex was no longer enough. There was a deep yearning in her heart for something more, yet she was too afraid to take a chance and discover what that "something" was.

"Mmmm, baby."

Bernard's moaning jolted her brain back to her latest problem. Reaching down between them, Simone took two fingers and gripped the base of his dick and held it firmly in place while she tried to lengthen her strokes again. She was anxious to get off this ride. The sooner Bernard came, the sooner she could rush home and scrub him from her body.

She met Bernard's upward thrusts pound for pound and eventually his breathing grew faster, hotter. She also panted heavily, pretending he was pushing her towards an orgasm.

"That's it!" he hissed, blowing air between his teeth. He rocked his hips, thrusting deeper, and she allowed him to set the rhythm while her mind wandered back to the façade she called her life.

What would her friends think if they knew her sassy no-nonsense attitude was a front to hide the wounded woman inside? Hurt and rejected so many times in her life, she just couldn't allow anyone to see how weak and vulnerable she really was. Been there. Done that. All it had gotten her was constant pain that eventually blossomed into the most humiliating moment of her life.

Reaching up, she wiped a teardrop from the corner of her eye. She refused to be a victim of love. Once was more than enough. All she had to do was to keep her heart under lock and key and she'd have nothing to worry about. Well, almost nothing.

"That's it, baby. Oooh-weee! Daddy's about to come!"

Simone's shoulders sagged with relief. *About time.*

2

"This is 107.5 WGCI coming to you live from Situations Nightclub—the hottest place to be on a Friday night. We've got drink specials, slamming buffalo wings and some of the finest women in the city of Chicago!"

Simone strolled across the floor, pleased at what she saw. There wasn't an empty seat in the house. The live broadcast from her upscale club was definitely going to be good for business. When a friend suggested that her cousin, DJ Rated R, come down to the club to do his Friday night *Grown & Sexy Show*, Simone had been a bit skeptical. She was afraid that the popular R&B station would draw the wrong type of crowd. Scanning the area, she was relieved to see that was not the case. There were no ball caps, do-rags, or white T's in the house. Everyone had abided by the club's rules. Men and women twenty-five and older were dressed to impress, and to her excitement, flooding the floor. Since she'd first opened her doors three years ago, business had been relatively good, but what she saw tonight was a dream come true. *Cha-ching!*

Noticing the crowd gathering around the bar, Simone

slipped behind the counter to give her staff a hand. Immediately, she took drink orders from one of her barmaids and got to work.

"Look at this crowd. We haven't seen these many customers in a long time!"

Simone looked up from the margarita blending and over at her bar manager, Amber. "I know. This idea was definitely good for business." Leaning in closer, she added over the booming music, "Now if only my sex life was this good."

"You're kidding," Amber replied as she pulled two frosty mugs from the cooler. "Weren't you supposed to have dinner with that handsome ex-basketball player last night?"

Simone rolled her eyes at the reminder. "You heard what I said."

"It couldn't possibly have been that bad," Amber said with disbelief.

"Humph! It was worse. He was huffing and puffing like some animal in pain. If I'd had a gun I would have shot his ass."

"Oh, my!" Amber was laughing so hard she was practically in tears. "Well, the night is still young. Mr. Right might be standing out on the dance floor," she said with a confident nod of her blond head.

"You're right," Simone began, then reached for a shot glass. "Mr. Right is here and his name is Situations."

Amber arched her brow. "A nightclub can't love you back."

Simone snorted rudely. "Neither can a man." As she garnished the drinks with lime, she glanced over at the woman she considered a good friend and scowled.

Amber Holland was one of the most beautiful women Simone had ever known. She had lovely alabaster skin and the most startling blue eyes. Her bar manager was also a romantic who'd been dating the same man for almost five years with plans to marry after he finished medical school.

If only I could be so lucky. After her string of bad luck, with last night being the icing on the cake, Simone had no desire to meet someone else.

"A man will love you if you allow him a chance. And you're not going to find that in a one-night stand," she heard Amber say.

Yeah, but at least I won't be in danger of risking my heart again, she thought. Pouring a glass of white zinfandel, she didn't bother to comment. Instead, she released a heavy sigh. This discussion wasn't new by any stretch of the imagination. Amber was determined to convince her to give love one more chance. But Simone just couldn't bring herself to do that again. Besides, after last night, she didn't need a man. She owned a successful nightclub, drove a BMW, and lived in a fabulous condo in Oak Park. What more could she possibly want? But as she reached for a clean shot glass, Simone asked herself if she was truly satisfied. The million-dollar question: did she really need a man to feel complete? After all, what use did a man have other than sex? Her vibrator was more than qualified to handle that job.

While Simone reached for a bottle of gin, she silently admitted that a vibrator did nothing to cure the loneliness in her heart. She missed the comfort of lying in a man's arms. There were nights when she cringed at the thought of going home to a big empty bed. At thirty-four she had hoped to have been married with at least one child by now. Instead, it was the complete opposite.

She loaded the drinks on a tray as thoughts of her college sweetheart came to mind. He'd broken her heart and shattered any dreams she may have had in believing there was such a thing as happily ever after.

"Did you hear me?"

"Uh-huh," Simone mumbled, although she had no idea what Amber was talking about. She carried the drinks over to the end of the bar, where one of her barmaids, Lee Ann, was waiting. The college student's bubbly personality was good for business, not to mention she looked fabulous in the uniform—a short black skirt and white midriff top.

"Thanks Simone. I also need two Heinekens."

Simone returned her generous smile. "Coming right up."

Amber brushed past Simone but not before whispering close to her ear, "Ignore me if you want to, but I promise you, tonight Mr. Right is going to walk right through that door."

Shaun Dutton strolled into the smoky nightclub and was tempted to run out the nearest exit. He didn't know why he let his co-worker and good friend, Javon Tate, talk him into coming out tonight. He hated crowded clubs and loud music and would rather be at home listening to Norah Jones. But as Javon had smoothly pointed out, at home he'd be faced with the same problem he'd been having every Friday night for the last two years—he would be spending it alone. Shaun released a heavy sigh. Javon was right. Besides, he had made a promise. Tonight was supposed to be the start of a new beginning. He just wished that chapter began somewhere other than at a nightclub.

"Man, I told you this was the place to be. Look at all these honeys up in here!"

Shaun glanced over at Javon's round, nutmeg-colored face, then allowed his eyes to travel around the room. Women in all shapes and sizes filled the room. "I have to agree there are some very attractive women in here tonight."

"Attractive? Yo, dude, these girls are phat. P-H-A—"

"I know how to spell it," Shaun interrupted.

"Hey. I'm just trying to school you with a little Urban 101," Javon said while rubbing a hand across his shiny bald head.

Shaun frowned. The two had been friends for almost seven years, yet Javon still felt like he needed to show him the ropes.

He might be white, but he knew a lot more than his friend gave him credit for.

"Yo, Shaun. You lose that ponytail, you just might get some pussy tonight."

"I didn't come here for that. Believe me, I'll get some when I'm good and ready." Getting pussy had never been a problem for him. He'd gotten his fair share when he was in high school. He'd screwed all the cheerleaders, dipping and dabbing in something new on a regular basis. But screwing just to be screwing had gotten to be a bore, and eventually he yearned for something more meaningful. Then he met Hannah his senior year and all that had ended. The only wet pussy he'd sunk his dick into was hers. Briefly, he closed his eyes and visions of his beautiful wife came to light. Raising his eyelids, he gave a heavy shudder. Since Hannah's death two years ago, he had been celibate.

All that is about to change.

He could feel it in his gut, but he wasn't settling for just anybody. He would wait. When the right woman came along, he would know it. Tonight, the only thing he was looking to wrap his lips around was an ice-cold bottled beer.

While Javon went chasing after a gorgeous chick with a set of double D's, Shaun strolled through the club. Glancing around, he had to admit the décor was rather nice. A large platform stage at the center of the room was surrounded by small intimate tables and chairs. To the far left was a dark, rich mahogany bar that stretched the length of the building. Mirrors adorned the walls while red and white tiles covered the floor.

He took a deep breath. The scent of cigarettes and alcohol surrounded him. A popular new rap song blared from a nearby speaker. Sweaty bodies were bumping and grinding on the dance floor. Shaking his head, he realized he hadn't been in a place like this since college, but even then it was nothing like this. The way couples were lip-locking and dry-humping, the behavior could definitely be considered foreplay. Times had definitely changed.

Reaching into his pocket, Shaun jiggled his keys, still contemplating turning on his heels and going home. But as much as he wanted to, he couldn't bail on his friend. Javon had been asking him to go out clubbing for months and each and every time he'd declined. However, this evening as he was preparing to say no, Shaun had this strange sensation that he needed to be here tonight, that his new life was about to begin. As much as he doubted this was the place, he'd come anyway. Hannah would have wanted him to start enjoying his life again.

Standing off to the side, Shaun's eyes traveled around the dimly lit room. Unattached women barely in clothes cluttered the room but nothing caught his interest until he gazed behind the bar and spotted the woman on the end. His breath stalled as he noted her slender neck and high cheekbones. She had smooth caramel-colored skin. Her delicate face was heart-shaped and framed by long, honey brown hair, which was in a neat French braid. Even in the dimly lit room, he could see enough to know she was beautiful. In fact, she looked so good she made his dick twitch and that startled him. He hadn't had a hard-on since his wife's death and had even begun to believe the overwhelmingly emotional experience had left him impotent. Obviously, that was definitely not the case. As he moved closer to the bar, all he could do was stare.

"She's the one," he breathed. The sweet thing came from behind the counter and he took in long, shapely legs meant to be wrapped around a man's waist. She was dressed in a white form-fitting dress that emphasized the delicate swell of her large breasts and small narrow hips. And damn! The woman had an ass that was like two ripe melons he wanted to sink his teeth into, certain it was just as juicy as it looked. He raked a hand through his hair and shook his head with disbelief. He was salivating. No woman had ever made him feel this horny but Hannah.

Shaun took several deep breaths. This was it. She was the reason why he was here tonight. He was destined to meet that delicious-looking beauty standing a few feet away.

"Yo, Shaun, you see anything you like?" Javon asked, coming up from the rear, breaking into his thoughts. "There's a cute brunette over there giving you the eye." He cocked his head toward a petite woman standing to his right.

Shaun gave the woman a brief look. Although she was attractive, he refocused his attention on the caramel beauty in white stilettos, who had moved back behind the counter. "Yeah, I want that one on the end."

Javon followed the direction of his gaze. "Damn! Now that sistah's hot as hell. But trust me, dude, she's not gonna to give you any play."

"Is that right?" Shaun replied. When his friend nodded, he added, "How about we put twenty on that?" He always loved a challenge.

Javon chuckled. "Fifty unless you're afraid you're gonna to lose."

"You're on." They shook on it, then Shaun took a deep breath and made his way over to the bar.

Simone was so busy she barely had time to think. She garnished what had to have been the tenth apple martini in the last half hour with a slice of apple and placed it on the bar. "That will be five dollars."

The woman handed her six ones. "Thanks."

As the woman slid off the bar stool and moved toward the dance floor, Simone noticed a man coming her way. The second she made eye contact, the air escaped her lungs in one big gush.

Damn!

The handsome stranger was looking at her as intently as she

was staring at him. He looked sexy as hell dressed in dark slacks and a cream-colored button-down shirt that showed off his tall athletic physique. There was something overpowering and aggressive about him and instead of backing away from it, she found herself drawn to it. Gulping, she reminded herself to breathe. Not stare like an idiot.

"What can I get you?" she asked, speaking loudly over the bass bouncing off the walls.

His eyes sparkled with humor. "Depends on what you're good at."

"I'm good at everything," she purred.

He smiled and she noticed the generous dimples at his cheeks "Good. Then there are two things you can get me—a Michelob, and your phone number."

Simone chuckled. "Let me get your beer." She turned and reached down into the cooler, conscious that he was staring at her ass. They all did. She definitely had plenty in the rear department. A quick glance over her shoulder revealed he had definitely noticed. Smiling, she reached for a bottle opener then turned and watched as his eyes traveled back up to her face. "That will be four dollars."

Shaun tossed a ten onto the counter. "Keep the change. Oh, yeah . . ." he began as he leaned across the counter. The position emphasized the thick muscles in his arms. "What about my other request?"

"What's that?" Simone asked, pretending she had no idea what he was talking about.

Interest sparkled in his eyes. "Your number, so I can take you to dinner tomorrow night."

His warm breath brushed across her face and his bold request made the muscles of her vagina tighten. Hell, the offer was tempting, and if she hadn't sworn off men, she would not have hesitated. But there was something unsettling about his eyes. It was as if he could see right through to her soul and that made her heart thump and her mouth go dry. In that instant she knew there was no way she could go out to dinner, fuck him, and simply walk away, her normal M.O. No, this instant attraction between them was much too strong to allow her to do that.

With an apologetic shrug she replied, "Sorry. Nothing personal, but I like my men like I like my coffee—strong and black." Enough said. She moved down to the other end of the bar to help another customer.

Javon was doubled over with laughter, as he'd obviously observed the entire exchange, when Shaun rejoined him. "Yo, Shaun, she told you."

Shaun wasn't fazed a bit as he brought the bottle to his lips. "Nah, I'll wear her down. I believe nothing ventured, nothing gained."

"You're not gonna do anything but make a fool of yourself," Javon said between chuckles. "Does she have to spell it out any clearer? She don't do the interracial thang."

"That's too bad." Because when Shaun looked at her he didn't see race. All he saw was a beautiful woman in four-inch stilettos and a body that screamed, "*Do me!*" He had come out tonight to meet her, and some way, somehow he was going to find a way to change her mind.

"Did he just ask you out?"
"Yep."
"And you turned *that* down?" Amber punched Simone lightly in the forearm. "What's wrong with you? He's gorgeous."
"Oww!" She rubbed her arm. "No offense but he's also white."
Amber pursed her lips and glared over at her. "If you haven't noticed, so am I. Since when has color been an issue?"

Simone gave her a dismissive wave. "It is when it comes to dating. It's too complicated."

"What's complicated about it?"

Simone didn't answer.

Amber frowned almost disapprovingly. "Race has got nothing to do with it and you know it. Don't I remember you mentioning once that you dated a white guy in college?"

Simone finished mixing the drink and didn't dare look at Amber because she would know she was lying. "That was a long time ago. People change."

"Uh-huh. We've been friends for too long. Being the wrong color is a lame excuse. Now come off it." She grabbed her arm. "Tell me what's really going on."

Glancing at her friend's questioning eyes, Simone sighed. There was no way she could let Amber know that just looking at him made her nipples hard and her kitty cat meow. "Okay, I'll admit I lied. But there is something about him I don't like."

"Could it be that a white boy has your juices flowing?"

Simone returned her grin. Amber was too smart for her own good.

"Come off it, Simone. He's gorgeous and you know it."

That was an understatement. He was *fine*. She sobered before saying, "It wouldn't work."

Amber frowned. "I don't get it. You've said you're not interested in a commitment. If that's true, what difference does it make what color he is? The only thing important is how much that gorgeous man is working with."

Simone's brow rose. "Speaking of dicks . . ." She purposely allowed her voice to trail off. "You know what they say about white boys."

Amber quickly wagged a finger in front of her face. "Uh-uh. Don't even start that mess about white men having small dicks. Michael's got more than any one man should be blessed with. Not that I'm complaining," she added with a light chuckle. "But don't forget I used to date David, who was black, and his dick was small enough to jack off with a pair of tweezers."

Laughing, Simone couldn't help gazing across the floor at her mystery man. He was talking to a black dude with a smooth bald head. Simone loved bald men but tonight he didn't do anything for her. The only thing she had eyes for was the man with the ponytail, standing beside him. His skin was dark, a strong olive. She couldn't tell if he was deeply tanned or whether it was his natural skin tone. Just watching him, her breathing became difficult. Her pussy pulsed and she could feel evidence of her arousal running down her inner thigh. *That's what you get for not wearing any underwear.* A customer waved for another round and she squeezed her thighs together, then moved to help him.

Even as she busied herself she was still utterly aware of the man barely twenty feet away. She knew every time he was staring at her because the hairs at the nape of her neck stood up and made her shiver inside. She couldn't help looking at him. Oh, he was definitely scrumptious. But she couldn't go there even if she wanted to. With one single glance, he had the ability to make her feel things that she didn't need to feel and that meant he was all wrong for her.

"This is DJ Rated R coming to you live from Situations Nightclub, the hottest spot on the South Side. We're about to slow it down and try to get a couple of love connections up in here, 'cause I got that Friday night fire! But first, let me introduce you to our lovely hostess, Simone Thomas. Simone, come on over and show us some love!"

Shaun was stunned when he saw the beauty from behind the bar sashay onto the stage. His dick bucked. She wasn't a barmaid, she was the owner.

"So tell us, Simone. You got a man?" the deejay asked.

Ignoring the catcalls and whistling, she shook her head. "Nope. I can't seem to find a man who can handle all this." She spun around to show what *all this* meant.

"That's a damn shame." DJ Rated R shook his head as his gaze raked her from head to toe. He then spoke softly into the microphone. "Tell me something . . . what's it gonna take for a man to get with yo fine ass?"

Simone took the mike, and a toe-curling smile claimed her lips. Shaun held his breath and waited.

"Well, Rated R, I'm gonna keep it real. I'm ready to put the vibrator away." She paused and gave a delightful giggle as the women surrounding the stage agreed. "I'm tired of faking it. I'm fienin' for a man who can satisfy me in and out of the bedroom."

"I know that's right!" a woman cried from the center of the crowd.

Simone laughed before continuing. "I tell you what. I've got a proposition for all your single listeners. I'll go out with any man who can tell me what B.S.A. stands for. If you can guess and you're up for the job, you'll get to spend the night with me." She handed the mike back to the deejay as loud murmurs spread across the floor.

"There you have it. Yo, fellas, you can have a night with this fine—and I do mean *fine*—honey. All you gotta do is tell us the meaning of B.S.A. What's it gonna be?"

All at once everyone started calling out possibilities. One short dude raced up to the stage and shouted, "Is it beautiful small ass?"

Simone turned around slowly and dropped a hand to her waist. "Do you see anything small about this?"

"Hell no!" someone shouted from across the club.

"Black sistah with ass!"

Again, she shook her head. Several more tried and didn't even come close. Shaun wasn't surprised. It just meant they weren't the man for the job.

From where he was standing, Shaun was close enough to see her face. Her eyes were wide, deep-set and chestnut brown. Her lush red lips were the color of cherries, plump and just as ripe. As she continued to stand there, listening to all of the pitiful answers, all he could think about was holding her in his arms while he licked and sucked her juicy lips. He wanted her and he wanted her now.

Shifting slightly, he wondered why he was feeling none of the hesitation he'd felt in the past about indulging in a one-night stand. Tonight, he wanted more than anything to bury his dick so far up inside her heat, he wouldn't know where she started and he ended. The overwhelming feeling was so unlike him. But he wasn't worried. Tonight he was going to allow his heart and mind to govern his actions.

After a few more tries, Simone waved to the crowd, then left the stage and headed back toward the bar. Shaun downed the rest of his beer in one swallow, then reached in his pocket for a stick of gum. "Excuse me, Javon. I've got some unfinished business to attend to."

His friend gave him a sympathetic smile. "Yo, Shaun, how many times she gotta tell you no, dude?"

"As long as it takes to get her to say yes."

Simone spotted him heading in her direction. Her pulse raced and breathing was now difficult to do. His muscular body moved with innate grace that made a woman pay attention. And his fine ass was definitely getting a lot of admiring looks. She swallowed as he moved close enough to brush against her knees, then gazed up at him with her mouth open like some starstruck teenager, which was so not her.

"Hey," he said in a husky voice that made her nipples tingle.

"Hello, would you like another drink?" she asked, shifting nervously from foot to foot.

He stepped closer. "No, I would rather have a dance."

Shivers coursed through her body as his minty-fresh breath played havoc with her mind. Simone glanced quickly over to the packed dance floor. The music had slowed down and hips were gyrating against each other. Swallowing, she declined. "I'm working."

His sexy lips curled in a playful grin. "I got the impression you were the owner."

"I am," she replied with a defiant tilt of her chin.

"Then you can take a break."

Quickly, she shook her head. "I don't think so." Needing to put some distance between them, Simone moved and retrieved a damp rag and started wiping off the bar. She watched the handsome stranger out of the corner of her eye and wondered why he was still standing there when she had made it boldly clear that he was not her type. He said nothing. Just stood there watching her.

Fine! Two could play that game.

While she worked, she took the opportunity to take a closer look at him. There was a small diamond stud in his left ear, and dimples that were visible even when he wasn't smiling. He had long, lush lashes, and sexy lips. Damn, she loved a man with nice lips. It took everything she had not to lean across the bar and press her mouth to his. *Girl, get it together.* Swallowing hard, she dropped her gaze to the counter. Yep. The man was all wrong for her.

She looked up again and found that he was still standing and waiting with his arms folded across his massive chest. He just stared and said nothing. Simone knew she should turn and go to the other end of the bar but her feet wouldn't move. Finally, unable to stand the tension, she asked, "Can I help you with something?"

"Yes. I'm waiting for you to get done so we can dance," he replied.

Simone dropped a hand to her waist. "Didn't I tell you I'm—"

"Go on, Simone, and dance," Amber intervened after ear-hustling on the conversation. She ignored Simone's frown and glanced over at the handsome stranger. "What's your name?"

"Shaun."

Her smile widened. "Well, Shaun, this is my boss, Simone. Simone, this is Shaun. Now that we're past the introductions, you're now permitted to take her out onto the floor," Amber said, pushing her from behind the bar.

Before Simone could object, Shaun took her hand and led her onto the crowded dance floor. As soon as he wrapped his arms around her, she forgot about being angry. Her body fit against him like a puzzle piece. A favorite Brian McKnight song was coming through the speakers and she closed her eyes and allowed Shaun to hold her tighter. Within seconds, a strong feeling of comfort cocooned itself around her. What she wouldn't give to be able to always feel this secure in her life . . .

Shaun was the first to speak. "So you've never dated a white man before?"

"Nope," she lied.

"That's too bad," he said close to her ear. "You have no idea what you're missing."

She blew out a disbelieving breath. "Can't miss what you've never had."

"There's always a first time for everything."

At the deep, sensual sound of his voice, Simone pulled back slightly. While gazing up at him, she felt a strong sensation that something was going to happen. Something exciting. Something amazing.

As if he could read her mind, he looked down into her eyes and said, "You're going to fall in love with me."

Simone sucked in a breath, surprised by the heat in his voice. She chuckled nervously, thinking he meant it as a joke. But the look on his face indicated he didn't. There was desire there. Only now it had intensified a hundred times over. After a brief, awkward silence she replied, "Sorry, Romeo. You can't find love unless you're looking for it. And I definitely ain't interested."

"What are you looking for?"

She shrugged. "At the moment, nothing more than a relationship that lasts as long as the moment. After an orgasm, I'm ready to move on to the next."

He chuckled as if he found her words amusing. "You can never find fulfillment that way. Sex has to start here." He gently thrust a finger to his chest. "Nothing beats love."

"That beer must have gone straight to your head," she said, trying to make light of the conversation.

"Nah. I know what I want and I won't settle for anything less."

"Well, then tell me. What is it that you want?"

"I want you. All of you."

He tilted her chin so she had to look directly at him. She didn't know why that tired line made her quiver. It was something about the way he said it that made it almost sounded true. Almost. "You're just trying to get between my legs."

Shaun ran the side of his large hand down her throat in a touch so soft the caress was lighter than a feather. The seriousness in both his tone and eyes made her uncomfortable. "Nope. I knew my wife was the one the instant I met her. And we were together until the day she died in my arms."

Her expression softened when she saw the pain in his eyes. "I'm sorry. What happened?"

"Breast cancer," he said barely above a whisper.

Simone stared up at him for a long moment before asking, "How long were you married?"

"Almost twelve years."

She leaned against his chest and rested her head on his shoulder. His voice and the emotions that shimmered in his eyes had said so much. He believed in love at first sight, a reason why he was wrong for her. But that did nothing to simmer down the attraction brewing inside. Lost in her thoughts, they fell silent until the beginning of the next song.

"You're beautiful," Shaun said, his voice thick and flirtatious.

"Thank you." She had heard the same compliment many times before but his soothing voice made the words sound extra special.

"What if I told you you're the first woman to make my dick hard in two years?"

Her jaw dropped open. Her kitty clenched. She was shocked and turned on by what he had said. Pulling back slightly, she stared up into his intense eyes. "What do you consider a dick?"

His jaw twitched. "Why don't you feel and find out?"

The other couples weren't looking at them. Boldly, Simone reached down and slid her hand across the zipper of his slacks. "Where is it?" she asked.

Shaun took her hand and guided it down toward his inner thigh. Almost halfway down his leg she found the head. She gasped. It was long. Thick. And hard as steel. The dampness between her legs grew warmer.

"That's eleven thick inches of pulsating dick that I'm ready to give you. All you have to do is say yes."

Oh, hell yes. She had to squeeze her lips tightly together to keep from blurting the words aloud. Dropping her hand, she moved it back to his waist as they swayed to the music. He pulled her closer and pressed the thickness against the juncture between her thighs.

"Speechless?" He chuckled lightly near her ear. "That's too bad. But fair is fair and now I get to touch you." He reached down between them and heat washed through her as his hand slipped beneath her short dress. Any second now and he was going to discover she wasn't wearing any panties.

Her knees shook as he pushed her thighs apart and rubbed against her wet pussy. Her lips parted, but instead of telling him no, she moaned. Boy, did it feel good. His fingers were warm and soothing to her ache. Skillfully, he parted her swollen folds and slid a finger inside.

"I want you to come on my finger so I can taste you on my tongue."

Oh, she was definitely coming. She rocked into him and followed his rhythm as his finger moved in and out. It definitely couldn't get any better than this, she thought, then he slipped another finger inside and plunged deeper. She closed her eyes, lost in the intense feeling spreading from the tips of her breasts down to her stomach and traveling lower. Simone knew she should tell him to stop, but she didn't want to, at least not yet.

"This is my pussy. No one will ever touch you here again but me." Heat rushed over her as he spoke just against her temple.

If anyone else had said those words, she would have deemed him a psycho, but not Shaun. She moaned against his ear while her nipples hardened against the fabric of her dress. It was his touch, his sexy whispering, and the feel of his warm breath against her cheek that had her turned on.

"You like that?"

"No," she whimpered.

"Quit lying," he said as he began to nibble on her ear, then dipped his tongue inside, matching the rhythm of his fingers. "You know that feels good."

She swallowed and fought for control. "I need to get back to work."

"Work can wait." With his thumb, he found her sensitized clit and rubbed against it. Her entire body trembled as he brushed it with the tip of his thumb. She arched against his hand and parted her legs even further, giving him complete and total access. The dance floor was too crowded for anyone to see.

"You want it?" he asked, his warm breath against her cheek as his thumb circled her clit. Once. Twice. Three times.

"Nooo," she purred.

"I told you to quit lying." He slipped a third finger in, increasing his rhythm. She rocked her hips to match his strokes. "I don't play games, baby. I want you. It's as simple as that. As simple as this . . ."

He thrust deeper and she cried out and clenched her nails into his arms. "Oh, yes!" Thank goodness, her cries were muffled by the loud music. Her head lolled back and her hips rocked to meet his fingers. Unconsciously she reached down and grabbed the bulge in his pants, yearning to feel it buried deep inside of her.

"It's yours. All you have to do is ask."

She knew Shaun well enough now to know he was serious. She tried to think of something sassy to say but her brain seemed to have totally shut down because it was blank. Then someone bumped her from behind. Simone's eyes flew opened and she realized the music had changed to a popular rap song. *What the hell am I doing?* She jumped away, but Shaun grabbed her before she could escape.

"Where's your office?" he asked.

"Back there."

He took her hand and with determined steps, led her through the crowd and down a hallway to the back of the club.

With her hand shaking, Simone punched the code to unlock her office and followed him inside. As soon as the door was shut, Shaun pulled her against him and claimed her mouth.

His mouth came down on hers, warm and so tempting a wave of hunger exploded through her body. *This can't possibly be happening.* He pulled her closer and then nibbled the corners of her mouth and cheeks before fusing firmly to her lips again. She tilted her head giving him greater access, then he pushed her lips apart and slipped his tongue inside. She savored the taste. *Delicious.*

Grabbing his shoulders, Simone welcomed his tongue, mating it with hers. She gave as good as she got and was rewarded for her efforts with a hand to her breast. He stroked and pinched her nipple, demanding access beneath her dress. She sucked in a breath. This was not supposed to be happening to her. She had never been drawn to a man this way, but there was something about him that defied logic. And, oh, did his hands feel good.

During the dance, she had wondered what his mouth would taste like and now she knew. The kiss went from gentle to possessive and her body continued to respond. His kiss tempted her to taste, and to feel everything about the man who held her gently. Simone held onto his forearms, appreciating the muscles beneath her fingertips. And when he moved to play with her other nipple, she dug her nails into his skin.

Trembling in his arms, she succumbed to the realization that this pleasure was beyond anything she had known. He had her doing things she never dreamed possible. She couldn't think straight and at the moment didn't care.

Shaun's hands traveled down past her waist, then he grabbed her ass and pressed her firmly against his arousal. "You feel that," he breathed against her nose. "That's what you do to me." He ground against her and she moaned on contact.

He had her so dizzy she had to hold on to keep from falling.

No man had ever kissed her this way before, and she knew that no other would ever kiss her this way again.

The kiss eventually came to an end when it became impossible to breathe. Shaun released a ragged breath and touched his forehead to hers. "Simone, you know something?" he asked, barely above a whisper.

She inhaled deeply, trying to catch her breath. "What?"

"The only reason why I haven't bent you over your desk and thrust my dick inside that sweet pussy of yours is because we've got plenty of time. I'm not going anywhere and neither are you," he said, then kissed her again.

Simone was totally at a loss for words. Fucking on her desk wasn't a bad idea. She knew she wouldn't be disappointed.

There was no telling what she might have said if the phone hadn't interrupted them. She pulled back, ending the kiss, but made no effort to pick up the receiver.

They were both breathing hard. Shaun watched her as if waiting for a reaction. He would be waiting a long time. She was completely floored by her horny behavior. Wasn't it just last night that she was riding little Bernard? It wasn't like she was lacking, although in Bernard's case, and the several before him, maybe so. Her shoulders sagged with frustration. *Damn, I'm fienin' for some real dick.* No wonder she had given in to the stranger's lips and hands.

Glancing up at him, she saw the longing. There was no way to undo what had happened. All she could do was make sure it never happened again. Silently, she was thankful she'd had the self-control not to slip her dress off and bury all eleven inches deep inside her pussy, right there on her desk. Instead, she stepped away from him and attempted to stand on her own. The dizziness had nothing to do with regrets and everything to do with the heat still flowing through her body and the cum running down her inner thighs.

His eyes were simmering with a promise that went beyond kissing. And damn, was she tempted. Her body was in desperate need of some satisfaction. But right now she was going to have to settle for her vibrator because being with this man was a risk she just wasn't prepared to take.

Shaun must have felt her anxiety because he reached out and cupped her face with his hands. He studied her eyes for a long moment before finally breaking the silence. "Whatever it is, we can work it out. Nothing or no one is going to keep me from you."

Simone shook her head. Damn, she wished it was that easy but what he wanted was impossible. "It won't work. I can't get involved with you."

His smile was slow and determined. "We're already involved, Simone. And now that I've tasted your mouth and your sweet cum on my lips there is no way I can do without. We'll find a way to get past your inhibitions, together." He pulled her into his arms again and placed a possessive kiss to her lips. Once again her body automatically responded to his. "All I want is your heart."

What he wanted she couldn't give. She pushed away from him and stepped back. She wished that she was willing to risk her heart again but she couldn't. "I've enjoyed your company but I need to get back to work."

He chuckled lightly. "I guess that's your way of telling me the party is over."

She couldn't even look at him. "I've got a business to run."

Reaching out, he caressed her cheek. "I'll give you a few days to think about everything I've said. Please keep in mind that I won't accept no as an answer." Leaning forward, he briefly pressed his lips to hers once more. "Goodnight, Ms. Thomas."

Simone opened her mouth, determined to make it clear that there was absolutely nothing going on between them. But she couldn't make the words come out so she pursed her lips and watched as he left her office.

The moment he shut her door, she slipped a hand under her dress and stroked her throbbing clit. He had her so turned on. With her other hand, she cupped her breast and worked at her nipple through the material. Moans slipped past her lips as she thrust her fingers deep within her wet kitty. Closing her eyes, she imagined that it was his dick buried inside. And what a dick it was. Thick. Long. Oh, what a ride it would be. She stroked hard and a scream began to build that raced through her body until her muscles tightened and clamped around her fingers like a fist. She bucked upward.

Remembering his smile, her body begun to rage its hunger again and she leaned back against her desk and sucked in a large breath as an orgasm shuddered through her body. When her breathing began to slow, she opened her eyes and moved on wobbly legs around her desk and lowered onto her seat.

For the next few minutes she tried to pull herself together. For once it wasn't regret that she felt, it was confusion. Simone leaned back in the chair. Tears pricked behind her eyelids. What in the world had she been thinking? Sure, she had flings all the time, but never at her nightclub. She didn't believe in mixing business with pleasure. It caused too many complications. But she was powerless around him. Simone knew that the exact moment she spotted him walking toward the bar. Usually she walked away feeling nothing, but this time her body hungered for more. With his scent on her skin and the taste of him on her lip, she released a shuddering breath and dropped her head to the desk. *Damn, that man!*

Her phone rang, startling her. She took a second to gather her composure and grabbed the receiver.

"Hey girl! I heard your proposition over the radio."

Her shoulders sagged with relief. It was her best friend, Lilliana. "Then I guess you also heard how many men tried and failed. At least I got a packed house tonight."

"Maybe you'll get lucky and someone will figure it out."

"No one is gonna figure out B.S.A. means big spankable ass. I've been running a personal ad for weeks and no one has even come close to guessing."

Lilliana laughed. "Now that it's on the radio, every horny man in the city of Chicago is gonna try to get a night between them caramel thighs."

"Good luck." She blew out a frustrated breath. "Damn, what's it gonna take for a girl to get a spanking these days?"

After ending the call, Simone lowered her elbows onto the desk while thinking about Shaun. She liked what she saw. What she had felt. She'd do anything to be able to love someone like him, but she couldn't. Lowering her head to her hands, she closed her eyes and tried not to remember but the memories never ceased. She could still hear her fiancé moaning and groaning only seconds before she had stepped into the room to find him stroking deeply inside another man's ass. At that exact moment, her whole world shattered. Her dreams of spending a perfect life with the only man she had loved were over.

Tears flowed down her cheeks. Cedric had moved on, accepting his sexuality. He was living a life with his lover, while she was fucking a different man every week, unwilling to risk her heart to another. She couldn't keep living like this. Something had to change. Dropping her head, she let heavy sobs break free. Simone knew it was time to leave the past in the past and find a way to move on with her life, no matter how scary it may be. *Yeah, right.* That was easier said than done.

Shaun stood outside the door. He was about to knock when he heard the sobs and froze. Someone had hurt her badly. Who, he wondered. He wanted to go to her, to kiss her tears away. To comfort her, but knew she wouldn't want that. Not yet. But soon. He was going to make certain of that.

As he reluctantly moved away from the door, despite the strong need to protect her, he felt a surge of excitement. He couldn't believe it! B.S.A meant big spankable ass. Simone wanted a spanking. He would have to give her exactly what she needed. With a determined smile, he moved down the hall toward the door.

3

It was all over the radio. Men were calling the station constantly trying to guess the meaning of B.S.A. In fact, the contest had gotten so hot, Beemster Travels was giving away a trip to Daytona Beach for Simone and the lucky winner.

She sat behind her desk listening to the radio, not believing how many horny men were trying to win. The entire city was intrigued by the outcome. Nibbling nervously on her lip, she was starting to worry that someone might figure it out. *Damn!* She definitely wasn't trying to go away for the weekend with some strange man. Simone raised her hands to her face and groaned. It was all her fault.

Several months ago, she and two of her best friends, Lilliana and Melinda, had come up with the ridiculous idea to find a man who could handle a big spankable ass. Keeping their personal safety in mind, each had agreed to post an ad and if anyone was lucky enough to figure out what B.S.A. meant, then they were obligated to go out with the lucky winner. First date in a public place. In daylight. No hopping into a stranger's car. No identifying personal information until the vibe was right.

Of course Simone was well-known, which made her situation trickier.

Lilliana had posted an ad in the newspaper while Melinda had placed her ad over the Internet. The only reason why Simone announced it over the radio was because she figured the chances of anyone figuring out what B.S.A. stood for were slim to none. Now she wasn't so sure. If she could get out of it, she would, but the radio producer had called and asked for the correct answer just so she couldn't change her answer at the last minute. In exchange, Simone had set Friday at midnight as the contest deadline. By the time the club closed Friday night, she would be able to breathe easily again.

For the next hour, Simone tallied receipts from the weekend and listened to the latest round of contestants. Bodacious scrumptious ass? She chuckled, then sighed with relief. She had absolutely nothing to worry about.

She resumed working and found her mind wandering back to Friday night and the sexy, olive-colored man. It had been four days and she still remembered that kiss. Hell, she still couldn't believe she let Mr. Sexy fingerfuck her amidst dozens of couples. She was a freak, but that went way out of her scope. *How stupid.* Someone could have seen her.

Simone took a deep breath and turned off the radio, needing just a few moments of peace and quiet to think. What in the world was she thinking? She had allowed a stranger to play with her pussy just because she hadn't had any qualified dick in months. She didn't know anything about Mr. Sexy except what he had told her and for all she knew he could have been feeding her a bowl full of lies. His wife could still be alive and he could also have a handful of kids. But as she stared up at the pastel border that circled her office, she knew there was something about him that told her he wasn't lying. Simone gave a frustrated groan. *What in the world was his name?* Shane? Shannon? Oh, God, what did it matter? She'd probably never see him again.

She pushed back from her computer and closed her eyes. Mr. Sexy's face wouldn't go away. Despite the risks that she took, she was drawn to him. The attraction had been overpowering and so unnatural for her. The first sight of him had been like a magnet pulling her in. Maybe it was because she had never met a white man with such a confident attitude. She found him intriguing.

Rubbing her hand across her temple, Simone took a deep breath, waiting for the pounding to go away. Fantasies of wild sex and heat had been filling her mind since the night they met and her head was starting to hurt from thinking about what's-his-name all the time. She couldn't remember his name but she hadn't forgotten his fingers. Magical. And she knew damn well if they ever crossed paths again, she'd want an instant replay. The man filled her thoughts and dreams. Although he had a big long dick that she would love to ride, her lack of good sex had very little to do with it. What intrigued her most was his personality.

Simone dropped her hand to her lap. Slowly she opened her eyes and images of Mr. Sexy finally began to fade. It didn't matter how good he had made her feel because it would never happen again.

Shaun couldn't stop thinking about Simone. He leaned back in his leather chair with his fingers laced behind his head and let out a heavy sigh. What had happened to him? After one evening, he couldn't get her off his mind. Her smile. Her scent. Visions of her were racing wildly through his brain. He was starting to understand how a schizophrenic felt.

Closing his eyes, he took a deep breath. He had piles of work to complete. As an architect for his father's company,

Dutton Custom-Built Homes, he had an eight-thousand-square-foot home to design by the end of the month, but he couldn't focus.

His stomach growled and he realized he'd forgotten to go to lunch. Frustrated and hungry, he realized he'd been forgetting a lot of things lately. All he could think about was Simone and the way she had felt in his arms, against his lips, and tasted on his tongue. The way she made his dick twitch.

"How about handing over the fifty dollars you owe me? My pockets are light. Us architects don't get paid enough."

Opening his eyes, he saw Javon standing in his doorway grinning from ear to ear.

Since it wasn't anyone's business but his own, he hadn't bothered to share the particulars of the other night with Javon. Not that his friend and colleague had noticed. By the time Shaun had come back from Simone's office, Javon was nowhere to be found. Obviously he'd hooked up with some honey he'd met and left for the nearest motel.

Shaun rolled his chair close to his desk. "I haven't lost yet."

"Yet?" Javon's eyes grew round with amusement. "Man, you lost the minute you left the club without her number."

Shaun arched an eyebrow. "How would you know? You weren't even there."

"Yeah, well, I was down the street getting these balls licked," Javon said and gripped his crotch.

"I just bet."

"Okay, so pay up."

Shaun gave him a long, thoughtful look. "Nah. I'm about to win." He picked up the phone.

"Who you calling?"

Ignoring Javon's question, Shaun spun around in his chair and faced the window. It wasn't long before he heard someone pick up the receiver.

"WGCI contest line, what's your answer?"

"Is it Big Spankable Ass?"

"Who am I speaking with?"

"Shaun Dutton."

"Shaun Dutton . . . you just won an all-expenses-paid week-end to Daytona Beach with Simone Thomas! What station hooked you up?"

"WGCI."

After he gave the station his information, Shaun hung up and grinned at Javon, who was standing there with his mouth wide open.

"Oh my God! Simone, are you listening to the radio?"

She had barely put the phone to her ear when her childhood friend started yelling in her ear. "No, Melinda. I'm working and turned the radio off. Why, what's up?"

"Someone just guessed what B.S.A. means!"

Simone dropped the pen from her hand. "You're kidding."

"No, I'm not. Some guy named Shaun Dutton just gave the correct answer."

"Shaun?" she repeated. Why did that name sound familiar?

"Yes, Shaun. The two of you are going to Daytona Beach next weekend."

Oh damn, she had to spend the weekend with a total stranger.

Melinda was cracking up. "I guess you're going to get that spanking after all."

It wasn't long after she hung up that the radio station contacted her with the news. Simone faked surprise, then slumped down in her chair. Shaun Dutton. Who the hell was that? she wondered. Leaning her head back, she wanted to scream. What in the world had she been thinking to come up with the stupid idea in the first place? What if the winner was crazy in the wrong way? Hell, she'd have the club bouncers jack him up and leave him in the gutter. Not a good plan. But better than nothing. Damn.

While working on next week's beer order, she tried to find a bright side to this whole mess. At least the publicity had been good for business. Last Saturday's crowd had been even better than Friday's. Hopefully, with word of mouth, business would continue to increase. With a heartfelt sigh, she rested her elbow on the desk and tried to picture what Shaun Dutton would look like. But no matter how hard she tried to put a face to the name, all she saw was the man from Friday night. Closing her eyes, she could still feel his fingers buried deep inside of her pussy. She had used her vibrator the last two nights, pretending it was his big, fat dick.

"Hello, beautiful."

Simone looked up and gasped. It was *him*. She gazed into his eyes and swallowed. *Lord, have mercy.* The other night the room had been too dark but now she could see his eyes were clear and leaf green, surrounded by the thickest lashes. She tried to pretend his appearance had no effect on her, but she would be lying if she did. "Hey."

He gave her a sexy, dimpled smile that instantly made her pulse race. "A little birdie told me we're spending the weekend at the beach."

Her heart hammered. His name was Shaun! How in the world could she have forgotten? Amber had introduced him to her at the club—and oh, that dance. She'd almost forgotten her own damn name after he was done with her. She stared at him for a long moment with her chin resting in the palm of her hand. "How did you know what B.S.A. meant?"

"Baby, it was easy. All I had to do was look down at that big spankable ass of yours."

She couldn't help blushing. "Shaun," she began slowly. "You take pleasure in making me nervous."

"I already told you, I know what I want."

"And that is?"

"You." He walked towards her, never taking his eyes from her. "I want you."

Simone shook her head, wondering what on earth she was going to do with this man. She had one idea but that would just get her in way over her head. "We need to get something straight."

"And what's that?" he asked as he moved behind her desk and took a seat on the edge.

"You think because you won the contest, I will now change my mind about you and spend a weekend on the beach together. But it won't work."

Shaun lifted a brow. "It won't?"

"No. So please don't waste your time. I'm sure there are lots of other women who would love to go out with you."

"But not you?"

She shook her head. "No, not me. I thought I had made myself clear about the reason why I won't get involved with you. It's nothing against you personally, but I have this hang-up about dating out of my race."

He nodded but she could tell by the way he looked, it didn't matter what she said. He was going to hear only what he wanted to hear. He took her hand and pulled her up from her chair. As soon as she moved, Shaun took her seat and lowered Simone onto his lap. She started to protest but he placed a finger over her mouth.

"Shhh! How you feel doesn't matter anymore."

She pushed his hand away. "It doesn't?"

"Nope," he said and placed his hands at her waist. "The radio station ran the contest, and I won, which means we *will* be spending the weekend in Florida together."

Her forehead bunched in a frown. She couldn't believe he could be that stubborn. "I'm going to Florida, but only because if I don't, it will be bad for my business. However, once we get there, I plan on getting another room."

His hand slid beneath her blouse and grazed her bare skin. "Afraid to be alone with me?" he whispered close to her ear.

Goose bumps popped up on her skin. His hand was creating havoc with her control. Shaun was right. She was more afraid of what she might let him do if she was alone with him. The attraction between them was too strong to ignore and that was a problem. "No, I'm not afraid of you."

"I think you are. I think you are afraid of what I plan to do to you." His tongue rimmed her earlobe.

She gasped at the contact. "And what's that?" she dared to ask.

Releasing her ear, Shaun reached up and cupped her chin, then turned her head so their noses were almost touching. "I want you to forget what it's like not to have me inside you." He reached under her blouse again, this time higher. Simone didn't move. Her eyes had grown large and round and she could barely breathe.

He cupped her breast possessively. "I know you want me." He leaned forward and pressed his lips to the side of her neck. "Have you been thinking about me?" He kissed her skin and more goose bumps appeared. "I've been thinking about you. How good it had felt being inside you."

Her entire body stirred all the way down to her toes when she remembered what happened the last time they were together. And as much as she wanted to deny it, her body wanted it to happen again.

"Unfasten your bra."

Simone didn't even bother protesting because her nipples were stiff and screaming for his touch. Reaching behind her, she unhooked her bra and freed the twins.

"Nice."

Shaun caressed her breasts and teased her nipples and she flinched. Staring into his eyes, she sucked in a deep breath and her lips parted. He lowered his mouth and pressed his lips firmly against hers.

She was in trouble. He was making her feel things that she had no business feeling. As soon as she gave him her heart and thought that maybe she had a chance at love again, he would hurt her. She didn't want to like him but she did. All sorts of warning bells were going off in her head. *Run while you still can!* The two of them weren't right for each other and the sooner he saw that the better. Even if he did feel so damn good between her legs.

"You're going to fall in love with me and there is nothing you can do to stop that, Simone," he whispered against her lips between kisses.

This was the second time she'd heard his warning and it had the same effect on her. The seriousness in both his tone and his eyes changed the rhythm of her heartbeat. There was no way she could ignore the desire flowing through her body. To top things off, a sexy smile turned the corners of his lips upward. He lowered his hand and slid beneath her skirt, then tugged her panties down past her knees.

"While in Florida . . . no panties. I want to be able to touch you whenever I want to." In one swift motion, he lifted her up onto the desk, tossed her panties to the floor, and then got between her legs. Her skirt was up past her waist, her legs spread and her pussy exposed. Shaun wasn't being shy about looking at her. Self-consciously, she tried to lower her skirt, but he grabbed her wrist. "Don't. I want to look at you."

He leaned forward until his mouth was only inches from the tangle of dark curls and blew a kiss. Simone began to squirm. "Shaun, this isn't the time or place."

His gaze shot up to her face. "No time like the present." He rose and pressed his weight against her. Tilting his head, he bit down, capturing both her blouse and nipple in his mouth. Simone arched her back and cried out. "Shaun!"

"That's it, baby. Surrender to me."

He released her, then traveled over and clamped down on

the other nipple. Reaching up, he squeezed them together and suckled one, then the other. He used his fingers and thumbs to tease her breasts until her hard chocolate nipples were exposed through her wet blouse. She quivered and moaned and he watched the expressions on her face. He would just have to do everything he could to get her to see that things between them were meant to be.

Abandoning her breasts, Shaun slipped his hands down over her hips. He lowered into the chair and draped her legs over his shoulder. With her pussy right in his face, he blew on her clit. Simone gave a startled cry. He then leaned forward, found her open and inserted his tongue.

"Oh, yesss!" she cried and arched off the desk.

She made mewing sounds that skimmed through his chest, settling at his groin. He dipped in and out, penetrating her with his tongue while he pressed his thumb to her clit and stroked. While still using his tongue he slipped a finger inside her. She was hot and wet, and whimpering. He felt the shudders begin and slid his mouth upward and captured her clit between his lips. Gently, he nibbled, then sucked.

"Shaun, please," she begged. "Fuck me!"

"All in due time," he said as he gritted his teeth. Despite his dick being hard enough to send a baseball flying across the park, he wasn't ready yet to slide all eleven inches into her damp, hot pussy. He would save that moment until he had her on a bed with her legs spread wide. Right now it was all about making her feel good.

He slid three fingers deep inside her and watched her head roll back and her eyes close. With one hard suck to her clit, an orgasm hit her hard and fast. She thrashed on the desk while he continued to work her until the last spasm drifted away.

Shaun rose, removed his wet fingers and slipped them into his mouth one after the other. Between moans, he licked every drop of her sweet cum from his fingers.

Her heavy lids finally opened and Simone stared up at him looking down at her. He cupped her face. "I want it to always be like this between us. I want to take you out to dinners and movies. I want to lie on the couch together with you in my arms, talking and getting to know you. Really know you. And as soon as the time is right, I want to buy you the biggest diamond in the store, and make you my wife, the mother of my children, and love you the way you deserve to be loved." His words were a cross between a promise and a plea. His eyes were intense and dead serious.

Oh boy. Shaun was making it so difficult for her to say no. Yes, they had a strong sexual attraction but that was all there was between them. What would happen after the sex wore off? She already knew the answer to that question. He would break her heart just like Cedric had.

Needing to put some distance between them, Simone finally slid off the desk. "Fine," she said between breaths. She was just going to have to show him. "You think you want me, yet you don't know anything about me. So why don't we find out what's what? Let's go out tomorrow night. My pick."

"You're on," he said with a lopsided grin.

4

Shaun pulled into the parking lot and glanced up at the flashing neon sign. EXXXTASY. No way. Their first date and Simone had taken him to a strip club.

Giggling, Simone climbed out of his Lexus. She was getting a kick out of coming here. *I can tell*, he thought with a deep, uneasy breath. Watching a bunch of sweaty, naked women dance across a stage had never been his thing, but if a strip club was what Simone wanted, then a strip club was what she would get. After all, he had agreed to let her pick the place.

Shaun turned the car off and got out just as she was coming around to her side.

"Come on, slowpoke," she said, voice bubbling with energy. "Tonight's swingers' night."

Was that bit of information supposed to have made a difference? Leaning against the hood of his car, he watched Simone sway toward the door. When she realized he wasn't following, she paused midstride and looked back at him. "Don't tell me you're scared."

His eyes lowered to the T-shirt that strained against her

round breasts and left her midriff open for the appreciative eye. He knew for certain she was not wearing a bra because her chocolate nipples were hard and visible. The short blue jean skirt she wore barely covered her assets and showed long, shapely caramel legs that traveled all the way down to a pair of red stilettos. She looked sexy as hell and knew it. In that outfit she could have easily climbed onto any stage and . . . No, that couldn't be the case. Simone wasn't a stripper. She had too much class.

Swinger? He swallowed a heavy lump in his throat. She didn't honestly expect him to fuck some stranger, or even worse, sit back and let some man slide his dick inside her while he watched. Studying Simone's face, he noticed the devious smirk. She was trying to intimidate the hell out of him. He chuckled inwardly. Well, she was in for a surprise because that was not going to happen.

"If you're scared, we don't have to go in," he heard her say.

Shaun swiftly moved over to where she was standing, leaned forward and kissed her neck. "I'm not scared of anything."

"Good," she purred. "Then step into my world."

He followed the sway of her big spankable ass toward the door. Together they stepped inside and his eyes immediately traveled around the large nightclub. Topless women were on platform stages, dancing suggestively. Below, couples were bumping and grinding on the dance floor. As they maneuvered their way through the thick crowd, Shaun couldn't believe what he saw. Without ceremony, a man bent a woman over the banister, surrounding the dance floor, and after lifting her skirt, thrust his meat inside of her. Another woman had a man pumping her from behind while at the same moment she took another man's dick into her mouth. To his right, two women were eating each other out. Others were in corners fucking. Lesbians, bisexual and even married couples thronged the club. Moans and cries echoes around him and the distinct scent of sex filled the air. Watching the group stroking and licking each other to orgasms, he realized this place was one big orgy.

Simone moved across the room, waving and saying hello. A few even called her personally by name. What the hell . . . he'd been to strip clubs before but never anything like this. And definitely not one where anyone knew him by name.

"Are you a regular?" he finally asked over the loud pop music blaring from a nearby speaker.

Simone gave him a wicked smile and nodded. Before he could ask her if she ever participated, she took him by the hand and led him over to the bar where a topless waitress with round pink nipples brought them both a Corona with lime.

"You want to dance?" Simone asked him, after she lifted the waitress's skirt and slipped three dollars in her G-string.

Shaun brought the bottle to his lips, then gazed over at the crowd of half-naked people dancing and doing each other, and shook his head.

"Then have a seat and watch the show," she cooed.

Carrying both bottles, Shaun found an empty table close to the dance floor and took a seat. He watched as Simone rolled her hips to the beat of the music. Her moves were sexy and seductive and he couldn't take his eyes off of her. Leaning back in his chair, he sipped his beer, and watched the show, getting even more turned on by the minute.

Simone gave him a come-fuck-me look as she caressed her body, sliding her hands down across her breasts to her belly button and hips. She was definitely enticing. Turning her back to him, she bent over and touched her knees while bobbing her round ass. Her hands slowly came around to lift the back of her skirt and Shaun almost came out the chair when he noticed her bare ass in a red thong. Holy shit! He was tempted to move onto the dance floor and show her exactly where she could back that thing up, but decided to hold his horses and enjoy some more of the show.

Two gorgeous blondes swayed over to where Simone was dancing and made a sandwich. One in the front. The other in the back. They rocked their hips and rubbed on each other. The blonde from behind ran a hand down Simone's belly. The other's mouth hovered naughtily behind her ear. The entire time Simone kept her eyes fixed on his face, gauging his reaction. Oh boy, he was definitely *reacting*. His dick had sprung to life. Watching the three of them together was better than a damn video.

"Take your shirt off!" Shaun yelled across the stage.

Simone took her time toying with her T-shirt, then slowly lifted the material just long enough for him to see she wasn't wearing a bra. His mouth hung open at the sight of her succulent breasts. They were full. Ripe. Dark chocolate nipples sitting high. They were beautiful and belonged in his mouth.

As if the blonde in front had read his mind, she lifted the shirt over Simone's head and tossed it over onto his lap. Shaun caught it without his eyes leaving the trio. When he had asked her to take off her shirt, he never expected her to go through with it. Damn, he was turned on by her bold behavior. It turned him on even more knowing she had a naughty side.

The blonde in front reached up and cupped Simone's breast. She rolled the nipple between her fingers, tweaking it until Simone's eyelids fluttered shut with pleasure. The other woman moved around and took a nipple in her mouth. Simone tossed her head back in heaven. Shaun gripped the edge of the chair and had to force himself to sit still. He released a low groan of appreciation. He wanted those big sweet breasts over here where he could touch them.

Taste them.

He unzipped his fly and freed his dick through the opening in his boxers and began to stroke it. Simone's eyes were fixed on him again. When she noticed what he was doing, a wicked smiled curled her succulent lips.

Being here, watching the three of them, was so un-fucking-believable. It reminded him of his wild high school days and ménage à trois fantasies. But now he couldn't dream of sharing his woman with anyone. Man or woman.

"Come here," he demanded while still holding his dick firmly in his hand. He wanted her on his lap, straddling him.

After saying goodbye to the two blondes, Simone swayed her hips in his direction and stopped barely a foot in front of him. "What can I do for you, boo?"

Shaun was so hard, he was ready to explode, but he would allow the moment to build a little longer before he'd plunged into her deep, warm pussy. Gazing up hungrily at her breasts, he shifted uncomfortably on the chair, and wonderful how far she was willing to go. "For starters, how about a lap dance?" he said.

"Coming right up."

Slowly, she swayed her hips in front of him while squeezing her breasts together. His breathing quickened as his eyes traveled from her face down to the stilettos that made her legs look a mile long. He released his dick and it stood up straight. Glancing up, he found Simone staring down at his meat while running her tongue slowly across her bottom lip. His dick pulsed. He had never been so sexually excited in his life.

Simone straddled him. She slid her way down his body and glided her bare breasts across his chest in a tortuously slow motion that was killing him softly. At the same time, her tongue trailed along his face.

Damn, she had skills. The look in her eyes said she knew what she was doing. She rocked against him. Her breasts bounced with every move and Shaun had to clench his teeth. Her big ass was doing wicked things against his groin. It had been too long. His balls were swollen, begging for release.

In time with a slow jam, Simone rocked against his erection. Her breasts were only inches from his face. Leaning forward,

Shaun drew a dark nipple into his mouth, then suckled hungrily. She moaned. Oh, man, they tasted as good as they looked. He gently bit down and she arched her back and leaned closer. Finally, he moved to the other breast and nibbled some more while Simone rubbed her pussy against his rock-hard dick. Her seductive lap dance was driving him crazy.

"Take off your skirt," he said as he struggled for air.

Simone rose, lowered the zipper and allowed the skirt to hit the floor, then kicked it away. Shaun gazed at the thong, which left very little to the imagination, and drew in a sharp intake of air.

"You like this?"

Her question inflamed him. His breath caught in his throat, cutting off his ability to think straight. "Like it? Hell, I love it." He reached up and squeezed her breasts, one in each hand. "And I'm going to love something else even more."

She gave a small laugh, then began dancing seductively again. His dick twitched, causing him to shift uncomfortably on the chair. She was doing an amazing job of teasing him. Hell, her moves were as good as any one of the strippers on the platform stage.

"You seem to be enjoying yourself. You been here before?"

Shaun shook his head. "Nope. But there's a first time for everything. Although you could have danced for me at your place."

Playfully, she wagged a finger, replying in a scolding voice, "Shame on you. The purpose of swinging is for us to meet other people."

To hell with that idea. "The only person in this place I'm interested in is you. What about you? You swing before?"

While still gyrating her hips, she winked and said, "I'll never tell."

Leaning forward, Shaun pulled her closer and slid the thong down over her hips. She tried to stop him, but he brushed her hands aside. Soon she was naked. "Come here, babe. It's been too long. I need to be inside you, now."

Simone took his hand and led him over to a private booth at the corner of the room. He didn't care who saw his dick hanging out of his pants because in a few minutes he was going to bury it inside her hot, wet pussy.

"Sit," she ordered.

Obediently, he lowered onto the chair. He then tried to pull her down onto his lap, but she stopped him with a hand to his shoulder and a firm, "I'm running this."

Simone let her hand drift down along his chest to the head of his dick, and he jerked under her touch. "Careful," he warned. "Otherwise it's going to be over before we get started."

She smiled and slowly slid her thumb across the head again and released a little pre-cum. "Don't worry, boo. I've got you covered."

She gave him a firm squeeze and he came off the seat. When he thought he couldn't take any more, she wrapped her fingers around his dick. He exhaled sharply. *Oh, shit.* He would explode with just the right touch.

"How long has it been?" she asked.

"Too long."

He raised his hips off the chair and Simone slid his pants down to his knees. His boxers went along with them, and every muscle in his body went rigid. "Take your shirt off," she said. He grabbed the T-shirt, pulled it over his head, and sent it flying. Where? He didn't care. When he tried to reach for her, she caught his hands and placed them against the sides of the chair.

He shook his head. "Simone, you can't expect me not to touch you."

"Yes I can," she whispered.

With a groan, he dropped his head back against the wall. He wasn't in the mood for teasing. He was ready to fuck. His dick stood upright like a flagpole. When Simone finally touched him again, his hips bucked off the chair. He could anticipate what would happen next. She cradled the base of his dick and slid her fist from the bottom to the throbbing red tip. Shaun dipped his head back and groaned.

"Straddle me," he commanded in a rough voice. But instead of granting his wish, Simone dropped to her knees in front of him. He spread his legs and she crawled closer with her gaze fixed on his pulsing dick. Her tongue slid over her bottom lip as if imagining how he would taste. His breath hissed through his teeth.

She took him in her hand again, her fingers teasing the tip, eliciting drops of pre-cum. His dick throbbed against her fingers and she continued to tease him. His need to be inside her was raging out of control. She gave him a smug half-smile, then slowly lowered her head. His hands left the chair and his fingers sank into her honey-brown curls, pushing her gently downward.

"I want to feel your lips wrapped around my dick."

She dipped her head then glanced up at him, her eyes shining with passion. "I've been waiting all night to do this." Before he could reply, she took him in her mouth. She teased the head, never taking in his fullness. Her tongue rolled around the tip, gathering droplets of pre-cum.

"Oh yeah. That's it," he said. It was even better than in his dreams.

She hesitated, then she let her tongue glide across his dick until she reached the head. She licked him, and he delved his hands into her hair. This was like a dream. Here he was in front of dozens of people, getting head from the most beautiful woman in the building.

His woman.

Simone opened her mouth and suckled up one side and then the other like he was a Popsicle on a hot summer afternoon.

"Damn, you got skills." The pleasure was so intense. Both

of his hands grabbed on to her hair, and he again came off the chair. He fought the urge to pump his hips skyward, driving himself even deeper into that luscious mouth. Cries of passion filled the room around him and all he cared about was the woman kneeling before him. He didn't take his eyes off her. Finally when he didn't think he could take a second more of the torture, Simone took him completely in her mouth to the back of her throat while her fingers squeezed his balls. Shaun had to hold on to the chair again to keep from collapsing from pleasure.

The sucking intensified. Up and down, then almost all the way out before she swallowed all of him again. Her head bobbed. His hips pumped. Having his dick sucked felt good, but he'd rather cum inside some hot pussy.

"Grab that condom out of my wallet."

She released him and fumbled around in his pockets before finding the green foil wrapper. "Now what?" she asked, gazing up at him with innocent eyes.

"Slide it on."

Simone tore open the package and Shaun ground his teeth and tried to restrain himself while she rolled it over his swollen dick. Once the condom was on, he reached down and pulled her onto the chair. She spread her legs wide to straddle his hips.

"Do you want me, Simone?" he asked.

"Yes," she groaned. Her lips were moist. Her eyes glazed.

"How do you want me?"

"Inside me," she whispered. "Deep inside me."

Moving a hand between them, he slid a finger across her clit. "Here?"

"Oh yes! Right there," she cried and rubbed her wet pussy against the palm of his hand.

"Tell me you never danced for another man like that," Shaun growled as he lifted her hips and positioned her over him. "Tell me!"

"You were my first," she panted.

No sooner than the words were out of her mouth, he plunged inside her.

"Shaun!" she gasped.

"I'm right here, baby."

Her body clenched around him each time he drove upward. Her legs were spread wide to accommodate every throbbing inch. Leaning forward, he kissed her deeply. She pushed her fingers through his hair and fisted the thick dark strands. As he plunged, Shaun felt her juices coating him. She was so wet. The pressure inside him was nearly overwhelming.

Simone's brown eyes were dazed with passion. "You feel *soooooo* good," she panted. She took over and rode him with her heavy breasts jiggling. She caught the chair behind his head and pumped harder. All the time, he held her steady by her hips.

"Fuck!" he hissed. Thrusting upward, he met each stroke, loving the way she looked as she took him in her body. Shaun knew their lovemaking could be seen from around the room, but he didn't give a damn. He was with Simone Thomas, and she was his.

While she rode faster, he reached down, slipped his thumb over her clit and rubbed. She screamed. Two more pushes, and her body quivered. Shaun met her eyes as he pounded inside her heat and took her over the edge. She cried out. Her pussy squeezed him tightly, and he called out her name as he came. With an expulsion of air, they collapsed in exhaustion on the chair. With a groan, Shaun waited for the room to stop spinning.

"Damn, baby," he finally said. "Anytime you want to come back, just let me know."

Simone laughed, then pulled back slightly and looked him in the eyes. "That wasn't the reaction I had expected. I was trying to scare you away."

"I know." He then captured her lips in a passionate slow kiss.

An hour later, Shaun pulled in front of Simone's condo and walked her to the door. As soon as the key was in the lock, she turned around.

"Thanks for a wonderful evening."

"The pleasure was all mine," he said, then she caught him peeking past her door into her living room. "Nice place. Next time I'll have to invite you over for dinner so you can see my place."

She stiffened slightly. See his place? She would never see the inside of his place, just like he would never see the inside of hers. Didn't he understand that this was a fling that ended as soon as they got back from Florida? She would return to her world and he to his. She wasn't looking for a relationship. The last thing she needed was to develop feelings for him.

It's too late for that. She liked him and the sex was the bomb. For those reasons, she couldn't take the risk.

"Why're you so quiet?" she heard him ask.

Meeting his gaze, she shook her head. "No reason."

"You've been quiet ever since we left the club," he began, then reached up and cupped her chin. "I know you were trying to scare me away by taking me to swingers' night. But what you don't seem to understand, Simone, is that I'm not going anywhere. We're meant to be together and nothing and no one can change that."

Before she could answer, he dipped his hand underneath her skirt and stroked her clit. She gasped as she stared up at him. "Don't forget what I told you—no panties in Florida. I want to be able to walk up to you and touch you whenever I feel like it," he said between strokes. "At any given moment I want to slide a finger inside and taste you. I want every man in the hotel

to know that the only one to have this is me." A smoldering
gaze met her and melted away any words of resistance. As he
tilted his head towards her, her knees felt like Jell-O.

Shaun's lips covered hers and made her so light-headed she
was glad he was holding onto her. She wrapped her arms
around his neck and leaned in to the kiss. His tongue stroked
hers, demanding access, and she opened eagerly. When he finally ended the kiss, she was breathing hard and all she could
do was stare. Lust shimmered from his eyes and Simone knew
from this point on there was no turning back.

"See you Friday," Shaun said. He turned and walked away.

On Thursday, Simone returned home tired and ready for a
hot bath and sleep. Ladies' night had brought on a crowd that
had kept the staff hopping all night, not that she was complaining. She pulled into her driveway and climbed out of her car.
Walking towards her porch, she stopped in her tracks. *Another
bouquet of red roses.* She couldn't resist a smile. As soon as she
turned the key in the lock, she reached for the vase and carried
it into the house. Her heels tapped across a hardwood floor as
she moved into the dining room and sat the bouquet down on
the table next to the other two.

Shaun had been sending flowers to both the club and home
all week, making this her fifth bouquet. Each came with a different message. She reached down, removed the small pink card,
and read it aloud. "Be prepared to surrender all to me." Blowing out a long breath, she shook her head. She didn't know
what she was going to do with him because the word *no* was
obviously not a part of his vocabulary.

She liked him. There was no getting around that, Simone
thought as she reached down and removed her shoes. She sighed
with relief as her toes sunk into plush cranberry carpet. She
loved high heels but that didn't necessarily mean they loved her
back.

She padded to her room at the end of the hall, where she shrugged out of her clothes and slipped into her robe. As she adjusted the lapel, her thumb brushed one nipple. It swelled and hardened and she moaned. Her breasts hadn't been the same since being in Shaun's mouth. In fact, her whole body hummed with anticipation of the weekend ahead.

With a weary sigh, Simone lowered herself on her king-size poster bed and closed her eyes. She hadn't been sleeping much since they'd gone to Exxxtasy. She'd been there dozens of times, so the whole erotic mood wasn't the issue. It was Shaun. All she could do was think about how good he made her feel, and not just sexually but mentally as well. For the last week, she had worn a smile on her face. The flowers and romantic cards warmed her soul. She truly liked Shaun. He was a man who knew what he wanted and didn't have a problem going for it. He was compassionate and romantic, and the icing on top—he could fuck.

Her pussy pulsed at the memories of him buried between her legs and a strong wave of desire raced down to her core. Simone squeezed her thighs together, waiting for the feeling to subside. Shaun was the type of man she could fall in love with. Leaning back on the bed, she took a moment to remember the last time she had allowed herself to feel that way and pain that came with it.

Love hurt. Her mother had told her so for years. She didn't want to believe it and for years she had thought her mother was simply bitter because she had loved a man who never loved her back. For twenty-five years, Linda Thomas played his games—here today, gone tomorrow—hoping and praying that he would get tired of messing around and finally want just her and Simone. Only it never happened. Instead, her father had married another woman and started a new family. Devastated, her mother never got over the rejection and had eventually died of a broken heart.

Even with everything that had happened, Simone had hoped that her mother was wrong about love. However, after Cedric rejected her for another man she realized to her disappointment that her mother was right. Through the pain and heartache, she had somehow pulled herself together and moved on. However, she had made a vow to never love again and she intended to stick by that.

Rolling onto her side, she thought once again of Shaun. He was trying to seduce her and it was working. Even now emotions raced through her body. She somehow had to find a way to deal with what was happening. Although there could never be a future between them, there was no reason why she couldn't go to Daytona Beach and enjoy the weekend, bumping and grinding on and off the beach. She would get him out of her system, and he would get her out of his, then they would go their separate ways.

Simone worried her lip as she realized that was easier said than done. After the other night, she knew he had changed her in some way, and she wondered if she'd ever be the same again. But there was no turning back. She had gotten into this thing with him and she might as well finish it. If she spent enough time with him, maybe the attraction she felt would fade away. She just hoped she could protect her heart in the process.

5

Simone arrived at the flight gate on Friday to find Shaun already sitting there. Her heart skipped a beat at the sight of him. He was so fine she just wanted to eat him up. Taking a deep breath, she headed his way. The sooner she set some ground rules, the sooner their weekend could begin.

Shaun rose when he spotted her coming. He was staring and her nipples tightened beneath her halter top. Damn, he looked gorgeous with his thick, dark hair hanging loose around his shoulders. His hair was extra wavy, as if he had just washed it. He was wearing jeans that hung low on his waist and a light blue shirt that emphasized his eyes. Her attraction to him was so strong she could feel her pulse beating in her ears.

A soon as she reached him, he draped an arm around her and pressed his lips to hers. Damn, he felt good. Simone held on to his waist as he kissed her passionately, the way a boy would on a first date. Long before two people had sex. They were in a busy airport acting like two horny teenagers and she didn't care who was watching. All she cared about was having his tongue in her mouth. Gently, slowly, the kiss went on forever, until Shaun lifted his mouth and she remembered to breathe.

A sincere smile spread across his handsome face. "I missed you."

Studying him, she was warmed by his green eyes. "I miss you, too." The words slipped from her tongue before she realized it. It was true. She had missed him. "Thanks for the flowers. All five bouquets."

"It was my pleasure." He was still holding her close in his arms when he smiled down at her and said, "My cousin owns a floral shop. We had a long talk this afternoon about you."

She paused as the announcement sank in. "Why did you do that?"

"I told you why. Because I plan on you being in my life."

He was watching her and waiting for a response. She groaned inwardly. Things were getting way out of hand. "We need to talk."

"Okay."

Simone moved and took the seat beside his suitcase and waited until he was sitting next to her. This was not going to be easy but she had to do something fast before this man had her walking down the aisle. She cleared her throat and glanced at the seats across from them to make sure no one was listening. "Shaun, I realize this may be a little late, but before we spend the weekend together, I think we should establish some rules."

His brows drew together in a frown. "We don't need rules. We're just going to enjoy the weekend and whatever happens."

She crossed her legs, then met his puzzled gaze. "But I want you to understand that whatever happens in Florida stays in Florida. And when it's over, we're over."

Shaun scratched his head, then chuckled. "A fling?"

"Yes."

There. She said it. Now they could enjoy a no-strings-attached weekend. Only Shaun gave her a long look that said he didn't like that idea at all. Simone sighed. The man was stubborn as all get out. With another breath, she decided to try a different approach. "I don't have time for a relationship. I like living for the moment with no attachments. I hope you understand that." She tried to smile but couldn't read his expression. Simone cleared her throat again. "You should be happy that a woman isn't putting demands on you." Only Shaun didn't look happy. He looked disappointed.

"Why are we having this conversation?" he finally said.

Why? Because I want to bounce up and down on your dick all weekend without you making more of it than it really is. "Because I don't want there to be any misunderstandings," she replied.

He looked angry. "If you want to pretend that nothing is happening between us, you go right ahead. But I'm not buying it." He then rose and strolled over to the nearest concession stand.

On the way there, Shaun prayed for strength. Dealing with Simone was just as bad as dealing with the flu. The woman was going to fight him to the end. All he could do was bide his time and hope it soon passed. Shaun pushed the last few minutes aside and concentrated on the weekend ahead. He planned on turning up the heat, and making her so hot, Simone would be melting in his arms.

He ordered a small orange soda and, while reaching for a straw, glanced over at the gate where Simone was fidgeting nervously on her seat. Good! He had her where he wanted her—scared of what she was feeling.

He admired her shapely bare legs in a short white ruffled skirt and high-heeled strappy sandals. The moment he'd spotted her walking across the airport, blood dropped to his dick. She might be fighting her attraction to him, but only minutes before he had seen the gleam of anticipation in the chestnut depths of her eyes, along with fear. The emotion was easy enough for him to recognize because he felt it as well. However, this weekend would tell all.

For now, even if she didn't agree, she belonged to him, and he intended to enjoy every minute, showing her how wonderful life would be together. He needed to use this weekend to brand a stamp on to her heart so deeply she would never run away again.

It wasn't long before they boarded their plane. After buckling up, Simone leaned back in her seat and closed her eyes. She was playing with fire and knew it. She pretended to be sleeping and tried to think of a way to control the weekend so things happened her way. All she could think about was having eleven inches buried deep inside her heat. Damn, he had her fienin' for him already.

Shortly after takeoff, she was starting to doze off when Shaun draped a blanket across her lap. Feeling his hand on her knee, Simone's eyes flew open and she looked over at him. There was a wicked gleam in his eyes.

"Are you wearing panties?" he asked in a low husky voice.

She swallowed and shook her head. Now she understood why Shaun had insisted they sit near the back of the plane. They had the last three rows to themselves.

Within seconds, she felt Shaun's hand traveling up the inside of her thigh. Her legs started trembling and her breathing got shaky as he reached her feminine folds and rubbed them. *Oh, damn!* She couldn't think when he did that.

"Spread your legs for me," he whispered.

He didn't have to ask her twice. She let her knees fall apart, eager for his attention. Shaun stroked her lips slowly, making her slick and wet. She could feel the creamy evidence of arousal sliding down her thigh. She squirmed on the seat. His fingers were just as magical as his dick. She whimpered as he inserted one long finger inside her, then two.

"I couldn't wait a second longer to taste your cum on my tongue," he whispered for her ears only as his fingers moved slowly inside her. Knowing he was watching her while he stroked made her tremble. Eyes locked, he removed his fingers and put them in his mouth, out and in, mimicking the undulations of sex, then reached under the blanket again. Before insertion, he circled her opening, now wet with her juices. This time, he inserted two at once and pushed them in past his knuckle.

Oh, yesss! She released a soundless cry, then tried to draw more air into her lungs.

"As soon as we settle in our room, I'm going to fuck you like there's no tomorrow," he whispered close to her ear while holding her apart with two fingers. "You'd like that, wouldn't you?"

Nodding her head, Simone had to bite her lower lip to keep from crying out. Slowly, he withdrew, then thrust again, and again, setting up a sensual rhythm. The sensation was incredible. His eyes never left her. When his thumb brushed her clitoris, a soft cry escaped her lips.

"Shhh! I promise to make you come so hard your head will spin," he said. His voice was low and deep, his breath hot against her cheek. "But right now, you have to promise not to scream."

Simone nodded and took the pillow from behind her head, squeezing it close to her mouth while he plunged deeper. She writhed, riding his hand as he slipped another finger inside.

"That's it. Enjoy."

Oh, she was definitely doing that. Her head rolled back and she muffled a moan with the pillow. His fingers felt so good. So gentle, and yet he'd started a fire that only his fingers could put out. She opened her legs wider so that he would have better access to her dripping slit. To her delight, he plunged even deeper. Oh, was she enjoying the ride. She tried to get a grip on her restraint. She tried to calm her racing heart, but she couldn't do that, either. She was too close to coming. So close to losing control. Thank God all the flight attendants were blocking the aisle rows ahead. Nobody was coming . . . besides her.

He stroked her clit some more and her back arched with pleasure. She tightened around him and cried out, her orgasm so strong she was thankful for the pillow.

As soon as she collapsed on the seat he slowly removed his fingers. They were slick and wet with cum. With a smile, he brought them to his mouth and lapped up the liquid from his fingers.

There was a long silence. He stroked her arm while she caught her breath. His body was warm and comforting, and Simone relaxed her head against his shoulder. She hadn't felt like that in so long she barely even remembered it. The thought was so shocking she had to force herself not to move away. She was in way over her head, but right now she was too tired to care.

Shaun planted a kiss to her forehead. "Take a nap. You're going to need your rest."

6

"Look at this place!" Simone was in awe as she stared out at the oceanfront view. "It's absolutely gorgeous."

"Yes, it is." *But the view in the room is much more attractive*, Shaun thought.

She swung around. "I'm ready to have dinner and walk out on the beach." Moving over to him, she placed her arms around his neck. "Who gets the shower first? You or me?"

Shaun cupped her face and leaned in, brushing his lips gently across hers. "How about us?"

Showering together was much too intimate. She quickly shook her head. "Oh no! We'll never make it out of this room, and I'm dying to go down onto the beach."

He brushed another kiss across her lips. "I promise to be on my best behavior," he said with a mischievous glint in his eyes.

Simone didn't believe him for a second, but as hot and sticky as it was outside, the thought of being under the spray of water was too tempting to ignore. "As long as you wash my back."

"Baby, I'll wash whatever you want," he murmured against her neck.

Her eyes closed and she leaned back and savored the light wet kisses along her neck and shoulders. If only things could always be this way. *Yeah, right.* Refusing to spoil her weekend, she pushed the feeling aside, and her smile returned.

"Come on." Simone stepped out of his reach and unfastened her sandals while he watched. Finding him staring, she frowned. "What are you waiting for?"

His gaze lingered on her breasts. "To see you naked."

She slipped her shirt over her head, then slowly removed her bra. "How's that for starters?"

His nostrils flared. Damn! Reaching out, he cupped one in his hand. "You're beautiful. They're beautiful." He moved closer and kneaded gently. Shaun heard her gasp as he leaned down and put a nipple in his mouth and suckled lightly.

"You promised to be good," she reminded while digging her fingers into his back.

He didn't stop. Instead he nibbled until he felt her shudder. "I can't help myself when I'm around you. You're gorgeous." He took the other nipple between his lips and bit lightly. Dick throbbing, he wanted to be slick and wet with her. It was time to start turning up the heat.

He captured her lips in a passionate kiss and she took what he offered greedily, winding her fingers into his hair. When he finally released her, they were both gasping for air.

Turning her back to him, she slipped out of her skirt. *Damn, she has a nice ass.* It was nice and round, and flared out delectably from a narrow waist.

"I'll meet you in the shower." She stepped around him but not before he reached out and smacked her firmly on the ass. Simone yelped. "Ow! What did you do that for?"

"You said you wanted to be spanked." Shaun slapped her other cheek. "So I plan to spank that ass every chance I get."

Laughing, she jumped out of the way before he could smack her again.

Simone dashed into the bathroom, turned on the water and adjusted the temperature. She slipped on a shower cap and pushed her chemically relaxed hair underneath. As soon as she stepped under the spray, she took a deep breath and tried to get her breathing under control. If she didn't slow it down, they would end up spending the entire weekend in bed. Which wasn't a bad idea, except it would just cause more complications and make it that much harder to part when the time finally came. Why did that thought suddenly sadden her?

Before she could find an answer, Shaun moved into the bathroom. As soon as he stepped into the tub, Simone turned away from the water and gasped. *Damn!* His shoulders were broad and his arms rippled with muscles. Dark hair covered his chest in a V. The same hairs circled the base of his dick. Shaun was also aroused. His meat was hard and thrusting toward her with uncontrolled need. She shivered, anxious to run her lips over every inch of him. Their gazes locked and the intensity in his green eyes was almost too much to bear.

"Glad you could join me," she said softly.

"I wouldn't have missed this for the world. This weekend I plan to show you why we're meant to be together." He reached out and pressed a wet hand against her breast. A cry burst from her lips. "I plan to show you why I won't settle for anything less than everything that you have to give, Simone. I won't be happy until you give all of yourself to me."

She shuddered. "I can't give you what you want." Why couldn't he understand that? Why couldn't he just accept what she was trying to offer?

Shaun grazed his thumb across her nipple in a slow rhythm that was driving her mad. "You can if you wanted to."

"I did once and had my heart broken," she whispered against his lips.

"He was a fool. I don't want to hurt you. All I want to do is explore this wonderful thing we have. All I want is to love you." He kissed her lips. "Tell me you feel nothing for me."

She swallowed between kisses. Desire flowed from her breasts down to her clit. "I'll admit the attraction I have for you is like nothing I've ever experienced before," she said truthfully.

"This is only the beginning," he said, voice low and thick with intensity. "We have a connection. I knew it from the moment I saw you." His hand moved to her other breast. "Do you know how much I want you?"

No. She didn't want to know because their relationship was short term. All she had intended to do was take what he had to offer, but as he gazed down at her, she felt something hard inside her crack open. It was that protective shell she had put up around her heart. Somehow he had managed to penetrate the hard exterior and had unleashed feelings that she had hoped to contain. She wasn't sure if she was even ready to acknowledge the emotions that she had tried so hard to hide because the thought of opening up and actually caring about a man was scary. She swallowed and finally heard herself say, "No, Shaun. I have no idea how much you want me."

Massaging her breast gently, his fingers sent a burst of pleasure through her body. Wet creamy cum slid down her thigh. "Then let me show you."

He captured her mouth in a hot, searing kiss. Instinctively, she closed her eyes and stood on tiptoes to lift her hips so she could press against his dick. Yeah, that's the way she liked it. Long and hard. The kiss became hotter and more demanding. His tongue slid inside her mouth in a sensual game of plunge and retreat. Reaching up, Shaun cupped her face and he took her fully into his mouth. The kiss became desperate and greedy. Oh, but he was delicious. Her inner thighs ached. Her pussy quivered. She wanted him to take her like an animal.

He turned her around and brought her close to him. Her ass rubbed against his erection. She trembled when his hands skated up her body and cupped her breasts. "Oh." His thumbs rubbed lightly, then pinched her nipples, and the sensitive peaks tingled and hardened until she started to whimper. *Please, baby please.* He played and kneaded her breasts some more before one of his hands traveled down past her belly button. Too much more of this and she was going to come, which was exactly what she didn't want. She needed him buried inside her first. One foot nudged her thighs apart and she thrust her hips back against his hard dick. "Please," she whimpered.

"Patience, baby. I plan on doing everything to you this weekend. Fuck you. Lick you. Caress you. You name it. I'm going to do it. And I guarantee you're going to love every tantalizing second."

"I thought you were supposed to be washing my back," she teased.

"I'd rather wash this instead."

He rubbed his dick against her ass, making her pussy scream for attention. His tongue was in her ear. His fingers played with her breasts. A moan escaped her lips as his palm slid down her abdomen past the juncture of curls. *Please*, she cried inward. He was driving her crazy and had her fienin'. She grinded against his hand before Shaun finally parted her folds with his fingers and slipped inside. One. Two. Three. While his fingers thrust in and out from behind, his thumb played with her clit. *Oh, yeah!*

He moved in a slow rhythm until she bucked against his hand, meeting the strokes and trying to encourage him to increase the rhythm. Her body was screaming for release. She craved the orgasm that only he could bring, but just as the intensity increased, he removed his fingers. She responded with a frustrated groan. "Please, don't go."

"Baby, I'm not going anywhere. I want to be inside you

when you come. But first I want to wash every part of your body."

Shaun turned her toward him. With the water pelting her back, she glanced up at him. Deep green, penetrating eyes stared down at her and long strands of black hair clung to his cheeks. She so loved his hair, she thought as she reached up and brushed it away from his face.

"Thanks, baby." Grabbing a bar of soap, Shaun lathered his hands and began soaping her shoulders. A moan rose from her lips. He worked down her neck across her arms, then grazed across her breasts, teasing her nipples. Shaun washed every part of her with such tenderness, it brought tears to her eyes. Damn, he was slowly reeling her in. She was in deep, deep trouble. But as his hands slid across her abdomen, she decided to worry about that later. Instead, she closed her eyes and savored the moment. Oh, damn, did that feel *sooo* good. Lowering, he pressed his slippery hand between her legs, massaging her clit and working back and forth between her folds. She sucked in air. She had died and gone to heaven. Her body was screaming *fuck me*, and she planned to have him doing just that in the next sixty seconds.

Shaun handed her the soap. Simone rubbed the bar across his pecs, soaping one tight pink nipple and the other, then slowly traveled down and followed the path of hair to his dick. Oh, yeah, she planned to have *that* buried inside her throbbing pussy real fast and in a hurry. Leaning forward, she planted light kisses to Shaun's chest and felt his intake of breath as her lips brushed his nipples. Dropping the soap, she reached down and fisted the base of his dick with her slippery hands and rubbed all the way up to the red tip, where she paid a little extra attention before moving down to his balls again. His dick jerked.

Hell yeah, come to mama! She licked her lips in anticipation and Shaun pulled her closer, then reached down and cupped her pussy. *Yes!* It was about to be on and popping.

"I want this," he said and squeezed.

She squirmed. "What if I don't want you?"

Shaun gave her a cocky grin. "I'd say you're a damn good liar." He reached down for the foil packet that she hadn't noticed he'd placed on the side of the tub.

"Let me do." She took it from his hands, ripped it open, and slowly slid the condom over his length. "Perfect fit."

"I know what else fits perfectly."

She didn't have time for a catchy comeback line, because Shaun caught her around the waist and lifted her off the floor of the tub. Simone didn't even remember wrapping her legs around his waist or her hands that cupped his neck. Without a second to waste, he leaned her back against the wall of the shower and before taking another breath, plunged all eleven at once deep inside of her. The fullness made her back arch.

"Oh, that's gooood," he growled.

Good was an understatement. In a matter of seconds, he had her shaking and speaking in tongues. He slid almost out, then pounded her so deeply he hit her G-spot. *Jackpot!* Finding a man who could reach her spot was an experience like no other. "Yesss!"

"That's, it baby. Give in to the feeling," he said. "Let me fuck you."

He began to pump in and out of her slick hot pussy in an intense rhythm. Again and again. Over and over until Simone couldn't catch her breath. *That's what I'm talking about.* "Damn, you feel good!" Before he'd stepped into her life, she hadn't had anything like this in weeks. Months. Hell, it had been years. And now she planned to enjoy every second. Shaun pumped in her, not letting up until she was sobbing with pleasure. Finally, he exploded. She slowly lowered her legs.

Shaun showered breathless kisses along her face. "Ready for me to wash your back?"

Her lips twitched with amusement as she nodded.

Hours later, they had dinner in the hotel, then decided to end the evening with a stroll along the beach. Moving through the lobby, they walked down to the shore and kicked off their sandals. Shaun took her free hand and Simone realized how romantic the setting was. It was a beautiful evening. The water was chilly beneath their toes, and a light, gentle breeze off the ocean washed against their skin. She needed that to cool off the feelings brewing inside her. She liked Shaun. She liked him too much. Enough to want to know more about him.

"What do you do for a living?"

As they continued their slow walk, Shaun glanced over at her and said, "I'm an architect."

"Really?"

He nodded. "I design high-end custom homes."

Startled, Simone paused in her tracks, then turned and faced him. "You're Shaun Dutton . . . of Dutton Custom Homes?"

He gave her a sheepish grin. "Yeah, that's me."

Her jaw dropped. *Good Lord!* They were not only the largest builder in the Midwest, but also one of the richest and most prominent families in Chicago.

Members of the Dutton family were regularly spotted in the society pages attending some important function. In fact, she had seen Shaun's picture in the paper relatively recently. The reason she hadn't recognized him was because he looked so much better in person.

Last week, St. Luke's Methodist Church had held a large fundraiser to renovate the Douglas Park Community Center, located in one of the worst urban neighborhoods in Chicago. The city had hoped that by having activities for the children in the neighborhood, it would keep them off the streets and out of trouble. According to the article, Shaun had generously do-nated his time and expertise towards the construction of a larger recreational facility that was to include an Olympic size swimming pool, a state-of-the-art computer lab, and a full-length basketball court. A man after her own heart. She gasped as the wall around her heart began to chip away some more.

"Who I am, does that bother you?" he asked, pulling her from her thoughts.

Simone blinked twice then glanced up at him. "That I'm sleeping with the son of a man who was listed in *Forbes* last year? Of course not." she said drily.

"Seriously?"

No. It bothered her because it showed how wonderful a man he was. His company built million-dollar homes, yet they had donated money, time, and materials to helping underprivileged children. She released a deep breath as her heart fluttered wildly against her chest. She was in a world of trouble.

Shaun must have sensed her uneasiness, because he draped an arm around her waist before resuming their stroll along the beach. "If it helps, I work eight to five just like everyone else. Even though it's a family business, I wanted to make my own mark in the world. Instead of starting as an apprentice like my brothers, I decided to become an architect. I've designed dozens of homes. I'm proud of our company. Especially my dad," he added with an admiring tone.

"What's he like?"

He took a moment to answer. "Tough, honorable, and quite honest."

They were all qualities she admired in a man. Qualities she was starting to realize that Shaun possessed as well. Knowing that made her want to yank her heart out of her chest and hand it over on a silver platter. She rose on her toes and kissed him. Her lips moved over his and savored the taste of sweet wine on his breath. When she finally pulled away, Shaun gave her a puzzled look.

"What was that for?"

"Just because." Damn, she couldn't believe that she did that. Who was this man? When she was around him she had no control of her actions. Instead, she was reacting on impulse, which would get her in trouble if she wasn't careful.

"You can kiss me anytime." He pulled her against him again and took a kiss of his own before pulling back. Hand in hand, they started walking again. Her cheeks were flushed and at that exact moment she was so happy, she felt like crying.

"What made you decide to open a nightclub?"

Simone smiled, pleased to hear he was interested in her life as well. "I have gone to hundreds of clubs that lacked class, and I always said whenever I could afford it I was going to open my own. It's been three years and I'm doing quite well."

"I could tell," he said with a look of appreciation.

"Thank you. It's a lot of long hours but it's worth it."

He brought her hand to his lips. "How often do you find time for yourself?"

She shrugged. "Maybe not often enough."

Shaun stopped walking and turned to face her. Without high heels, she suddenly felt very small with him staring down at her.

"I hope you'll find time for me in your busy life. I really want to see where this relationship goes."

He was talking about a future again. Her heart skipped a beat. This was not supposed to be happening. Why was it so hard for him to understand that a serious relationship was not what she needed?

"I guess I should take your silence as a no."

Simone released a heavy sigh. "No, it's not that. I just wish you would understand that I don't want another serious relationship."

"If you tell me why, maybe I'll understand." Taking her hand, he moved over to a bench facing the ocean and lowered her onto his lap. Simone stared off into the water as she gathered her words.

"I met my fiancé in my first year of college. We dated for four years before he finally asked me to marry him. I was so in love with that man, I don't remember life before he was there. One day I thought I would surprise him, so I went over to his apartment and found him in bed with another man."

Shaun tightened his grip around her waist.

"I was devastated. When I confronted him about it later, he tried to deny it, then finally came out and said he'd been that way for a while and didn't know how to tell me." She scowled. "He planned to marry me and continue to live a double life because he didn't want to hurt me or his family."

"I'm so sorry."

She brushed the tears away as she continued. "I was so hurt and humiliated. It took me a year to get over the hurt and because of that I'm determined not to feel that type of pain again."

"All men aren't like that."

"True, but I'm not sure if I want to take that chance again. Love hurts too much and I don't know if I could survive another rejection."

Reaching up, he stroked the side of her face. "I don't want to hurt you. I want to love you."

Simone turned on his lap and studied his eyes. "Why me? What would your parents say if you brought home a black woman?"

"They would be happy to see that I've finally fallen in love again. I shut down after Hannah died and my family has been very worried about me. They would be relieved to know that I'm happy."

Her pulse raced. Loving a man like him could be so easy if only . . . "Was Hannah black?"

Shaun hesitated. "No, but it wouldn't have mattered to my family if she was green. I was raised to understand that we are all human beings. What makes us different is what's inside." He emphasized his point with a finger to her heart. "My family would love you for you. They would love you even more if we had a few grandbabies."

She couldn't help but giggle. The thought of having his child caused her to yearn for a future with a man. She had always wanted children, a big house, and a dog, and, most importantly, a loving and devoted husband. She just wished she could take that chance.

They sat there for the longest time with her head resting on his shoulder. He held her tightly in his arms.

When they finally returned to the room, Simone was quiet. Shaun knew she was thinking and fighting the strong attraction between them. Why? He understood her reason for being scared, but he wanted her to give them a chance. Deep in his heart, he knew she was the one. He was just waiting for her to figure that out as well.

Simone stood over at the balcony. The wind was tossing her hair around her head while she stared down at the beach. Shaun walked over, pressed his chest to her back, and enclosed her in the circle of his arms.

"I've never been to Florida before," she said, barely above a whisper as if she didn't want to disturb the world in front of them. "It is so beautiful. I could stay here forever."

He held her closer. "My parents own a beach home in Miami Beach. Anytime you need to get away, I'll be more than happy to bring you back."

"Okay," she whispered, but her voice lacked conviction. She was telling him what he wanted to hear, not the truth. She had

no intentions of going anywhere with him again after they returned home. He felt a sting of jealousy at the thought of her
being with anyone but him. Shaun wanted her in his life, and he
knew if he wanted her to stay, it was up to him to show her
how good they were together.

Shaun lured her into the room, then turned her around and
walked her backwards until she bumped into the bed and fell
back with him on top of her. With one quick push, his tongue
parted her lips with hard strokes. For the longest time they lay
in each other's arms, kissing and touching, then they quickly
shed their clothes. Shaun moved between Simone's legs and
pinned her arms over her head as he ran a trail of kisses along
her neck and face.

She gasped. Her need for him was so overwhelming. She was
so wrapped up in the moment, she didn't realize what Shaun
was doing until she felt pressure around her wrist and a click.

Her eyelids flew open. "What are you doing?"

"Handcuffing you to the headboard," he said with a wicked
gleam in his eyes. "You want to play games and pretend our relationship is just a weekend fling. Fine. I'm about to show you
that what we have is much more that."

Simone pulled and sure enough, she was completely at his
mercy. She stared up at him. His dark, silky hair was wild around
his shoulders and hunger burned in his green eyes. Swallowing,
she knew she was in trouble. Despite knowing that, her pussy
pulsed with anticipation.

Dipping his head, Shaun ran his tongue along her earlobe.
"I'm crazy about you, Simone," he whispered.

The words made her pulse race. Reaching down, he rolled
and pinched her nipples between his forefingers and thumbs,
and the combined pleasure and pain was intense. Squirming,
she yanked hard against the handcuffs and tried to free herself,
but it was useless. Shaun was in complete control and she was

helpless to do anything about it. The thought made her wet and she felt cum slide down her inner thigh.

He laughed low and a mischievous gleam lit his eyes. "Baby, I think you're crazy about me as well." Rolling onto his side and resting on one elbow, Shaun allowed his fingers to wander. His hand left her breast and tickled her underarm, feathered her nipples, then swept down past her stomach to her apex where he combed his finger through the dark hair, causing Simone to cry out.

"Your hair is darker down here and curlier, too," he reported between caresses. "I like that."

The light feathering of his fingers was driving her insane. His hand traveled to her clit, and her back arched. She couldn't escape his touch. With her hands bound, Shaun could do anything he wanted to her. And dammit, she wanted him to do just that. "Yes," she moaned.

He brushed his thumb back and forth against her clit. "You like when I touch you like this, don't you?"

"Oh, yes," she whimpered.

Shaun chuckled, then lowered his head toward her breasts. She waited impatiently for the warm, wet touch. Her nipples were swollen and screaming *suck me*. She arched off the bed trying to meet his lips halfway and cried out when his teeth finally grazed her puckered flesh.

"You taste good," he said. He licked. He teased. And finally, he suckled her. Simone closed her eyes and gave in to the pleasure. What he was doing felt so good, it was terrifying. With every flick of his tongue, his name spilled from her lips.

"That's it, baby. Remember the night we met?" he crooned while he continued to tease her clit. "Did you play with yourself after I left your office?"

Hell, yeah. Heat flowed between her legs as she remembered masturbating on the edge of her desk. But there was no way she was going to admit she fantasized about him, so she shook her head.

"You're lying. I know you did because on the ride home, I could feel your hot pussy clamped around my dick." His tongue delicately licked her nipple. "Did it feel good pretending I was inside you?"

Yes, it had. All week, she had masturbated. But now she wanted the real thing. "I did no such thing," she panted. "Now free my hands so I can touch you."

Shaun lifted his head and shot her a hard look. The caramel beauty was driving him crazy. He ignored her request and, using his teeth, gently pinched her nipple. "Did you tell your friends about us?"

She flinched at the wave of pleasure. "No. Why should I?"

"Because I told mine about you." Okay, he thought. He'd just have to turn up the heat a little higher and see if she continued to downplay what was happening between them. He planned to enjoy every inch of her to the max, before taking her again.

Slowly, he slid further down her body, his gaze locked with hers. "Make sure when you tell them about me you don't miss a single detail," he said with a smug smile. Shaun blew across her damp skin and her head jerked away from the pillow. "For instance, you'll have to tell them that I did this."

When she felt his lips glide across her skin, her belly quivered and a moan escaped her parted lips. Chuckling, Shaun opened his mouth and licked and nibbled his way across her abdomen. She began to whimper, but he kept the pace slow and easy, hoping she would be frantic by the time he plunged inside her.

"And they'll want to know about this," he whispered.

Shaun teased her nipple with his tongue before capturing the whole thing in his mouth. He sucked hard. Simone squirmed, demanding to be freed, but he ignored her request and moved his mouth to the other breast. He sucked and nibbled for so long she was bucking her hips beneath him.

"Dammit! Let me go," she pleaded. "Please!"

"Baby, not yet. I still have to give you some more to talk about."

Desperately, Simone tried to kick him, but he caught her legs and spread them wide. She cried out when his hands gripped her ass and lifted her hips up off the mattress. "Shaun, let me go!" she screamed between pants.

"Not until I taste you."

Within seconds, he had her completely powerless. Hands above her head. Legs draped over his shoulders. Shaun glanced up from his position. Was she finally ready to let whatever was meant to happen between them, happen? "Stop fighting it, Simone," he said. "There is nothing you can do about fate."

She began to wiggle but he held her still. Moving closer, he slid his tongue across her swollen folds and she jerked forward.

"That's it. Let go."

The tip of his tongue snaked out and he took quick licks. She squirmed and cried out his name. "Shaun!"

"That's it, baby," he said. "Enjoy it." His tongue swept over her in slow strokes, probing, separating, and teasing her clit. She thrashed about.

"Ohhhh!" she moaned. "That feels so good."

Mmmm. She tasted delicious. He licked, stroked, and sucked again and again until her body was rocking against him. Replacing his mouth with a finger, he coaxed cum from her pussy. Simone screamed. She arched upward and he slid first one finger, then a second finger into her. When his mouth joined in, he heard a sharp intake of breath. His tongue circled her clit, then slid lower and plunged back into her soaking wet pussy. Out and in. Again and again with slow, deliberate strokes. He could feel the walls of her pussy contracting. His tongue dipped inside again, and she sobbed.

"Shaun!"

"I'm yours, Simone," he said against her skin. "All you have to do is give yourself to me."

He could feel her beginning to come undone. Her orgasm was only seconds away. Deliberately, he returned his attention to her clit and firmly licked. The pressure seemed to push her over the edge. Her back arched, and her muscles tightened around him.

"Oh, yes!" she cried in a strangled voice. He pushed his face hard against her bucking hips. Her body heaved and mewing sounds rose from her throat.

"That's it, baby. Let it go."

Finally, a powerful orgasm ripped through her body and he kept on sucking until the last palpitation subsided. When she went limp, he lowered her hips gently to the mattress.

Shaun rolled off the bed. Simone watched as he reached for his wallet and removed a condom. While standing directly over her, with their eyes locked, his meat overhead, he tore open the package and rolled it over the fat rosy tip.

Yum yum. Her pussy dripped and more cum ran down her inner thigh. She knew that in the next few seconds she'd be taking that big dick deep inside her.

Shaun crawled onto the bed and pushed her knees apart, then rubbed the head of his dick across her wet opening for what felt like forever.

"Please," she said softly.

"Please what?" he asked as he teased her some more. "Simone, tell me what you want."

"I want you, Shaun, inside me, now," she said between breaths.

Without a second to spare, he drove deeply into her. Simone cried out at the sudden penetration. "Ohhh!" She panted, then bit her lips. He felt so good. She opened her legs wider to accommodate every inch of him.

"Oh, yeah, babe," Shaun crooned, then pulled out and plunged again. He grabbed her ass and held her at just the right angle for his thrust. Leaning forward, he pushed her knees back to her chest and forced her to take him deeper. When he plunged again, Simone felt every inch of him.

He loved the way she looked when he slid inside her body. "Damn, you got some good pussy," he panted with broken breaths as he pumped faster. She was gripping him tight. He didn't want it to end so soon. He wanted to take his time. But she was too hot and wet and felt too damn good to hold on. "Fuck!" he said.

"Ah, yes!" she cried. "Oh!"

He dropped his head into the side of her neck and drove into her hard again and again. The headboard banged. Handcuffs jingled. Simone screamed and with a curse, he came. His fingers bit into her ass and her back arched like a bow as she came again.

Shaun collapsed on top of her, and they both struggled to catch her breath. When his heart rate finally slowed, he lifted his head. He smoothed her hair out of her face and looked down at her. "You okay?"

Simone nodded, still too out of breath to speak. Why did it have to be this way with him? Somehow, he managed to reach a part of her that she had kept locked up for so many years. If he kept this up, she was going to fall in love with him, and that would be a mistake that could cost her.

"I think we can take these off now," he said as he ran his hands up to her wrists. He slowly pulled out of her and reached for his pants, removing a small key and unlocking the handcuffs. As soon as she was free, she buried her hands in the dark strands of his hair. Shaun stretched out beside her on the bed, kissing her as he cradled her in his arms.

Something spiraled through her body and plagued her heart as she held on to him. A connection had been formed that went beyond sexual attraction. Could her feelings have something to do with love?

7

Shaun brushed a lock of Simone's hair away from her face and watched as she slept on the pillow beside him. He wasn't sure how long they stayed up last night, making love, talking and laughing about nothing in particular before they had finally drifted off to sleep. Gazing down at her lovely face, he could tell Simone was in no big hurry to get up. That was fine with him. As far as he was concerned, they could spend the weekend in bed.

Reaching over, he lightly caressed her face and she turned her head slightly before resting comfortably against his body. While watching her, he thought about what he had confessed before drifting off to sleep.

Simone, you complete me.

If someone had told him two weeks ago he had a second chance at love, he never would have believed it. But her lying next to him was proof. It made no sense, but he felt it in his heart. Even though he knew so little about her, he knew enough to know that he could no longer imagine his life without her.

Hearing a knock at the door, he scowled. Room service. He

had put in the request the night before. Slowly he moved from beneath the covers, trying not to disturb Simone, but he was unsuccessful. By the second knock, her beautiful chestnut eyes were staring up at him.

"I ordered coffee and rolls."

She rolled onto her back and did a full-body stretch, knocking the covers away and revealing two chocolate nipples. His dick rose to the occasion. He was ready to dive in again and would have if there hadn't been another knock.

With a scowl, Shaun reached for his shorts, hoping he could hide a serious hard-on, while Simone rose from the bed and slipped the robe around her body. "You better get that. I'm starving." She stepped into the bathroom while he groaned and moved to the door. He tipped the waiter, then carried the tray over to the desk in the corner of the room, next to the sliding-glass door. A gentle morning breeze flowed through the room, ruffling his hair. By the time Simone came out, Shaun had coffee poured in two mugs.

"Man, that smells fabulous," she said with a brilliant smile.

There was juice, two kinds of Danish, bacon, and, of course, coffee. She took one of the mugs and took a seat on the end of the bed.

"As soon as we're done eating, let's go hang out on the beach," Simone suggested between sips as she stared out the window at the white sand below.

Shaun nodded. He couldn't wait to see her in a bikini. However, gazing down at the way her robe gaped open in front, he had a better suggestion. "How about we save that for this afternoon?" he began as he pushed her thighs apart. "I've got something better planned for this morning."

Simone gave him a knowing smile as she slid further onto the bed. "What do you have in mind?"

Shaun took the mug from her hand and sat it back over on the desk. He then stepped out of his shirts and moved onto the bed between her legs. "I can show you better than I can tell you," he whispered against her lips just before he slid inside. "Aahhh!" he growled, glad to be home again.

Her bikini turned out to be the kind to make a man lose his mind. Simone removed the cover-up and instantly Shaun's mouth went dry. God, she was beautiful. He'd never been with a woman with skin so amazingly rich and creamy. It reminded him of a piece of saltwater taffy that he was dying to sink his teeth into. While Simone spread sunscreen on her arms and face, Shaun watched her over the tops of his sunglasses, shaking his head. He didn't even know how she got the suit on. A small gold triangle took care of the bottom front and two more triangles took care of the top. The rest was all her. Curvaceous hips. Flat belly. Large breasts. And a sweet spankable ass.

He gave a wolf whistle and Simone simply blushed at the compliment. Getting comfortable on the beach chair, she tilted her head and stretched out her long legs. Shaun's eyes traveled from the peaks of her breasts down to her sparkling orange toenail polish. He was speechless, which was probably a good thing, because with all the blood flowing to his groin anything that came out of his mouth would sound childish.

Simone looked over and smiled when she caught him staring. "You ready to go get wet?"

Hell, yeah. He wanted to get wet. Shaun was ready to bury his dick in her dripping wet pussy. But she was talking about swimming. In that case, hell, no. There was no way he was getting up. He shook his head. "Go ahead. I'll wait." Shaun then shifted on the chair to conceal the front of his trunks. Leaning back, he watched her race across the hot sand.

Simone frolicked in the cold water. The feeling was refreshing. After three hours at the beauty shop on Thursday, she had no intention of getting her hair wet, but that didn't mean she couldn't appreciate the water surrounding her. Besides, swimming had just been an excuse to put some distance between her and Shaun for a few minutes. Noticing the tent at the front of his trunks, she knew there was no way he was going to follow.

Staring down at the water, her mind returned to the last several hours. Being with Shaun was like nothing she had ever imagined. He was the type of man who would love a woman with all his heart. *So then what was the problem?*

Simone released a shaky sigh. If only those feelings would last. Cedric had once felt the same way and then he changed. She'd learned the hard way that nothing was ever meant to last forever. Only this time she wished things to be different. If Shaun could give her some kind of guarantee that he would always love her, she might be willing to take that chance. She liked him. He challenged her mind, body and soul. She wanted so badly to be everything he wanted her to be . . . yet she was afraid that if she did, she would never recover.

Coming back on the shore, she found Shaun lying on a large beach towel with his legs stretched out in front of him, bracing his weight on his elbows. His hair hung loose around his shoulders. He looked like a Greek god with muscular legs sprinkled generously with hair. The hair on his chest sloped down and grew thicker before disappearing inside his trunks. *Lord have mercy.* "You should have come in, Shaun," was all she said. "The water feels good."

"I was trying to take advantage of the sun," he said while Simone moved over and lowered onto the blanket beside him.

"Is this your natural color or a tan?" she asked curiously.

"Tan. I spend a lot of time visiting our construction sites."

"Without a shirt?"

He grinned in reply. "Yeah. Gotta strut my stuff."

"I would love to see one of your designs." And she meant it.

"I plan on showing you." He leaned in and kissed her. "What

about you? Are you naturally this beautiful or have you been visiting the same tanning salon as my mother?"

She found his compliment amusing. "Nah, this is all na-tu-ral."

"I can see that." Shaun pressed his lips to hers again and Simone felt it all the way down to her toes. When the kiss ended, he rose. "Wow! Baby you've got my soul on fire. I better go cool off," he teased. Shaun rose and raced across the hot sand, out into the water. As soon as he was deep enough, she watched in amazement as he cut the water gracefully, then did a back-stroke. He was an excellent swimmer.

Tears clouded her eyes and before she realized it, they were streaming down her cheeks. She didn't know why she was cry-ing, except to say that Shaun had a way of making her feel things she never thought she'd ever feel again. He was also compassionate, kind, and romantic. Yep, he definitely was not going to be easy to forget. And a big part of her didn't want to.

Carrying his towel, Simone moved back to her chair and took a seat. She slipped her sunglasses on and leaned back. It wasn't long before she spotted Shaun headed in her direction, his skin glistening with water. Her heart hammered against her ribcage. Fine as hell was the best way to describe him. Glancing to her right, she noticed two women pointing, and damn if they weren't staring at Shaun. A wave of jealousy surged through her before she looked up and greeted him with a smile. "How was your swim?"

"Wonderful." He shook his hair and water splashed across her.

"Hey!" Simone cried, while laughing and trying to block the water with her arm. "You're getting me all wet."

Leaning towards her, Shaun gave a devilish grin. "I would love to get something else wet." He scooped her up into his arms and kissed her soundly on the mouth. Simone glanced over to see if the two women were watching. They were. Chuckling, she deepened the kiss.

* * *

After they left the beach, they quickly changed clothes and strolled over to the Ocean Walk Village to see a movie. They gorged on popcorn and candy and held hands during the horror flick. Afterwards they visited the shops, then returned to the room and made slow sweet love, then showered and went two doors down for dinner.

Shaun glanced at Simone sitting in the booth across from him at Bubba Gump Shrimp Co. Tonight she wore a burnt orange halter dress that tied around her neck, then plunged low in the front and left her back bare. Her hair was up in a ponytail that made her look years younger. He reached across the table and touched her hand. "Do you know what it is to have a soul mate?"

Her brows rose. "Soul mate?"

Shaun nodded. "Everyone has a soul mate. That one person who completes you—mind, body and soul. The hard part isn't finding that person, it's holding on to them when you do." Simone opened her mouth to respond, but he pressed a finger to her lips, then said, "Love comes with a price and sometimes it hurts, but if you want it bad enough it can also be quite rewarding." He lowered his hand and for the longest time she was quiet, apparently thinking about what he had said.

Simone reached for her lemonade, then shook her head. "I watched my mother die of a broken heart," she began between sips. "All my father wanted from her was sex, and nothing more. That was all he wanted, period. She spent years waiting for him to love her, but he never did."

He allowed her words to simmer for a moment before saying, "Are you afraid that the same thing will happen to you?"

She lowered her glass and looked up from the table with frank eyes. "No, because I will never allow it to happen."

Simone's eyes quickly darted to the table while he took a

moment to study her. She was lying. *She's still running.* Shaun took a deep breath and decided to change the subject.

"Do you have any siblings?"

Simone shook her head. "No. My mother never had any more children. She was too busy waiting for my dad to come home," she replied bitterly. "What about you?"

"There are six of us."

"Six?" She practically choked.

He nodded just as their waitress arrived with their food. After she left, Simone dug into her food and listened while he talked about growing up with the Brady Bunch—two brothers and three sisters.

"Did your wife want children?" she asked while chewing a rib.

"Yes, we wanted a big family. What about you? Do you want kids?"

"I love kids."

He watched her eyes cloud with tears before she looked down at her plate. In that instant, he knew a family was what she wanted most, despite all her protests. Why would she deprive herself of happiness? he wondered. But he already knew the answer. Fear.

Shaun eased them into a light conversation about sports and found that she was a die-hard Bears fan. It wasn't long before he had her laughing about dozens of the team's blunders over the years. His eyes held hers for the longest time before he reached across the table and clasped her hand. "I'm glad you're here with me."

Simone couldn't help but smile. "I'm glad I'm here as well."

After another moonlit stroll along the beach, they returned to their room. They'd left the air conditioner off and the sliding door open to enjoy the warm breeze.

"Take your dress off."

His directness zinged straight to her clit. Simone slipped the dress over her head and stood before him. No bra. No panties. Just what the good Lord gave her.

Shaun shed his shirt and shorts, then backed her against the wall. Her body shook with anticipation. He lightly kissed her lips and moved down her neck to her shoulder. *Tonight he is mine.* Boy, did she want him. Shaun was a total package—handsome, funny, and compassionate.

His hand slid to her breast and the arousing touch sent liquid desire sliding down her thigh. *Oh, yeah.* He leaned back slightly, and she stared up into his eyes, filled with a hunger and something else that she wasn't ready to define.

Tonight, she would enjoy every second with Shaun. Every kiss. Every touch. Every loving word. Then tomorrow they would return to Chicago and the fantasy would end. Man, how could she like someone she just met so much and so soon?

"You knew the moment I first held you in my arms you were mine," he said as if he read her mind.

Simone nodded. Yes. While at her club, she had known something special was happening between them.

"You're mine, Simone," he began between kisses. "I want to hear you say it."

"I'm yours." *Even if it is just for the night.*

"Good. Because when I'm done with you, any doubts you may still have will be gone." The words vibrated as he kissed the length of her neck. She prepared to say something, but he silenced her. "Let me have you for as long as I can," he whispered against her damp skin.

"But—"

"No buts." He raised his head and stared down at her. "Tonight, let me have you." His eyes snapped to her lips. "All of you." He lowered his mouth again. "Surrender to me, Simone."

He wanted her to surrender her heart as well? She swallowed while his hand slid along her inner thighs. If only she could trust him not to hurt her, she would surrender forever. "I—"

"Shhh." He touched her mouth with his finger, running the pad along her bottom lip.

Simone surrendered to his touch and decided to believe she was truly his. Until they boarded that plane tomorrow, she would pretend she was his, and he was hers. The fantasy was possible as long as she kept her heart out of it.

Reaching down, her fingers brushed the length of him. His dick was hard, erect and ready for her. Shaun crushed his mouth to hers again, only this time the kiss was hard and hungry. Wildly, Simone combed her fingers through his hair and was half-crazed by the time the kiss ended. Shaun swung her around so she was facing the wall and nudged her legs apart.

"You're not surrendering, Simone." He pressed his dick against her ass.

Yes, I have. At least for the night. She could barely think straight as his hands worked up to the juncture between her inner thighs. He rubbed against her dampened pussy. Simone shuddered and rocked against his hand.

"I need you to give me your heart." Shaun slid a finger inside her wet heat.

Then another.

And another.

Simone cried out while she met each delicious stroke.

"Tell me."

She didn't feel like talking. All she wanted was to see what he was about to do next. It wasn't long before Shaun pressed the pad of his fingers to the top of her tender walls and stroked her G-spot. "Oh, yesss!" Her heavy breasts jiggled with the rocking of her body while her nipples brushed the wall.

Shaun then used his thumb and pressed firmly against her clit. She bit the inside of her mouth to keep from screaming.

"Answer me, Simone."

She groaned, clenching his fingers that continued to move in and out of her pussy with slick insistence.

"Are you ready to surrender?"

"I can't," she whispered. "Not completely."

He removed his hand and she cried out at the loss. He was going to deny her until she surrendered her heart as well as her body. Taking her hand, he led her over toward the chair. "Have a seat," he demanded.

She lowered and waited. Determination hardened his features.

"Now put your legs over the armrests."

She did as he said and swallowed. Her pussy was wide open and exposed. Juices flowing freely. While she sat there waiting, he moved over to the bed and removed his boxers. Eyes never leaving her. Her clit twitched. She was in a world of trouble. There was no way she was going to be able to deny herself *all* of that.

Shaun moved in front of her and gripped the back of the chair, one hand on either side of her head. Leaning forward, the head of his dick teased her inner thighs. "Ready?"

She wiggled her hips back and forth, rubbing her clit against him. "No."

"Look at me." Eyes locked, he plunged inside, then stilled his body. "Do you want more?"

"Please." She was begging and didn't care.

He eased out halfway, then slammed inside her. "Tell me you're ready to risk your heart. That you're ready to love again."

She arched her back off the chair at the contact. "I can't," she gasped, while squeezing the muscles of her pussy tightly, never wanting to let him go.

"Yes, you can." He pulled out completely. His thick length

was wet with her juices. She gazed down at it as her body screamed for him to come back.

"Please, Shaun," she whimpered.

"Please what?" While waiting for an answer, he slid the head of his dick across her clit, teasing her. "Tell me what you want, Simone." When she didn't respond, he lowered before her.

Intense heat flowed through her. "I—" she gasped when he licked a nipple with the tip of his tongue. "I—"

"I can't do anything until you give me your heart." Gently, he suckled. "Trust me to love you."

She let out a long, low moan. He was demanding more than her body. He planned to open her up until she had no other choice but to confront everything she was feeling. Surrendering meant trusting and giving without fear of what pain might come after everything was said and done. "I surrender." And she meant it. As much as she tried to deny herself, she wanted everything he had to give, even if it was for one night. She wanted him tonight and was not afraid to say so. "I surrender to you."

Shaun brought his mouth to hers. She cupped his neck and wrapped her legs around his hips. "I want you inside of me," she said. He lifted her into his arms, then carried her over to the balcony, and she lowered her feet to the floor.

"Turn around, baby. I need to see that big ass."

Simone turned and faced the ocean, then leaned over, holding on to the rail, and stuck her ass out. He smacked her left cheek and she cried out, the sound echoing through the night.

"You like when I spank that big ass?"

"Yes," she moaned as he smacked her again and again until her ass stung with pain.

"Now bend over. I need to taste you."

Obediently she lowered her chest to the rail and parted her thighs. Shaun dropped to his knees and spread her butt cheeks wide open. He then worked his tongue all the way down to her clit. "Yesss! Oh, God, that feels so good!" She thrust her hips back to meet each sensual stroke of his tongue. "Fuck me! Please fuck me."

He rose. "Baby, tonight we're making love." With his firm hands at her hips, he rammed his dick inside her. "This is my pussy," he chanted as he moved in and out, slowly. He smacked her ass. "Tell me whose pussy it is."

"Yours," she whispered.

Smack! "Whose?"

"It's your pussy, Shaun."

"And don't you forget it." Shaun then gave her a long and thorough spanking, causing her to cry out with pleasure. He pulled out to the tip and plunged deep inside again. "You belong to me." He increased his speed and she met him stroke for stroke. His breathing increased while she screamed out his name, her voice floating out into the night. He plunged harder until she peaked and jerked. Her muscles clenched around him. With one final thrust, he released a deep growl and came.

Shaun withdrew slowly and carried her over to the bed. Once under the sheets, he pulled her into his arms as he had done several times this weekend. It felt like heaven to be held while she felt so fulfilled, so all alone. Again their strong connection scared her and caused silent tears to stream down her cheeks. Shaun was everything she had ever wanted in a man.

It wouldn't be easy parting tomorrow. Once back in Chicago, she would probably be miserable. The thought was unbearable. Nevertheless, that's the way it had to be.

"What's wrong?" he whispered close to her ear.

What's wrong? Simone wanted to say. *What's wrong is how complete I feel with you and how scared I am of this wonderful feeling.* "Nothing."

His expression told her he didn't believe her. However, he didn't press for answers. Instead, Shaun rolled her onto his chest, her breasts pressed against his steady heartbeat. Squeezing her eyes closed, she forced herself not to think about the sadness tomorrow would bring.

"What do you fear most?" Shaun whispered.

Her heart clenched and it took her a long time to answer. "Falling in love again. What about you?"

"Losing love a second time," he replied as he pressed his lips to her forehead. Shaun pulled her tightly into his arms and Simone wished she could hold on to the moment forever.

8

On the flight home, Shaun sat near the window. Taking Simone's hand, he laced their fingers together. Simone rested her head on his shoulder and closed her eyes.

Shaun had made love to her until the wee hours of the morning. Then they'd fallen asleep for a few short hours and had just enough time to share breakfast in the hotel before they caught a shuttle to the airport. Taking a deep breath filled with the scent of Shaun, Simone buried her nose against his shirt. She wanted every detail of him embedded in her brain. Memories of him would always be a part of her heart. He had become quite special to her and she would not forget that. When the pilot's voice came over the intercom, her stomach sank.

They were beginning their descent. The fantasy was officially over.

As soon as they departed the plane, Shaun walked beside her. He placed a hand at the small of her back to steer her toward the parking garage and her body stiffened.

"Simone, what's wrong?"

"Nothing," she mumbled without bothering to look at him.

"No, it's something and we need to talk about it." He caught her elbow in a firm grip and guided her across the floor away from the flow of traffic. She turned and looked at him. Frustration was prominently displayed on his face. "I love you. Can't you see that?"

"Love me?" She shook her head with disbelief. That wasn't possible. He hardly knew her. "You couldn't possibly love me."

Reaching out, he cupped her elbow and pulled her closer. "Why not? My father knew he loved my mother the second he met her in the checkout lane at the grocery store. They've been together ever since."

She shook her head. "That's wonderful, but that doesn't happen often."

"It happened with us. I love you and I know you have feelings for me. The sooner you realize that, the better off we'll be."

Simone stared up at him, stunned by his words. She wanted a life with him. "It won't work, Shaun," she said softly.

"Why?" he asked as he pressed his lips to hers.

"It just won't," she managed, then gasped as he pulled her in his arms. "I can't risk feeling that way again."

"I don't want this to end."

Neither do I. But she had to because it was easier now than it would be later. It was way too soon for love. There was no way Shaun could be sure of his feelings. And she wasn't prepared to take that risk. Making the break now would give her memories instead of heartache.

He nuzzled her neck with his lips. "At least have dinner with me tomorrow night."

Simone pulled back from him and nodded. "I'll call you." Turning on her heels, she moved toward her car on the second level of the parking garage before the tears started falling.

9

It had almost been a week and Simone still hadn't called. Battling his frustration, Shaun swiveled around in his office chair and stared out the window at the hurried traffic below. For five days, he'd sent flowers and handwritten notes expressing his love and gotten nothing in return. Not a peep. Not a phone call.

Shaun forced himself not to call her, even though he constantly watched his cell phone. Her departure from his life made him face the painful truth. It had been what she said it would be—a weekend fling. Not a relationship or commitment. Just sex. He wanted a life that as far as she was concerned would never work. And after a week of nothing, he was starting to think that maybe it was time for him to face the strong possibility it was over.

"What do I do now?' he murmured in his empty office. He didn't have a clue. He couldn't sleep or eat. Everything about Simone haunted him. Her scent. Taste. Wet, hot pussy. He just couldn't seem to get her out of his mind . . . because he didn't want to.

Leaning back in his chair, he let his head loll to the side, feeling defeated as he recalled their last conversation together. He couldn't be angry because from the very beginning Simone had been totally honest with him. He was the one who refused to believe that what they had wasn't real. It was hard for him to admit, even to himself. He had been brought to his knees by a woman who refused to love him back. Simone was too afraid and there was nothing he could do but wait and hope that she would come to her senses and follow her heart. He also needed to face the fact that it might never happen. If not, he would have to be thankful for the memories. Shaun raked a frustrated hand across his face. Who was he trying to fool? He didn't want memories. He wanted Simone.

Only time would tell if she wanted him as well.

"Want to go and grab a bite before the beer distributor arrives?"

Simone glanced up from her desk at Amber and shook her head. "No, I'm not hungry."

"But you need to eat. You don't look well."

Yep. She looked like shit and knew why. She missed Shaun. All week he'd been sending roses with personalized messages to the club but not one phone call.

Isn't that what you wanted?

Simone briefly shut her eyes and inhaled deeply. She didn't know what she wanted anymore. She had told Shaun it was over and had gotten what she wanted—a weekend of knockin' the boots. Only it wasn't as easy as she thought it would be. Since Sunday, all she could do was think about him. Shaun interrupted her every thought, haunted her dreams, and filled her mind until she couldn't even take a single deep breath without remembering how good he had felt inside of her.

Amber walked across her office slowly, keeping her gaze locked with her boss's. "Simone, you need to quit fooling yourself. You're in love with that man and you better call him before it's too late."

She was right. Logically, the time frame was too short to fall in love but Simone had. Shaun *was* the other half of her. He provided comfort and strength. He gave her friendship and love. They were a good mix. She hugged herself, wishing his arms were around her. In her mind, she could hear his voice. As she took a deep breath, his smell flooded her senses. With her lids shut, she saw those magnificent green eyes staring into hers with the same explosive force as his erection when it penetrated her body. Who was she fooling? It didn't matter if he was white or black, rich or poor, she was miserable without him and the sooner she admitted that, the better off she would be.

"Should I take your silence as a sign that you're thinking about what I said?"

She returned her tearful eyes to Amber and couldn't resist a smile. "You think you know me."

"I do know you. That's why I know you need to give that man a chance. Sweetie, I hate to see you so unhappy when you don't have to be. I've read his notes and that man loves you."

"What if it's too late?" Simone asked with sudden apprehension.

"It's never too late for love."

She took a deep breath and prayed that what Amber said was true. Maybe love hadn't worked out with Cedric, but for the first time in years, she was willing to take that chance. She wasn't her mother and Shaun was absolutely nothing like her father. Shaun was worth the risk. As soon as the club closed tonight, she was going to tell him how she felt.

Shaun stepped out of the shower and heard the doorbell. His brow bunched. It was after midnight. Who in the world was at his door this late at night? After wrapping a towel around his waist, he moved downstairs and swung the door open.

Simone.

"Hello." She glanced down at his towel and he saw her swallow. "I'm sorry—did I interrupt something?"

He shook his head. "No. Come in."

She gave him a tentative smile, then brushed past him and entered his foyer. He watched as she moved into his spacious living room, her eyes traveling around. While he waited for her to get to the reason for her visit, he stood back and admiring her body in black gauchos and a white blouse. High-heeled sandals were on her feet.

"You have a beautiful home. Is this one of your designs?" she finally said, breaking into his thoughts.

He nodded. "Yes, it is."

Shaking her head, she took a deep breath. "You're probably wondering why I'm here."

"That thought has crossed my mind. Shouldn't you still be at the club?"

She shrugged. "I left Amber to close up."

"Why?"

"Because I couldn't wait to ask if you'd go out with me tomorrow night."

Taken by surprise, he reared back. "Tomorrow?"

She nodded. "Yes, or the day after. Whatever day works best for you."

He hesitated. "Is this another visit to Exxxtasy?"

"No, nothing like that. Dinner . . . at my house." Simone chuckled and he realized how much he missed hearing her laugh.

He shifted his weight onto his other leg and nodded. "I'd like that."

Her shoulders sagged with relief. Shaun stared at her for a moment, fighting the urge to hold her. "Is there anything else?" he asked after several seconds had passed.

"Yes, there is." Simone began as tears welled in her eyes.

"I'm tired of being alone. I'm tired of running from relationships. Things didn't work out with Cedric, but I can't give up on my life because I am afraid." She paused and moved toward him. "I'm crazy about you, Shaun."

He nodded, then waited impatiently for her to finish.

"This has been the worst week of my life. Without you, my days and nights have had no meaning. All it took was one weekend for me to get so used to sleeping with you that my bed feels cold and lonely." She shook her head. "I can't go back to that."

A husky laugh escaped his lips as he felt the weight on his heart lighten. "I've missed you."

"Then why haven't you called?" she demanded to know. Shaun found her pouting lips quite sexy.

"Because I wanted you to figure out what you wanted and then show me how badly you wanted it."

She sniffled. "I do want you. I've missed you so much."

"Come here."

Simone practically ran into the circle of his arms. Shaun pushed his wet hair away from his face and brought his lips down hungrily against hers. His tongue slipped inside, touching the tip of hers in a teasing caress.

Finally Simone pulled back to look at him. "I've been a mess without you."

"So have I, baby." He stole a quick kiss then pulled back and stared into her eyes. "You think you're ready to meet my family?" He was ready to share her with his world.

"Yes! I look forward to it." Shaun started unbuttoning her blouse, and she jumped back, giggling. "What are you doing?"

"Taking your clothes off."

Desire brewed through her. "Why?" she asked quietly.

"Because I'm going to carry you up to my room and make love to you," he answered as her gauchos fell around her ankles.

"But I . . ."

His smile turned devilish. "Baby, it's been a long week. Too long." He lowered her panties and his knuckles brushed across her clit. She gasped at the contact. "I gotta have you now. I'm—"

Simone reached for the towel around his waist and snatched it away. At the sight of his arousal, her eyes sparkled, then rose to meet his again. "The word is fienin'. And good, because I'm fienin' for you, too."

Epilogue

Simone stepped out of the ladies' room and was heading back to her table when someone tapped her lightly on the shoulder. Looking to her right, she met a wide, dimpled smile.

"Excuse me, sexy, but I was curious as to what B.S.A. means."

Briefly, she glanced down at the letters proudly displayed on a T-shirt she'd personally designed and back up to the appreciative gleam in the young man's eyes.

"Sorry, sweetheart, but if you have to ask then obviously you're not the man for the job." She brushed past him and moved over to the booth where her friends were sitting.

"What did he say?" Melinda asked, eyes burning with curiosity as Simone lowered onto the seat across from her.

She pointed to her friend's matching shirt. "He wanted to know what B.S.A meant."

"And what did you tell him?"

"I told him that job has already been filled," Simone replied with a triumphant smile.

"I know that's right." Reaching across the table, Melinda gave her a high five.

Lilliana agreed. "The only ones who know are the men who matter most."

While reaching for her lemonade, Simone glanced down at the platinum engagement ring on her finger. She had discreetly slipped it back on her finger while in the bathroom. It was the reason why she had invited her two best friends out to lunch, wearing their B.S.A T-shirts.

It had taken her almost a year to get past her insecurity and trust that what she had with Shaun was real, and now she was ready to spend the rest of her life with the man of her dreams. Just like her friends.

Lilliana and Joshua eloped last year and now her very pregnant friend was due any day now. Melinda and her husband Nicholas were now the proud parents of a beautiful baby girl, named Sophia. Both women had given love one more chance and each had been blessed with a wonderful new life.

Melinda leaned back on the bench, eyes glittering with excitement. "I can't believe that it's been more than a year ago that we sat at this same booth and came up with that silly ad idea."

Lilliana nodded and laughed. "What I can't believe is that it actually worked!"

"Neither can I," Simone murmured. She then reached for her lemonade again and made a show of waving her left hand in front of their faces, hoping it wouldn't be long before they noticed her engagement ring.

Lilliana's eyes grew round. "Oh. My. God! What is *that*?"

Simone wiggled her fingers and couldn't resist a smirk. "This little old thing? Just something that Shaun gave me last night while down on one knee."

Lilliana started kicking and screaming, and Simone gave her a worried look. The last thing she needed was for her to go into labor. Melinda jumped out of her seat and grabbed her hand for a closer look.

"Simone, it's gorgeous. I'm so happy for you." She wrapped her arms around her.

"Thanks, Melinda."

While she returned to her seat, Lilliana pulled her arm across the table and took a closer look. "Girl, I must say, that man has good taste."

Simone snorted rudely. "Of course he does. He chose me."

"So modest," Lilliana laughed. "When's the big day?" she asked as she placed her hand back on her protruding stomach.

"We haven't set a date yet, but we're thinking about a Christmas wedding. Shaun and I are anxious to start a family as soon as possible." Simone's eyes clouded with happiness.

"I'm so happy for you," Lilliana said and Simone saw the tears shimmering in her friend's eyes.

"I want to make a toast." Melinda held up her glass of lemonade. Lilliana and Simone reached for their own glasses and held them up as well. "Here's to a lifetime of happiness." Gently, they tapped their glasses together.

Simone quickly jumped in. "Oooh! And to our big spankable asses."

Lilliana chuckled. "Okay? If it wasn't for B.S.A. we wouldn't be as happy as we are today."

Melinda nodded and raised her glass again. "All right. Here's to B.S.A."

"B.S.A.," Lilliana repeated.

"To our big spankable asses!" Simone shouted with glee.

The three clicked their glasses again. Noticing the stares coming from the nearby tables, the friends looked at each other and then started cracking up laughing.

Wasn't nothing wrong with having a big spankable ass, Simone thought on a happy sigh, as she and her girls took healthy swigs of their drinks and settled back into their favorite booth at Hooters. It was the same booth they'd sat at over a year where they'd hatched the crazy plan to find men who knew how to handle a B.S.A.

What they'd found in the process was love and happiness beyond their wildest dreams.

Watch for some BODY MOVES,
from Jodi Lynn Copeland!

Coming soon from Aphrodisia!

Jordan Cameron sank back in his office chair and glared at the reflection of his father's profile in the eighth-story window of the New York City investment firm. For the first time in over a decade, John Cameron wore no beard and every trace of gray in his hair had been covered with dark blond. He looked more like Jordan's older brother than his father. It wasn't right and, clearly, neither was his father's state of mind.

Jordan swiveled in the chair, curling his fingers around a brochure for the medical tourism resort his father returned from three weeks ago and had yet to stop talking about. He respected his father and never questioned his choices aloud. However, this latest decision wouldn't allow him to bottle his exasperation. "Jesus, Dad, think about what you're doing. It's a passing fad at best."

Inspecting himself in the golf green-etched mirror hanging on the wall kiddy-corner from Jordan's desk, John rubbed his first finger and thumb along his clean-shaven chin. "Oh, I think about it. Every time your mother sneaks up and pinches my ass. I forgot how strong my sex drive was until I spent a week at

Private Indulgence. Thanks to that 'fad' our marriage and love life are stronger than ever."

Jordan sighed. For the way his father talked, you would think the resort staff had restructured his entire reason for being and not just his underdeveloped chin.

"Fine. Let's say this place is the real deal and will be around for years to come, that doesn't explain why you feel the need to sink your entire life savings in it." Not when he'd spent the last five years refusing Jordan's investment advice because he claimed the only safe place for his money was in the bank. "Split the money. Let me put 70 percent of it into annuities."

Barking out a laugh, John looked over. "Back in the day we considered a split to be 50/50."

Back in the day there wasn't an endless supply of lowlifes coming up with every scheme under the sun in the hopes of getting their hands on an old man's money. Jordan had heard the buzz on the medical resorts—Private Indulgence had never been among those said to be taking off. Even those resorts who claimed to be doing well had yet to provide convincing proof of their longevity. "At least give me some time to check this place out. You got to know too many of the staff to view it objectively."

"Not to mention I was strung out on Percocet 90 percent of the time I was down there."

"Exactly."

His father crossed to the twin tan leather chairs opposite Jordan's desk and slammed his hand down on the back of one. "By God, son, you've gotten so stiff, you don't even recognize sarcasm anymore."

"Oh, I recognize it. I just don't find it humorous when it mixes my father with habit-forming drugs."

John closed his eyes and pinched the bridge of his nose—a habit Jordan had picked up from him. Opening his eyes, he let his hands fall to his sides. "All right. You've got four weeks. Only because I want to see you away from this damned desk for more than a few hours at a time. This place is sucking you dry, stealing your zest for life—"

"And worrying Mom sick she'll never have grandkids," Jordan finished drily. He'd been through this song and dance too many times to count. Sorry to say for his parents, he wasn't one of those kids who lived to please them alone. "She'll get her grandkids when I'm ready. Right now, I'm enjoying the zest for life you seem to think I've lost by dating whatever women appeal to me."

His father snorted. "Whichever ones are willing to come in second to your career is more like it."

"Dad . . ." Jordan warned.

"I'm leaving." John went to the door, turning back when he reached it. "Four weeks. I don't hear convincing evidence against the resort by then and I'll be on the first flight to the Caribbean to share my investment decision with Dr. Crosby."

With the *snick* of the office door, Jordan turned his attention to his laptop. He clicked on the bookmarked resort informational page for Danica Crosby, M.D., the plastic surgeon cum owner of Private Indulgence who'd someone convinced his father to sink his money into her resort.

Calling the plain-looking, glasses-wearing redhead who appeared on his screen a surgeon was pushing it, considering she was barely out of her residency. The sudden ache in Jordan's gut told him calling her business dealings with his father reputable would be pushing it even farther, and in less than four weeks he would prove it.

"What in Hi'iaka's name are you doing?"

With her friend and assistant's question, Danica Crosby released her death grip on the alarm clock radio and set it on her desk. Lena stood in the doorway of Danica's office, eyeing her as if she'd lost her mind. For now, her sanity was intact. God only knew what would happen in the next few minutes.

Danica pushed aside one of several wayward envelopes and grabbed a chocolate-covered almond from the starfish-shaped candy dish on her desk. She popped the nut into her mouth, letting its soothing taste and texture work their magic on her tension before giving the alarm clock's red digital readout another glance. "Waiting. Three minutes from now something bad is going to happen."

Lena's brown eyes flashed with hope. "You became psychic last night?"

"Wouldn't you have felt some sort of psychic friends' connection if I had?" Lena gave the expected dry laugh and Danica continued soberly, "I grabbed my morning Pepsi out of the refrigerator this morning only to discover there was no Pepsi to grab, even though I know there was one last night. An hour later, I almost cut my nipple off shaving."

Day glow pink and lime green hula girl earrings—what Lena claimed to be her twin talismans, since her supposed visionary powers began the day she'd put them on—swayed with the scrunching of her nose. "Ew. Your breasts are hairy? I just thought you'd given up on dating because you realized you were a lesbian and were afraid to come out of the closet."

"Not everyone's a date addict like you." Probably because not everyone had Lena's cute build, which had only gotten cuter with the recent chopping of all but the last couple inches of her hair and subsequent dye job that turned her locks from near black to dirty blond with fuscha streaks.

"I prefer 'serial dater.'"

"Whatever, I'm not one. I also don't have hairy breasts. I was shaving my underarm and fumbled the razor. It nicked my nipple on its way down." Danica winced. The memory hurt almost as much as the real thing.

Lena frowned. "A nipple ouchy tells you something bad's going to happen in three minutes?"

Danica gave the alarm clock a glance. Her stomach tightened

forebodingly, so she popped another almond. "One minute now and yes. Haven't you ever heard bad things happen in sets of threes?"

"Sure, but I never knew there was a timetable."

"Well, there is. In fifty seconds, mine's due up." Judging by the fact that last almond didn't even touch her anxiety, whatever happened at the end of those seconds was bound to be a doozy.

Lena studied her so long and thoroughly Danica thought another of her friend's questionable visions was about to strike, but then she just smiled, calling out the exceedingly cute dimple in her right cheek. "You know, most of the time you're as boringly normal as they come, and then you go and say something totally whacked like this and I remember there's hope for you yet."

The alarm clock rolled over to ten o'clock. Any amusement Danica might have found in Lena's word was forgotten in the wake of her heightened unease. "Time's up."

She looked around the office, half expecting the overflowing bookcase to fall on her, or the chaos on her desk to blow up in her face, or the bay window behind her to shatter, or . . . She swiveled in her chair, praying her customized golf cart hadn't gone up in flames.

Nope. Still there, parked two stories below.

"Looks like your timetable's off—strike that." Lena inhaled audibly. "Trouble's headed this way. Don't look like no cowboy, but I'd know the smell of Stetson anywhere."

Danica swiveled back in her chair in time to see her friend exit her office as an unfamiliar man entered it, bringing with him the mouthwateringly spicy tang of cologne. Her belly did a slow warming, her inner thighs mimicking the intimate response as she took in the newcomer.

Lena was right. With his black power suit, which was completely inappropriate for the humid island weather, and polished Kenneth Coles, he didn't look like a cowboy. Danica still had the urge to climb up his long legs and take him for a ride.

Wow! Where had *that* come from?

She never thought of sex while on the clock and nearly as seldom while off it. Not because she didn't share Lena's perfectly cute everything or the natural tan complexion of her friend's Hawaiian heritage. She just had too many other, more important things to fill her days, namely seeing Private Indulgence, the elective surgery medical tourism resort she'd started up three years ago, continue to thrive in a way that would eventually allow for expansion into nonelective areas.

The guy moved into her office, assessing each inch before moving on to the next one. His measuring gaze landed on her. "Interesting place you have here."

Holy killer eyes! They matched the turquoise waters of the Caribbean right down to the sparkle.

The way Danica's sex grew moist with the striking shade suggested his walking through her door might well be the third bad thing to happen to her this morning, by making her focus on something other than work. Even if she did have time for dating and he lived locally—doubtful given his attire—and showed an interest, things would never work.

From his carefully styled dark blond hair and neatly trimmed mustache to the perfectly symmetrical divot in the knot of his gray silk tie, there was an order about him his delectable appearance wouldn't allow her to look past. Danica and order went together like Lena and celibacy—both would be happening the same time pigs sprouted wings.

She relaxed with the knowledge they wouldn't be having sex. All but her churning stomach relaxed anyway. It was a little too coincidental he'd shown up right at ten. "May I help you?"

"I have a meeting with Dr. Crosby. I was told at the front desk you're her."

"You do?" Pepsi withdrawal had to be playing hell with her memory. She didn't do visual order, but her mind usually had a firm grasp on things.

Danica stood, offering her hand over top of her desk, along with an apologetic smile. "Sorry, this week had been hectic. I recall it now, Mr. . . . ?" Shoot, So much for correcting her oversight.

His lips twitched as his gaze slid the length of her, eyeing her in a penetrating way that renewed the wetness between her thighs and made her want to squirm.

His gaze returned to hers and he took her hand in a firm shake. "Jordan Cantrell."

She made it a point to personally greet as many resort guests as possible, shaking dozens of hands each week, many of them male. Not one of them rendered visions of strong, warm hands sliding over her aroused, nude body the way Jordan's did. Her jean skirt would allow easy access. The thin barrier of her panties barely an obstacle. She glanced at his fingers—ringless, and long like the rest of him. Able to easily slide between her thighs and deep inside her slick pussy.

The increased twitching of his lips broke though Danica's reverie. Heat flooded her face and undoubtedly flushed her fair skin with the reality of where her mind had traveled. As if her thoughts weren't bad enough, he was silently laughing at her. Mocking would be a better word.

Damn it, she'd worked hard to see the resort gained a foothold in the fast-growing medical tourism industry and had come far in the time since its launch. Too far for her to be made to feel incompetent by a man who didn't know her from the Easter Bunny. Yet incompetent was exactly how she felt.

"I'm here to check out the resort for potential surgery," Jordan supplied, his derisive tone making it clear how unimpressed he was so far.

She wanted to give him a tone of her own. Or forget the tone and tell him off outright. For the sake of the resort's reputation, she refrained. "Of course you are." Ignoring her damp panties, she forced a smile and rounded her desk. "Let me grab your file from my assistant and we'll get started."

Danica entered Lena's next-door office as her friend stood from behind a desk so efficiently organized it made Danica feel dysfunctional by comparison. Lena flashed a smart-ass grin. "So is he here to repossess your villa, or tell you an active volcano was discovered in the resort's backyard?"

"Neither. He's a potential patient." *And not even close to a gentleman.* Danica ran a hand over her belly. God, she needed an almond, or maybe a handful of them. "He says he has an appointment with me this morning."

"If he's J. Cantrell, he has a ten fifteen. He took over a late cancellation spot a few weeks ago. I was about to pull his file when you walked in.'" She went to the rear wall, which was lined floor to ceiling with shelves of patient files, and pulled a thin manila one from the Cs. Halfway back to her desk, she stopped on an indrawn breath and gasped out a "Whoa!" that in Lena talk meant she'd had a vision.

She crossed the rest of the way to Danica, handing her the file and sitting down without a word. Completely unlike Lena, who compensated for her small stature by being as vocal as possible. "Well? What was it about?" Danica prompted.

Lena didn't look up. "You don't want to know."

"I asked, didn't I?"

She looked up, her lips curving in an impish smile. "A Pepsi-aholic with one hairy armpit because she was too afraid to go back and finish the job."

"Cute, Lena. Very cute." Despite her follow-up groan, the friendly jab eased Danica's tension . . . until she returned to her own office to find Mr. Hot, Blond, and Oppressive waiting in front of her desk.

Jordan happened to walk in right at ten—fifteen minutes

early for his appointment—and made her have sexual thoughts for the first time ever while on the job, but that didn't mean he was trouble. He could just be a pain in the ass.

She sat down on her side of the desk, popping two chocolate-covered almonds into her mouth before opening and quickly reviewing his file—all one and half mostly blank pages of it. She looked up at him. Damned if a bolt of lust didn't shoot through her with the brilliance of his eyes. "There's nothing listed on what you would like to have done."

"I didn't say."

"The facilities vary a great deal depending on the type of procedure you're considering. Showing you the entire resort would require hours, possibly days."

"It's a"—he glanced down—"sensitive matter."

"A sensitive—" Danica's gaze landed on his crotch. For an instant, as she thought about the anatomy behind his zipper, the heated state of her body returned. Then his meaning settled and she barely subdued her gasp.

She didn't exactly like the guy, but there was no denying he was a stunning specimen of masculinity. Was it possible he could be equipped with an undersized penis?

Of course, it was possible. She'd scrubbed in on several phalloplasty surgeries where the patient was bigger body-wise than Jordan yet minuscule below the belt.

The irritation in her belly let up some, knowing he was here because of body issues beyond his control—something she could relate to well. "I understand. The facility for that surgery is quite a distance from here. If you don't mind going for a ride in the open air, we can use my golf cart to take a shortcut."

"You golf?" He sounded impressed.

"Actually, I bought the cart because I only live a half-mile from here and figured it a more economical choice than a car." Technically, her rationale had been the more she saved on auto expenses, the more she would have to invest in the resort. Since he actually looked impressed now, she kept that tidbit to herself. Not that she was trying to impress him. Even if she could get past the whole "order" thing, he probably had performance-anxiety issues.

How small could he be?

Her gaze strayed back to his crotch, lingering for a few seconds before intelligence caught up with her Pepsi-starved brain. "I do golf, when time allows for it."

"Same here. It's been a while since time has allowed for it," Jordan admitted, perhaps a bit grudgingly.

Danica closed his file and pushed her chair back from her desk. "Work has a way of taking over."

"That it does."

"Having a job you love helps."

He gave a noncommittal murmur. She took it to mean he wasn't comfortable with the conversation any longer. While the casual talk had lifted the oppressive air and mostly relaxed her stomach, it was time to get on with the tour.

She gestured to the door, then made it a point to lead him to the elevator and out into the parking lot, so she wouldn't be tempted to peek at his ass.

"Have you tried a natural approach?" Danica asked as she slid into the driver's side of her golf cart.

After climbing into the cart, Jordan looked over with a frown, "Natural?"

The breeze wreaked havoc on his previously flawless hair. The sun baking through the roof of the cart already had perspiration gathering on his forehead. He should look like an imbecile for how warmly he was dressed. Not to mention completely unappealing with that frown. Instead he looked sexy and sweaty and he smelled downright appetizing.

It was a good thing he probably had performance issues, because Danica was aching to let passion rule her in a way she hadn't allowed in ages.

"Have you tried exercising your . . ." She sent a covert glance at his groin. "The area in question."

"Yeah. Sure. Didn't work."

She started the golf cart. "What about pills?"

"Didn't do a thing."

"There are a lot of placebos being illegally marketed as the real deal. It's an easy mistake to make."

Jordan wanted to view the words as an insult. The reassurance in Danica's greenish gray eyes when she told him it was an easy mistake made that hard to do.

She wasn't what he'd expected. For one thing, she didn't wear glasses—not at present anyway—and for another she did play golf. Her behavior skirted from strange to skilled to sexual. She kept staring at his crotch. No way in hell could he be imagining it—his dick would know the difference and not be in the process of tenting his pants. Then there was her appearance.

The Internet hadn't done her justice. In person, her layered, shoulder-length hair was more fiery copper than dull red, her nose narrow and straight with a charming bump and even more charming freckles near the tip. Her mouth was soft, pink, lush, and wide and he had more than one idea of how she might use it on him.

Danica reached across to a small compartment in front of him. The back of her hand brushed against his knees, jetting heat up his thighs to his stimulated groin. On a sharp inhale, Jordan retracted his body into the seat. He was acting like a pubescent teen, but he didn't want to like her and he sure as hell didn't want to want her.

"Sorry." With a sympathetic smile, she lifted a pair of wire-framed glasses from the compartment. "You don't want to ride with me when I'm not wearing my glasses."

As it turned out, Jordan didn't want to ride with her when she had her glasses on, either. The golf cart had clearly been modified to go beyond traditional speed. Twice, on the mile or so ride, he'd been certain she was going to need to call 911 to come scrape his remains off the ground.

Danica braked the cart to a halt in front of a wooden foot-bridge surrounded by tropical underbrush and trees. "It's easier to walk from here."

He jumped out and hoofed it across the bridge, wanting the hell away from the psycho driver who had overtaken her body. The bridge opened up on the other side to reveal a number of pale gray and slate-blue villas detailed in sky blue and separated from one another by a good-sized yard and towering palms. A three-story, mostly glass building loomed past the villas. He headed in that direction, guessing it to be the facility she planned to show him.

She surprised him by sprinting past, developed muscles in her bare legs constricting enticingly. His gaze lifted to a high, round ass cloaked in a short jean skirt and his blood heated. She could owe her body to faithful jogging. More likely, her muscles and the ample breasts filling her knit pink tank top were the result of implantation.

"In a hurry?" Jordan called after her.

"I thought you were." Danica dropped back to match his reduced pace and gave him an openmouthed smile. "I'm all yours till noon, so anything you want to know"—she looked at his crotch—"don't be shy about asking."

The glimpse of her moist pink tongue and the suggestive words would have been enough to have his shaft hardening again after the hellish ride's deflating effect. The continued ogling of his groin had his cock stiff as a board.

He considered stripping away his suit coat and dress shirt under the pretense he was roasting his ass off—technically not a pretense but a reality he owed to the airport for losing his luggage during flight transfer—and seeing how she responded. Learning she slept with prospective patients in the hopes of ensuring their patronage would be as good of a way to start unveiling the resort as a bad investment as any.

"We have a fully equipped hospital," Danica said in a voice that sounded both professional and proud, "but the majority of our surgeries are done in ambulatory facilities, which are housed in the same building as the surgeons' offices for the associated procedure. Using these facilities is one of the ways we're able to keep our costs substantially lower than most public practices."

"Should I be worried ambulatory and ambulance sound remarkably similar?"

Her throaty laugh was an unexpected as her appearance—totally enticing, totally dangerous to his mission. "Not at all. Ambulatory means you arrive and leave the facility on the same day. Your phalloplasty surgery . . ." She sent him another of those damned apologetic looks that made it difficult to remember she was the bad guy, or rather woman. "I didn't mean to put it into words."

Jordan sent a pointed look around. The closest person lounged on the front porch chaise of a villa over a hundred feet away. "I don't think anyone heard."

"I'll still be more careful."

"You said same-day facilities are one of the ways the resort's able to keep costs down," he rushed out, needing to get the apologetic look off her face. "What are the others?"

"Unlike a lot of the islands around us, we're not governed by the United States."

Now they were getting somewhere. "In other words, you're able to avoid licensing fees and training staff in the latest procedures."

Danica stopped walking to shoot him a frosty glare. "All of Private Indulgence's facilities and staff are accredited and operate under International Standards, Mr. Cantrell." The icy look softened, along with her tone. "The cost of living is simply lower here, which allows us to charge less overall while providing first-rate, state-of-the-art services by top-notch specialists. Many of our procedures are discounted 70 to 80 percent as compared with the national average."

Well, fuck. Instead of uncovering a skeleton in the resort's figurative closet, he felt impressed for the second time since meeting her. He couldn't stop his smile. "I'd prefer you call me Jordan."

"Like the almond." Cheeks gone rosy, she leaned close to release another of those dangerously enticing laughs. "That probably sounded odd." Her eyes warmed as she confided in a husky whisper. "It's just that I have a nut fetish."